"Harrell takes you into the very essence of his characters, their training, their thoughts, and their loyalties."

—Mark Berent, author of
Rolling Thunder and *Steel Tiger*

INFILTRATORS

MacIntyre ducked, as rounds pinged the tree trunk by his head, blasting pine bark into his face. "Keep the Blackhawks away from here," he ordered. "They've got SAMs in the AO of the Redeye type. I say again, *Redeye,* over."

The pitch of the tilt-rotor changed to a shrieking whine as it prepared to take off. Santo leapt out from his protective cover and rounds pinged all around him as he planted the Redeye's sight against his right eye. He thumbed the arming device into the fire mode, trying to ignore the heat of the battle flaming all around him. A bullet burned its way into his calf. Santo tried to ignore that, too. But an explosion threw him to the ground like a discarded doll . . .

**Don't miss these remarkable thrillers by
Mark D. Harrell, coming soon
from Jove Books . . .**

Penetrators
and
Operators

Infiltrators

MARK D. HARRELL

JOVE BOOKS, NEW YORK

INFILTRATORS

A Jove Book / published by arrangement with
the author

PRINTING HISTORY
Jove edition / January 1991

ISBN: 0-515-10501-5

Infiltrators

PROLOGUE

The night had grown long. The sand in Border Patrol Sergeant Martin Clayne's eyes scrubbed his corneas with a vengeance, as he drove his El Paso Border Patrol Blazer down Highway 18 westward toward the New Mexico border.

Headlights approached, making his eyes burn even worse. Glancing at his watch, Clayne felt the acid from the chili burrito he'd eaten at a truck stop two hours earlier kindle a fire across his solar plexus. The uniform tailored for him last year was already too damned tight around his gut. Twelve years on border patrol was taking its toll.

The approaching vehicle passed by, much too fast.

"Hey!"

Clayne looked to his right, exchanging glances with his partner, who was suddenly very awake and very excited. Then he looked up into the rearview mirror. The desert night was clear enough for him to make out a van receding in the distance, closing in on El Paso to their rear. "Well, sport? Wanna be a hero?"

"It's worth a check. Dispatcher radioed in earlier to watch for all vans."

Martin Clayne sighed. His partner was both green and right. The two made an exasperating combination. He slowed the Blazer down and prepared to turn back. "You're gung ho, Sonny, know that?"

They sped down the road. It was mostly deserted, but they did, after all, have orders from the dispatcher to watch for all late-model rust-brown vans coming their way from the New

Mexico side. Christ, that meant . . . that meant . . . well, it meant it was time to liven their evening up a little. He just wanted the shift over with, so he could go home at dawn, drink a few Coors, and go to sleep.

"Excited, Sonny?"

Clayne's partner grinned nervously. "It's probably dope, you know. Most of the wets have foot routes across the Rio."

"Sure, Sonny." Clayne thought that Sonny Benton looked just marvelous in *his* tailored issue. Young, fresh out of El Paso Tech—he'd been there once too. *Give him time*, he thought. *Give him a spouse, a couple of rug rats, a divorce and alimony—give him time.*

Speeding the Blazer up to ninety miles per hour, they gained on the van enough to see it careen suddenly off to the left and then gather speed along the dirt road that would eventually lead whoever was driving it up to the Fort Bliss Military Reservation's boundary. Clayne followed suit and put on the strobe lights. The van speeded up to fifty, and then sixty miles per hour. Clayne edged the Blazer up closer. Already, twin dust clouds in column rose ten feet above and around the vehicles, making it hard to see.

So it was going to be a chase.

Just as Clayne was about to call in the dispatcher for backup support, the van skidded to a halt on the other side of a dried-up arroyo, clouds of dust billowing all over. Long seconds passed as Clayne tried to make out the outline of the van shrouded in the dust before he approached it.

Clayne would show his younger partner how to handle what would probably be a dope bust this time, instead of illegal aliens. He stopped the Blazer fifty feet behind the van beyond the arroyo's bridge, his Blazer's strobe lights painting red and blue streaks through the dust.

"Keep to my right, and watch for any sudden movement."

"Okay, Marty."

Clayne kept his eye on Benton's face. He still had a mustard smear on the corner of his mouth from the truckstop. It reminded Clayne of his own thirteen-year-old son at the El Paso Border Patrol picnic last week. *Christ, Benton's young.*

They got out and walked slowly toward the van, Benton a few

steps behind and to the right of Clayne, just as he'd been taught at the academy. He constantly shifted his eyes from left to right, keeping them away from the taillights of the van to preserve his night vision. Benton nervously unhooked the retaining strap over the hammer of his .357 service revolver. He drew it out. Clayde did the same.

Clayne kept a watchful distance, a careful two feet at an oblique angle away from the driver's window, and aimed his flashlight inside. He saw a Mexican in his thirties, maybe his forties, sitting very still behind the wheel, staring dead ahead, the muscles along his jawline working. With the window rolled down, marijuana smoke wafted in the cool desert air.

"Come out of the van."

The Mexican said nothing, just kept staring ahead. Footsteps shuffled from behind the Border Patrolman. Clayne glanced nervously around his shoulder. Benton was creeping toward the rear of the van. "Heard something back there, Marty."

Clayne put his attention back on the driver. "Watch your ass, Sonny. I don't like this." He refocused his flashlight back on the driver. "Come out of the van."

The Mexican stared at Sergeant Martin Clayne for the first time. He had thin features, lank black hair, a hawk nose. "Fucking gringo," he muttered. "Fuck you."

If Clayne hadn't heard a scuffling sound from the other side of the van where Benton had gone, he would have bashed the flashlight into the Mexican's face.

"*Sonny? Out of the van, grease-ball!* Now! *Sonny, answer me!*"

The Mexican slowly opened the door, revealing a smoldering joint. Clayne stared at it. The guy was begging for a bust.

"*Sonny, get over here!*"

A shot rang out.

Suddenly, wire looped around Clayne's neck, cutting it, slicing it open, arterial blood spray shooting a foot out from him as tiny sawlike teeth cinched around his neck vertebrae. Sergeant Martin Clayne was then hauled over his murderer's shoulder, and he crumpled in a heap by the hub of the front wheel.

His partner, Sonny Benton, had served only thirty days with the El Paso Border Patrol before suffering the same fate. On the other side of the van, he too lay dead and bleeding in a gully. He'd only gotten one round off before dying.

Five minutes later, the area was cleaned up, and both vehicles took off into the night, heading north toward the El Paso Military Reservation.

CHAPTER ONE

"Where did they go, then?" Scott Crossley asked, low and menacing. He looked coldly at the undercover operatives chief for the El Paso region standing by the situation map. Then he got up from his desk and moved his blocky hulk over to him. Crossley had not become Southwestern District Chief of the Drug Enforcement Administration by being young and timid. He could be garrulous when he wanted; it depended on the circumstance. He usually got to the heart of the matter by never raising his voice, and that gained more results than being overbearing. But now he was running out of patience.

The other man pored over the situation map, trying not to let the bigger man intimidate him. "Sir, the only way they could have gone is north."

James Wiggins was the quiet intelligence type, a slender man in his mid-forties. Right now, he was a harried man with thinning gray hair flying all askew, who'd received no less than a dozen intelligence analyses from the think-tank department concerning the murdered Border Patrolmen. Ever since a prospector had discovered the two bodies and their burned-out vehicle in the mountains north of El Paso twenty-four hours ago, all hell had broken loose. They'd never caught smugglers in those mountains before; they were entirely too rugged. Besides, their man in Juarez—El Paso's sister city across the Rio—had given them startling, yet incomplete information just before being killed, not three days ago. Now, the El Paso District DEA chief wanted answers.

"North to what? All that's up in that direction belongs to Fort Bliss and White Sands." Crossley clasped his hands behind his back, glaring at the map. The pipe he never lit ground audibly in his clenched teeth. "Two Border Patrolmen on a routine check-over found strangled to death with garottes," he muttered. "Christ, one of 'em's head was almost popped off. Now why the hell would whoever'd done that take off into the mountains toward White Sands instead of making a beeline for the highway? There were two sets of tire tracks, right? What about aerial reconnaissance? Why aren't there any sightings?" Crossley swung around and glared at Wiggins. The other man looked away. "You mean to tell me there's been no sightings at all?"

"No, sir. I mean, yes, sir, that is correct."

"Well what in the name of sweet Jesus have your people been doing?"

Wiggins clasped his hands together at his front and stared at them. Then, ever so gently, he said, "Sir, we have only so many agents to cover so much terrain. Most of them are combing the Rio south of Las Cruces with the Border Patrol where that massive drug roundup is going on." Wiggins locked eyes with Crossley.

"What about the FBI? No, forget that. We can handle this without the FBI."

Wiggins looked up at the department head, wanting to say, "Are you crazy, bub?" but didn't. "Sir, we need to get FBI involved. It's their area. It is my opinion that someone is trying to get into White Sands Missile Range complex. There's no other explanation."

"Why are you so sure about White Sands?"

"Sir, we have a massive operation going on at Las Cruces. That's about twenty miles west of White Sands. Those patrolmen's bodies had all the signs of a drug execution. But it makes no sense for ordinary smugglers to have gone up into those mountains." The intelligence man pointed at the map. "Those mountains lead directly north into the missile-range complex. Our man in Juarez—"

"Rivera?"

"Yes, sir, the man who was tortured and executed. His last communiques—"

"Of course!" Crossley rubbed his temples, trying to remember. "He implied that the drug organization in Juarez was with the

KGB, which was linked with narco-terrorism, and so on. . . . "

Wiggins knew when to keep his mouth shut. Fortunately, he'd planted the right thing in the boss's ear at the right time. He'd always had the theory that narco-terrorism was bigger, much bigger than the Latinos usually involved.

"Goddammit, this is big," Crossley muttered. "I can feel it in my gut." He paced back and forth before the map. "Okay," he said finally, calming down. "Okay, just who do we have down there?"

"Sir—this may be a possibility," Wiggins said, relieved. "We have tentative Congressional approval to use pilot teams from the military on drug-enforcement operations. We've gotten requests from the Army's Special Operations Command for active participation, and of course, the Marines are competing to—"

"Spare me, Wiggins, I know all that. Get to the point. "

"Sir. There is a Special Forces battalion conducting its annual desert training at Oro Grande, New Mexico, right now. That's only twenty-two miles due east of the White Sands Missile Range. They know the entire area inside and out, especially those mountains where the suspects have gone."

"Special Forces, huh?" For the first time that morning, Scott Crossley looked surprised and at a loss for words. "Why didn't you tell me that earlier?"

"Uh, sir, what about—"

"To hell with the FBI! Don't you realize what this could mean for the DEA? If we catch these people, we'll get the—" Crossley caught himself short, almost saying, *"we'll get the credit."* He calmed down and in no uncertain terms told Wiggins: "This is our baby. And I will personally be held responsible for it. You get our man in Raleigh, North Carolina, over to the Commanding General of 1st SOCOM at Fort Bragg right now. I'll clear the path with DEA headquarters from my end."

Furtive movements in the night. Heavy civilian backpacks creaking with weight. From the summits and ridgelines and caves looming high above them, a bat wheeled crazily into the midnight sky, silhouetted against the moon; then it dive-bombed a backpack, steering away from it at the last second, but still brushing the cordura nylon of the backpack. Whispered curses followed the bat's exit from the area, as the target plodded heavily onward, step by step, limping past the cactus, slipping on rotten, loose rocks and gravel underfoot, trying to keep up with his comrades ahead who were steadily outdistancing him. The pain in the gun-shot calf muscle of his right leg throbbed and ached, infection setting in.

In front of him, three other men and a guide dressed in outdoor wools, cottons, and canvas clothing—looking no different from American hikers—climbed slowly up a rocky mountainside twenty kilometers southwest of the White Sands Missile Range. The only light beaming down upon them through the chill desert night air was from the stars and full moon above. Presently, they would take a break within a jumble of boulders near the mountain's broad summit, the north ridgeline of which would lead them into the main complex of the Organ Mountains.

One of those men up front, the leader, turned around and looked down the rocky ridgeline. Moonlight glinted off his high cheek-bones, and his thick, hooded eyes squinted as conflicting emotions boiled deep inside his solar plexus. The leader was in his mid-thirties now, and the man he watched struggling below was the oldest team member by at least seven years, yet the toughest and the wisest. They'd been through so much together.

Would he make it? Could he make it?

The team had been together now for over five years, and they all had shared many tough situations during their stress training in the Karlovy Forest outside Moscow where the original four-man team had come together, and also, similar to their current environment, in the mountain passes of Afghanistan. Their team had been bloodied by Mujahideen guerrillas in rocky, desolate passes high above Kabul; their team had been replenished and decimated; but the team's core, the leader staring from above and the other man struggling far below, had always remained intact.

Now, as Major Sergei Antonov stared at Senior Sergeant Vladimir Grodniko below as he struggled with the pain in his calf where the Border Patrolman's bullet from the night before had grazed him through his flesh, Antonov's heart told him one thing and ingrained discipline and standard procedure told him another.

He did not want to make this decision.

He turned to face the others, who had automatically spread out in a perimeter around him, the Mexican guide out front, and Antonov's chief communications sergeant at his nine o'clock position. "Break!" he whispered. Antonov leaned against a boulder.

Another man approached Antonov. Expect for the senior sergeant below, this man had been the last to catch up. Boris Pushtkin. Antonov glanced at the man with contempt. Pushtkin was the computer specialist from the KGB who had been attached to his team upon arrival in Juarez days before. The KGB man was also, technically, mission commander, despite Antonov's tenure and ability. He had wispy brown hair, and dull green eyes that constantly cut in quick stares of calculation, then assessment; medium height, medium weight, a bland, nondescript face with little pockmarks on his nose. Pushtkin constantly surveyed his surroundings, thinking out his actions three and four moves ahead, like a chess player.

The man's character and political loyalty were identical—party line all the way, not a cynic like Antonov, who was a commando. Pushtkin was not one of them, and neither was the Mexican, yet Antonov had his orders. Take the KGB man and his Mexican guide. Use the former's computer expertise to confirm the RAIL model; use the latter's knowledge of the area to get them in and out of the rendezvous site. The KGB man professed to have had Spetsnaz training, but he was no commando. As far as Antonov was concerned, he was excess baggage. His team could conduct the mission without either of them. But . . . orders were orders.

"You might as well get it over with," the man told Antonov. "Comrade Senior Sergeant knows what must happen."

Antonov's right eye twitched. "The senior sergeant has a name—*Vladimir Grodniko!*"

In the moonlight, the other man thought that Antonov might disembowel him on the spot. Antonov was forbidding enough to look at. He was taller than average at six feet two, and lean and sinewy from years of training. The Muscovite knew the Spetsnaz leader could easily break him in half. Yet the KGB man too had orders:

There were to be no traces of the mission left. The Spetsnaz team was expendable.

"Besides, he is keeping up all right," Antonov muttered.

Pushtkin stared at the mission's ground commander, then slunk away. There would be another, more appropriate time. He found his own rock, and pulled out a lighter and a pack of cigarettes from his shirt pocket.

Antonov leaped toward him and slapped the lighter out of his hand before Pushtkin could spin the igniting wheel. "*Fool!*" he hissed. "You would give our position away?"

Pushtkin fought to maintain his composure. Antonov was right. It had been a while since he'd been out in the field—he was more accustomed to urban aspects of unconventional warfare—but still . . . the Spetsnaz major had crossed the line. "Do not do that again, Comrade Major."

Mutual hate, mutual distrust. *That had been a mistake,* thought Antonov. *But this KGB idiot will be our ruin. How could he be so . . .*

He leaned closer to Pushtkin, allowing the other men the full blast of his own foul breath. "I know my orders," he told him, glancing at the senior sergeant making his way into the perimeter, where he limped off to the side of them. Antonov glared at the KGB man until Pushtkin looked away.

Antonov stalked off and pulled a flask out of his American manufactured backpack. Then he joined his senior sergeant on the perimeter. "Vladimir, drink. . . . "

"Sergei Antonovich! You will lead this mission!"

Antonov slapped the heels of his jackboots together. "I serve the Soviet Union!"

"You will take this man with you. . . ." Antonov's Group Leader paused, letting his most able officer within the 2nd Combined Arms Army Spetsnaz Company of the 2nd Directorate read between the lines; read the tone in his voice; understand the danger involved. He knew that Antonov understood the role of the KGB contact he would take along on this mission. Things were not so simple when GRU (Chief Directorate of Intelligence of the General Staff) headquarters sent a directive to pull Antonov, his senior sergeant, and the chief communicator out of his unit operating the perimeters of Kabul. And when working with the KGB, well, orders simply had to be followed. After all, the KGB was in charge—at the top of the Soviet Union's intelligence hierarchy. The Group Leader did not envy the young man standing before him, immaculately turned out in the simple uniform of a

Communications officer, a cover within their own Army for the Soviet Union's elite and secretive Spetsnaz commando forces. He began again.

"You will establish contact with this man in Juarez and then proceed to his residentura—*KGB headquarters in Juarez." The general handed Antonov a picture.*

Antonov studied the picture, and then he burned it in an ashtray. "Comrade General, when will I receive this mission?"

"In Juarez upon meeting that contact. He will be in overall charge. You and your men will report to him in five days. You know your route and have your papers."

"I serve the Soviet Union!"

Areoflot got Antonov's men to Havana, and from there, Mexico City. They'd split up then, melting into the crowds surging in the Old City Square, mingling with the tourists and the beggars. Differently located dead-letter drops stuffed with the necessary papers gave them new identities, and then they became tourists among Mayan temples and in the resorts of Acapulco and Cancun. They became migrant workers en route to the north. They became refugees escaping from the crushing poverty in the northern provinces. Separately, they traveled north to Juarez— north to the KGB residentura *there controlling cross-border operations.*

One by one, they arrived in Juarez and became Mexican citizens with a supply of forged documents at separate dead-letter drops. Language was no problem. Mexico and the southern half of North America had always been Antonov's team's specialty area, and they had been relentlessly drilled throughout their careers in Spanish, and in different dialects of Spanish that were spoken in Mexico, Nicaragua . . . Texas and California.

The safe-house network operated by KGB operatives from the Juarez/El Paso residentura *had not been good to them. The mission they received there increased their three-man team's size by two others. The KGB man and the Mexican guide who would lead them through the mountains en route to the missile complex were the unwelcome, secretive additions. It had been pointless to argue, Antonov would later recall. The KGB overruled the GRU and ultimately the GRU's Spetsnaz units. This mission would happen, and the way it would happen demanded Antonov taking along the KGB man and his computer expertise . . . and acquiesce to Pushtkin's command.*

Initially, during the infiltration, they were common Mexican laborers crossing the El Rio del Norte bridge in tandem with thousands of other daily bridge-crossers; they were driven in beat-up old Chevies from the fifties—cars on their last gasp with odometers reading the second iteration of a hundred thousand miles. A mere wave by the American border guard got them across, one by one, as they flashed him their work visas.

The next linkup was in a barrio in El Paso, the next safe house. Papers were exchanged for American identities. Chevies were exchanged for a van that lost itself in the pending American Labor Day weekend crush of traffic north of the Rio, and ultimately they became American backpackers and rock-hounds combing the mountains north of El Paso.

But when they split up—the Mexican, the senior sergeant, and the KGB man having gone into Las Cruces to pick up the motorcycles—the first mistake was made. It had been decided earlier to use three cross-country dirt bikes as an emergency escape measure, should their mission be compromised while still on foot in the mountains. The operative in Las Cruces had the motorcycles standing by, legally purchased and registered in a dead man's name, the owner of which had been long forgotten.

Once having established and secured the rendezvous site in the Franklin Mountain range south of the Organ Mountain network that would lead them to their target, the others had departed to bring back the bikes for their cache. Antonov and his communications sergeant, Chelstovsky, had waited. And waited. Finally, the others had come back over six hours late, as dawn cracked over the desert horizon. They had killed two American border guards during the night.

Compromise! Killings! Abort the mission now while there is time!

"The price of failure . . ." the KGB man had reminded Antonov.

Antonov knew failure's reward—it was in the jaws of an oven in Moscow, deep within the bowels of a monolithic aquarium, a dark, secretive building located next to the old Khodinka Airfield. Once, a very long time ago, when he had been inducted into the

Spetsnaz, he had seen a film at GRU headquarters, home of the Soviet Military Intelligence. During that film a man strapped down to a stretcher was fed feet-first into a crematorium. Alive. A traitor, who had betrayed the organization. Though it was a silent film, Antonov reflected on how the man's patent-leather shoes had melted almost instantly and how his screams must have sounded.

"We must proceed. We will proceed!"

Antonov was not willing to depart from this world through a blackened chimney. He nodded his head and then turned away. "The senior sergeant's leg . . . Vladimir, can you—"

"It is a scratch."

"You were lucky, my friend."

The obtrusiveness of Pushtkin. "We hid the bodies and abandoned their vehicle in another canyon to the west. They will blame it on the drug people."

Mutual distrust, mutual hate. The party man and the commando. The agent and the soldier. The cunning and the strong. "Yes, the drug-smugglers," Antonov had agreed.

"It is one of the reasons we use them. We must move."

Now, there was infection. Antonov shared his flask with the senior sergeant for three minutes, then glanced at his watch, shivering in the brisk desert night air. He felt Pushtkin's eyes on the back of his head, and dreamed of killing him. This was no team. This was a game, a mission puppeted by the KGB.

"We must move, Vladimir." Antonov grabbed his senior sergeant by the arm. Vladimir Grodniko moaned as he put his weight on his leg.

"Sergei Antonovich!" a voice whispered to his left. Antonov glanced around. It was Chelstovsky. The communications sergeant approached them. He was younger than the senior sergeant by twelve years, scrawny with youth, a dark, black-haired Ukrainian.

Antonov pulled his communications sergeant off to the side. "What is it? And keep your voice down!"

Chelstovsky clapped his hand on his leader's shoulder. "Do not turn around to look. They are talking together again, Major. I do not trust them."

Antonov pondered this. The Mexican and the KGB man

conversed often, away from the rest of the team. He cupped the back of Chelstovsky's head with the palm of his hand and rocked the younger man's head back and forth, as if he were his younger brother. "Then, my young friend," Antonov said, "let us both keep a wary eye on them tonight. And the rest of the nights to follow."

CHAPTER TWO

Oro Grande had gotten more than its normal share of rain that summer. Desolate, bleak, harsh, austere Oro Grande, New Mexico. The town of Oro Grande consisted of a post office, gasoline station, a roadside cafe that had a round and rusting Coca-Cola sign from the fifties hanging on the door that people back East would pay good money for.

Oro Grande. Those two words conjured lizards, rocks, sand moguls covered with thorns and scrub brush, cactus. And mountains. Rotten, rocky mountains that would sprain your ankle in a New York minute, and take your Texas time healing it back up. Lying at the foot of the Organ mountains, Oro Grande had been the site of an impromptu and short-lived gold rush a hundred years earlier. Unkempt mine shafts still ventilated the rocky, cactus-laden mountainsides, and sometimes, careless rock-hounds would disappear in those mine shafts.

Forty miles north of El Paso across the New Mexico state line, air-defense units from Fort Bliss often used the Oro Grande Range Camp as a forward base for extended field problems. It lay four miles to the west of town en route to the White Sands Missile Range complex along the secondary road adjacent to the north-south Highway 54 linking El Paso to Alamogordo. The range camp itself included a tiny PX in a temporary tin shelter that had been temporary since World War Two. The rectangular, tin-covered mess hall and two sets of twenty-odd quonset huts and a makeshift motor pool, all equally temporary, constituted the bulk of the grounds. The only permanent structures at the Oro Grande

Range Camp were the half-dozen desert-tan brick buildings aligned with the east-west secondary road linking Oro Grande to White Sands Missile Range.

Most of the year, air-defense artillery units from nearby Fort Bliss trained there. And, most of the year, individual battalions from one of the Special Forces Groups at Fort Bragg deployed to Oro Grande Range Camp for sustained desert-operations training. Survival, military mountaineering, combat, and reconnaissance operations, mortar and machine gun and small-arms live-weapons fire . . . by the time the average Beret came back to wives and girlfriends on the East Coast, he'd be thoroughly tanned and trimmed. Enough time in the desert thinned and dehydrated anyone. Cooked his brain a little too.

But this summer had been unusual. Enough rain had saturated the desert to turn the tumbleweeds green. The mountains, usually sweated light brown and rocky underneath the relentless sun, had rejuvenated with greenery and flowers. Lizards feasted. Snakes sunned. Skunks sprayed. Jackrabbits multiplied. It was a good time for the desert when Oro Grande's dust clouds settled—a rare occasion indeed.

And it was a damned good time, that Labor Day weekend, for a battalion's worth of two hundred or so Green Berets who had deployed to "Orfice-fucking-Grande" earlier in August to stand down for the weekend and make their first run down to El Paso for two nights of flat-out partying. Not that the SF guys were ever a nuisance or caused problems for the locals; for the most part they were mature, hardened men, bronzed and fit, just ready to blow out some of the sand that had caked inside their ears and throats from the hard training, ready to go down to El Paso and Juarez and throw a few Coronas down their necks.

The camp had come alive this morning with men scurrying from one end of the camp to the other in preparation for the stand-down. Within the next half hour, two buses waiting by the one-bar-and-two-pool-table excuse for a club would depart for El Paso.

One of those Green Berets stepped out of an elongated shack in the quonset-hut-barracks part of the range camp that served both as a shower and latrine. He squinted at the morning sun blinding the entrance.

He was a well-built man in his late thirties standing just under six feet tall. His physique was hardened from the rigorous physical-training program his avocation as a triathlete and his profession as a soldier demanded. He'd had a Cuban father and an Anglo mother, and his features and skin had been burnt even more creased and bronzed during the past month of desert training. Some would have said that he was an unattractive man, given his pock marked face and broken nose, three times mended, from the battles won and lost, with street fights fought growing up in Miami. But it was the man's calm self-assurance and steady manner that had made him a leader, a man to be trusted, a man with charisma.

It had not come easily. His rites of passage were consummated in Southeast Asia just before the final American pullout in 1975, when he was younger. Now, sixteen years later, Santo was a master sergeant in the United States Special Forces. Throughout, he had gained a certain wisdom about men, leadership, and everything there was to know about things military.

He was a lonely and saddened man as well, having been widowed two years before when a drunken driver killed his wife and thirteen-year-old daughter.

But this man was also an intellectual and a warrior. He was a leader who taught officers and junior NCOs alike who had the sense to listen to him. He was his team's mentor.

He was their team sergeant.

Master Sergeant Timothy "Manny" Santo shielded the front of his face with one hand and looked for a few seconds at the team hootch fifty feet away from the rear entrance of the shower-latrine building. He'd taken his time during his shower, and the wind had picked up. Dust devils from thirty-mile-an-hour south-of-Mexico winds swirled between him and the quonset hut which had been his home in the desert for the past month.

Santo licked his lips. He didn't know this time whether to run and stab himself in the foot with a desert thorn that would easily pierce his shower thongs, or carefully pick his way across and risk getting sandblasted by the wind. He was glad to be going into El Paso later on. He'd had all the Ramen noodles and mess-hall B-rations he could stomach. It was time, by God, to get to town and swallow a T-bone at El Paso's Great American Land and Cattle Company.

He opted for the first course of action. Santo braced himself for the dash to the quonset hut. Before he leapt out into the wind and the dust, the door to his quonset hut banged opened.

It was Greeley, the team medic. Comedy was due to happen soon. He watched the young blond-haired man sprint in his birthday suit across the area to the latrine. Greeley flew past Santo and burst to the latrine, his toilet kit in one hand, towel in the other.

"Have you no modesty, little Teddy?"

"Manny, you old Geritol sucker . . . this happens to be the only way you can get inside this here latrine." He covered himself up with his towel. "Besides, modesty or no, I have my coin on hand." Greeley pawed inside his toilet kit and then flashed Santo a huge coin, slightly larger than a silver dollar, that had the Special Forces Group designation on the front inscribed over a beret. Greeley's rank, initials, and team number designation were engraved underneath the beret. On the back was an insignia of a Trojan horse with three lightning flashes. Inscribed there was Greeley's motto—a concise , personal philosophy the soldier lived by.

"Get that thing outta my face." Santo was not inclined to indulge in trivial affairs like coin checks. It was an overused custom in the Forces. The custom dictated that whoever was found without his coin, despite the circumstances, state of dress, or activity, owed all those present a beer. But the rapid expansion of Special Forces during the previous decade had lowered training and unit-acceptance standards. Even support personnel—non SF-qualified clerk-typist, cooks, and intelligence attachments—were now prone to coin-check anyone in their vicinity. They would show up at the Green Beret Club on Smoke Bomb Hill, their berets carefully stowed in the cargo pockets of their fatigues, so that the flash showed everyone their Group of assignment.

The wanna-bes. Santo snorted. The coin-check custom has been used and abused.

"You owe me a beer, big Sarge." Greeley stuck his coin in Santo's face. "Read it and weep."

"I don't believe in that bull—" Santo broke off in mid-sentence and grabbed Greeley's wrist, bringing the coin closer to his eyes. "What's this? You got this at a pawn shop, right?"

"It's authentic!"

"My ass. You got this at the Mike Force Pawn Shop back in

Fayetteville, didn't you? I hate to break the news to you, kid, but you'd better buy a real coin at the PX. Okay, let's see what it says." Santo squinted. "Omigod, Teddy. 'We, the Professionals'?"

"That's my motto," Greeley said proudly.

"What kind of grades did you make in school? That's not even a complete sentence. Besides, you're just a no-time, no-grade buck sergeant."

Greeley grinned and stuck his coin back into his toilet kit. "You're a cynical man, Sergeant Santo. Have you no romance, no tradition, no customs?"

Santo grinned. "Sergeant Greeley, I've got more time in a—"

"I know, I know, you've got more time in a T-10 parachute than I've got in a T-shirt. Har-de-har-har. I was creaming mustard when you were creaming Commies. I know 'em all, fossil-face."

Santo laughed and let Greeley pass on by. Looking back out the door, he braced himself for the mad dash for his quonset hut. And then he went for it!

Immediately, a gust of wind whipped his towel off from around his waist. It gathered dirt and thorns along the ground, and finally plastered itself against the chain-link fence surrounding the compound. Santo chased after it with a tube of Prell in his right hand and his thongs flapping on the soles of his feet.

"Hey, Chief, get a load of this!" a gleeful voice yelled out from the doorway of his quonset hut.

Santo glanced around. *Hanlon and his big mouth*. He grabbed his now-filthy towel off the fence, and headed back for the barracks.

In the doorway stood Maslow and Hanlon. Maslow watched Santo with the corners of his mouth slightly upturned, the largest smile the warrant officer could muster. The man who had spoken, unlike Maslow, was dressed like a surf-party reject in Sony headphones, a madras shirt, and baggy shorts. Tears streaked down Sergeant First Class Randy Hanlon's cheeks, and he clutched his sides and brayed in a way he knew would bring the fullest attention to his team sergeant's predicament.

Santo scowled. It was the only clean towel he had.

"I believe that is the smallest penis I've ever seen," Maslow said in perfect solemnity.

Santo couldn't help but grin a little. Wintz Maslow, the only black cowboy he'd ever known, wore his typical deadpan expression, and was already dressed in his civilian uniform of pressed Levi jeans, Tony Lamas, and a blue demin shirt. This was a weird but predictable combination for the local intellectual, the high-domed forehead computer nerd, and also the best damned warrant officer in Special Forces.

Santo approached the quonset hut's entrance and paused, grinning a little. "What're you laughing about, Lurch?"

"What?"

"Take off the damn earphones!"

Hanlon pulled off his earphones, still grinning. Santo recognized heavy metal blasting through them. He often wondered how Hanlon's ears took it.

"I said, what are you laughing about, asshole?"

"Why, *you*, Team Daddy."

Santo redirected his attention to the warrant officer.

"Chief," Santo announced gravely to Maslow, imitating Maslow's way of speaking like a judge in the Supreme Court, "you know I respect *all* warrant officers, and you are second in command of this team, but sir, the reference to the size of my penis—as you so clinically refer to it—you don't even qualify to be a dickhead. You're just a walking penis with ears."

Hanlon roared and slapped Maslow on the back, knocking the smaller man off the doorstep and into the dust. Santo joined in the laughter.

"Hey, Manny."

Santo glanced to his left at the first bunk. His team leader was busy plowing through his wall locker.

"Sir?"

"What did you say the name of that place was?" Captain Matt MacIntyre found the polo shirt he'd been looking for and pulled it on. Then he reached into his toilet kit and retrieved a bottle of cologne.

"My God, sir, what's that you're putting on your face?"

Hanlon and Maslow reentered the team hootch. The warrant officer examined his team leader, one eyebrow arching. "I think I will kiss this man. It's been entirely too long."

"Back off, you degenerates," MacIntyre told them. "Manny, you could probably use this stuff."

"Sir, I take offense."

"Big Sarge, I was taking serious offense before you finally showered up a while ago."

"Now I'm crushed. So much for officer-NCO rapport."

MacIntyre had what Santo called that Ivy-league look, a look of careful groom and polish that six months ago made him think that the new team leader was a full-fledged member of the West Point Protective Association. Hell, he had to ride the new captain about something. And what better than his looking like a preppie with the polo shirts and slacks rounded out with Docksiders?

Actually, in MacIntyre's own words, he'd been a rotcee-nazi. An ROTC product from the University of Oklahoma. He'd spent his summers roughnecking out on his old man's oil-well sites to help pay for school. MacIntyre was from an immensely wealthy family, but never talked about it. Everything MacIntyre did, he did on his own without his father's help. It hadn't taken long for Santo to realize he'd initially misjudged the personality of a man he'd almost called "Skippy" to his face when they'd first met.

"Sir, the first stop tonight will be The Great American Land and Cattle Company," Santo said, answering MacIntyre's earlier question. "Best steak and pinto beans in El Paso."

"Juarez later, right?"

"Sir, before you get laid, me and the team are gonna get you tequila-qualified tonight. Might even let you eat the worm."

"Tuh-kill-ya," Hanlon roared from his bunk over Walkman-induced AC/DC.

"Hu-yah," MacIntyre said weakly. He had absolutely no intention of getting laid in Juarez. He combed his hair in front of his wall locker's mirror, and tried to think of a way to stay on the U.S. side of the border that night.

Grinning, Santo walked over to his bunk next to MacIntyre's to get dressed. That had been a weak "hu-yah." The last date MacIntyre had brought to the team party before deployment had been one of the post dependent schoolteachers. *Very* nice. He did have to hand it to MacIntyre for his taste in women. But! He'd have to make sure that the captain got his butt squeezed by some Mexican wench in Juarez tonight. Yeah, he'd personally insure that.

Santo had expected less in his new team leader. MacIntyre was green, fresh out of the Q-course at Bragg, but over the past six months he'd been with the team, the officer had listened and pulled his share of the load. And with Santo's guidance, MacIntyre seldom made mistakes in operations and planning when they jointly prepared their briefbacks and missions. The past two STRIKE operations on the previous deployment to Helena that year had confirmed the new team leader's ability. MacIntyre knew his communications and how to by God encrypt and decrypt a one-time pad, and that was more than he could say for a lot of the team leaders he'd served with in the past.

The door to their Quonset hut banged back open. Greeley again. The team medic strolled down to his bunk and picked up a well-thumbed magazine. Santo glanced at it. *Hustler.* "Teddy!"

"Yo!" Greeley was youngest member of the team, looking more like a fresh-faced Eagle Scout.

"What'cha reading there, big Ted?"

"Uh, *Hustler.*"

Christ on a crutch, Santo thought, grinning, pulling his shirt on. *He's actually embarrassed.* "You gonna be a gynecologist someday, Teddy?" Santo thought the team medic's face looked like the kid in the barber's chair straight out of that Norman Rockwell painting.

At only twenty-two, Sergeant Ted Greeley was the youngest, the boldest, and the skinniest man of the team; he instigated most of the jokes and towel-snapping wars. But Santo had been half-serious when he'd made the crack about Greeley becoming a gynecologist. Or an orthopedist. Or a pediatrician. Or a dentist. Special Forces medics were trained to do surgery, major surgery if necessary, in a bad situation when no doctors were available. Members of the team, including wives and pets, rarely had to go to the hospital. Greeley would just administer the right drug if he had it in inventory, splint the sprain, stitch the cut—and if you let him (but no one volunteered), even pull your wisdom teeth. He knew how, after a year and a half of medical training. In the "goat lab" Greeley had shot, scalded, lacerated, burned, and fractured his "patient." Every time the goat healed, Greeley would torture it some more under the close supervision of his medical trainers, and if Greeley's "patient" died while being treated, then he would have flunked the course—the fate half his medical training class suffered. But if a Special Forces medic was to perform surgery in a combat environment and heal not only the members of his own team but the indigenous populations in the countries his team was deployed in, then he had to know his stuff. There was no substitute for the experience his goat-lab training offered him.

Greeley put the magazine down and did his toughest swagger toward Santo's bunk as the team sergeant pulled his Levi's on. "Nope. But I'll give ya some free medical advice, pilgrim—if ya'd quit slammin' that Geritol down every mornin', ya wouldn't be such an *ugly* fuck."

"Teddy, you're not John Wayne. Sorry to break the news to you kid. Go wake Barkowitz up, it's time to get on the buses."

Greeley kicked Barkowitz's big toe the next bunk over, and interrupted the steady snore Santo had noticed upon entering the hootch. "I stand corrected, Manny," Greeley informed his team sergeant. *"This* is the ugliest fella on the team. It's hard to believe, but yes, he's even uglier than you. Wake up, Barko."

Staff Sergeant Edward Barkowitz was a big man with a barrel chest and heavy, Polish features and frame. Barkowitz stirred in his bunk and sat up. He glared at Greeley, his physical and psychological opposite.

"Out of my face," he growled, low and deep. Barkowitz rummaged through his locker to get ready.

Barkowitz, aside from Maslow, was the only other married man on the team, with a gorgeous wife back home and two girls—a set of six-year-old twins—who fortunately took after their mother. Broad at the brow—one brow, that is—wide at the forehead, and high on the cheekbones, Ed Barkowitz was the team's senior communications sergeant, who could carry his communications gear the way he slept—anytime, anyplace, and in any position. He could send code at twenty-five groups a minute. He could make commo from the West Coast to the East Coast. Intercontinental commo, when necessary. Whenever their team deployed, they always made commo back to their headquarters, when other teams couldn't. Barkowitz personally ensured that.

Back by his locker, Santo pulled on a pair of biker boots to go with his Levi's and Harley-Davidson T-shirt. He smiled and tuned out Greeley's litany of past heroics. Life was good, and he loved his family. They were a *team*, even if there were only six of them deployed out to Oro Grande this year instead of the normal twelve. The six others were either attending language school at the Defense Language Institute or going through NCO professional-development courses at Fort Bragg and Fort Benning.

On this deployment Santo's detachment was a split-team—the normal complement of manpower was twelve—but a team nonetheless. There were few things in life Manny Santo held sacrosanct, but Special Forces was the one thing no one could ever change, augment, tear away, or update. These Green Berets were his team. And that meant they were family.

Who had gotten him through some rough times.

It was an unspoken thing, their philosophy. Once you'd been in Special Forces for a while, then you knew. You understood. A common, healthy respect for all existed on a good team, born of mutual sweat, experience, sacrifice. Maturity, without empty boasting. Never quitting, regardless of the task, whether it was pulling support details back at Fort Bragg, or going the full length of a desert-survival course at Oro Grande. It was the team way. It was the soldier's way. The green beret they all wore was just a sloped and rounded forest-green wool hat that was cold in the wintertime and hot in the summertime.

The headgear did not make a man into a Green Beret. It was the man underneath. It simply did not matter what your rank was, or how much experience you had—what mattered was whether or not you were a *soldier*, a soldier who contributed and trusted those who had earned your respect and vice versa. What mattered was being a hard son of a bitch when the choppers broke down and you had to go it cross-country over the cactus and rocks with minimum food and water. To travel light and freeze at night.

It was easier in Special Forces than in any other kind of unit to figure out who had the big egos and who had the strong egos. There was a difference. Respect within the team came more from merit than from authority and position. Every man counted.

Santo had seen other guys with state-of-the-art web gear, with brand-new Randal knives and Silva compasses; guys who looked good on the instructor stand but were worthless in the field; guys who made careers out of hiding in headquarters staffs and training assignments. Most of them never amounted to a hill of beans when the dude was walkin' and walkin' and humpin' that ruck and that radio and that demo and that medical kit bag to wherever they had to go, and then driving on with the mission once they got there. And if necessary, doing it all over again, even if it meant living on nothing more than a ration a day and drinking iodine-purified stream water.

But the team—*the team*—was what mattered. No prima donnas. No hypocrites and ego-trippers. *The team*. And if necessary, the individual, to drive on and accomplish the mission when the team was no more. His teammates would expect no less.

That was their philosophy.

Santo lived by that and when he was hurting, he prayed by it. It had cost him his marriage shortly before his wife and daughter were killed, but he more than most team sergeants in Group could look himself in the mirror every morning.

Minutes later, they were all dressed, ready and about to leave for the buses. Then a head poked through the door, belonging to the Company Sergeant Major, Ed Denny, the oldest man in the company, in his mid-forties. His face had the creases, graying hair and eyebrows, and scowl of a man twenty years older. But he was lean and strong, and he competed every year in the New York City Marathon.

"Sergeant Santo!"

"Yo!"

"Bad news, Manny."

Santo knew what was coming. Murphy's Law: What can go wrong, will go wrong. MacIntyre strolled over to the doorway, meeting Santo and the sergeant major there. The others clustered behind them. "What's up, Smaj?" Santo asked him.

The sergeant major walked inside, seeing the disappointment on the team's faces. No one liked to be told that they had a shit detail to pull while others played. Already, the buses outside were revving up for the trip into town. "You know that ADA unit that pulled in here a week ago?"

"Yeah." Santo knew all about the air-defense artillery from Fort Bliss—cocky young kids, out of shape, pretending they were bad; potbellied NCOs leading them—they often came out to Oro Grande to conduct their training. What the sergeant major had to tell him obviously included working with them.

"The battalion commander and *their* commander worked out some sort of agreement that we'd provide them some foreign-weapons training in return for the support they've given us out here at Oro Grande."

"What support?"

"They own this range camp. They cleaned it up and prepared it for our training out here this year. The CO's got the details."

"Bullshit. This place was a pigsty when we got here. We spent two days just mopping the sand off the floors. Besides, we've pulled every shit detail on this exercise. Hell, we've run the survival course, just last week we planted all those caches behind White Sands for the strike ops going out next week—"

"Well, Manny, you know as well as I do that the CO thinks you're his golden boys. Your team's already trained up to standard, and that's why he's had to put you in charge of running the drop zones, the caches, survival, and so on. Now he wants to put his best foot forward with the ADA. You know, improve unit interoperability and all that."

"Yeah, yeah." The other team members quietly returned to their bunks, satisfied that at least their team sergeant had tried. What the hell. Sometimes you fell on your sword, and other times you just sheathed it and said "Airborne!"

The sergeant major glanced at his watch. The others were out of earshot. "Manny, " he said, quieter this time, "time is now 0950. You and the Captain need to report to the FOB's war room at 1000 for your briefing."

Santo immediately noticed the gleam in the sergeant major's eye. "What do you know, Ed?"

"Nothing." The sergeant major grinned. "Absolutely nothing, but keep acting pissed off." The sergeant major left.

MacIntyre stepped up alongside Santo as he watched the sergeant major walk back to the company headquarters hut next door. "What was that all about?"

"Support, sir. Detail support." The two men looked at each other.

"Right."

"Let's go find out about it."

CHAPTER THREE

Ten minutes later, Santo and MacIntyre had walked across the compound to the battalion headquarters and FOB—Forward Operations Base, the battalion's command-and-control nerve center located along the highway linking Oro Grande Range Camp with White Sands Missile Range. En route, the buses had passed by, members from other teams leaning out the windows and laughing at their predicament. The compound was desolate, and the only vehicles left were a civilian Dodge K-car and the battalion commander's CUC-V—a four-wheel-drive military version of the Chevy Blazer—parked in front of the headquarters building.

"Wonder what the Mad Russian's got in store for us?" MacIntyre muttered, as they walked inside.

"No telling," Santo replied. "He keeps a pretty good secret."

Volensky was a legend in Special Forces, and even though Santo and MacIntyre's team was going to have to pull a detail in support of whatever crazy scheme the Mad Russian had cooked up, they'd do it and do it well. Even if it just entailed teaching privates from some Fort Bliss air-defense artillery unit how to fire AK-47 assault rifles. Even if it meant missing out on The Great American Land and Cattle Company and Juarez.

Lieutenant Colonel Andrei Volensky commanded the respect of every man in his battalion. Born of Russian parents in the Ukraine shortly before World War II, he had led a colorful and at times desperate life. Deserting the Red Army in the mid-fifties when he was barely nineteen, he eventually crossed all Warsaw Pact borders into West Germany, emaciated and ill with pneumonia, where he was given sanctuary by the U.S. government. By the time he was twenty, he had been recruited for the Army Special Forces, first as an enlisted man and then, after pulling a tour in Vietnam where he earned a battlefield commission, as an officer. More combat tours in Southeast Asia followed, and then multiple tours with Special Forces and the CIA during the seventies and eighties. He'd never married. Special Forces was the only family Volensky had. Now, having just turned fifty-two, he considered all soldiers in the battalion as his children.

He led by example, and fought for his children when they were in trouble. At Group headquarters, he continually insisted upon the most arduous training for them in preparation for war, demanding decentralized command and control to the lowest level. Team leaders and team sergeants appreciated that about him most of all, in a day when even Special Forces fell prey to careerist-minded senior officers at the command level who paid lip service to decentralized training, while micro-managing them from the top of the same time.

Volensky was not afraid to let people make mistakes. That was how they learned. However, if a man lied to him, or cheated on reports, or violated his integrity, he'd have his nuts. He was a hard man, but fair. Loud and temperamental at times, he often intimidated those officers and NCOs at Group headquarters into submission if desk-jockeying interfered with his unit's training or with the progress of one of his teams. He had no patience with petty bureaucracy.

Volensky had a policy that everyone in the battalion respected. He preferred not to utilize the conventional norms of non-judicial punishment for minor offenses within the battalion such as a fistfight or the minor wreckage of a vehicle. He'd just have the battalion Command Sergeant Major notify and escort the offend-ing NCO to his office (and he did not discriminate between ranks—officers as well, as notified by their company commander) with a sixty-pound rucksack full of water and a couple of rations. He'd always listen to the individual after calling him on the carpet, and—since the man was usually "guilty as charged"—have him walk.

Therein laid a choice: walk or leave the battalion. Without exception, they always chose to walk.

Volensky's attitude was that men were basically good men; that they, like him in the past, would occasionally commit a sin and transgress the boundaries of propriety—as anybody could. He detested other commanders who'd hand Article 15's (non-judicial punishment) out like candy which took away a man's pay and time off, and often ruined a professional soldier's future career in the Army.

So Volensky would just make the guilty man walk out into the desert for fifteen or twenty miles, and while he sweated and baked and humped, an assigned driver would check up on the transgressor to ensure he would not become a heat casualty. Then, upon completion, the man would report back to Volensky in his office. During this painful walk, Volensky philosophized, the man had time to reflect on where he went wrong, and no one in the battalion wanted to experience a repetition of the walk. After the walk, the NCO's or officer's "sin" was permanently forgotten and never mentioned again.

Santo and MacIntyre's team would never let Volensky down; neither would they complain to the other detachments upon this unwanted detail's task completion. But something in Santo's gut told him that it wouldn't be any ordinary detail.

MacIntyre and Santo strode down the hallway into the primary staff room, where the operations staff NCOs and officers normally clacked away at their typewriters, writing plans for the next month's series of missions. But the place was deserted. Only one unlucky buck sergeant stood guard at the door. He didn't have a weapon with him, but his presence indicated that they wouldn't pass through the operations section into the war room for their briefing until he checked their identification cards for clearance.

"Okay, Smitty," Santo began fishing for his billfold, "what gives?"

The young sergeant, valiantly trying to sprout his annual desert mustache on an otherwise smooth face, said, "Old Man's orders, Sergeant Santo."

Weird, Santo thought. Pulling his identification card out of his billfold, Santo presented it to the young NCO. MacIntyre did the same.

"Okay?"

"Yeah. Pass on through."

As Santo and MacIntyre walked in, they saw the war room spotless and ready. Ready for something. Usually, it was total chaos during their training mission briefings, with the S-2 intelligence officer scurrying around clutching operations orders and weather reports in his hands; the S-3 operations officer would be flipping through the briefing chart by the podium before the gargantuan situation map behind it; and of course the Old Man, Volensky, would be sitting in front of the situation map, slouched and smoking a long, brown *More* cigarette, yelling at them to hurry up.

Not today.

This was definitely unusual. Everything was ready—no last-minute rushing about. Santo thought about the wiseass smile on his Company Sergeant Major's face fifteen minutes before.

"Ah! The trolls from the trenches!" Lieutenant Colonel Andrei Volensky bounced up from his chair and waved them inside, where Santo and MacIntyre took their seats to his left before the situation map on the wall.

Volensky's brown hair was turning gray at the temples, yet his bushy eyebrows still retained the dark vigor of his youth. On his face was a sardonic half-smile. Santo looked at that smile and thought to himself, *Oh, shit.* He immediately checked the Old Man's hand and confirmed the omnipresent dark-skinned cigarette. Already the ash had grown a full inch without, for some reason, falling off and scattering ashes across his fatigue blouse.

MacIntyre was about to take the seat immediately to the colonel's left when Volensky said, "So tell me, Team Leader, how have you enjoyed the desert?" Santo smiled to himself. Volensky always had that habit of addressing his subordinates by their position. It was kind of a test, to see if the lower-ranking officer or NCO could be intimidated. Volensky did not like mental or physical weaklings.

MacIntyre stuck out his jaw. "It's fine, sir."

Volensky squinted at MacIntyre over his reading glasses. "You're testing me, Team Leader?"

"Actually, sir, it sucks."

Volensky smiled and pinched MacIntyre's cheek, slapped it gently a couple of times. "And why does it *suck,* Team Leader?" Santo drew in a deep breath, glad he wasn't an officer. Volensky always tested his officers in this none-too-subtle way. It was effective.

"Because, sir, my detachment deployed with the advance party to sign for these barracks. We covered the drop zone when the battalion jumped in. We ran the survival-instruction phase of training. We've been setting up these caches the whole past week, and sir, we haven't even pulled a real mission yet. That's what we came here for. That's why it sucks."

"Enough!" Volensky barked. "Sit down!"

MacIntyre took his seat, his cheeks flushed. Okay, so he'd laid the ol' scrotum sack out on the chopping block for that. What the hell.

Santo caught MacIntyre's eye and winked at him. MacIntyre grinned a little, but not much. Volensky walked out to their front and stood before the podium.

"And what do you think, Team Sergeant?"

Santo straightened up in his chair. He knew how to play the game. "I fully agree with my team leader, sir."

Volensky scowled at them. "Maybe you'd rather be in Lebanon, or perhaps down south in Honduras, eh?"

"Yes, sir," MacIntyre and Santo replied in tandem. Santo almost smiled.

"Or how about *here*."

No one replied. *Christ,* Santo thought, *they already* were *here*.

"Here to support my ADA friends," Volensky continued. "I need good men to show them a good time."

Santo glanced behind him. The only people he'd seen since entering the war room was a civilian slipping a round tray of slides into a projector by the Old Man's seat. Another civilian, a silver-haired skinny man in a three-piece suit, sat at the rear of the room, listening to them. At first, he'd only concentrated on Volensky, but *this* was unusual. Something was up. A briefing, a mission. Something.

Volensky sat down next to MacIntyre and slapped the team leader's knee. "Listen to what my friend has to say, and then if your detachment wants to get drunk in Juarez or El Paso tonight, you may go if you want. No questions asked." Volensky waved his hand at the civilian.

The civilian proceeded to their front, holding a control box wired in to the projector through a long cable. He was a robust, stocky man with an animated, reddish face. Blond hair and a dark brown mustache with a ruddy complexion. Young, about MacIntyre's age. Business suit, with his jacket off and necktie loosened.

ADA, huh? Santo thought. *My ass.*

"Good morning," the civilian said to them in a slow, measured voice, an Arkansas accent. He turned back to the situation map. He studied it for a moment and then faced them again, putting his hands in his pockets. "My name is Terry Saxon, and I am *not* an ADA puke."

They all grinned at that. Volensky's face kept its impassive stare, and Santo noticed that the Old Man's cigarette ash was about to drop all over his lap.

"Used to be in the Army, but I was a platoon leader in the Ranger Regiment. Got to participate in the Grenada FTX back in '83. Now I work for the Drug Enforcement Administration." He paused, looking at them, holding everyone's interest. "Right now, the rumor mill in your battalion has it that you guys are pulling a detail, crapola extreme, in training your ADA friends from Fort Bliss while everyone else is having a good time in town for the next two nights during this Labor Day weekend. That's good. What you will be doing in reality is helping me out."

Santo glanced at Volensky and smiled inwardly. Volensky, inscrutably Russian to the core, was still in his slouch, smoking his cigarette, peering over his reading glasses at Saxon, saying nothing. It was as if the Old Man was bored. He was anything but bored. Because Volensky had once been his team leader a million years ago, Santo knew this. He knew exactly what the battalion commander was doing right now—even as he slouched and smoked and watched.

Saxon was unknowingly the target of Volensky's intense character analysis during this briefing. It was always that way when Volensky met someone new. Why? Volensky had told him long ago: A man's character tells everything; the way he looks or does not look you in the eye. Nervousness. His physical conditioning. Does he tell you what you want to hear—or the truth? How often Santo had found himself adopting the Old Man's habits during his own supervision in the training and leadership of his team. The following hour would be a constant, unspoken ballet of chemistry, a certain inflection in the briefer's voice, the measured glance at Volensky's eyes to gauge his reaction to the briefer.

Saxon turned on the slide projector and then pressed a button on the control handle he held. The screen by the situation map illuminated, showing a blowup of the southwestern United States, Mexico, Central America, and the top half of South America.

"As you know," Saxon continued, "the Caribbean basin and Central America are of vital importance to the security of the United States. Fifty-five percent of our crude oil and almost half of our exports and imports flow through this area. In the event of war, sixty percent of our matériel and manpower would pass through this area in support of a conflict in NATO or in the Persian Gulf. The Soviets put Castro and Ortega in power in Cuba and Nicaragua. By continuing to subsidize those bankrupt economies, the Soviets' ultimate goal was the spread of Communist revolution throughout Latin America. Of course, as recent events have shown, the Soviets have wound up bankrupting themselves. Nevertheless, it is still much more economically sound to continue sponsorship of their proxy Latin American war machine as opposed to maintaining their huge buildup in Eastern Europe." Saxon pressed the button again, and this time, a picture of the island of Grenada occupied the screen.

"Seven years ago, I was a platoon leader with elements of the 1st Battalion, 75th Rangers, who initially jumped into Grenada in October '83. During the mop-up which followed the rescue of American medical students at the university, we captured vast supplies of arms and ammunition sent there by Cuba under the guise of Cuban economic aid. My platoon alone secured over 800,000 rounds of 7.62-mm ammunition, 1000 rounds of RPG-7 warheads, one hundred RPG-7 launchers, machine guns, mortars—that was all in just one warehouse. Overall, my battalion secured a dozen storage sites such as this. Likewise, the Panama incursion in December 1989 revealed that Noriega had ample dealings with Soviet arms trading. U.S. forces captured over 73,000 AK-series assault rifles and machine guns." Saxon walked directly to the front of the team and locked eyes with them. "It was a good thing the Administration sent us into both those places. Grenada and Panama were plainly to be used as launch-sites for the export of Latin American revolution in our own backyard."

Volensky cleared his throat suddenly, making an irritated sound. He wanted to remind the young ex-Ranger standing before him that Grenada was one of the most poorly executed military operations in recent history. Almost thirty American dead, most of them from helicopter accidents and lack of common sense. Faced only with a lightly armed Cuban force, American casualties for the most part had resulted from a lack of realistic, and yes, dangerous, peacetime live-fire training.

"Sir?" Saxon asked him.

Volensky waved his hand. "Go on, go on."

Manny Santo thought to himself. *Strike one.* Saxon's last lengthy statement had been awkwardly phrased, dogmatic. It had not been spoken in the way someone would normally say it. It had been formal, canned, as if Saxon was quoting a party line, like a redundant justification. *Besides,* he thought, *why are we talking politics and strategy?*

Saxon paused and beeped another slide onto the screen, reflecting data that listed many different types of Soviet weaponry discovered on the island. Santo let out a low whistle.

"Central America writhes in anarchy," Saxon continued. "Eleven years ago, Somoza abdicated and fled Nicaragua. That country promptly fell inside the spheres of influence of the Soviet Union, through their proxy state of Cuba; the leaders of Nicaragua's revolution were hand-picked and trained by Moscow. Now, those Sandinista revolutionaries export their revolution in the same style throughout the rest of Latin American. One of their chief allies are the Colombian drug cartels"

Another slide. This one showed a picture of Lenin and a quote beside it. Saxon picked up a pointer and and underscored the quote. "Lenin once said, *'Probe out with the bayonet—if you encounter mush, go deeper, if you encounter steel, withdraw.'* American resolve, fortunately, made the Communists abandon their adventure in Grenada, and blew the lid on Panama's involvement with the drug trade and Soviet proliferation of arms for narco-terrorism. But, following Lenin's doctrine, Latino insurgents had a backup plan: one that is in full effect today and has been for quite some time. That backup plan is manifested in drug money and narco-terrorism as run by the Colombian drug cartels, headquartered in Medellín and Cali. It's very simple. The Cuban intelligence apparatus, dominated by the Soviets since 1966, subverts the morale of the American population through drugs, creating a festering domestic problem at home that undermines U.S. foreign policy abroad. The Cubans provide the Latino drug cartel safe haven and ports throughout the Caribbean for their smuggling operations. In return, the cartels subsidize revolutionaries throughout the Western Hemisphere with drug money and weaponry. Those profits also help fund ongoing Cuban intelligence initiatives hostile to the United States."

Santo stole another glance at Volensky, who had leaned forward in his chair after Saxon's last statement, his eyes narrowing. Volensky turned to his left and caught Santo staring at him. They locked eyes for moment, and then Volensky inhaled deeply, let it out, and returned his attention to Saxon. Santo thought, *Strike two,* and knew that he would be talking to Volensky first chance he got.

"Now for the big picture in a nutshell," Saxon said. "Communist-inspired revolution is therefore funded in great part by drug money. Nicaragua and Cuba and, ultimately, the Soviet Union reap a two-sided benefit—profit for their revolutions, and the undermining of U.S. security in the Western Hemisphere."

Saxon glanced away from the team, turned around, and stared at the screen. "And we Americans continue to snort that white stuff up our noses and pay for it all." He faced them again. "It's getting worse, gentlemen. Now there's crack, and now a new designer cocaine-based drug called ice. Instant addiction. Instant slavery. What better way to subvert an indulgent, spoiled society?"

This time Santo saw the glint of confirmation in Volensky's eyes, as the Old Man nodded his head and then leaned back in his chair, as if he had just made his mind up about something. *Strike three.* That last comment smacked of one voicing a personal crusade. Personal crusades in the government—like the Iran-Contra affair a few years back—led to scandal, political infighting, all that garbage.

Saxon pressed for the next slide. The screen now showed the original layout of Mexico, Central America, and the top half of South America. This time a series of arrows linked the countries of Colombia and Peru ultimately to key border cities along the Mexican-U.S. border.

"Recent intelligence reports from our agents in Juarez reveal that a tremendous operation is under way near an area immediately west of Las Cruces, New Mexico. The eastern extent of this smuggling operation includes your desert-training area here, near Oro Grande—the border of which is delineated by the Organ Mountains leading south from the White Sands Missile Range. The DEA needs help to cover the mountains south of White

Sands. For years, we have been trying to get Congressional approval to use elements of the American military in support of our counter-smuggling operations. We now have both an opportunity and permission to use a team of Special Forces who specialize in desert operations—yourselves—to assist us in reconnaissance."

"This is where you come in," interrupted Volensky, getting up. "Through Group headquarters, I have been tasked by the Special Operations Command back at Fort Bragg to support the DEA."

Santo nodded his head. For years, he had been told to plan and train for the next war. For years, he had trained his team to the best of his ability, but now veterans from the Vietnam War were steadily retiring from the Army, and the edge in experience had been lost. The Army had become a careerist-minded, bureaucratic system of paperwork and stifled training. It was time for the real war to be fought—the war against insurgency and terrorism in Latin America, against drug subversion in the U.S. and against the drug money that paid for it. He liked the idea. But still, there was something amiss: something in the way that Volensky had caught his attention and in their earlier conversation outside that showed that something was not right. He comforted himself with the knowledge that Volensky would get back with him later.

"Gentlemen, I have presented to you the overall situation. You will receive your mission shortly." Saxon glanced at Volensky, who nodded.

"Thank you, Mister Saxon," Volensky said, rising from his seat. He faced the others. "Still want to go into El Paso tonight, Team Leader? Team Sergeant?" Santo noted there was no humor in Volensky's voice. It confirmed his suspicion.

MacIntyre was the first to speak. "No, sir," he replied. "My team will be more than happy to support the ADA pukes this weekend."

"Everyone take a few minutes for a piss break and some coffee. And then you shall receive your mission." Volensky glanced sharply at Saxon. "I guess you'll want to rearrange your slides for the remainder of the briefing."

"Why, uh . . . yes, Colonel."

Santo waited for a moment, and then followed his battalion commander outside.

Volensky's boots crunched on the gray compound gravel

surrounding the FOB building, as he walked away from the front door. Turning right, he faced due west and stared at the White Sands Missile Range complex twenty-two miles away, lying at the base of a series of sharp, jagged peaks comprising the Organ Mountains.

The FOB's front door opened again and Santo approached Volensky from behind. Absently, Volensky patted his pockets for his cigarettes.

"Those things are gonna kill you, sir."

Volensky lit up, keeping his eyes on the missile complex and the mountains. "It has been a while since we've last talked, Team Sergeant."

"Then let's crack a bottle of cognac tonight, sir."

"No time. Your team is moving out tonight."

Santo glanced at his watch. Already, it was 0930. "Tonight? What about isolation? Isn't this supposed to be a drug-intercept mission?" Isolation was the planning phase for each mission, where a team would draw specialized equipment, analyze the mission, terrain, and previously gathered intelligence, and rehearse specific mission requirements and actions on the objective.

"Orders from SOCOM," Volensky muttered. "Saxon is going with you as well."

"Strange . . . think he can hang?"

Volensky looked at Santo for the first time. "The Group Commander thinks so. He's on the team, so any resistance to that idea is moot. Yes. It *is* strange, Manny. So far as I know, this *is* a drug mission—you are to identify a suspected smuggling route somewhere behind White Sands."

"Why there? That doesn't make sense. It's pretty damned hard to move around in those mountains, let alone smuggle drugs. Unless . . ."

"Unless it's got something to do with White Sands," Volensky finished, shaking his head. He didn't have to add the words— Strategic Defense Initiative—for Santo's benefit. How many times had Volensky faced this before? His last assignment before assuming command of the battalion had been at the Pentagon, where he'd seen more than this share of inter-service rivalry, constant jockeying for government fundings for newer, gold-plated weapons systems. There, he had also seen the same inadequacies in the civilian civil-service branches as well—the

NSA, DEA, CIA, FBI. Why? Why could there not be smoother, better-coordinating factions in the American government? Was it a national trait?

"Sir?" Santo was used to his battalion commander's spells of silence, but it was time to receive the rest of the briefing.

Volensky returned his gaze to Santo. Despite inter-service and inter-agency rivalry, the bottom line still dictated that he had to send the best team in his battalion into the mountains on this no-notice reconnaissance-and-intercept mission. Santo and his men were that team.

Volensky clapped his hand on Santo's shoulder as they entered the FOB. "Just do your duty, Team Sergeant," he told Santo. "Aside from that, I want you to think about accepting a direct commission."

Santo blinked. Volensky had a habit of catching people by surprise. "Don't wanna be no officer. Sir."

"Screw your enlisted-man superiority complex. I was a sergeant first class myself, once, you know that. We'll talk about that later, Team Sergeant. For now, you just do your duty, conduct this mission, and bring every man back whole and sound. I've got a battalion party scheduled and I don't want your team to miss it."

But a battalion party was the farthest thing from Santo's mind. It was only another eleven hours before infiltration.

A clatter and a stifled moan of pain. Glancing down from where his backpack was wedged between a chute of rocks, near the rim of the canyon, Major Sergei Antonov watched his senior sergeant tumble down past the cactus and the scree and rocks on the slope they'd been climbing. He looked back up. The terrain was difficult, but not that difficult. They had been ascending a long talus and scree slope, and were now almost out of the canyon. The remaining obstacle was a twenty-foot band of crumbling rock at the canyon's lip. Pushtkin and the Mexican guide were already up and over. Grodniko, unhurt, could have made this in a quarter of the time it had taken the team to reach just the band of rock.

A face appeared over the rim and stared down at him. Pushtkin. Antonov could read the KGB man's face, and he hated him for it. But they were moving entirely too slowly. Vladimir was hurt, and his knowledge of Spetsnaz standard operating procedures concerning wounded personnel, now that they had reached the moment of decision, had been the only thing to keep the senior sergeant going.

Antonov glanced at his watch. It was 2100. The sun had gone down barely twenty minutes ago, and they had only been moving for the past fifteen. It was to be this way for the rest of the night? *Damn him! Damn him for getting shot! Vladimir, you fool! Pushtkin, you incompetent ass!*

Despite his intense dislike of the KGB man, Antonov knew that Pushtkin was right. Right that he had to kill a man he'd fought with and led with and trained with and bled with over the past five years.

He had to follow regulations.

"Sergei Antonovich," a voice floated up to him. It was Chelstovsky. The communicator had scrambled downslope, and was now kneeling where Vladimir Grodniko lay bleeding and semi-conscious in the cactus and sand. "His bad leg, Major . . . the senior sergeant cannot go any further. It is now broken. He may have a concussion."

Antonov glanced back up at Pushtkin. The KGB man pulled away and rejoined the Mexican at the top. Antonov spat against a cactus growing on the side of the rock chute to which he clung. Then he slowly climbed down, descending to his communicator and senior sergeant on the scree slope.

Grodniko was breathing heavily, his eyes glassy. He was conscious, but in pain. "Your flask, Sergei Antonov," he rasped.

Antonov fished two items out of his backpack: his flask and the medical kit. Chelstovsky turned away, clenching his teeth.

"Get the others," Antonov told him. "We'll need their help." Bitterly, Chelstovsky shrugged off his backpack. Before leaving, he grasped his senior sergeant's hand and held it tightly for several moments. Then he started climbing.

Antonov stared off into the night, blinking his eyes, saying nothing for several long moments. Then a strong hand, calloused and gnarled, grabbed his wrist.

"It is all right, Sergei Antonovich," Grodniko rasped. "You know I would do the same if the situation were reversed."

Antonov tried to grin, but couldn't. Then he forced himself to. "You were always a hard bastard, Vladimir."

"And since when have I ever taught you anything that was not hard," Grodniko chuckled. He grimaced from the effort it took, and reached down to his leg. It was swelling rapidly, ballooning out of his mountain boot like a sausage cinched tight at the end. "We are running out of time, and you know what you must do. I gave it my best, but now . . ." Grodniko paused and picked a cactus barb out of his kneecap, swearing quietly under his breath. "Now, I wish for a drink."

Antonov unscrewed the flask's metal cap and pressed the opening to his senior sergeant's lips. The man gulped down better than half of the flask, and some of the scorching clear liquid dribbled out of the corner of his mouth. Then the older man abruptly sat up, in pain, but now with a slow fire spreading across his belly, and with it, the accompanying numbness. When the pain started to subside, Grodniko settled back on his elbows. He stared at his commander, a man he had taught everything he could over their five-year liaison together. A man who at times was more like a younger brother than a superior officer.

"Do it, Major," he finally said.

Antonov, silent, morose, unzipped the cotton bag of his medical kit. Inside, vials of drugs were strapped in individual pockets by velcro pull tabs. He pulled out one of those vials and a syringe. Looking away from Grodniko, he loaded the syringe. In school, in his Spetsnaz training, they had called it the shot of bliss. A hated rule. You go into an area sterile, so they can't identify you. If you're compromised, the first man who gets it by any means available is the communications sergeant, with his knowledge of frequencies and crypto. If anyone is injured and cannot keep up with the others, he must—he must get the shot of bliss. Morphine. Too much of it, an overdose.

Antonov eyed the syringe against the light of the moon above the canyon walls, measuring the amount. Then he unplugged the syringe from the vial and strapped the vial back in the medicine bag. He was ready.

The sound of slipping boots, of gravel cascading down, creating tiny avalanches of scree from above. They both looked up. The others were descending. Antonov spotted Pushtkin's silhouette, and wished more than anything that *he* was the one to receive the shot.

"Get back," Antonov snarled. He looked back at Grodniko.

Grodniko averted his eyes. "Do it," he repeated.

Antonov hesitated and stared into his senior sergeant's eyes, begging forgiveness. Then he plunged the syringe into Grodniko's exposed forearm, operating on reflex and training. He blanked his mind of any friendship or camaraderie he had ever felt for the man he was now killing. Grodniko's grip on his upper arm relaxed. Then his hand slipped away. Antonov gritted his teeth and became an automaton, a robot, a man with no compassion nor . . .

Minutes later, he glanced back down. A sudden gust of wind whipped coldly against his face. Grodniko was dead.

After scraping out a shallow grave inside a cut in the ground near the canyon wall, and piling it high with rocks, they left the senior sergeant. They left him and they climbed the slope without him, and they continued their mission.

CHAPTER FOUR

"Wow, man, check it out. . . ."

A dark girl, with long, black, French-braided hair, loped past two runners on the track. Minutes earlier, the sun had risen, glinting against the park's pond and the flesh of her tanned and toned legs.

"Yeah, that's her, all right. Jesus, look at those legs."

Two runners slowed down on their final lap inside El Paso's Memorial Park to look at the girl. Both of them were young, maybe out of college a year, fully into the yuppie mode, on the hunt at the park's cross-country track. They'd been seeing *this* one every morning for the past week.

"Go on, Josh," the shorter man said. He was dark-haired, well-built. A weight lifter, not interested in running. About the same height as the girl they were watching.

His partner said, "Jesus, Larry, hold your water. I'm waiting for the right moment."

"Okie-dokie. You lose, strong-man." The man called Larry started to walk toward the girl, who ran the last few steps to a tree by a water spigot where she would stretch.

Josh, Larry's lightweight partner, red-faced, and with hair equally red, was having none of it. "Outta my way." He trotted toward the girl. Chuckling, Larry let him by. It was about time his ol' buddy, ol' pal took the bull by the horns.

Josh trotted slowly past the girl, who had stopped not too far away from the parking area. She spread her legs out wide, locked her knees, and stretched out her hamstrings, bending way over.

Josh slowed down, enjoying the view. Finally, he walked over to her, standing a careful ten feet away, trying to act nonchalant.

A tall blond man sprinted toward them on the track, doing a four-forty.

Ignoring him, Josh strolled over to her, trying not to notice the blond man's possessive glare as he ran by.

"Hi."

The girl bobbed down, holding her elbows perpendicular to the grass, maintaining her stretch. Josh's jaw sagged. The place where her sweatshirt opened at the neck revealed her breasts. They were firm, not large, not small. Just right. She looked up at him and caught his stare. Josh's cheeks flushed, as if he'd been caught kicking a mirror underneath his fourth-grade teacher's dress. She said nothing for a moment. Then: "Hello."

"Uh, run here often?"

"Every now and then. It's a beautiful day." Her voice was low, soft. Traced with a Mexican accent.

"Yeah, except it gets too damn hot later."

She smiled at him, but not nicely. He saw the look of contempt. And that hurt, coming from a face that belonged on a cover of one of those—well, not *Vogue*. She wasn't *that* pretty. More like on one of those outdoorsy magazines, like a nature chick. Granola, and all that. The healthy, wholesome look.

Josh glanced around, hoping Larry wasn't watching. The blond man sprinted back from the opposite direction, this time looking at him and letting him know in no uncertain terms that *this* babe was already with someone. Josh knew all was a no-go. No way he could compete with that guy's chest and looks. He too had that fresh, wholesome, and also confident look. Long, straight nose, high cheekbones, a face that had never known acne. *Back to the showers, stud,* he told himself.

"Well, have a nice day," he said to her lamely.

"You too," she said. The smirk hadn't left her face yet. At least Josh didn't see it. He was already dragging his feet back to his partner Larry, who was shaking with laughter. They ran on, working out that last two-miler that would do them in for the rest of the day. They had beer calories from the night before to burn off. Better luck next time, kid.

"Hey, fox." The blond man was back. The girl straightened up, arching her back, sticking her behind out. She put her hands

around the back of her head and stretched her sides. "Hi, Blake,"
she replied, smiling.

"Can't leave you alone, gorgeous. Lotsa sharks out here."

Victoria Sanchez dropped her hands and walked over to Sorens.
"Scared to go in the water?"

He put his hands on her waist. "Not after last night, gorgeous."

She glanced down. "Oooh, Blake. Look at yourself."

"Oh, shit." Sorens glanced around, embarrassed. She ran her
hand across his ass. "Hey, quit that, you'll make it worse!"

"Ow!" She suddenly grabbed her calf and limped away to the
tree.

"What's the matter?"

"My calf muscle is cramping."

"Are you going to be all right?"

"Yes. Just give me a minute to stretch it out. I'll be right with
you."

Blake Sorens walked over to his Jeep Cherokee, in the parking
lot, to towel off the morning sweat and get ready to drive Vicki
back to her place. It was a beautiful day. The whole summer had
been cool, green, lush. Unusual for El Paso.

Reaching the jeep, he was suddenly reminded that it was
actually paid for. He'd always wanted a jeep. He felt good about
it, and realized that for the first time in his life he had damned near
everything. He opened the door of the jeep and got the towel. As
he wiped off his torso, Blake Sorens glanced over at Vicki, who
was stretching her calves against the tree by the water spigot. He
admired her lithe, slender body. For a man almost forty, he hadn't
done too badly.

He had money, and he had Vicki, a beautiful, intense woman
almost ten years his junior. A totally sensuous woman who
listened to him. He had the Cherokee and he had her body. He had
a house full of furniture back in San Francisco that was all paid
for. He couldn't afford to pay off the house, though; now was not
the right time. The IRS would. . . .

The only thing he did not have was time, he reminded himself
once again, growing bitter. Time and choice. Time and choice to
do the things he wanted, when he wanted, and how he wanted.
But compared to a year ago—well, to hell with a year ago. Debt
and alimony meant no more to him. Besides, all that had been

different. Things were better now, if only . . . well, the White Sands assignment, regrettably, would last another year.

Sorens's mood changed into a slow, seething anger toward the missile complex and the desolation . . . the rape of his mind. He focused his anger on the government civilians and the Armed Forces officers who stood behind him, watching, asking naive and stupid questions about his project. *His* goddamned project. Not IBM's. Not the fucking government's.

No. His. RAIL had been his baby, born of sweat, creativity, restless energy. A desire to excel. A desire to finally be recognized in IBM's massive hierarchy. And what did those fuckers do? Management? Executive Branch? The goddamned fucking *chairman?*

Army, Navy, Air Force, Marines. He'd been sold out. His project had been sold out. At first, he'd been told to go to work at White Sands on the computer refractory link project for aeronautical guidance systems. He was going to use his breakthrough, *his* fucking breakthrough, to help make airplanes easier to fly. Right.

And Star Wars was just a movie.

Well, by God, Blake Sorens had gotten his. Fuck the government.

He glanced back at Vicki, now bending over next to the tree she'd been stretching her calves against, holding her ankles. He loved her ass. God, she had such an ass. "Ready whenever you are, babe," he said to her.

Victoria Sanchez glanced back and melted Sorens with a smile. "Coming."

"We'll be late for work."

"Start the jeep. I'll be right with you."

Sorens got in the Cherokee and started the engine. He glanced at his watch. Maybe there'd be time before they left for work. Then they'd make the drive to White Sands in different vehicles. His mood became lighter. Then they would spend one hell of a Labor Day weekend together in El Paso, in bed, in each other. For sure.

When she was sure he wasn't watching, Victoria Sanchez moved her hand from her ankle into the hollow inside the crook of the tree's trunk where the tree halved in two. After scraping away the dirt and the bark, she retrieved a thin metal matchbox and stuck the matchbox in her running sock.

Then she stretched her hamstrings one final time, wondering if today was the final day.

They'd been steadily humping all night. The loads weren't too bad, but now that the sun had risen, MacIntyre's ruck bit deeply into his shoulder blades, weighed down by the seventy pounds he carried. Ever since they'd been dropped off by the CUC-V seven hours previously, Santo and Maslow, in front of the file, had led the team on a steady but grueling climb out of Soledad Canyon onto the north-south ridgelines. Those ridgelines would lead them to their positions along the southern avenues of approach bordering the missile complex.

MacIntyre glanced to his rear and nodded with approval at the way Saxon was keeping up. He was also maintaining an even fifteen-meter distance, automatically homing in on correct movement dispersion.

MacIntyre then remembered Saxon saying he had been a Ranger. That was good. MacIntyre had taken Ranger training on completion of his initial basic officers course when he entered active service. It was the hardest leadership course he had ever attempted.

Saxon had done the same, and had served in Grenada. Some said Grenada was only a short-lived field training exercise for the Rangers and the 82nd Airborne Division, but the guys who jumped in while ZSU-99 flak guns flung green-tracered rounds at their C-130's hadn't known what kind of fighting would be involved.

At first, MacIntyre had been hesitant, accepting an outsider on the team. But Saxon was the team's liaison, and the DEA agent who had gotten authorization for his team to go on this mission, and that was good. Now that he was proving himself by keeping up with the team, it was even better. MacIntyre paused before going on and let Saxon catch up with him.

"How's it hanging, pard?"

Saxon grinned at MacIntyre, and swiped a hand across his face. "You're not gonna let a Ranger pass one of you SF wimps, are you?"

"Suck my shorts, Saxon."

Saxon laughed quietly. It was one of the team sergeant's signature quotes, and the rest of the team had picked up on it. He was glad to be with a good team. Their professionalism during isolation and this hard-driving movement underscored the point.

The two men pressed on up the rocky mountainside, silently joining the competition. Behind them, Greeley and Barkowitz brought up the rear.

"How you doing with the prick, Barko?"

Barkowitz shrugged his shoulders in complete nonchalance. The "prick" was a PRC-70, their main radio, and it weighed a few pounds. Maslow humped the backup radio fifty meters to their front. "I'm okay."

"I'll carry it for you if you get tired."

"Sure you can handle it, little Teddy?"

"Quit callin' me little Teddy! Hey, you remember the time we were in Juarez during spring deployment, and we got the chief drunk enough to go up on the stage with that stripper and then he—"

Looking down at them from above, Santo grinned. Greeley weighed no more than a hundred and fifty pounds wringing wet, but he'd seen the medic carry hundred-pound loads before with absolutely no complaint.

The night-long hike into the area of operations had allowed Santo time to reflect on the mission and what Volensky and he had talked about during isolation. First, there had been Volensky's concern about the legality of the mission the previous afternoon, during the mission briefing.

As usual, he had been prepared to listen closely to Volensky's Byzantine reasonings, the twistings and turnings of a flexible and imaginative mind constantly analyzing all situations and crises. Indeed, Volensky had warned him about the gray areas surrounding this DEA operation and the possible connection with SDI and White Sands, but had also popped the question to him about accepting a direct commission. Santo snorted and shook his head. A direct commission! He tried to picture himself as a major in charge of a Special Forces company.

To his surprise, the image fit. Despite the bureaucracy and the politics and the paperwork of an officer's career, even in Special Forces, he could have a much greater impact on the training readiness of his command—a company of six teams, and a company headquarters split-team, a total of seventy-eight men.

Plus, he could immerse himself in even more work. He

maintained an apartment in Fayetteville, and it was a lonely place. It was not like going home. After Sally and Ellen had been . . . had been . . .

Santo tore the image of his wife and daughter away from his mind. After the initial months of grief and an overpowering sense of guilt and apathy, he had sold the house and moved into a Fayetteville apartment complex close to Fort Bragg where mostly junior officers and NCOs lived. It was a spartan and dark place with no decorations or woman's touch, designed only for sleeping and eating. He could not bring himself to live with reminders, to hang up the picture of Ellen's junior high school band concert, when she had played a flute solo, to look at the seashells gathered and snapshots framed from the time five years ago when he and Sally had lazed away an entire week on the beaches of Cancun while Grandma Cunningham—Sally's mother—took care of Ellen. The pictures and memories of that second honeymoon were once warm and nice to think about. But that was before they had started fighting, and that was before the drunk had killed his family.

No, he had decorated his apartment with none of those memories. Instead, there was a stereo he never listened to and a television he never watched, some pots and pans, a few sticks of second-hand furniture. He didn't spend much time in his apartment. His work and his fourteen-hour days on post came first.

As it always had, Santo thought bitterly.

Santo ground his feet into the mountainside and let the physical effort drown out the bad thoughts, the thoughts that always came when he was alone. But it wasn't enough, he reasoned. He had to learn how to think new thoughts, different thoughts. He had to live and grow and learn how to be . . . if not happy, then satisfied.

So what about that direct commission, Manny Santo thought. He already had almost seventeen years in the Army—from the time he was seventeen and faced with the prospect of staying in Miami and working for his father's family. His father's . . .

After his father, Cesar Santo, had been killed in the Bay of Pigs when he was only six, Manny had been raised in his paternal grandparents' home. His mother—a white Southern girl from the University of Miami where his father had met her—had succumbed shortly after his death to a binge of amphetamines and barbituates and the alcohol she washed the pills down with.

Orphaned, and being raised by strict, wealthy grandparents still loyal to Batista and exiled in Miami, Manny Santo had been afforded the best Catholic schooling money could buy. It was decided that he would attend Notre Dame someday, maybe even Yale or Princeton. It was decided that he would date only Cuban girls during high school, and seldom, if ever, was his Anglo mother mentioned in his grandparents' house. It was decided that he would excel in sports . . . tennis, football, baseball . . . and education was equally important. A Santo had to be a *whole* man, both intellectually and physically. Someday, he would inherit his father's and grandfather's legacy of Cuban nationalism. While the Santo family's Miami dry-cleaners and restaurants funded the future patriots who would eventually wrest Cuba from Castro's grip, Manny Santo would prepare himself for the mantle of leadership and provide a shining example of the new Cuban man who would finish what the patriots in the Bay of Pigs Cuban exile force had started but failed to complete.

Manny Santo escaped from his grandparents after high school graduation and joined the Army. Pleas, letters, accusations followed.

Yet Private Santo was now responsible to no one's expectations, save the government's. He liked the Army. No more grandparents clutching and expecting and demanding. Of course, he was proud of what his father had done in the Bay of Pigs. Cesar Santo had shown courage, even if he had died in a brave folly. Santo's own ingrained sense of *machismo* led him initially toward the paratroopers and then the Green Berets. Special Forces—some of the last remaining troops in Southeast Asia—afforded him an opportunity to taste the combat he sought—how could you be a *real* soldier and not see combat?

As Lieutenant Colonel Andrei Volensky had often told him later on in his career, Santo found out indeed that "you should be careful of what you want . . . you might just get it."

Santo discovered enough death and destruction along the Thai-Laotian border to last him a lifetime. There he had initially met Volensky on his first combat mission against a jungle heroin and opium processing lab. That had been the start. Throughout the seventies, he had fought the contained, covert wars no one back home paid attention to, like the ongoing patrol firefights in Korea's demilitarized zone after his year in Thailand, the joint

CIA/Special Forces missions in support of Joseph Savimbi's band of freedom fighters during his tour in Angola during the late seventies, the mobile-training-team missions in Latin America supporting the Contras during the early eighties.

Santo had indeed found war and smelled its stink and seen its depravity. He paid the price with a broken marriage. His soul, hollowed by what he had seen already, became an even thinner membrane of what was good and sane. Then Sally and Ellen were killed. Manny Santo peered into the abyss, wanting to lean away, to let go; the rungs of the ladder to which he clung were rotten and crumbling.

Through work, he strengthened. His heart and his soul still became open wounds when depression reoccurred, but each time, a thicker band of scar tissue made him stronger and gave him hope.

Now, Master Sergeant Santo had reached the peak of his career at only thirty-six years of age. Though he was in superb condition, his dark, brooding eyes, the creases networking around the corners of his eyes, and the set of his jaw displayed a much older man's coutenance. What was left for him careerwise . . . sergeant major? If he stayed in past twenty, he'd have no problem making promotion. An assignment as a Company Sergeant Major would be rewarding—at least you got to be around troops—but that would only last a couple of years.

Santo tried to visualize himself as a Battalion Command Sergeant Major with his own office situated directly across from his battalion commander's office, replete with a "glory wall" crammed with pictures showing past teams he'd served on, free-fall parachuting shots, honorary awards and plaques from foreign government military forces he'd "advised," the coffeepot gurgling in the corner, just waiting for the next boring command and staff meeting he'd have to attend, looking wise and ceremonious . . . occasional forays through the battalion's company and team headquarters areas searching for stray cigarette butts that had been missed during the morning police call . . . chewing out his Company Sergeant Majors for not paying enough attention to detail . . . doing the same if he spotted a troop with a borderline haircut or bushy mustache . . . .

No. Thank you, but no.

Santo knew he'd accept the commission. At least he could be useful.

Sweat stung Santo's eyes, as he rounded a switchback in the canyon's trail, and the desert sun would soon make its debut over the canyon walls. Pulling out of his reverie, he knew that a patrol base would have to be established soon. At this hour, no hikers or backpackers would be moving around, but soon the shadows would leave the team no more cover from the sun. They'd get too hot and use up all their water before reaching the first cache site. They'd also be seen. Glancing ahead, Santo saw that the rest of their route out of the canyon angled up a steep scree slope, over a lip of rock and then onto the exposed ridgeline.

Santo swung his gaze around and spotted a hole in the canyon wall about fifty meters over to his left. It was a cave. Beside it was a platform of rocks. If they climbed up to the foot of the scree slope and traversed to the ledge, they'd get to the rock platform next to the cave. There, they'd be out of sight from anyone, and this particular canyon was just too desolate and non-scenic for hikers. The place was as good as any for the day's rest..

Maslow met him at his position, breathing deeply and evenly. The weight of the backup radio hadn't drained him at all. "About time, isn't it, Manny?"

"Yes, sir." Santo pointed to the cave. "I was thinking about the cave over there."

"Let's do it."

Santo watched the warrant officer take off for the cave. For such a slender, little guy, Maslow kept up.

Ten minutes later, they had established their rest position and had put Greeley on first watch with the binoculars. Everyone else crapped out against their rucks, catching Zs, or were heating up Ramen noodles with a mountain stove.

Santo was about to doze off, his eyes safely shielded by the rock buttress looming above their heads. Then, he felt someone brush past him. Peering out from underneath his bush hat, he saw Maslow walk out to the edge of the rock platform and examine the scree slope for several long moments.

As the coffeepot ceased gurgling in the kitchen, Victoria Sanchez rose from the couch in her living room, her instructions from the dead letter drop in the park in hand. Finally, the message was decoded: A meeting was to take place behind the complex over the American Labor Day weekend. Bring the model and all the papers secreted away since the last handoff and evacuate with the contact. Bring the scientist. Establish communication via the television homing device today at 1000 hours and receive the exact grid coordinates for the rendezvous behind the missile range in Ash Canyon. Walking into the kitchen, she burned the message in her sink and rinsed the ashes down the drain.

She looked at the kitchen's wall clock. Already, it was half-past seven. She undid the waist belt of her white terrycloth bathrobe and let it hang open at her breasts, barely concealing the rest of her naked body. She knew that Blake Sorens liked that—her dark skin, her black hair still wet from the shower, the outline of her strong hips and leg muscles, and the smooth, flat hardness of her belly—he would be more receptive to both her and the message that way.

She poured coffee into two cups. Sorens would soon be out of the shower. What about the contact? Would it be just one man or several? There were too many unanswered questions.

"Hi, gorgeous."

Startled, she turned and saw Sorens smiling at her from the doorway of the kitchen. He had padded across the shag-carpeted living room to where she stood, silent and waiting. She saw the look in his eyes and knew exactly what he wanted.

"Oh. You scared me."

Sorens walked into the kitchen and closed his arms around her, feeling for her waist, slipping his hands down to her bottom. He wore only his bath towel, wrapped around his waist. Beads of water glistened on his tall, athletic body, and his blond hair was slicked back. She responded to him, and pressed her body close to his. They kissed. Then she broke away and led him by hand back into the bedroom.

Later she climbed on top of him, as he dozed belly down. She knew he would soon be asleep, and then he'd be late for work. That was good. His guard was down. She kneaded his shoulders with her strong hands, massaging the back of his neck and then working her way down his spine. Sorens groaned in contentment.

"Do you like that, Blake?"

"Mmm? Yeah . . . I sure do." He reached behind him and ran his hand across her thigh and on up the curve of her hips. He liked the way she felt on him, cool, warm, and moist in the right places. He stirred and tried to twist around to greet her caress with his own. She gently pushed him back.

"You will be late for work, Blake."

"I guess."

"You will. Just five more minutes, then you must leave."

"Okay, sugar."

"Blake?"

"Mmm?"

"I need you to do something for me." She leaned forward and bit his earlobe.

Blake Sorens tensed. "What?"

"Tomorrow, we need to go backpacking," she whispered into his ear. "We'll go behind the range complex where the trails lead up toward that abandoned gold mine."

This time, Sorens turned around and grabbed her by the wrists. His eyes pleaded. "Why?"

She said nothing for a moment, and then she leaned forward and kissed him. "Because we must meet somebody."

Sorens sighed. "I can't do that, Vicki."

"Yes, you can. You must."

"No!" Sorens pushed her away and sat up against the headboard. "No!" he repeated. "You and I will go into El Paso or Juarez, as we planned. We'll take in a bullfight, go shopping . . . *Christ*, Vicki . . ."

Sanchez let him finish. Soon, he would quit arguing and complaining and being hurt. Just like a spoiled child, he always did that whenever she wanted him to "do something" for her. But she knew how to handle him, and now, she looked at him long and hard, her dark brown eyes casting an almost hypnotic spell over a man she had beaten a long time ago.

"Blake," she began again, "tomorrow we will go backpacking up in the mountains behind White Sands. It will be beautiful, and the rains this summer made it especially nice up there. We will camp out and make love underneath the stars. Please, Blake . . . you know how I feel about you."

"You use me," he said bitterly.

She stared at him, and began kneading the muscles in his chest. This time, he stirred underneath the sheets and let her do it.

"What . . . what do I need to bring?"

"The model, Blake. The model you've been working on. You've done such a beautiful job of it."

Sorens looked away from her. "I need to go." He made no move to get up.

She kneaded his temples and looked deeply into his eyes, allowing her breasts to brush against his chest. "This is the last time, Blake. Then you won't have to deal with me anymore."

"Won't . . . have to what?"

"I won't ask you to do anything more for me, Blake. You'll be paid and then you can forget about me and all the pain I have caused for you."

"Vicki, I . . . I *love* you. I . . . Christ, Vicki, I don't want to let you go."

She veiled her contempt for him by making her eyes mist over and letting her breath hitch in her chest. "Blake, don't make it hard. You know we can't go on."

"Wait a minute, dammit," he said. "Just wait a minute. I'll do it, okay? But after all we've gone through together, let's not throw it away, okay? Okay?"

She flattened out on him and nestled her face in his neck and let him feel the moistness of her tears against his neck. She drew in a deep breath. "Just this last time, Blake. Then we'll see. I do love you, Blake."

Then, after they had made love again, she knew she had him. Blake Sorens realized this as well. The terms remained unspoken. It would be the same as before. And before that . . .

"Dark girl, late twenties, outstanding kind of shape, you know, like, I mean she's hot. She's Mexican, you know."

"That's her?" Blake Sorens asked his buddy at the White Sands cafeteria before rising from the table to go to work. He raised his coffee cup to his lips and stared at a slender, athletic woman going through the breakfast line. When she paid at the cash register, she looked in his direction and held Sorens's stare for a moment before sitting down at a table not too far away. She smiled at him and looked away.

"Yeah," Rob Chase told his buddy, his good friend, his partner in divorce and alimony, the great Silicon Valley computer whiz Blake Sorens, who hadn't been laid since he'd arrived at the fucking "Sands" over a month ago.

"She was looking at me."

"No shit?" Chase, forty and looking it with a gold chain around his neck that had gone out of style ten years ago, shifted his bulk around and glanced at the woman. He turned back to Sorens. "Yeah, well, good luck. I tried talking to her last night at the club here on post. She was cool, man, real cool. Didn't give me the time of day."

"Where does she work?"

"That, my friend, is prized information."

"C'mon, sluggo, where does she work? You're chief of civil service assignments. Where does she work?"

"Down, boy, down, I think she goes to work in your lab tomorrow."

"Doing what?"

"Secretarial pool."

"Make sure she gets assigned to my section. You're right. She is hot."

Overtime, late nights, unnecessary papers to be typed. Chance meetings in the hallway. Blake Sorens was not a man to be stopped easily. The woman attracted him, and she was about the only goddamned thing around this godforsaken hell-hole of an assignment that he really cared about—apart from his project. Even that was losing its appeal. He felt like he had been raped by the government for his RAIL brainchild in the first place.

Finally, the walk out to her car one night, where they talked for a while out in the parking lot. Discussions in the lounge. A first date. Then others. Who was she? Oh. Was it that bad back in Mexico? Yes, I understand. You speak English so well. You are so beautiful. Yes, I know what you mean about how our government takes advantage of Mexican resources. I was once in the Students for a Democratic Society in school, you know, and we used to say. . . .

By God, finally, he was seeing a woman who listened to him, who liked him, who would go outdoors with him into the mountains for backpacking trips, who listened to his points of view on the rat race, politics, the nuclear arms race, the criminal war in Southeast Asia that America was trying to sweep under the rug as if it never happened; how the same was happening all over again in Central America, and, and, and . . .

She listened to him about his sellout by IBM, his involuntary *reassignment to White Sands, the military officers and specialists and scientists, all working with him on RAIL. Oh, you don't know about it? Well, not that many people do, perhaps I shouldn't . . . oh, to hell with it. The acronym means Radiated Alloy Integrative Lithography. The point if that whoever comes up with a way to galvanize semiconductors on computer chips through X-ray stimulation first, and then refracts a laser into a series of mirrors backed against a magnesium alloy, will send computer technology into an evolutionary spiral superseding that of all existing technologies. The goal is to miniaturize chips and make them more powerful with this process. Then, when integrated into guidance systems of missiles, said missiles would become much, much more accurate—accurate enough to guide in on incoming missiles—and thus give the much vaunted Strategic Defense Initiative a credible and realistic feasibility.*

But who gave a shit about missiles, he had told her, when the same could be used for exact, precision automation in aircraft navigation, the new computer laser-optics microprocessors, seismograph calculations, and data processing? What about peaceful usage of the technology?

Why missiles?

Oh, no, he hadn't been told about missiles at first. At first, IBM gave him a bonus and promises of more, pending his acceptance of an assignment to work on aircraft navigation systems with RAIL in New Mexico.

"Where?" he had asked his employer.

"The White Sands Missile Range complex, forty miles north of El Paso."

"Why the government? I'd rather do it here."

"Why, my boy? Because the government's just given us one hell of a contract. You will do it, won't you? Won't you?"

Yes, he had told the new woman in his life, he had done it. And he told her about his marriage, his broken shell of a marriage that was no longer a marriage, but a never-ending series of alimony checks and long-distance phone calls ending in spite and greed and pettiness. No, there was no love lost, that part of his life was ruined and dead, best to be forgotten.

And then he met Vicki. For the first time in a very, very long time, he felt more alive, more energetic, and more wanted. His ego demanded it. His body needed it. They worked out together.

They attended rock concerts together in El Paso. He took her to her part-time classes at the University of Texas at El Paso, and waited for her in the cafeteria.

Once, he even gave her a paper he had written years ago as a college student on the evolution of computer technology.

Of course, it was not classified, or anything like that.

Of course, it didn't relate to RAIL.

Of course, she could use it in preparation for the economics class she was taking on campus.

And then there were the notes expanding his college paper into a reality, while working for IBM as a college graduate in the research department. More papers, more research. He liked helping Vicki. She was always interested in him, his mind, his body, his papers.

He tried to help her out any way he could. He could tell she was different, and that she had not come to America from Mexico as a common alien. Roots in El Paso and Juarez, hence the move there. She'd initially had a job as a secretary in the El Paso Chamber of Commerce, where she'd become highly valued. From there, she'd eventually become an American citizen. Her resume had gotten her into White Sands.

A self-made lady, and he admired that. She had done things in a way that he hadn't but secretly envied. College for him was a way out of the madness in Southeast Asia, a way to expand his mind and develop his true love for research in computer science and physics. There were rallies, demonstrations against Vietnam—and he damned sure kept up his grade-point average. And his parents damned sure kept the silver spoon in his mouth while he went to school at Berkeley.

He graduated, and was immediately accepted at IBM in the forefront of the computer industrial boom of the late seventies. But Vicki? Yes, she too had become successful—in her own way. Her moving around, her application for citizenship in a land where anything was possible. Unlike himself, she had earned everything on her own. He admired that and he encouraged her.

"Blake, I have an uncle in Mexico City who will come to Juarez for a visit. He too is in the computer industry."

"Your uncle?"

"He's an important man in Mexico City. I think he will lead Mexico's venture into the computer industry."

"That's great."

"Will you help him? He needs help."

"What do you mean?"

"He needs an American scientist's viewpoint on the development of a faster microprocessor—how silicon chips can be made more powerful and smaller at the same time. I've told him of all your help for me."

"I see. Vicki, I don't know. . . ."

"Blake, he'll pay."

"Pay? For what?"

"If you can write a paper similar to what you gave me that time for my economics class in El Paso . . . he'd be very interested in what you have to say."

"For what? Payment for that?" Automatically, he calculated his budget for the month. He was always tight, even though he made over $50,000 dollars a year.

"Well, it won't be much. Will you at least see him?"

"Hell, no, he doesn't have to pay me anything. Anything for you, babe. Who does he represent?"

He met the man in Juarez, where he was impressed with her uncle's cool intellect, yet warm manner. It was best to keep the meetings discreet. They were no more than probings of the mind, of what could happen, not what was happening. Of course, Vicki's uncle did not pry about about his ongoing work at the missile range. It was in extremely bad taste to even hint about that. The man even protested when Blake ventured opinions in comparison to his current project.

Out of the meetings developed notes. Simple notes on his opinions and possibilities about what could be developed within computer technology and the enhancement by radiation of smaller silicon chips. He was paid, and as Vicki had warned, he was not paid much, but still, he was paid. Five hundred dollars for a consultation here. One thousand for another . . .

Blake Sorens came to depend on those payments.

"Sign for our receipts, if you would, Mister Sorens. You understand, records for our budget people. I'm just sorry we can't offer you more."

"I . . . don't think that . . ."

An insulted look. *"What do you think we're doing, Mister Sorens? Something illegal?"*

"No . . . of course not."

Uneasy feelings, a continuous, gnawing apprehension way back in his mind, needles in his gut. What was it all about?

"Vicki, I'm starting to think twice about these consultations."

She gave him a blank look.

"I mean . . . something does not seem right about this. I'm basically bullshitting my opinions around with this guy, and he always wants to pay me for what I think. I don't mind talking to him really . . . I really don't need to be paid for this," he lied.

"You are a very smart man, Blake."

"But why? How did all this develop?"

He still kept seeing Vicki's uncle, though, and the others who came in her uncle's stead during the monthly visits to Juarez.

Then one Friday night, after making love in her house in El Paso, she told him. Out front. In the open. His most hidden suspicions were confirmed.

"Why, goddammit? Why? You—you set me up!"

"Please don't say that, Blake. I love you."

"The hell you do! You're using me!"

He had stormed out of her house, out of El Paso, out of Texas into Juarez, intent on sucking down as much beer and booze at all the clubs he could find. To forget, to analyze, to make a new plan, to counteract. What to do? Turn himself in? He tried to find the answer at the bottom of a mescal bottle in a conversation with the worm. Eventually, he blacked out.

He was driven back to El Paso by an unknown, unseen taxi driver. He was in too much of a blind stupor to tell. He was sick, incontinent. Delirious. Something in his booze. He allowed himself to be poured into Vicki's bed, where he slept all day the following Sunday.

It hadn't been just alcohol polluting his system.

She cared for him and loved him. No words were spoken. She sponged his forehead and bathed him. He let her do it. He had to hang on to something, and now he needed a friend, even if that friend had used him.

He went to work that week intent on calling the post-operational security people.

"Rob Chase, please." Sorens drummed his fingers on his desk outside his lab, waiting for the personal director's secretary to page him. "Rob? Hi. Something I've got to talk to you about,

buddy. Listen, who's the spook around here handling operational security? Edwards? Good. Okay, that's extension 9824. Naw, there's no problem."

After hanging up the phone, the mail distributor came through, handing out his bills and bills and bills and—wait a minute . . . what's with the magazine?

Deciding it must be some subscription program with National Geographic, *he tore open the brown manila slipcover posted with his address—no return address—and discovered his new magazine was anything other than* National Geographic.

Porn. Disgusting porn. He thumbed through the pages with glossy photos stuck in between the pages showing sex acts between transvestites. Men with breasts, long hair, feminine faces—but still men, and what they did with each other in varying and unspeakable positions disgusted him. Yet, he thumbed through the pages.

And found himself in a five-by-eight glossy, sandwiched between the pages. It was obscene.

He grabbed the magazine and dashed to the bathroom, where he threw up again and again. He sat in one of the stalls for a very long time, trying to collect his thoughts. He reopened the magazine. There were others. A half-dozen pictures in all. Paper-clipped to the pictures was a check for $60,000 dollars.

He had only one recourse.

He went back to Vicki and reassured his manhood that night, trying to forget about the picture. She was understanding, and neither ever again mentioned his drunken foray into Juarez. The meetings continued. The pictures were burned. The check was cashed.

And thus, RAIL was compromised.

"Whattya think it is, Chief?"

Maslow studied how upslope, next to the canyon wall, a pack of coyotes were clawing at the scree trying to get at their meal underneath. The warrant officer turned and faced Santo. MacIntyre had joined them along the edge of the rock platform, which was to be their bivouac site for the day.

"Something is buried up there," Maslow said finally. "And it's fresh enough for the coyotes to fight over."

MacIntyre thought about it, looking at his watch. "It's daylight, Chief. Think we ought to take a look and risk exposure?"

"Recommend just two of us up there, sir. It might have something to do with our mission."

"I'll go with you, then."

CHAPTER FIVE

MacIntyre and Maslow scrambled up the scree slope toward the spot where the coyotes were digging. Upon spotting them the animals ran, bounding and clawing their way into a fissure that led up and over a twenty-foot band of rock comprising the canyon's rim.

It was a gravesite. A foot stuck out of it, and the coyotes had been gnawing on the foot. What was once a Raichle heavy backpacking boot was now a gluey mess of leather, bone, tendon, and raw, red meat with splinters for toes. Already, flies buzzed the area, and both men could smell the decay, feces, and intestinal gases of a dead man.

"Good God" MacIntyre said, his face turning pale. Beads of sweat slowly dripped down Maslow's nose, and down from his temples into the hollows of his cheeks. His jawline worked, and MacIntyre could hear Maslow grinding his teeth, which was the only sign of tension MacIntyre ever noticed in the man.

"We'd better dig him out, sir," he told MacIntyre.

Minutes later, they had uncovered a broad-shouldered grizzled bear of a man stiff with rigor mortis, wearing boots, a khaki shirt, and canvas pants. Ants covered and ate their way into his eyes, and he had swollen from the gas building up in his circulatory and digestive systems.

MacIntyre did his best to keep from throwing up when they had the dirt and rocks clear. "Kind of . . . kind of looks like the Michelin Man," he said weakly.

"Sir, you'd better turn your head."

MacIntyre agreed, and promptly heaved his guts, splattering the scree slope. Maslow felt the corpse's pockets for a wallet and found nothing.

"I'll go get a rope, sir," Maslow offered. "We'd better drag this guy down out of view and check him out."

"Allow *me*," MacIntyre countered, springing to his feet. He slipped down the mountainside back to the ledge where the others stood by at the cave.

Maslow took one of his canteens out of his web gear and splashed water on the corpse's face, clearing away the dirt. He analyzed the situation: a body with no identification, hastily buried on a mountainside. The border guards dead two nights earlier that Saxon had briefed them about. The mission. He examined the corpse for blood, for a bullet wound. He found both in the man's calf muscle of his right leg, where the wound had evidently been bandaged. He ripped open the pants leg and felt around the bone, which had also been broken. Yet the man could have been saved—whatever had happened to him. Whoever had buried him could have traveled a few short kilometers downhill and flagged someone down on one of the range roads.

Whoever had buried him murdered him.

Maslow was uneasy. Who was this guy? Then a thought came to him about, of all things, dental work. He clenched his teeth tighter, and grabbed hold of the man's chin with one hand and the sockets of his eyes with the fingers of his other. He started to pull the corpse's mouth open, fighting the rigor mortis, straining, sweating. Slowly, it gave. Maslow cocked the head into the angle of the sunlight.

When he saw the steel inside, the first of his suspicions was confirmed.

They all gathered around the body, protected from the sunlight by the mouth of the cave. MacIntyre sat crosslegged near the cave's entrance, recoiling the climbing robe they'd brought with them around his knees. They had used it to bring the body down. Everyone was wide awake now, and the previous night's exertions were forgotten, as they all stared at the open-mouthed body.

"Kinda looks like you, Barko," Greeley said. His feeble attempt at humor met no response.

Barkowitz stared at the corpse's gnawed foot, saying nothing.

Then his gaze swept up the corpse's legs, across the barrel-chested torso, and up to the face with its high cheekbones, narrowed eyes, and sloping forehead with a low hairline. "Looks Slavic," he said. "Is that why you pried his mouth open, Chief?"

Maslow had been squatting down next to the face, staring at it, asking it silent questions. Now he got up and turned away. "Yeah. He's probably Russian. You can tell by the steel in his teeth. They do rotten bridgework." He glanced at Hanlon, who was guarding the cave's entrance. "Randy, keep a sharp eye out there." Hanlon nodded, and spat a stream of tobacco juice on the ledge to his front.

Maslow turned his attention to Saxon, who stood by Santo and MacIntyre next to the body. "This guy's a Russian, Mister Saxon. I think he might be one of the agents you're looking for."

Saxon regarded the thin, sinewy warrant officer before him and then glanced back down at the body. "Yeah. One of them."

"There's a party of them. I'd say at least four or five. Whoever they are, they buried this guy in a hurry." Maslow squatted down next to the corpse, and pointed at its leg. "The only wound I found on him was this bullet hole in the fleshy part of his calf. The same leg is broken too, but not from the bullet wound. Apart from where the coyotes got to his other leg, those are the only wounds I see."

Santo grabbed his canteen from his web gear and dribbled some water on the corpse's arm after rolling up the sleeve. Then he scrubbed at the skin until it was clean. On cue, Maslow did the same to the other arm.

"Teddy, come take a look at this," Santo said.

Greeley examined the exposed crook of the corpse's arm. He nodded slowly.

"How long do you think he's been dead, Teddy?"

"Less than a day."

"Is that a needle mark?"

"Yeah. Whoever did this guy put him out with a shot."

Maslow slowly nodded his head. "The shot of bliss . . ."

MacIntyre got up from where he'd been coiling the rope and walked over to Maslow. "What's the prognosis, Chief?"

"Spetsnaz."

The team fell silent for a few moments. They all knew about their Soviet counterparts. Maslow had made it part of his duties as the team technician to ensure all the men knew their enemy. The Soviet Spetsnaz were commandos who had remained unidentified and virtually unknown to the world until the past ten years, when a defector from the Soviet military intelligence community had written papers and books about their existence. They specialized in deep reconnaissance, assassinations, terrorism, sabotage . . . all proven commandos on various battlegrounds from World War Two through Afghanistan.

Born of partisan units formed in World War Two, the Spetsnaz were the most elite, toughest, and most dependable of Russian soldiers, carefully screened for qualities much like commandos and special operations forces around the world had to possess: initiative, endurance, intelligence, foreign language skills, and the motivation to see a mission to its completion—regardless of risk. Theoretically, if the combustion of international tensions were to ever warrant superpower deployment of troops in Europe or the Middle East—the genesis of World War Three—the Spetsnaz's primary mission was to penetrate NATO nuclear storage and missile sites in Europe and destroy them.

"Well, I'll have to say one thing for them," MacIntyre said, breaking the silence. "They've got balls, crossing the border like this. And it's pretty goddamned important if the Sovs are willing to stick their necks out in our territory." He looked back at Saxon. "So that's what we're up against, Mr. Saxon. I think your intelligence assets underestimated the threat. Or else you know something you're not telling us. This is no drug operation. We're dealing with a goddamned Spetsnaz team."

By now the team had clustered around Saxon, who was studying his watch. "In this business," Saxon said finally, "you should always have a cover within a cover. More than likely, there were no bugs in the war room back at Oro Grande where you received your original briefing, but what I have to say now is between you, me, and these cave walls. Your battalion commander already knows what your real mission is."

"What kind of bullshit is this?" MacIntyre demanded, irate. "You could have told us back at headquarters."

Santo said nothing. His earlier suspicions were now confirmed. Volensky had given him all the warning he needed during the briefing.

Saxon stuck his hand inside his pocket and fished out a note. He gave it to MacIntyre. "Read this."

MacIntyre read the note. It said: *Just do it, Team Leader. The less said, the better. Volensky.* He glanced up at Saxon, and then passed the note on to Santo, who read it, nodded, and passed it along.

"Like I said," Saxon continued, "in this business, you've got to have a cover within a cover. Everyone in town now believes you're training with the Air Defense Artillery from Fort Bliss over the weekend. Those people back at the war room, excepting your battalion commander, thinks you are pulling a drug security/recon mission in the Organ Mountains south of White Sands." Saxon paused, and then locked eyes with MacIntyre. "Well, that *is* what we're doing. But, more specifically, we're going to be reconning the major avenues of approach into the White Sands complex itself for anybody that looks like they're exchanging documents and cash for services rendered."

MacIntyre's face clouded. "Wait a minute. Haven't we just overstepped the boundaries of the DEA and entered the realm of the FBI here? You're talking about counterespionage."

"That's right," Saxon replied. "When you're in special projects in any of the paramilitary services—whether it's DEA, FBI, or CIA—you share a lot of information, and sometimes projects overlap. Simply put, we're going to watch for a couple of suspected enemy agents to rendezvous up in the hills behind the missile range."

"How'd you get that intel?" Santo interrupted. "And how many enemy agents are we talking about?"

"Remember that DEA agent that was murdered in Juarez a few years back? Mexican authorities tried to cover it up?"

"Yes."

"He was in special projects too. Yeah, he stumbled into a big-time dope deal when he was caught, but there was more to it than that. His communiques before he was killed involved one of the scientists that work out at the missile range, but we haven't identified him yet. It has something to do with the drug cartel, but we have yet to put all the pieces together."

"Wait a minute," Maslow said, getting up from his seat. He walked out to Saxon's front. "We were planning for a drug op.

That I can accept. Now you are saying there is a link between the Juarez drug people and the White Sands Missile Range?"

"That's exactly what I'm saying. We think someone's been selling SDI secrets to the Soviets. We think that some agents are up in those mountains for a rendezvous off the southern boundary of the missile range, while the DEA and the Border Patrol are concentrating on the massive drug roundup near Las Cruces I was telling you about earlier, back during your initial briefing." Saxon turned back toward Santo. "To answer your earlier question, we don't know how many agents there are. All we're going on is a suspicion, a hunch. There may be none. There may be a dozen. We don't know."

"Pretty thin, Saxon," Santo said quietly.

"That's all the information we've got, but we can draw up some theories as to what's going on. Suppose—just suppose that the KGB residence in Mexico City's Soviet embassy decided one day to contact key members of the drug cartels throughout Mexico and Central America. Hell, South American drug organizations as well. They tell them that they will assist their organizations in the acquisition of weapons, hand-held surface-to-air missiles, state-of-the-art night-observation devices, anything to help them defeat the American Border Patrol and the DEA in smuggling their goods across our borders. Of course, they wouldn't come right out and say, 'We're doing this because the Soviet Union loves you.' Hell, no. The Sovs would make the transactions as if they were independent arms dealers. The main reason they're doing this is because the continued flow of drugs in the United States steadily undermines the morale of the citizenry; it's a destabilizing factor, and it's a threat to our national security. They can pull their tanks out of Eastern Europe, look like good guys to the entire world for so doing, and still pose a threat to our national security at a fraction of the original cost. But there is another benefit as well.

"Now suppose that over time the Sovs *penetrated* those various drug organizations with some of their own people, people who become drug-smugglers. While working under those new identities, they discover dozens of infiltration routes across U.S. borders. They rise in their respective drug hierarchies, but always as a planner, a logistician, an intelligence-gatherer. The resultant information they send back to their KGB bosses in Soviet embassies throughout Latin America, and, ultimately, Havana and

Moscow, gives the Soviets an open-ended spy pipeline into the United States. When the Soviets want to send agents or terrorists across American borders through the drug-cartel pipelines, they can do so."

Maslow slowly nodded his head. "That makes sense," he said. "That also gives the Soviets a chance to recruit key people within the drug cartels—a mole in place to carry out a mission on orders from Moscow if any situation in the future warrants. Maybe even take some of the people they recruit back to Mother Russia and train them at the terrorist training center they've got at Odessa. Update them on weapons, clandestine communications systems, techniques, and principles of unconventional warfare."

MacIntyre examined his map, and motioned to Santo. "Let's get back to the mission. We find whoever's coming in and radio intelligence reports back here to the FOB. Then the reaction force goes in and picks them up." He glanced up at Saxon. "Right?"

"Right," Saxon said, moving away from the group and approaching the mouth of the cave.

MacIntyre followed him. "Wouldn't it make more sense to follow them and see where their trail goes?" he asked. "Uproot the network they've got with the drug cartel?"

"Good question, sir," Santo said, joining MacIntyre and Saxon. "We'd be getting only a short-term benefit by capturing enemy agents on the spot."

Saxon nodded, pensive. "That's something to think about. But right now, we'd better just concentrate on the mission at hand and play the rest by ear. We need to be in position within the next twenty-four hours."

MacIntyre turned his attention to his communications sergeant. "Barkowitz!"

"Yo!"

"Let's make commo back to the FOB, big guy. Volensky's gonna be real interested in this Spetsnaz body."

As MacIntyre and Barkowitz exited the cave with the team radio, Santo pulled Saxon aside.

"I guess there was something you didn't learn in Ranger school, bud."

Saxon tried to shrug away from Santo's grip, but found he couldn't. "What—what are you talking about?"

"You can lie to anyone you want about the Rangers, but you

don't *ever* lie to another Ranger or a Ranger officer. You're with Special Forces now, DEA man. Same thing applies. Remember that it's *our* asses on the line out here. No more surprises, Mr. Saxon."

When Sorens finally left for work, late, Victoria Sanchez beat a hasty retreat for the shower and scrubbed for the next ten minutes to wash away all traces of a man she despised. She despised him as all agents despised the informers and traitors and sell-outs they recruited in affluent societies around the world.

She rubbed shampoo into her hair and let it fall in one thick tail over her glistening right shoulder down to her breast, where she worked the lather. She found two gray hairs right next to each other. Surprised, she started to pull them out, but then stopped, realizing that she too had made the inexorable transition from girl to young woman to mature woman, a woman who would see thirty years the following month.

But Victoria Sanchez was a woman who had been an American from the age of twenty-two, when she was still Tanya Canberra.

In the late 1930's, when Franco finally crushed his opposition during the Spanish Civil War, her grandparents had fled with their Russian sponsors to Moscow. Devout Communists, they had established themselves with the rest of the Spanish community the Soviets had made for them, just like the Czech community, the Polish community, the German community, and other communities of nations and cultures either swallowed up or controlled within the Soviet Union's sphere of influence, as their empire expanded westward following the thirties.

Those communities were farming grounds for ethnic spies.

Tanya Canberra was a natural athlete, with a flair for languages. As a child, she had been provided with the best schools, clothing, and medicine. A developing leader at sixteen within the Young Pioneers, she had been selected for early membership within Komsomol, the Communist Party's youth organization.

Tanya Canberra was a bright young girl with flashing black eyes who learned Lenin, Marx, Engels. An energetic, charismatic young woman who scored top grades in Gymnasium. And as top fighter during her summer military training, she learned how to fire an AK-47 assault rifle and prime conventional explosives.

Then, as it was carefully explained to her, she had been honored by the state with attendance at a very special school, a school that trained her wits and initiative for placement in foreign and unknown environments. She learned how to stalk without being seen, how to watch without seeming to watch, how to get on a bus at the last second and dismount equally fast, and how to jump off moving vehicles and trains without hurting herself. She learned how to deliver a quick, sharp blow to the trachea to crush it; she relearned her native Spanish, and learned how to spice it with Mexican pronunciation and accents.

Upon graduation, she was destined to become a master spy. Her selection was an honor, and her government praised her for it.

And then she was a woman of twenty-two, and upon the silent and secret evaluation by her Party leaders, was chosen to attend a graduate school deep in the south of the Tatar Autonomous Soviet Republic. A secret place.

She made a short trip back home first to her parents. There were reunions, meals, vodka, caviar, a graduation present, relatives, friends—and an unspoken commitment. There was throughout a strong, relentless restlessness. She left after a one-week stay and never returned.

Gaczyna.

Tanya Canberra had never heard of the place, and she was tired from the long, three-day train ride to get there. Dust, open steppes, unused grainland. Where was this university? The instructors, the buildings, the trees? A bus met the new students at the train station. As she neared town at the end of the thirty-minute ride, she finally did see trees and houses. And that wasn't all!

Cars! Restaurants! People walking on the sidewalks with Western clothes! Along with the rest of her comrades, she gaped at the opulence and beauty of a town she had never heard of before, an island of Western civilization deep in the heart of the *Rodina*—the Russian motherland.

When the babbling among the students became louder, the instructor in the front of the bus jumped up and faced them, her glowering face a study in severity.

"Enough!" cried their escort—a hatchet-faced woman, her severe, sexless lips pressed tight together and thin, old-maid's body defying the occasional lurch of the bus as she clenched the hand rail. "*Enough!*"

The voice of authority. They stared at her in obedient silence.

"You have spoken the last word of our beloved native tongue! Never again, as long as you live here—for the next three years, mind you—will you speak Russian!"

The students exchanged glances, bewildered. No one dared to whisper when they passed the town's border, whose welcome sign informed them that they were in the city of Stewart, Texas.

Tanya Canberra learned how to speak English, and it was okay if she interjected some Spanish in her dialogue. Her instructors—Communist defectors from the West, cipher clerks, wives, artists, and recruited and discovered spies—guided her and helped her become an American.

The first year, Tanya Canberra learned how to be an American in the make-believe city of Stewart, Texas, population 10,014, citizenry consisting of a mix of Anglo and Spanish. She went out on dates, held a job as a secretary in the local bank, danced to the disco of the late seventies. She wore Levi's. She watched a great many Western movies and learned Western slang. She confided—in English—to her best friends about her sex life, and learned how to select and color-blend the right kinds of Western clothes for the right occasion. At all times, they were under orders to correct one another for any slip in the nuances of the language spoken by the inhabitants of Stewart, Texas. She mastered both Tejano Spanish and English. She mastered her own personality and character makeup as a Mexican-American.

She mastered the art of death and covert operations.

She became an expert with the employment of toxins and how to make booby traps consisting of ordinary kitchen supplies. She became an expert with clandestine communications and in how to encrypt and decrypt code. She learned how to transmit and receive messages with modern, burst-communications devices. How to conceal microdots, computer chips, and microfilms inside tooth-paste, clocks, belts, fountain pens, book covers, wine-bottle corks. She learned how to assassinate with the jab of an umbrella loaded at the tip with a tiny syringe filled with the chemical Ricin: a sharp jab, the result of an accidental bumping—and then a prolonged, undiagnosed death for the target. She learned how to kill with her hands or with a pistol, and how to snipe with a silenced rifle from eight hundred meters away, and how to manipulate people with her sex or with the results of her excellent photographic skills.

In three years she was ready.

The infiltration of the United States was easy enough during the mid-eighties—many devout Catholic parishioners in the south of Texas believed in what they were doing, and the KGB agents stationed along the Mexican border towns used them to their advantage.

Aliens, illegal, yet honest, hardworking, and desperate—especially a young and pretty if somewhat thin girl of twenty-five—deserved a Christian chance in a land that could offer her much more than what destitute Mexico offered. She stayed in a series of Catholic safe houses, learned more about Jesus, smiled a lot, and prayed and went from one hiding place to another. By the time she reached San Antonio, she broke contact with the smuggling network after mixing in with the crowd one day at a mall.

Once free of the Christian underground, she made her way to her first designated dead-letter drop and obtained her temporary papers. And that was the last time she would make a contact for the next six months, until she "acclimatized."

She found work eventually as a secretary in El Paso. She had to start with El Paso. It was the jumping-off point for the missile range she would eventually infiltrate. Her illegal-alien status was soon rectified with the American illegal-alien amnesty program.

She'd spent her first year with the City of El Paso's Chamber of Commerce, typing letters, making contacts, seeing generals from nearby Fort Bliss and majors and captains and scientists from the White Sands Missile Range forty miles to the north. Good secretaries were hard to come by out at White Sands, she learned, for what the government paid.

After stacking her resume, she got a job there.

Dead-letter drops in trees and parks; messages tucked inside magnetic match boxes under the fourth shelf in the second aisle facing the left of the store in her neighborhood 7-11; messages concerning missions, information, dossiers, microdots; occasional trips to Radio Shack for circuit boards and remote detonators for booby traps, demolitions, counter-surveillance technology. She bought camera equipment, hiking equipment, became an avid backpacker, became one with the terrain for the mission.

The mission was Blake Sorens.

America had what their newsmen parodied as "Star Wars." But

disaster for the *Rodina* was in the making at White Sands. The Soviet Union was devising "Red Umbrella," with which they were determined to surpass the West's ability, the same as they had done in the space race of the sixties, and with the conventional and nuclear arms race throughout the Cold War.

Sorens was the spur the American program had needed for so long, what with his genius for irradiated silicon manipulation and his know-how for its practical integration between radioactively stimulated microprocessors and refractory lasered guidance systems. He was politically aware, was a member of the Sierra Club. In the university, he had been a member of the Students for a Democratic Society. An outspoken liberal when it came to things like Watergate, Vietnam, CIA exposures, nuclear arms. He was a prime target who could be motivated to turn both ideologically and financially.

Upon meeting him, and upon seducing his mind and his body, Sanchez had capitalized on his opinions and unhappiness, drawing out his bitterness about his career, exploiting his intellect and integrity. Computers, lasers, radiation—their technological blend with engineering—all for war. All for American arms superiority.

When she had finally drawn him in, setting him up, little by little, like a salesman getting people to repeatedly say yes prior to closing a deal—or moving in for the kill—she had begun to control his emotions. The pictures she'd gotten on him when he threatened to go to security had been as easy as notifying her contact in the Juarez KGB residency. Drugs in his alcohol, their earlier confrontation when she had asked him to work for her, his confusion . . . it had been the classic recruitment.

Now, for the past few months, there had been a steady supply of documents, pictures, analyses, theories. Sorens had even been making a model, a working model without radioactivity, yet replete with computer chips, that easily demonstrated how RAIL worked. The model, which was the "brain" that could be placed into the guidance systems of anything—airplanes, rockets, fire-and-forget artillery shells—could fit inside a shoe box.

Sorens had made the RAIL model on the sly in his laboratory, and had gotten into the habit of carrying a large briefcase with him every time he entered the lab. The security guards out front had at first inspected the briefcase thoroughly, but turned up nothing more than a smaller bag of gym clothes and a toilet kit inside, mixed in with his files and papers. Day by day, eccentricity gave way to habit, and the security guard at night when Sorens left would now just pop open the latches, give the briefcase's contents a cursory glance, and then promptly hand it back to Sorens. *Just orders, sir, sorry for the inconvenience*.

Victoria Sanchez found herself staring at the drain as shower water rinsed off the lather in her hair and spiraled soap bubbles into the drain underfoot. She did not know how long she had been staring, with the steady pounding of water against her skin, the rushing noise in her ears. She had been trying to come up with her sum total. The sum total of her success. And she *was* successful. Thanks to her efforts, her countrymen now possessed America's most closely guarded secrets. And, according to her message, they would soon possess Sorens's model and RAIL blueprints.

But . . . why would American citizens, with their wealth, sell out their country's secrets for more wealth?

She had enjoyed her assignment. America was the most choice of all assignments, with clothes, money, food, cars . . . she had hated queuing up back home for even toilet paper and toothpaste. Why did Americans, even though they were greedy, capitalist pigs, prostitute their secrets? Sorens had been naive and reluctant, yet steady with his contributions, once he'd been recruited. She would always despise him for being a traitor. And that was what he was, a traitor. Well, she would continue her work and see it through.

Her plan was a simple one: He'd stay late tonight in the lab, put the model inside his briefcase, and she'd meet him out in the lobby, after talking to the security guard for thirty minutes or so. The appearances would be there. The security guard would be lulled by the sheer consistency of Sorens's pattern with the suitcase, and would even envy him for taking a woman home who would actually wait half an hour just for him to finish work. A cursory glance, and that would be it. Then, they'd sneak RAIL up into the mountains an hour or so before sunup by hiking the trails behind White Sands. There would be a handoff. Then she would go home, back to the motherland, back to the *Rodina*.

Victoria Sanchez bent and turned off the shower faucet, pensive. The crux of her mission in America was at hand. She had worked long and hard. According to the message, she was to be evacuated—the scientist too. Would he go peacefully? He'd get a dacha, a car, rubles . . . working on Red Umbrella, he would indeed be privileged. Maybe he would learn to like Russia.

She wrapped herself up in a large beach towel, cinching the ends together over her breasts, and then stepped out of the shower. Soon, it would be time to establish radio contact with the team which had infiltrated the country for the evacuation.

Going into her bedroom, she retrieved the digital radio from her bedside and a Poloroid camera from her dresser, and walked back into her living room, where she wired the radio into the antenna wire outlet in back of her television. Then she unplugged the headphones from her stereo set and plugged them into the radio. Turning the television on, she then opened the channel-tuning door covering the channel changer and turned one of the dials, which normally would have fine-tuned channel reception. Her actions now raised the frequency level of the channel, and changed the snow effect on the screen into a humming, steady field of solid gray. She turned on the radio and then leaned back against her recliner, glancing at the wall clock above the television. In three more minutes, she would receive her 1000 hours communication as the hidden message from the park had instructed.

She bit her lip and realized for the first time in her life that she was scared. Before she started to communicate, she knew she would have to think of a contingency plan, in case the mission went bad.

"Sergei Antonovich, we are ready to communicate," Chelstovsky told him.

"Good." Antonov leaned back against a huge pine tree brushing the side of the cliff face before him, and looked thirty feet up at his communicator. With only five more kilometers to the rendezvous, this place was as good as any to observe the canyon approaches leading into the missile-range complex for any unwelcome intruders. They were near the summit of the largest mountain in the vicinity. Ribs of rock and spires and walls and pinnacles of reddish granite sprinkled the top of the ridgelines leading away from the summit into the canyons below. Their current position afforded them both good communications for a straight-line-frequency shot back to El Paso, and good security—that is, they would see someone first before being seen.

Antonov glanced at his watch, as the second hand swept toward 1000 hours on the dot. The rising sun, moving over the ridgeline which had kept them in shadow all morning, pierced through the canopy of trees, and now splashed on his face. It felt good to have the sun on his face. But inside, uncertainty boiled in his guts, and he realized that there was absolutely no turning back from this mission now. His communicator on top of the small cliff looked down at him expectantly, ready for the go-ahead to send their message to the agent they had been instructed to contact. This message, though important and necessary, also represented commitment, a symbolic touch with a friendly deep inside enemy territory.

But to hesitate now, to consider the mission compromised, would demand his head. His life would be exterminated in the furnace of a GRU crematorium back in Moscow (if they made it back at all)—hopefully, after having been shot. He glanced at Pushtkin, the KGB man, who sat leaning against the tree twenty feet to his front and left. Pushtkin had been staring at him.

Again.

He thought of the border guards and of his senior sergeant, and he focused his hate on the KGB man and his civilian sloppiness. What was he thinking? What was Pushtkin plotting? His type always plotted. Then they rose in power, and this mission would ensure that.

Antonov was a cynic. If they were caught, then they were caught. He would be liquidated, but as a Spetsnaz soldier, he accepted that risk. The Party Chairman and President would be disgraced when the world public was told of Soviet aggression across United States borders. If his team were not caught, then their mission would be accomplished to the detriment of American national security, and Antonov and his team would receive appropriate gratitude from the *Rodina*. The organizers of this mission—his GRU leaders and, ironically, their competitor KGB counterparts—had deemed this mission necessary in light of recent successes in the American SDI program, and the Soviet President's radical, sweeping changes that threatened to emasculate KGB and GRU control of the Soviet Union's organs of national security.

But Antonov's team *was* good—he and Chelstovsky anyway— and therefore, they would *not* be caught. The bottom line, though:

No pig of a KGB idiot would cause the failure of this mission. Pushtkin and the Mexican guide sitting with him by their civilian backpacks could one way or another be disposed of during the exfiltration. Antonov smiled for the first time that day.

The second hand swept past the twelve mark on his watch. Major Sergei Antonov locked eyes with his communicator above and said, "Send your message, Nicholai Chelstovsky."

Barkowitz and MacIntyre squatted together on top of the summit ridgeline above the cave and the scree slope, breathing heavily. The altitude—5,000 feet above sea level—and the stiff wind that had picked up had depleted their energy, compounded by the infiltration into the canyon from the previous night-long hump. But they had to get on top for the straight-line shot back to Oro Grande across the other ridgelines and mountains which would otherwise have masked communications.

Now, after having encrypted and sent their team status and notification about the Russian corpse through their radio's DMDG attatchment—a secure, burst-communications device that could relay a forty-six coded message back to the FOB in seconds—they waited for the reply.

Five minutes passed as Barkowitz patiently listened for a reply, his headphones plastered over his huge head onto his ears. MacIntyre glanced at him. The stout, blocky team communications sergeant never failed to amaze him with his strength.

Back at Bragg when they weren't deployed, his team had a physical training routine of five- and six-mile runs on Mondays, Wednesdays, and Fridays during the week. Greeley, the team runner, always led the pace—his thin man's frame tough and sinewy, like Maslow's. Barkowitz, on the other hand, led the team in weight training on Tuesdays and Thursdays. The huge pecs on his chest and his bulging arms clearly displayed his expertise.

Hanlon and Santo conducted the team's calisthenics every day prior to the main event with what Maslow liked to refer to as Doctor Mengele's warm up—only a twisted Nazi doctor working the "special experiments" ward at Dachau could think up the torture that Santo and Hanlon had devised in their perpetual triathlon training: pushups, situps, upper crunches, lower crunches, V-ups, body twists, flutter kicks—they were all exercises, one immediately following another, designed to torture your gut into the eventual washboard it would become.

They had to stay in shape. It was the only reason they could have hiked ten kilometers with heavy loads the night before and still drive on. There were no quitters on the team. Different personalities, different strengths, few weaknesses. One man in the team complemented another, both physically and mentally. It was moments like this, when MacIntyre pondered his chosen profession while watching his team in action, that he knew why he put himself through the stress of leading a team of commandos.

Beside him, Barkowitz suddenly glanced up, holding his right hand over the headphone covering his ear. "We got through, sir," Barkowitz told him. Then, whipping out his pen and paper, he wrote down the FOB's reply from Oro Grande as the readout appeared on his DMDG.

"Good," MacIntyre said, glancing at his watch. It was already 1005 hours, and it was starting to get hot. Minutes later, Barkowitz translated the code he'd received.

"The Old Man says to skirt the mountains, sir, to forget the ridgeline route. It'll take too long. He wants us to locate whoever's out here before they get close to White Sands."

"Then let's get the hell off this mountain and haul ass, my man."

Sanchez aimed her camera at the television set. Suddenly, the burst transmission came through: six sets of four digits per set created a platoon of numbers on her screen. As she began to depress the button on her camera, they suddenly jumbled, disorganized, chaotic.

What?

She listened hard with her earphones. She was to receive only two shots from the communications her linkup team was to have possessed. Why did the first shot jumble up? She aimed her camera again, and prepared to take another picture.

Another grouping of numbers. This time she snapped the picture. Then, while she still had time, she stretched out toward the radio she had hooked up to the TV and threw three of the tuning switches on the control panel on line with each other, which freed the fourth switch to be used as a tapping device.

In Morse code, she tapped out the emergency send-back message for a reiteration.

MacIntyre and Barkowitz slipped back down the scree slope en route to the others at the cave. Barkowitz had been silent since relaying the last message. MacIntyre looked at him, curious.

"What's up, Ed? You look like you're pissed about something."

"Hell, I'm not pissed, sir."

"What, then?"

"That last message I sent back to the FOB. I got some sort of radio interference and a weird beeping sound, like Morse."

"Could you interpret it?"

"Didn't make any sense at all. I don't know how it could have even come close on my frequency. Just a jumbled set of a half-dozen letters."

"Sergei Antonovich."

Antonov looked up from where he'd been leaning against a tree at their hide site below the cliff and saw Chelstovsky approach him from the trail he'd taken. "What is it?"

Chelstovsky glanced toward the others and then looked back at Antonov. "Our contact will meet us at the linkup site as planned. She confirmed receipt of our message."

"Then why do you not look happy, Nicholai?"

Pushtkin approached them. "Yes, what seems to be the problem?"

"Go ahead, Nicholai," Antonov prodded, impatient with the KGB man's interference.

"Our message was interfered with by another radio. We made contact, but still . . ."

"Impossible," the KGB man retorted. "Your radio has too high of a frequency. It should have cut through any other traffic."

"Comrade Pushtkin," Antonov said wearily, getting up to his feet. "That is *not* impossible, and it bothers me. Show him your radio, Nicholai."

The communications sergeant shrugged off the backpack which carried his radio. "This, comrade, is an R-350M radio. It is similar to American Special Forces radios, which operate on high FM and AM frequencies, has a burst device for quick transmissions, and it can receive and send Morse code on a frequency so high it can only be detected by like-type radios. The design was copied from American technology."

Pushtkin rubbed his jawline, scratching the stubble of his beard. "Were we so monitored, do you think?"

Chelstovsky retrieved the radio and strapped it inside his backpack. "I cannot say for sure. But can we take the chance?"

"We—we have problems then," Pushtkin replied nervously.

Antonov regarded Pushtkin with contempt, noting the worry in his face. "Then we must be in position soon, if we are to carry out this mission."

"We will be spotted in the daylight!"

"Not if we move with stealth and with great attention to our surroundings."

"But we have moved all night!"

"I'm sure you are up to it," Antonov said, smiling a thin smile at the KGB man.

"If you think we should take the risk . . ."

"I do. If we move out now, we should be in position by nightfall."

CHAPTER SIX

Sergeant First Class Randy Hanlon paused and leaned against a huge granite boulder, the day's steady wind blowing hot and loud around his ears. At the point of their staggered-file movement formation, he'd been leading his team into the lower reaches of the canyon that would eventually take them to the uphill approach to their commo site. He was tired. The day's hump was steadily draining him, the wind sucking moisture from his body. But the long, grinding hike from the night before was only tiring at the worst.

When he and the rest of his team had first deployed out to the desert a month earlier, they were all confronted with the basic, initial acclimatizing factors—blisters, dehydration, and salt stains on their fatigues, not to mention the strawberries on their backs where seventy-pound rucksacks rubbed flesh into open sores. But like all good soldiers, they quickly overcame the initial misery and inward sniveling and summed it up in one word: Fuckit. Now, a month later, the team was in the kind of rugged, toughened shape that only the desert and its harsh, unforgiving environment could mold them into.

For the past four hours since the discovery of the corpse, they'd been threading a trail through canyons and boulders and cactus, the occasional tree. It had been rough going, especially when trying to stick to a route that would shield them from the desert floor and highway two kilometers to their east as well as possible observation from the main north-south ridgelines above them.

Hanlon faced to his rear, leaning against his M16. The rest of the team plodded toward him, each man separated by twenty-five to thirty meters, sweating and weary from the effort of the day's body-sapping movement through the heat. Greeley looked like a pinched-face orphan from a Charles Dickens novel as his lean body struggled with his rucksack. Barkowitz, his one eyebrow furrowed into an angry scowl, stomped forward heavily, one boot after another crushing tiny cacti into greasy smears against the sandstone and rocks underfoot. The rest—all basically the same. But they all had one thing in common: as tired as they were, their senses still maintained an air of inspection and analysis of their surroundings. They were alert.

Hanlon grinned. His team was all right, and they'd all still keep driving on until, simply, they got to where they had to go. But first, a break was in order. He caught MacIntyre's eye, and made a circling hand and arm signal above his head. MacIntyre nodded and made the same signal to the rest of the team, and then pointed at Hanlon.

Eventually, they reached his rest spot and spread out into a tight security perimeter, each man moving behind a rock, shrugging off his ruck, and surveilling their outside perimeter with weapons at the ready. No one had to tell them to do it; it was team SOP.

MacIntyre met Hanlon in the center. "Okay, guys," he said. "Take about fifteen minutes and get something in your gut. We've got another couple of klicks to the cache, and then one more kilometer to the commo site." He looked at Hanlon and winked. "You too, macho-man."

"You got it, Boss." Hanlon rummaged through his ruck and came up with a can of tuna fish. After ripping it open with his Swiss Army knife in fifteen seconds flat, he proceeded to wolf it down, drinking the base and water the tuna was packed in as well.

MacIntyre turned his attention to Santo. "How goes it, Manny?"

"Just call me Festus, Marshal Dillon. I hurt all over."

"You and me both."

"We'd better recon the next klick before moving the team any closer to the cache."

MacIntyre squinted at his team sergeant. "Think so?"

"Yes, sir. I want to make sure it's secure before unloading it. We don't have to go the whole way; we have pretty good observation. But—it's the best thing to do."

MacIntyre nodded his head. Santo had an instinctive nature, an almost uncanny ability to anticipate things, but really, when you got right down to it, the man simply had a wealth of experience and common sense. MacIntyre had learned early on when he came to the team that he'd be a fool not to listen to his own sergeant. "Sure, Manny."

"I'll take Randy and be gone for about half an hour. It shouldn't take long."

"Wrong, Team Daddy. *I'll* take Hanlon. You could use a break."

"Me? Take a break? Shit, sir, I smoked *your* ass on that Oro Grande-White Sands death run."

"Relax, old man. Take some Geritol and rest."

Hanlon blew tuna fish through his nose. "That's tellin' him!"

Santo grinned. "Captain, with all due respect, fuck off."

Ten minutes later MacIntyre and Hanlon, sans rucks, glided past the boulders and rock walls and scree slopes en route to a high point where they would be able to see the cache site.

They moved five meters apart, Hanlon out front. MacIntyre never ceased to marvel at his heavy weapons and demolitions sergeant's physical prowess and stamina. He himself was no weak man, but Hanlon had that certain Irish stubbornness donated from ancestors who knew what it was like to work and suffer and plod on.

Hanlon's father had been in Special Forces, one of the old guys. Randy had come from a broken home, no other brothers or sisters, a mother who had remarried when Hanlon was fifteen, his father succumbing shortly thereafter to leukemia—a by-product of exposure to Agent Orange while serving in Southeast Asia. Hanlon's father had died the year before Randy Hanlon had graduated high school back in California. In an outpouring of grief and frustration, Hanlon had screwed up his life for the next two years before enlisting in the Army. There had been drugs, DUIs, misdemeanor charges. Once, a month spent in the county jail. And then, he'd gotten his act together. He'd joined the Army, seeking out all the hardest courses and assignments. Airborne school, followed by a three-year stint in the Ranger Battalion at Fort Stewart, Georgia, Ranger School, early promotion to sergeant. A natural leader and soldier, Randy Hanlon inherited his father's legacy of the Special Forces and excelled. He became an overachiever in an elite organization. As with MacIntyre, Greeley, and Santo, Hanlon was unmarried—no prospective wife would want to compete with his Porsche 911 and his chosen profession. Yet Hanlon was the local heartbreaker in that respect as well. Now, with less than ten years of service, Randy Hanlon was the de facto team sergeant in Santo's absence. MacIntyre was glad to serve with him.

Up front, Hanlon paused. MacIntyre walked up next to him, and they both took a knee on top of a rock ledge. Angling steeply below them was a slope of smaller boulders that led into a series of rock ribs a hundred meters away, rising vertically from the valley floor into small east-west canyons climbing adjacently into the main north-south ridgeline.

Hanlon took a swig from his canteen and then put it back into his canteen pouch on his web belt. "When we get to those rock ribs over there, we ought to be able to locate our cache and see the commo site we're headed toward at the same time. Then it'll take us about thirty minutes to go back and get the others."

"If we get good enough observation."

"That's the point."

"How you feeling, Randy?"

Hanlon dug a paw into his trousers pocket and retrieved a tube of chapstick. "Okay, Dai-uy," he said rubbing the chapstick against his mouth. "You?"

MacIntyre rubbed his hand over the darkening stubble on his jawline and grinned. Hanlon always called him Dai-uy (pronounced *Die-wee*), which was Vietnamese for Captain. It was a common reference for a captain in Special Forces originating from the Vietnam days, and it was always spoken with affection and acceptance—but only if an officer deserved that kind of respect within an elite unit that relied on a healthy spirit of meritocracy for morale and mission accomplishment. "Kinda tired, Randy."

"Yeah, me too."

"See that shelf of rock over by the rock ribs?"

"Yeah. That's where we want to wind up."

"Let's do it."

Ten minutes later they had reached the rock ribs, which bulged out of the ridgeline like a drawn bow. The wind whipped incessantly around the two men, flapping the loose material of their fatigues. They climbed up and over boulders, down into twisting gullies that often flash-flooded during sporadic but torrential spring and summer thunderstorms. Glancing at the horizon and the gathering clouds, MacIntyre guessed that tonight was as good as any for one of those thunderstorms.

They climbed up a shallow apron of granite, and then they reached the shelf at the base of the pillars spotted earlier. The mountaintop where they'd emplace the commo site came into view.

MacIntyre, who had stepped out ahead during their last movement, stopped just short of their lookout vantage point. "Almost there," he gasped. Both of them sought shade beneath a cliff face and rested for several moments, draining half a canteen apiece. Overhead, the sun, hot and searing like a steel mill's furnace, bore down on them with its mid-afternoon intensity. But as the sun traced its inexorable journey to the west, it would eventually hide behind the ridgeline and cool things down, sometimes by as much as forty degrees. Already, the shadows grew long over their route.

"It's 1500, Boss," Hanlon told MacIntyre, as they rested up. "Got about another thirty minutes before we ought to head back."

MacIntyre squinted at their objective, which was still half a klick away. A major canyon angled up from their direction of approach that would take them eventually into the main north-south canyon where the agents they were following would more than likely set up their actions against the missile range. "I want to get a closer look at the cache site."

Hanlon peered down the slope at the shelf of rock set at the foot of the east-west canyon, shaded and deserted. "That'll be a good recon spot."

They entered the small canyon, the wind swirling tiny puffs of dust kicked up by their boots. Then they were there.

"Yeah," MacIntyre said, gazing at a small cut into the ridgeline by some rock cliffs. It was where they had emplanted the cache the week earlier. "That's the ticket."

As they looked past that, their evening's destination was in plain view, near the top of a mountain comprised of a series of gullies and boulders. Off to the east was the huge diamond-shaped cliff face that was one of White Sand's main landmarks. Behind it, up the canyon and near the top of the mountain, was where they'd put the commo site.

A tinkling sound filtered throughout the whine of the wind.

MacIntyre was immediately reminded of cowbells from one of his father's ranches back in Oklahoma while growing up. Both he and Hanlon glanced to their left inside the canyon. Where was the noise coming from?

Two rock climbers stared down upon them from a hundred feet up the cliff face. They had been masked by the shadows and the wind and the corridor of the canyon. The clanking sound came from climbing gear strapped over their shoulders and around their waists. There were two of them, one male and one female, both in their early twenties. The woman was near the summit of the rock rib, belayed from the top by another person sitting on the summit's ledge. A fourth man looked down at them, hands on his skinny hips. MacIntyre could make out wire-frame glasses and a red bandanna tied around his forehead.

"Oh, Christ," Hanlon muttered. "This is all we need."

The man on top yelled something unintelligible at them.

"Let's scram," MacIntyre told Hanlon.

As they picked up to move a small rock chipped at their feet, bouncing away and down the slope below them. Seething, they looked back up. Another missile pelted down from above, barely missing them. They trotted out of the area back for the others.

David Court glanced up from the last twenty feet of his climb at the idiot chunking rocks at the soldiers below. He was at a good position, the angle of the rock face not quite as steep, and he had good jug-handle holds. "What in Christ's name are you doing?"

"Fuckin' Army pukes," came the reply. Newton Rasmin chunked another rock from above.

Court's girlfriend, Wendy, who had just reached the top and was waiting for him to come up, said nothing. She was embarrassed by her sister's boyfriend's behavior.

"Well, cut it out, you idiot," Court yelled.

The other man laughed and walked over to the belay site, where the other woman belayed Court up the remainder of the rock face. "Aw, they're just Army pukes," he repeated.

Angry and indignant, David Court scrambled up the rest of the climb and met them on top, where he glowered at the other man, who wore round granny glasses over mocking light-brown eyes that sparkled with intelligence. A smooth, light complexion was framed by light blond hair, longish in back and banded into a small ponytail.

"What is your problem? You could have hurt someone."

"What are you so tender about? Those fascists are always crawling around the desert, you know. They ruin the ecology with their tanks and stuff. To hell with them."

Court shoved Newton Rasmin, and gladly watched him fall ass-first onto a boulder laced with prickly-pear cactus. Rasmin howled and clutched at the seat of his pants. "Don't forget, asshole, that *I'm* an Army puke," Court informed him. "Or fascist, if you'd rather pin that label on me too."

Court's girlfriend stomped over. "Quit it, both of you! You've been digging at each other ever since we came out!"

"We *shouldn't* have come out, Wendy," Court told her.

The woman who had been belaying Court glared at him contemptuously. She was her boyfriend's female counterpart, wearing a T-shirt with a slogan emblazoned upon it proclaiming the need to ban the nukes. "You didn't have to shove him," she snapped. "Newton has his own views about the military and ROTC," she sanctimoniously added, knowing beyond a shadow of doubt that David Court was just another rotcee-nazi.

From the start, Sarah Donahue had disliked almost everything about her sister Wendy's boyfriend. He was thick and powerful, his short hair bleached blond from the sun, with an easy, athletic gait gained from years on the wrestling team. He was UTEP's golden-boy athlete and, according to present company, an Army fascist to boot.

"ROTC's got nothing to with it, Sarah. Your boyfriend was chunking rocks at those guys down there."

"What were they doing with guns then?"

"For Christ's sake, we're on a military reservation! What do you think they were doing?" He gave up and skulked over to the other man. "Look, Newton, you just don't throw rocks at people like that."

Newton Rasmin puffed up, ready for a shoving match, but knew what the outcome would be. Instead, he slowly got up and tucked his Save-the-Whales T-shirt into his blue jeans. "Let's go back to camp."

"Yeah, let's go back to camp."

"Don't shove me like that again."

"Yeah, no problem," David Court said wearily.

The weekend was turning rapidly into a disaster. Wendy and her sister Sarah would be going camping and climbing with Sarah's boyfriend. Oh, sure, you'll get along with him, he's just got some liberal views, David Court had been told. No fucking problem.

First, there'd been all the anti-military innuendos on the drive up. Anti-establishment all the way. The acidic comments about ROTC. About how David Court would someday kill Latinos for the American Fruit Company in Central America, since he was another Army (puke) pawn in the clutches of a reactionary administration. Court had put up with it all, saying nothing, for Wendy's sake. Even her sister, Sarah, had more than once told Newton to shut up.

There had been the long hike from the car park on the western slope of the mountains to the abandoned gold mine where they'd set up camp the night before. Then, with the climbing today, things had gotten more relaxed and tensions eased. It would be a good weekend of climbing after all. But the Army guys had shown up out of nowhere, and the rocks that Newton had thrown had just pushed David Court over the limit. That was it. The following day, they would, by God, drive back to El Paso.

They all gathered up their equipment—coiling ropes, rearranging chocks, and climbing gear—on their equipment slings. Boots were relaced, water drunk, granola bars munched. All in silence.

Newton Rasmin extended his hand. "Hey, look. I've got no quarrels with you."

Court chewed on the inside of his cheek and decided to take the offered hand—if anything, just to keep himself from busting the idiot's face. Then *he'd* be the idiot, and Wendy would probably tell him to go take a hike. *Well, what the hell*, he thought.

The handshake turned into one of those thumbs-up, palms-around-the-backs-of-hand handshakes, power-to-the-people style. Court grimaced and put up with it.

Then they started the thirty-minute hike back to camp. The shadows were growing longer, and the temperature was cooling down. Soon, it would be dusk.

". . . out of nowhere, Manny," MacIntyre told his team sergeant after he and Hanlon had gotten back to the security perimeter.

"Ah, Christ, I just walked us into the area where they saw us, fat, dumb, and happy. Wasn't paying attention."

Hanlon came to his rescue. "Could have happened to anybody, Dai-uy. Wouldn't worry about it none."

Santo nodded. "Yes, sir. We knew the risk about moving around in daylight. It would have happened sooner or later."

MacIntyre picked up his ruck. "Well, we'd best get moving. I want to establish the commo site before it gets dark. We'll make sure those people aren't still climbing when we reach the cache."

The team moved out.

The Soviets stopped near a mountain stream high up. The rest of the trip was downhill. One more kilometer would take them to the abandoned gold mine, and then they could put surveillance on the area and wait for the scientist and the mole.

Antonov watched with disgust and contempt as Pushtkin, the KGB man, bobbed his head into the rivulet of water, slurping and gagging. As predicted, he'd gobbled up his canteen water much too soon. Throughout their movement, the Party man who supposedly had military and even Spetsnaz experience had exhibited no discipline, no self-discipline at all in the ways of the field.

His silent partner, the Mexican, lazily watched over Pushtkin as if he expected Antonov or Chelstovsky to jump him. *As well he might*, Antonov thought. *If there is a weak link on the team, it is those two*.

"You'll make yourself sick, comrade."

Pushtkin gulped more water.

"As you wish then," Antonov snorted, turning away. He withdrew his canteen from his backpack, squatted uphill from the stream, and reloaded the canteen full of water. He would only drink it twenty minutes later when the purifying iodine tablets he put in the canteen with the stream water took effect.

A mighty barf. Grinning, Antonov watched Pushtkin stumble away from the stream and vomit the water he'd just drunk onto the dried pine needles, cactus, and granite pebbles comprising the side of the mountain they had stopped on. Miserable, Pushtkin stumbled over to his backpack, weary and beaten. He lolled his head in Antonov's direction. Antonov studied him from his position by the stream, filling his other canteen. The major looked like a cobra ready to strike—silent, staring, coiled.

"We have to have been compromised," Pushtkin croaked.

Antonov stared at him, saying nothing.

"This daylight movement. . . I'm dehydrated. . . it's hard. . . ."

"I'm sure the Spetsnaz cadre that trained you in Moscow hardened you once. You've done this sort of thing before. Comrade."

"Do not be flippant with me, Major Antonov. We must plan an escape route . . . we must. . . ."

"You ordered me to continue this mission earlier, comrade. Why the sudden change of heart?"

Chelstovsky listened to the Muscovite's bickering from his position, slightly uphill, busying himself with sharpening his spade. It was an ordinary-looking trooper's field spade, painted matt green—fifty centimeters long, with a blade that measured fifteen centimeters wide and eighteen centimeters long. He treasured his spade and was quite good with it. But in order to keep good with it, he had to keep it sharp. And all three sides were kept razor-sharp.

Chelstovsky stopped stroking the blade of his spade with the file from his medical kit and stared at it. The file had many uses, like his spade. It was one hell of a sharpener, and many a Mujahideen rebel babbled after a few strokes against his front teeth. But as for someone like Pushtkin—over there leaning his back against his rucksack gasping for breath, sweat-soaked hiking clothes clinging to his body, the gleam of self-pity melting in his eyes like putty—someone like Pushtkin would not last a minute under torture. Not with the file. Not with the spade. Not even a second.

"Man, you do not plan on defeat," he heard Antonov continue. "If you cannot keep up, well . . ."

"How dare you even *suggest* I can't keep up!"

The Mexican stirred from the stream where he too had been filling his canteens. He walked over to the eastern side of their tiny security perimeter, watching the interchange between Antonov and Pushtkin, fumbling around with something in his right front trousers pocket. Chelstovsky kept a wary eye on him as he continued sharpening his spade.

The Mexican was obviously KGB, Chelstovsky thought, and that made sense. Chelstovsky prided himself on being a soldier, a paratrooper, a commando. To hell with the politics. Politicos, commissars, Party men—as far as the young Ukrainian was concerned, the Mexican and Pushtkin were both military-trained party-line quoters—the Mexican more of a mercenary, though. His own attitude was simpler and more to the point when it came to a mission: get in, do what had to be done, and get out. Ruthless. Professional. Unfeeling. Do not let politics get in the way.

Yet now, unfortunately, politics drove this mission. Pushtkin was in charge. But the KGB man would not have lasted long in Afghanistan.

"I'll keep up!" Pushtkin yelled. "How dare you insinuate—"

"The mission will be accomplished, Comrade Pushtkin. There is no other way, and besides, it is too late to turn back now."

Chelstovsky tensed as he watched the Mexican pull out a knife handle from his trousers pocket. He knew automatically what kind of knife it was—one aimed the knife handle, pushed a button, and a four-inch blade, spring-loaded, would shoot out, thunking into a target with great accuracy up to ten meters away.

He drew his spade back, ready.

Antonov gasped, his eyes growing wide.

"Why do you look at me like that, Major Antonov?"

And then Chelstovsky saw the diamondback rattler, thick as his wrist, raising up like a phoenix behind Pushtkin's head. It had been slithering up his backpack, and now it was in plain view parallel with the thick pine tree trunk Pushtkin leaned against with his backpack.

Twin blades shot through the air, each plowing into the pine within a split second of one another. The first blade, the spring-propelled knife blade, came from the Mexican, which impaled the rattler onto the tree, and the rest of the snake's body writhed and snapped against Pushtkin's head. A fraction of a second later, Chelstovsky's spade had whistled across the perimeter and chopped the snake's upper head and body clean through. The blade quivered in the tree trunk, and the snake's head, its mouth snapping open and shut, rolled down from the top of the blade onto the top of Pushtkin's head.

Pushtkin shrieked.

Spinning away from his rucksack, he tumbled downslope along the mountainside, clawing at the top of his head. He crashed to a halt against a tree five meters away, prostrate and trembling with adrenaline.

Antonov looked at the snake, looked at Chelstovsky uphill with his fists opening and closing, looked at the Mexican with his hooded eyes. The Mexican's arm was still outstretched, aiming the knife handle.

Then he roared with laughter.

No words were exchanged after that. Minutes later, they reformed their perimeter and ate their evening rations. It was a time to gather strength for the night's surveillance. A short rest, water, food. Already, it was 1600.

When it was 1700, Antonov moved them out.

This time, no climbers spotted them, unseen and hidden in the cracks and crevices and canyons of the Organ Mountains. The team crept through their route carefully, threading through the boulders, stepping gingerly over the cactus, stopping for a few minutes to verify the climbers' absence along the granite apron by the rock ribs where Hanlon and MacIntyre had spotted them earlier. They unloaded the cache and replenished their canteens with water. Finally, at 1823 hours that evening, they had reached their communications site.

From their vantage point on a rocky ledge on the eastern side of the mountain's diamond-faced summit, Master Sergeant Manny Santo watched the sun filter its last rays between a three-peak-pronged mountain massif over ten kilometers away along the western boundary of the missile complex. White Sands Missile Range sprawled in plain view below them in a cluster of houses, laboratories, and mock missiles. In another two hours, it would be dark.

The mood and atmosphere of the quiet of dusk calmed him, and Santo marveled at the way the desert and the granite peaks spread before him turned golden, then a purplish pink in the sun's fading rays; the way the shadows blued the valleys and desert plain darker and darker until finally the stars came out—the Milky Way, Orion, the dippers, the planets. . . .

Sighing, Santo turned to his rear. He did not like moments of quiet and beauty. It reminded him of . . . his wife. And his daughter. It reminded him of how. . .

He shook his head and tried to think of the mission. Upon securing the commo site, he'd had everyone take care of three simple soldiers' priorities after Barkowitz set up his communications relay station: clean weapons, eat their assault ration for the night, and sleep. He had taken first watch. The only man still up was Maslow.

Santo broke out of his dark mood and grinned, watching him. The team technician was busy stretching in only the way a martial artist could—limber, Oriental-style, his kneecap brushing against his chin while the toes of his foot were planted against a small cliff face above his head. Maslow was weird. One, he was a cowboy nut from New Mexico; two, he was definitely a computer nerd always gizmo-ing around with his state-of-the-art Apple back at Bragg, coming up with exotic spread sheets, training plans, and equipment and personnel rosters; and, three, he somehow managed to combine all elements of his personality into a man who was half brain, half animal, and all mystic. It was a wonder how his wife put up with him.

But thinking about wives again returned Santo to his original depression.

Maslow eventually made peace with the world in a lotus position by his rucksack and drifted off to sleep.

MacIntyre stirred and woke up when the tiny beeper of his Casio watch sounded off. It was 1900 and his turn to pull guard. That's the way it was on an "A" team—no exceptions for rank; everyone pulled their share of the load. He sidled up to Santo and leaned up against the rocks beside him for several moments, not wanting to break the peace and quiet of early evening.

"Look at 'em, sir."

MacIntyre stared off into the distance, at the pines growing at the foot and shoulders of the rocky peaks around them, the gorge rushing hundreds of feet below. "Look at what?"

Santo turned around. "The guys."

MacIntyre grinned. "They're all crapped out, Manny."

"They're good guys, Matt. The best."

MacIntyre's grin faded upon hearing the tightness in Santo's throat. Santo must have been thinking about his family again— and the loss he'd suffered two years before and the hurt that would remain with him for the rest of his life. MacIntyre clapped his hand on Santo's shoulder. "Better catch a few Zs."

Santo sat down on a boulder, leaning up against the small cliff face forming the peak of the mountain Maslow had been stretching against earlier. He breathed deeply. "They're like . . . family . . ."

MacIntyre looked away. He'd never talked with Santo about how his wife and thirteen-year-old daughter had once been home for the team sergeant, how they once had all celebrated Fourth of July picnics with some of the other families on the team, how—

Christ, how once they'd been *alive*. . . .

"They're . . . great guys, Manny."

Santo didn't answer. MacIntyre watched him feign sleep as the team sergeant leaned against the small cliff and sealed his eyes shut.

Chapter Seven

Major Sergei Antonov, on point, treaded softly through the pines. The ground was finally starting to level out, and soon, they would enter the final canyon where the stream and rendezvous site was located. The stream ran the length of what his American map told him was Ash Canyon.

Then it came into view—a rusted mining sluice, once used to filter the mud and rocks apart from gold picked out of an abandoned gold mine high up the west face of a huge mountain across the canyon. The sluice stood guard near a rim of boulders and trees encircling a natural dam in the stream where the water pooled out for several meters behind a barrier of rocks, before cascading downward.

Movement to the front!

Antonov shot his fist up in the air, held it. All four of them—including Pushtkin, the Mexican, and Chelstovsky, bringing up the rear of their staggered file—froze in position. Had they been seen? His eyes ran over his periphery, instantly gauging the possibility. No, not if they stayed put. Already, it was late, and within the next half hour, it would be completely dark.

Antonov slowly sank down to one knee, turning to his rear so he could face the others. It was hard to keep his balance. They had been walking downhill off the last mountain whose northern ridgeline would lead them into the rendezvous site. Antonov locked eyes with the other men and got their attention. Putting a forefinger to his lips, he slowly waved his other hand from left to right, palm down and perpendicular to his chest.

Pushtkin and the Mexican silently lay down in the prone behind trees, facing outward. Chelstovsky crept toward Antonov and met him at the front.

"Four of them, Nicholai," Antonov whispered to his communications sergeant.

Chelstovsky squinted through the shadows at the ridgeline on the opposite side of the stream where the rusted iron sluice hovered over it, ghostlike and skeletal. He heard and then saw four American civilians draped with climbing gear and ropes stomping loudly through the deadfall and rocks down toward the stream. They were only fifty meters away. They entered what seemed to be a tiny cave by the rocks at the sluice and came back out with their backpacks.

"Campers," Chelstovsky muttered.

"Yes."

"We are . . . at the correct position, Sergei Antonovich?"

"Yes."

"This is a difficult situation. Our rendezvous will be compromised."

"No."

The pair exchanged glances. Then Antonov dragged his forefinger slowly across his throat.

As the climbers went about with the talking and activity of setting up their camp, the Spetsnaz team silently pulled back up the ridgeline from where they'd come, and established another security perimeter completely out of site. Backpacks were camouflaged with pine needles and deadwood. Weapons were drawn.

Weapons. They had traveled light, but what they carried was deadly. They had been issued Western arms, none of which were of Soviet or Eastern Bloc design, in case they were captured or killed. Antonov had a German submachine gun, a H&K MP-5. Chelstovsky had the same. Pushtkin carried an Uzi. The Mexican, an Ingram MAC-10. All carried Browning nine-millimeter Hi-Power Pistols.

They clustered together in a tiny circle, ready.

Antonov's mind raced as they waited for his instructions. He knew he could not trust Pushtkin, who seemed to have had his earlier arrogance and cocksure attitude knocked out of him from the movement and the afternoon's comedy with the snake. The Mexican remained silent and anticipating. Antonov knew that it was best to keep the pair separated.

He laid a conciliatory hand on Pushtkin's shoulder. "Comrade, you and I shall sneak into their camp and listen to them, gather information." Antonov examined Pushtkin's face closely.

He detected a gleam of fear in the man's eyes. He was no longer in his urban environment; he was no longer playing the urban guerrilla's game of terror and covert espionage and assassination in the streets. Pushtkin then stuck his chin out, no doubt remembering his earlier loss of face, now determined to go through with the demands of the operation. Antonov played on this.

"Your mastery of English is much better than mine, comrade. We will decide whether or not to dispose of the civilians pending our reconnaissance." Antonov glanced at Chelstovsky and the Mexican. "You two shall remain here and secure our position. Comrade Pushtkin and I shall return. . . ." Antonov glanced at his watch. It was 2000 hours, and almost dark. "No later than 2200 hours." Then Antonov remembered the need to placate the KGB swine "commanding" his team. "What do you think, comrade?"

A slight pause, a shifting of the eyes. Then: "Yes. Of course." Pushtkin glanced away and stared at a pine cone on the slope near Antonov's foot.

Antonov repressed a grin of contempt. The answer had been too hasty, the gulp in Pushtkin's throat too visible. He nodded sagely and said, "Then let us be on our way."

Before they left, Pushtkin approached the Mexican, who squatted outside the perimeter with his binoculars, watching for any outside movement coming toward them.

"Remember the contingency plan?" Pushtkin asked him.

"*Sí.*"

"We must be very careful. When I give you the signal, take advantage of the situation when we split up. Do not let him suspect you, understand?"

"*Sí.*"

The hiss of four propane-fueled stoves warming their evening dinner seemed to calm the thick veil of antagonism between David

Court and Newton Rasmin. The hike back to their campsite had
been silent and unhappy, especially for the sisters, as both had
boyfriends who were simply making a mess out of the weekend.
But once they had set up camp and gotten the evening meal under
way, tensions relaxed. Now, as the water was heating into a tepid
boil, they lay back against their rucksacks in a circle around the
stoves.

Newton Rasmin happily whipped out a plastic bag from his
rucksack and thumbed through its contents. He pinched what
appeared to Court to be several chopped up and dried leaves and
sprinkled the lot into the hot-water pot.

"What's that stuff you're putting in the coffee water?" he asked,
afraid of the answer.

"Well, in the first place, David, we don't drink coffee. It's
unhealthy, you know."

"So what is it?"

"Tea."

"Tea, huh? What kind?"

"Natural, man. It's pretty good stuff."

Court sniffed the air. It *did* seem to have a pleasant, orange-
and-spices-like-his-Grandma-used-to-brew odor to it.

"Go ahead and try some, David," his girlfriend told him.

"I prefer coffee."

She withdrew her hand from his thigh, where she had been
stroking him. He caught the signal.

"Well, maybe some." He gave his tin hiker's cup to Rasmin.

Minutes later, the tea was ready, and Rasmin gave him back the
cup after filling it. "Enjoy, dude."

"Thanks." Court took a sip. It *was* good.

"You know," Rasmin told him, "I really am sorry about
chunking rocks at those two soldiers today. That was childish."

Court perked his ears up. He couldn't believe the same guy who
had been strumming his guitar and lamenting the U.S. presence in
El Salvador with the other protestors on campus last week was
apologizing for throwing rocks at a couple of soldiers. He thought
it was hilariously funny and said so.

"What's more," Rasmin continued, "*I* even thought once about
becoming a soldier."

"No!"

"Yes!"

Court guffawed, sloshing his tea out of his cup. Rasmin said, "Yeah, really!" The two women laughed with them.

Antonov and Pushtkin lay hidden in the rocks ten meters away from them, listening closely, for the subject of soldiers interested them greatly. But were there more than two?

"I'm hungry," Court said, breaking out his Mountain House foil of beef Stroganoff. On cue, the others opened their packages of freeze-dried food and poured hot water inside the plastic bags. "This is like the MREs we eat on our FTXs."

"FTXs?" Rasmin's girlfriend, Sarah, asked. "What's that?"

"Field Training Exercises," Court solemnly intoned. Then he broke up in laughter again. He thought it was hilariously funny that this earth-mother Wendy had for a sister didn't know what an FTX was. "You see, when you're in the Army, you go on field training exercises where you fight war games with each other and you have blank firing adapters on your M-16s and we're all acting like John Wayne in *The Sands of Iwo Jima*. Then we eat these MREs, and . . . and . . ."

The girls exchanged mirthful glances. Rasmin brayed with laughter.

"What's so funny?"

"You, man. Got the munchies, David?"

"I'm so hungry I could eat three of these."

Rasmin reached back into his backpack and took out another plastic bag. This one was filled with joints.

Court quit laughing and stared at it. Rasmin pulled out four of the rolled cigarettes and passed them out to the others. He held the final one out to Court. Court slapped his hand away. "You're not gonna smoke that shit in front of me."

"Feel kind of numb, David?" Rasmin put away the joint and picked up the tea pot. "Here, have some more." Rasmin poured the tea into Court's cup, which was lying on a rock by the stoves.

Court paled and stared at his cup. "What kind of tea did you say this was?"

"Tea, man. As in T-H-C."

"THC? What the—what the hell is—"

"Pot," came the solemn reply. Rasmin then grinned again through his beard. "You're drinking marijuana leaves in your tea. It's a mix I made with some regular tea from the store."

Court's eyes bulged. "I'm drinking—I'm drinking—"

"Afraid so, man." Rasmin leaned back against his backpack and chuckled. "Be cool, David. Mellow out."

"You son of a bitch!" Court scrambled up, jumped over the stoves, and grabbed Rasmin by his T-shirt, hauling him up. "Why'd you do that?"

"Let me go!"

"To hell with you!"

The girls scattered, trying to keep the men from knocking over the stoves. Rasmin, petrified, managed to sock his knee in Court's groin.

David Court grunted and doubled over. He raised his head and shot Rasmin an evil look. Rasmin backed slowly away.

"Hey, man, take it easy. *Take it easy!*"

Court bounded over to him and threw him on the ground, shaking him furiously. *"You stupid son of a bitch. Say your prayers, fuck-face!"* He drew his fist back and planted it squarely in Rasmin's mouth.

Rasmin shrieked. The girls screamed and pleaded with Court to quit.

Antonov and Pushtkin took advantage of the noise and crept back up the mountain for the others.

Court only socked Rasmin once, but it was enough. Disgusted, he finally got up, leaving Rasmin bleeding and whining against the pine needles.

"David!"

Court wheeled around. Wendy was pissed.

"David, you didn't have to do that!"

"This asshole's been begging for it all day."

"How can you be so violent?"

"What? *Violent?* Hey! All right! I've had enough of this shit!" Court stomped over to his backpack and stuffed his cup back in it, and turned off his stove and put that in his backpack too. He jerked his head in the downslope direction. "To hell with all of you!" He stuck his hand in his pocket to make sure his car keys were still there. They were. "I'm camping away from you pot-heads tonight. You want to leave with me tomorrow, then you can meet me back at the car."

"David," Wendy pleaded, "don't . . ." She glared at Rasmin, who had stood up and was shuffling back over to the others, keeping a wary distance from Court. "Newton, you apologize to David! You shouldn't have done that to him!"

Rasmin felt his lips with one hand, already feeling them swell, and then extended the other like before. "Hey, c'mon, man, I didn't—"

"Back off, asshole."

"David . . ."

"To hell with it, Wendy," Court said indignantly. "You're no better than this idiot and your sister. I'm leaving."

With that, he walked off in search of a new camp.

During Antonov's and Pushtkin's reconnaissance, the Mexican had kept a subtle eye on the communications sergeant, Chelstovsky. He was careful, and by being careful ever since his recruitment by Pushtkin in Juarez five years ago, he'd reaped Pushtkin's rewards of more pesos than he possibly could ever have earned across the bridge as a migrant worker like his father and his grandfather. In fact, the thought of once having been a migrant worker so repelled him that he spat on the ground.

A lizard scattered through the rocks, having been rousted from his hiding place in the pine needles. The lizard crawled up the boulder where Chelstovsky had leaned his ruck against and stared at him. The Mexican chuckled.

"Eh?" Chelstovsky turned around and looked at the Mexican. Then he saw the lizard by his rucksack. He grinned at the Mexican. "Go on. Get him with your knife too."

The Mexican shrugged. "It's not worth the effort."

"You are not a man of many words, friend."

The Mexican's ears perked up at that. Chelstovsky had called him "friend." New possibilities were in the making. An idea began to form in his mind.

"You're pretty good with that knife."

"As you with the spade. Where did you learn that?"

Chelstovsky beamed with pride. It was an unusual technique,

the technique with the spade. The compliment stroked his ego. "The Soviet soldier's spade is his best friend. In minutes, and at all halts during a troop movement, the Soviet soldier is required to dig into the ground in case of attack. The common soldier, that is."

"But you are no common soldier." The Mexican turned toward the center of their security perimeter and rested his full attention on Chelstovsky. "You are from a special unit."

Chelstovsky's chest swelled. "Yes. In my unit the spade is our trademark. We are never without it. You dig with it, you use it as an ax, and . . . if thrown properly, you can kill with it. A silent way for killing sentries when breaching perimeters."

"I prefer my knife."

"Yes, I see you do." Chelstovsky did not say so, but he knew where the knife came from. He had one himself, but did not display it like the other man. It was of Soviet design and manufacture, and every Spetsnaz soldier possessed one. Had Pushtkin given him the knife?

"You are quiet much of the time, friend," Chelstovsky continued, fishing for information. "I do not even know your name."

The Mexican lifted his chin, looking hard at the Russian. Then the corners of his mouth upturned slowly. "Jaime Navarro."

A moment's silence, as each man appraised the other. Navarro decided to press on. "You seem to have a wealth of experience— friend. All those places you must have seen . . . Afghanistan . . . I have only known Mexico."

"In my country," Chelstovsky told him, "a peasant boy growing up on a collective farm is not afforded much choice in his destiny. My father was a farmer. I will never be a farmer. When I was inducted in the Soviet Army, I was chosen for special training." He shrugged his shoulders. "Ten years passed by. I served in Czechoslovakia, then Afghanistan. Now I am here."

"Then, in that way, we are alike. I will never work for the American pigs across the Rio Grande. I will never slave in the fields like my father and grandfather. This," he added, fingering his MAC-10, "is the key."

Chelstovsky beamed. "When we get back across the border, Jaime Navarro, we will drink vodka together."

The Mexican's hooded eyes twinkled at the corners, belying a cold spark of calculation in his pupils. He uttered a premeditated chuckle. "I will match your vodka with my tequila. One for one."

"Done! Until then!"

The soft scrape of footsteps picking through the pines and the gravel underfoot greeted their ears. Instantly, both men fell silent and aimed their weapons back out on the perimeter.

Chelstovsky saw Antonov and Pushtkin come into view, materializing through the oncoming darkness. They walked inside the perimeter, sweating and breathing hard from the elevation and the climb back up the canyon from the gorge where they had reconnoitered the campsite. They huddled in the center of the perimeter.

"Four people," Antonov said evenly. By contrast, Pushtkin beside him was still gasping for air. Antonov acknowledged the other man's physical prowess with a quick, amused glance and a wink at Chelstovsky, then continued. "Two men and two women. They were arguing about throwing rocks at two soldiers and so on."

Chelstovsky was puzzled. "Throwing rocks, Sergei Antonovich?"

Antonov nodded his head. "Yes, at two soldiers in the area. Apparently they had been climbing earlier in the day when they saw the soldiers."

"Yes!" Pushtkin hissed. "Yes! There are American soldiers here in the mountains! They are looking for us!"

Antonov glared at the KGB man and Pushtkin fell silent, intimidated. "It is a possibility."

"The campers . . ." Chelstovsky interjected. "Sergei Antonovich, they are located at our rendezvous site."

"Yes, yes," Antonov said, weary of complications. He was tired of complications, and especially tired of the KGB man's continual bickering about possible compromise. They had no choice. If they returned to Juarez without the scientist and the RAIL device and their agent—if they failed their mission, Pushtkin would surely fabricate lies to cover his own tracks for mission failure.

The reward for failure was death. And he'd been warned about working with the KGB . . . to hell with complications. To hell with Pushtkin! To hell with the Party men in Moscow. They knew nothing of challenge and stamina and victory. They were snivelling party-line quoters who would backstab their own mothers to cover their asses. Swine!

He would carry out this mission if it killed them all.

"Now that we have masturbated our intellects, comrades, here is how we will succeed." Antonov slapped a hand on his communicator's shoulder. "Nicholai!"

"*Da!*"

"You and he," Antonov said, glancing at the Mexican, "will locate these American soldiers who are supposed to be in the area. I trust your judgment, Nicholai Chelstovsky. You will kill these men if you deem it necessary, but if they are nothing more than soldiers on a training exercise, don't do anything unless they appear to walk near the rendezvous site. If they have been sent in to observe us and report back to their headquarters, or worse, if there are more of them ready to capture us, you will tie down their operations and evade your way back to the border. In any event, do not let them know of our existence. Should everything turn out all right, return at 0600 tomorrow morning, an hour before the rendezvous. If you do not show up by then, I will assume you are dead or en route to the border."

"*Da*, Sergei Antonovich!"

Pushtkin said nothing. At this point, he was more than willing to let Antonov run the show. When they got the scientist and the agent, he could settle accounts with Antonov then—in Las Cruces with the others, where Antonov and Chelstovsky would be outnumbered and easily disposed of. He thought of *his* lieutenant, Chelmno Grzniecki, who was running the Las Cruces operation, and Boris Pushtkin smiled.

"Meanwhile," Antonov said, casting a cold eye on Pushtkin, "you and I will take care of the campers and get ready for the rendezvous in the morning." He glanced at his watch. "It is now 2000 hours. Prepare to move out in fifteen minutes."

"Sergei Antonovich," Chelstovsky said, "about communications . . . the possible American location . . ."

Navarro felt a crawling sensation flush his cheek. He looked up and saw Pushtkin staring at him, while Antonov talked with

Chelstovsky. Pushtkin nodded once at him, tight-lipped, taut, eyes burning with intensity and hate for Antonov.

Navarro acknowledged the signal, and then his eyes hooded back over, reptilian and cold.

Greeley made the 2100 hours commo check to the FOB back at Oro Grande and sent the team's location and status report. Then he shook Barkowitz awake. It was time for the team to split up and move into their respective R&S (recon and surveillance) sites.

The wind was picking back up, and now, it was completely dark. At their commo site, on top of the mountain, Greeley rousted the others awake. In ten minutes, web gear was strapped on and readjusted, hamstrings and calf muscles were stretched, tight from the past twenty-four hours of movement, and hastily brewed cups of coffee were drunk. They were alert, rested. They were ready.

MacIntyre gathered everyone in tight around a terrain model he had made depicting Ash Canyon's layout. With this, he'd go over the last-minute adjustments to the plan.

"Okay," he began, his voice rising above the pitch of the wind, "the next forty-eight hours are crucial." He glanced up at Maslow, Saxon, and Barkowitz. "You three will maintain the commo relay site up here on the mountain. Remember—commo checks back to the FOB every three hours, 2400, 0300, 0600, and so on, until I give the word for a linkup when the reconnaissance is over, or until the time Colonel Volensky comes over the air and gives the say-so."

MacIntyre picked up a stick and pointed at the terrain model. "Okay, everyone see how this is set up? Good. Here's the mountain we're on. Randy," he said, glancing at Hanlon, "you and I make up R&S team number one. Manny, you and Greeley are R&S team two." He dragged the pointer from the top of the mountain depicted in the terrain model down into the simulated canyon. "All four of us walk down to where the stream at the bottom of the canyon starts to open up into the gorge farther down. We've all been in this area before. Our route passes about three hundred meters north of the remains of an old mining shack and sluice where they used to filter gold ore. Once we get to that vicinity, Manny," MacIntyre said, clapping his team sergeant on the shoulder, "we'll all split up into our R&S teams. You and Greeley will position yourselves at a good vantage point by morning to observe the White Sands approach into Ash Canyon. Randy, you and I will cross over to the far-side ridgeline and establish surveillance up there where we can observe both Ash and Texas Canyons." MacIntyre glanced around at the other men. "Okay, everybody got it so far?"

"One thing we need to think about, Dai-uy," Santo said. "Those climbers you and Randy saw earlier today . . . they'll more than likely be camped somewhere in the canyon. Watch out for them."

"Good point, Manny. They'd be near the stream in the center of the canyon if they are in fact still around. Anything else?"

"When we spot 'em, sir . . ." Hanlon offered.

"Right. When we see what appears to be any kind of unusual activity—equipment, documents, dope, some guy who looks like a scientist or whatever—we report it back to the commo site to you guys," he said, nodding at Maslow and Barkowitz. "We'll contact you with the PRC-68s at least fifteen minutes before the scheduled commo checks back to the FOB—at 2345, 0245, and so on." MacIntyre held up his PRC-68 hand-held radio. "Both R&S teams are on channel six, which we pre-tuned to the PRC-70 during isolation two days ago. We'll have three-way commo at all times."

Everyone exchanged glances. They had already known the mission from heart, as Santo had put the word out earlier. But, as Murphy's Law dictated, what could go wrong, would go wrong. It never hurt to re-hash the plan immediately before execution. "Any questions?" MacIntyre asked.

"Enemy contact, sir," Maslow said. "You know how it is. You've got your regular plan, like what we've just discussed, and then you've got to have your go-to-hell plan in case the feces strikes the fan."

Santo hefted his M16 in front of him. It was the new M16A2 model, more reliable, accurate, and with greater range than the A1 model. "That's why we've got live ammo this time out, Chief. But don't let the bad guys get you into a firefight. If you're compromised, make commo back to the FOB and shag ass for the missile range. We'll hear you on the PRC-68's and stay in the area to maintain observation. We're here to make a recon, not to slug it out with the Russkies."

MacIntyre looked from man to man. "Anything else?"

No one spoke.

"Then let's, by God, do it."

CHAPTER EIGHT

Security Guard Ray Bloodworth stretched back in his swivel chair in the office guarding the entrance to the laboratory complex's access door and burped contentedly, having just polished off the peanut-butter-and-jelly sandwich he'd passed up at lunch. Glancing up at the wall clock above the building's entrance, which now read 2000 hours, he wondered if all the overtime he'd been working lately was worth it. Sure—he'd be eligible for retirement in another couple of years, and then the bucks would come in pretty handy. Yessir, that's right. He and his wife Maria would settle down in the small ranch house they had up in the Sangre de Christo Mountains up by Taos and just take things easy. Trout fishing, elk hunting in the fall . . .

Bloodworth's mind drifted, wishing that the scientist he had let into the Guidance Research lab earlier in the evening would hurry up with *his* overtime and be gone. Then he could relax a little more and not pay so much attention to the monitors he scanned inside his Plexiglas office.

The double doors at the building's entrance swung open slowly. Bloodworth's eyes widened. It was one of the secretaries, one of the *good*-looking lasses. She walked slowly inside the building, clutching a bible in one hand she kept pressed against her bosom. In her other hand, she carried what appeared to be a to-go order of hamburgers in a greasy snack-bar paper bag. *Now what on earth . . . ?*

"Hello, Mister Bloodworth."

Bloodworth swung his feet down off the counter and opened his office door. "Miss Sanchez . . . out kind of late tonight, huh?" He stretched in the doorway and stifled a yawn, then patted the broad expanse of his gut that strained and puckered the buttons of his shirt. Company was welcome, especially when it was one of the secretaries. He wondered if she was here for that scientist, Sorens. Everyone knew they were seeing each other.

Victoria Sanchez walked closer, and Bloodworth saw dark circles pooling beneath her eyes and the pallor of her skin. Even though she was dressed in a beautiful ivory and lace Mexican dress and high heels, with her ebony hair draping over her shoulders, she didn't look so well. The tiny gold crucifix nestled in the hollow of her throat added to the frailty of a woman who was normally athletic, healthy, alive with inner reserves of energy, coupled with sensual grace. Now, her gait was without vigor.

Bloodworth became alert with concern, and he stepped out of the office to meet her. "You don't look well, Miss Sanchez."

Sanchez shivered slightly, and Bloodworth's heart clutched watching her naked shoulders tremble. No, he didn't like this at all.

"I've just returned from the chapel, and wanted to drop these off to Blake on the way home tonight," she told him. She blanched suddenly, and reached out to support herself against the doorjamb.

"Miss Sanchez!" Bloodworth supported her by the arm and guided her to an easy chair in the lobby a few feet away. He liked the feel of her, and even in her condition, he could not help but feel aroused by the smooth texture of her skin and the clean fragrance of the bathwater she must have used that evening before going out. "The virus that's been going around—is that it?" he asked her.

"Well, it just seemed to come on rather suddenly, while I was in Bible Study a couple of hours ago," she replied, smiling gently at him as she sat down. "Mr. Sorens is expecting me." Sanchez set the bag of hamburgers she'd been carrying on the floor and clasped the bible to her chest with both hands, as if it would warm her.

"If that don't beat all. Ol' Mister Sorens in there just don't know how good he's got it if he has a lady friend as nice as you are." In the back of Bloodworth's mind, he cursed the preppy-looking scientist with his superior, patronizing attitude for being the object of this young woman's devotion. "I'll just give him a ring and tell him you're here."

"No, please, let me do that." She started to get up.

"Are you sure?"

"Yes . . . please . . . can you just let me use your arm?"

He walked her over to the office and dialed Sorens's number for her.

The phone rang. Sorens knew it was coming, glad when it finally did. He'd been ready for the past hour, after having gathered the irradiated microchip circuitry he had needed for the handoff up in the mountains. The model he had built was a simple one; nothing more than a plastic black box with circuit panels in it and the irradiated microchips that galvanized the process he'd pioneered with the RAIL project.

The phone rang again, and he reached for it.

"Blake?"

"Yes . . ."

"Blake, please drive me home tonight. I'm not feeling well."

"Sure, Vicki," he said mechanically. "I'll be right out."

Sorens stuffed the model into the shoe box he'd let the security guard see earlier in his gym bag. Then he grabbed his briefcase, locked up his office, and walked out the lab toward the lobby.

When he pushed the door open, he saw two things: one, that the security guard's office door was ajar; two, that Bloodworth was standing near Vicki in the center of the lobby as she waited, looking like hell.

"Blake," she said unevenly, taking a step forward, "Blake, please take me. . . ."

She fainted.

"Vicki!" Sorens bolted inside the lobby. The security guard held her tightly to keep her from collapsing on the floor. They hovered over her, as they half dragged, half carried her to the big easy chair. She came to.

"Oh, Blake, I feel so sick. . . ."

"Better get her home soon, Mister Sorens," said Bloodworth. He pointed at the bible. "Said she came up early tonight for Bible Study. Now's she's sick with that virus that's been going around."

Sorens went back to the door where he'd dropped his briefcase and gym bag, then returned. "Thanks, Mister Bloodworth. We'll be on our way."

"Take care, folks." Bloodworth pulled on Sorens's arm. "You ought to get her to the dispensary, you know," he muttered.

"Thanks. Yes, I will. C'mon, Vicki." Sorens helped her up from the chair, grabbed his briefcase and gym bag, and they walked slowly toward the lobby entrance.

"Wait."

"Huh?" Sorens turned around. The security guard looked at him sheepishly, his hands thrust deep in his pockets.

"Still have to look at your bags, Mister Sorens."

"You—you looked at them earlier, remember?"

"Hell, Mister Sorens, you know procedure. Sorry, but . . ." The security guard's face suddenly clouded and his eyes narrowed. "Just put them on the cage counter, please, sir." It was not a request.

"Sure, but . . ." Sorens glanced at Vicki. She gave him an imperceptible nod.

"I'm okay, Blake," she told him, still clutching the bible.

"Just take a minute, ma'am," Bloodworth told her. He turned his back as he and Sorens walked back toward the cage. "Regulations, Mister Sorens. You know the procedure." They reached the counter. "There you go. Now if you'll just—"

Victoria Sanchez pulled a tiny syringe out of the hollow she had carved in the bible earlier and walked up to them.

Sorens caught her movement out of the corner of his eye. He stiffened when he saw the syringe.

She stuck it in the security guard's back.

Bloodworth let out a wheezing gasp and staggered to one knee and then the other, clutching at his heart with one hand and using the other to keep from toppling over. Perspiration beaded on his forehead in huge, wet drops. He made a croaking sound deep in his throat, and then crashed to the floor.

Aghast, Sorens stared at the body. "Vicki . . ."

Sanchez calmly opened her purse and placed the syringe inside. She withdrew some trace paper. "He had a cardiac arrest, Blake."

Sorens remained frozen. He hadn't expected this. "Vicki . . ." he repeated.

Sanchez put the trace paper on the sign-in-sign-out logbook on the cage counter and drew over the security guard's initials in his own handwriting. Then she transferred the forgery onto the logbook, indicating that Sorens had left two hours ago. She grabbed him by the arm. "Quickly now. You *do* have everything. . . ."

"Vicki . . ."

She slapped him. "Pull yourself together! We have to move quickly!"

"You killed him!"

"It had to be done! Now do you have everything!"

"Yes . . ."

"Then move!"

He picked up the bag and briefcase and they hustled out of the building, where they climbed into his Cherokee.

Within minutes they had exited the missile complex and were driving toward the dirt roads leading to Ash Canyon.

Thunder rumbled threateningly in the distance. Looking up, Captain Matt MacIntyre realized that the clouds they had seen on the horizon earlier had now blotted out half the stars above. Looking past the expanse of the missile range below them on the desert floor, he saw the firefly glimmers of lightning spark all along the incoming front's advance.

"It's gonna pour like ten motherfuckers," Santo said to him just loud enough to be heard over the wind. The pine trees above wheezed in agreement, and the smell of ozone permeated their nostrils.

Having just reached the gorge, MacIntyre knew that it would not take long before the oncoming downpour would turn the swift-running stream at their feet into a roaring death trap. They would have to find high ground fast. But first, the commo check.

For the past hour, the four of them—MacIntyre, Santo, Hanlon, and Greeley—had crept through the rocks and pines, slipping down the ridgelines into Ash Canyon. If anyone had been there, the sound of their footsteps would have been deadened by the noise created by the oncoming storm and the stiffening wind preceding it. MacIntyre squeezed the talk button on the PRC-68 and said, "Charlie-Sierra, this is Romeo-Sierra One, over." He glanced at his watch. It was 2345, and that meant that Barkowitz would be on watch. They had to make commo back to the FOB in another fifteen minutes. He repeated the transmission.

Static broke through the brick-sized radio in MacIntyre's hand. *"Romeo-Sierra One, this is Charlie-Sierra."*

"Charlie-Sierra, this is Romeo-Sierra One . . . we're at the release point, and are now en route to respective positions. Negative situation-report so far, over."

"This is Charlie-Sierra. Roger that. Anything else, over?"

"This is One, negative. Out."

The commo check was complete. MacIntyre had informed Barkowitz of the two R&S teams' location—they were now at the release point, where they would split up into their respective surveillance sites. MacIntyre nodded at Santo. "Ready, Manny?"

"Yes, sir." Santo squinted through the darkness, and looked off to his left, uphill, toward the top of the canyon. "There's a cliff face not too far away from here, and a trail off to the side that'll get us up high enough for observation. That's where Greeley and I will be."

"Okay. Hanlon and I will scoot on across the gorge and climb up the next ridgeline."

"You two be careful. This storm looks like it's gonna get pretty bad."

"No sweat, Manny. See you when I see you."

Then the two R&S teams separated.

Taking advantage of the noise created by the incoming front, Chelstovsky and Navarro climbed steadily toward the rim of the canyon where they had seen the climbers descend earlier in the day. They paused for a few minutes to catch their breath.

Chelstovsky glanced back at Navarro, who had been climbing behind him. "We will climb until we reach the ridgeline that leads toward the last mountaintop. There, it overlooks the desert on the other side. Major Antonov and I decided earlier that the most likely point of surveillance and communications will be in that general location. We will see if in fact anyone is there, and then complete the search by combing the mountainside back into the canyon."

The Mexican grunted noncommittally.

"Ready?"

"Sí."

The two climbed on. Presently, they were on the ridgeline leading to the mountaintop spotted earlier. The trees thinned out.

They concentrated on moving in the shadows of the scores of boulders and cliff faces lining the ridgeline. In another few minutes they would be on top.

Chelstovsky halted.

"What is it?" Navarro asked him.

"It is too barren up here."

Both of them strained their eyes, using their peripheral vision and moving their eyes around to garner the full usage of their natural night vision. Moments later, Chelstovsky unslung the small daypack he had been wearing and withdrew a cylindrical object with rubberized caps on both ends.

Navarro looked at it quizzically.

"It is a night-vision device," Chelstovsky informed him. "It operates on infrared and enhances what we see to our front." He brought the telescope up to his right eye and scanned his front from left to right. Several seconds later, he froze the device on a spot to the right of the summit.

"What do you see?"

"Some type of . . . incandescent light. There's nothing to our left, but on the other side . . . there might be something."

Chelstovsky handed the telescope to the Mexican. Navarro pointed it in the direction where Chelstovsky had seen the glow. The phosphorescent green display inside the night-observation device highlighted the ridgeline sloping down from the summit. Then, in accordance with what Chelstovsky reported, he noticed the rounded glow of soft light arcing over the ridgeline in one concentrated area.

"What could it be?" Navarro asked him. "It is not a campfire. We would have seen that with our naked eye. A flashlight would throw a beam."

Chelstovsky pointed at the area where he had initially spotted the glow, where several trees met on a ridgeline connecting an adjacent peak. "There might be someone on the other side of this saddle, in between peaks. We will move toward those trees and reconnoiter them from above."

"Yes, that is a good idea."

Chelstovsky shoved the night-vision device back into his daypack, ensuring his spade was strapped on within easy grabbing reach. "And then, my friend, we will see who and what they are."

• • •

David Court woke up at 0233 with the initial, deafening crash of thunder and with huge drops of rain splatting on his face every other second. He came to, cursing the developments of the weekend. He had been in a fight, lost his girlfriend, gotten high on pot, and now he was due to get soaked from the pregnant cloud cover above. The thin tree line he had set his bivouac in would provide no shelter at all when it started to pour.

He crawled out of his sleeping bag. After rolling it up and sticking it in his backpack, he swallowed his pride and started hiking the hundred-odd meters back to the others, who no doubt were quite warm and toasty in their tents.

"Two tents," Antonov muttered to Pushtkin, as they lay hidden in the rocks by the sluice.

Pushtkin shivered in discomfort. "Let's get it over with." He pulled his pistol out of his shoulder holster and chambered a round.

Antonov clasped his calloused hand firmly over the receiver. "No. This must be done as silently as possible. And with no traces."

Even in the black of the moonless night, Antonov could see the way Pushtkin paled. Enjoying the other's discomfort, he pulled out a hunting knife, and held the long, serrated blade in front of Pushtkin's face. "This way."

"Yes. Of course." Pushtkin pulled out his own knife, his hands shaking. The rain had wet him through. The wind howled through the canyon with an occasional clash of thunder. Bolts of lightning overhead illuminated their silhouettes. His nerves were shot. He dropped the knife and it clattered noisily against a rock.

Antonov held his anger in check and picked up the knife. "I'll do it," he told Pushtkin, handing back the knife. Antonov swung his attention back to the camp, not ten meters away. Two dome tents had been erected upon a platform of dirt and rock near the streambed, which was due to be flash-flooded soon. An idea suddenly occurred to him. He would break their necks. They wouldn't be armed, they were only civilians. With all the other noise, neither tent could hear the commotion in the other. Then, when it flooded, the bodies would be carried downstream, their necks appearing to have been broken from the bashing the corpses would receive lower down in the gorge.

He glanced back at Pushtkin, and then pointed at one of the tents. "Listen to them. The couple in one of the tents are making love—they won't pay attention to what's going on out here. The other tent is quiet. I'll do that one first. You follow me inside their perimeter and stand guard with your pistol."

Jabbing his walking stick into the ground with each rain-soaked step, David Court climbed up the trail leading back to the campsite. He had only a few more meters to go. Finally, he saw the skeleton of the mining sluice that marked the site. The trees thinned out as he walked closer.

And then he saw two men steal inside the campsite, dark, blurry shadows. One silently entered the tent Wendy was sleeping in. The other squatted outside, holding what appeared to be a pistol.

His bowels turned to water. Swallowing, he pulled off his backpack and quietly lay it down, his heart racing. Then he stared at his walking stick, his knuckles gleaming against the hickory.

Wendy stirred in her sleeping bag, glad to hear the zipper release the opening. It meant that David could warm things up for her and that they could make up. Then she wouldn't have to listen to Sarah and Newton next door keeping her up all night.

When the U-shaped opening came undone, a dark figure blotted out the trees and rocks beyond.

"David?" she moaned. "Come on in, baby. It's so cold."

The figure moved closer, and Wendy could smell the mustiness of his body odor. That wasn't David!

Before she could scream, Antonov had already straddled her and clapped his hand around her mouth, the knife edge of his hand against the cartilage of her nose. When he cradled the back of her neck with his other forearm, he snapped her spinal cord with one quick jerk.

Heart pounding, David Court watched as the man who had gone into Wendy's tent returned outside. After muttering something to the man on guard, he then unzipped the opening to the other tent. The realization that something very, very wrong was happening numbed Court to the wind whipping at his hair and the rain which was now pounding down in sheets. Streaks of lightning flared nearby, illuminating the area in brilliant flashes that seared his eyesight with their silhouettes.

David Court knew what he had to do. He crept toward the campsite slowly, moving from tree to tree, clenching his walking stick.

Pushtkin wheeled around when he heard padding footsteps immediately behind him, but it was too late. A thick-trunked, muscled, blond-haired man, more a boy than a man, whipped his walking stick through the air and struck him on the crown of his head. The pistol flew out of Pushtkin's hands. Reeling backwards, the KGB agent fell on his back, scrabbling at the rocks and loose gravel underfoot with his hands to keep from falling in the swelling stream below.

The moaning sounds from the other tent increased in their intensity. When Antonov entered, he saw the woman first; she was on top. The man beneath her, initially gasping in pleasure, gasped again when he saw the Russian.

Newton Rasmin screamed.

The girl spun around in surprise and Antonov grabbed her head in his huge hands. He promptly twisted her neck, the audible pop of her severed spinal cord and broken vertebrae standing out with the noise outside.

The noise outside! Antonov tore out of the tent, and immediately saw a blond-haired man kicking Pushtkin with rib-cracking enthusiasm.

Court spun around and leaped to the side before Antonov could reach him, striking the Russian soundly on the cheek with his walking stick. Dizzy and bleeding, Antonov staggered about, warding off more blows with his forearms and fists. Then he grabbed the stick and planted a kick in the other man's midsection. The blond man doubled over and careened toward the tent where Antonov had just killed the other woman.

"*Newt!*" Court screamed, falling against the tent. Rasmin popped out of the entrance and lunged away from the two fighting men.

He stood paralyzed, watching them, his mouth opening and closing with fear.

"*Newt! Help me!*"

Antonov had Court on the ground now, and was pressing the stick toward his throat.

"Get this guy offa me—"

Antonov rammed his knee into the blond man's groin. David Court screamed and his grip weakened on the stick. Antonov pressed it closer to his throat. Closer. He rammed his knee into Court again.

Court shrieked.

Newton Rasmin, clad only in his blue jeans, tried to say something, anything, tried to move, but he froze. The big silent man on top of Court was going to kill him. It was simple as that. Already, the man had Court's walking stick pressed up against his larynx, and now, Court was choking under the pressure.

Terrified, Rasmin glanced wildly at his right. Another man was sitting up on the ground clutching his ribs. He looked up at Rasmin, and locked cold, red eyes on him. Immediately, he reached out and grabbed the pistol lying by his feet.

Rasmin's sphincter muscles lost all control. Screaming, he bolted out of the campsite, his fear and horror and adrenaline numbing him to the cactus barbs and rocks slashing at his feet.

CHAPTER NINE

A black figure in the crisp air left behind from the storm's spent fury slithered on his belly into the trees by the summit. It was Chelstovsky. In another minute, he'd stop and wave at Navarro following behind to join him. But first, he had to see what the origin of the glow was that he'd spotted earlier with the night-vision device.

He crawled deeper into the trees and made for the top of the ridgeline. It was quiet now with the passing of the storm, and every movement had to be calculated for the amount of noise he'd make. Five more minutes in the trees brought him to the top of the ridgeline.

Then, moving to the left and downhill into the mountain's saddle, he spotted the stove. Chelstovsky took in the position. One man leaned against a rucksack and was draped in what had to be an American Army-issue poncho. A primus stove boiled water by his feet. As far as Chelstovsky could tell, there was only one other man with him, sleeping over by the rocks beside a small cliff face leading toward the mountain's summit. Chelstovsky nodded his head in satisfaction. These men had to be the two soldiers Antonov had told him about earlier after his reconnaissance of the climbers' encampment.

After studying them for several minutes, he quietly crept back from where he'd come to retrieve the Mexican.

When the full force of the cloudburst had passed on into the canyons and ridgelines and summits south of their communications site, Terry Saxon poked his head out from underneath his poncho and shivered, watching his breath steam out from his mouth. No matter what time of the year it was in the desert, the nights were always cool, if not downright cold. Especially after a cloudburst.

He glanced at the two prostrate figures of Maslow and Barkowitz, who had been sleeping huddled up in their ponchos. Little rivulets of water ran off the small cliff face from the mountain's summit and gathered into gullies farther below. Saxon turned his stove on again, ready for another cup of coffee. The sandman was doing his best to make him go to sleep.

Saxon let his eyelids rest halfway across his corneas, trying to relieve the gritty feeling created by the wind and the lack of sleep. The hiss of the stove boiling water by his feet lulled him into letting his eyelids close all the way. When he felt his head droop, he jerked awake, spastic and angry for letting himself relax. Soon, it would be 0400 and time for Barkowitz to take the commo watch with the PRC-70.

When the water had boiled past the tepid point, he poured in a packet of dehydrated ration coffee that had enough caffeine in it to zap him fully awake for at least the next thirty minutes. Already, he had two empty packs lying by the stove from past battles with the clock inside his mind dictating that the hours between 0300 and 0400 were definitely for sleeping.

A grunting noise to his front left. Maslow. He had sought the shelter of a hollowed-out portion of the cliff shielded by an overhang that had offered him more protection from the storm. The warrant officer stirred into wakefulness, crawled out from underneath his poncho, tramped wearily up to Saxon with his M-16.

Saxon held out a cup, and Maslow took it, shivering, letting the hot metal of the cup warm his hands.

"Good God," Maslow muttered.

"Storm was pretty violent."

"Yes." Maslow stretched and arched his back, letting his vertebrae snap and pop from twenty years of accumulated aches, healed bones, and sprained joints from too many airborne drops. "You have a choice with a poncho, you know. You can remain somewhat warm inside, but the condensation alone will still make you as wet as if you didn't have one."

Saxon poured more water into another canteen cup and re-lit his stove. "Keep it, if you want. Can't go to sleep?"

"No. I usually have a bad case of insomnia like this when I'm out in the field. It's weird. What's more, I've been putting off taking a crap all day. No way I can hold it any longer."

Saxon chuckled. "Some things never change when you're in the field." He leaned over to the radio beside him and squeezed the mike, listening for the sound of breaking squelch that would tell him the radio had weathered out the storm all right.

Maslow set the canteen cup down and stood up. "This coffee does no good at all either. But—it warms you up a little." He then took a small tin of Copenhagen snuff from his fatigue trousers cargo pocket and went through the ritual of thumping and shaking the can's powdered tobacco contents to one side of the can, where he could grab hold of a good healthy pinch before sticking it in his lower lip.

Saxon watched him, fascinated. "You're going to do that?"

"Black people chew too, you know."

"But you're drinking coffee."

"Ah, that's the best part. One receives the nicotine rush and the caffeine rush at the same time that way."

"Oh."

Maslow grinned. "Mother Nature calls. Once I return from the tree line, my morale will boost one hundred percent."

"See you later."

Maslow walked downslope into the trees.

On the opposite side of the ridgeline, Chelstovsky leaned close to Navarro's ear. "They are only fifty meters away," he whispered.

"They?"

"Two soldiers—one is sleeping, and the other is on radio watch. They have M16 rifles, and a radio similar to the one I packed in. They obviously are sending communications back to other elements of their detachment who must be down in the canyon somewhere."

"How can you know that?"

"I suspected it when we had transmission difficulty earlier, upon contacting our agent. Plus, I study my enemy. There is only one kind of American Army unit that uses the type of radio I saw."

"Who?"

"The American Special Forces."

Navarro spat. "Fucking gringos. They're all the same to me."

Chelstovsky grabbed his arm. "Lower your voice. And *never* underestimate your enemy."

Navarro twisted away from Chelstovsky's grip, eyes flashing. Then he remembered to keep things on an even keel with him and relaxed. "Yes, of course. Well . . . we will put surveillance on them like your major instructed, no?"

Chelstovsky nodded his head. "Yes. Be ready for anything, my friend. Your knife . . ."

"I still have it. And my pistol and machine pistol."

"If we have to kill these men, then we must do so quietly. Do you understand?"

"Yes." They stared at each other for several long seconds.

Chelstovsky took off his daypack and Navarro did the same. Then, in tandem, they crawled up to their new point-surveillance site.

A sharp whisper cut through the quiet of their position, moments after they had arrived and set up observation. "Sir!"

MacIntyre picked up from where he'd been watching the gorge below with his nightscope and crept over to Hanlon, who was studying the area to the right of their surveillance site. They were located on the western side of Ash Canyon in the trees, high up on the mountain where a long, sloping granite apron on their left merged into the tree line. From there they were able to watch the mining sluice at the foot of the stream fifty meters below them and higher up the canyon.

"What is it?"

Hanlon lowered his M16, which also had an AN/PVS-4 night-observation scope attached to it. "There's a campsite down there. My bet is that it's the climbers we saw earlier."

"Those voices we heard—"

"Yeah. They came from there. We'd better check it out with the thermal."

MacIntyre opened his rucksack and retrieved what looked like an olive-drab green metal box with a rubber eyepiece on one side and a lens on the other, resembling an oversized camera. When he flipped on the activation switch, it fluttered into a hum, the motor inside activating the thermal-imagery technology that illuminated all objects to their front radiating heat—rocks with the previous day's heat, animals, and humans. He pressed his right eye against the rubber eyepiece, and the campsite down by the sluice and its surrounding terrain transformed into a glowing, green-hued outline. He spotted the tents. Phosphorescent green glows indicated the prostrate forms of two of the tents' occupants. Off to the side of one of the tents, another figure lay unmoving. Three, in all. He handed the thermal imagery device to Hanlon. "Take a look, Randy—I only see three people."

"It's gotta be those climbers, sir," Hanlon said, swinging the device from left to right. Suddenly, he held the thermal imagery device very still on the left, spotting another glowing figure. This one was moving. "Dai-uy! I see the fourth . . . he's running through the woods on the opposite side of the stream. And two others seem to be chasing him." He glanced up at MacIntyre. "Over by Santo's position."

MacIntyre unclipped his hand-held radio—a PRC-68—from his web gear. "I'd better tell Manny."

Squelch broke on Santo's radio. He and Greeley exchanged glances.

"Romeo-Sierra Two, this is Romeo-Sierra One," a tinny, static voice crackled over the PRC-68.

Santo picked up the radio and pressed the talk button. "Go ahead, One."

"We heard voices a while ago, roger that?"

"Roger. We heard 'em too, but we can't spot their origin from our position."

"We've just located a campsite with three personnel in it. None of them are moving, and one of them is lying outside of a tent. It doesn't make sense, with the storm and all. Something's happened there."

Santo's mind raced. Three bodies—the climbers Hanlon and MacIntyre saw earlier in the day. What about the fourth?

"One more man is running down the mountainside toward the gorge in your direction—and it looks like two others are chasing him, over," MacIntyre continued, finishing his transmission.

Santo nodded at Greeley, who immediately raised his M16 and scanned his front with the night sight.

"Roger that, One," Santo replied. "We'll go check it out."

"Romeo-Sierra One, out."

Santo got up, stiff and weary, preparing to move out. He took out another night-vision device from his rucksack, this one an AN/PVS-5, which resembled a face mask with telescopic goggles for eyes. It operated on the same principle as the starlight scope on Greeley's rifle, a system which enhanced available star and moonlight, lighting up the terrain before him in a bright, phosphorous green hue.

"Manny!"

Santo squatted down next to Greeley, switching on his night-vision goggles. "See something?" He lined up the PVS-5 with Greeley's rifle.

"About a hundred meters below us and to the left, higher up the canyon directly below MacIntyre's line of site."

"What about the other two?"

"Don't see 'em."

"Okay, I'm going down for a look. I'll be back in thirty minutes. If I get fired on for any reason, stay put and maintain surveillance on the area. Report to the chief back at the commo relay site. If you get compromised up here, break contact and haul ass for the commo site. Advise the captain on the situation. I'll meet you there."

"Roger that, Manny."

Santo paused before leaving. He clapped his hand on Greeley's shoulders. "Be careful, Ted."

Greeley looked up at him incredulously. "For Chrisakes, Manny, *you* be careful."

Santo grinned. "I'll be okay." Then he slipped on down the mountainside.

Logs, brush, loose rocks. Santo creeped silently along. A pine bough scraped along his forehead, and he ducked under it, the branch swaying in the cool breeze channeling up from the gorge below. He angled off to the left, where MacIntyre and Hanlon had spotted the figure. What had happened? The voices, a couple of shouts, then silence. He'd been about ready to move out when MacIntyre had called anyway.

Finally, Santo spotted moonlight glinting off the sparkle of the storm-flooded stream several meters below in an open area. The sound of rapids rushed in his ears. It was hard to pick out the padding sound of a running man. He stopped inside a stand of pine trees and put the night-vision goggles to his eyes, scanning the area.

A twig snapped. Then another, accompanied by the sound of something breaking through the brush below. A figure popped out into the opening; it stumbled and fell. Santo saw him now—a skinny man, bare-chested, his hair drawn back in a ponytail, who was hobbling across the clearing in ragged blue jeans.

Santo paralleled him through the trees, close to where he'd fallen. Then he circled around and crept up to him from behind.

Newton Rasmin picked himself up from where he'd fallen, gasping for breath and clutching his knee, which he'd bone-bruised from the fall. Cactus spines in the seat of his pants, scrapes on his arms from where he'd bounced into huge pine trees during his flight, gouges from sticks and rocks in his chest—he knew he couldn't make it much longer. He was done for. Whoever had killed his friends back at the campsite were coming for him, and he didn't know if he could—

A hand closed around his mouth and he twisted violently away trying to scream, but then a hairy, thick forearm caught him in the hollow of his throat just beneath his Adam's apple, and when the crook of the other man's elbow snugged off his air and blood supply, he thrashed for a few seconds and then passed out.

Sergeant Ted Greeley heard Santo coming, and he peered through the trees at him with his night scope, his thumb itching at his M16's safety. Then he confirmed that it *was* Santo, and that he was carrying something draped over his shoulders.

Santo reached the position and quietly laid Rasmin on a bed of pine needles. "That's him," he explained to Greeley.

"What gives?"

"Keep your night sight trained on the perimeter, Teddy."

As Greeley continued scanning to his front, Santo searched through the young man's pockets for identification. Nothing. Rasmin stirred, coming to. For a moment he stared vacuously at the stars. When he saw Santo leaning over him he gasped deeply to scream. Santo clamped a hand over his mouth.

"Don't even think about it," Santo told him softly. "Just relax, I'm not going to hurt you."

Rasmin stiffened, straining feebly against Santo's hold. Then, when he realized he was no match for Santo's strength, he sighed through his nostrils, blowing a strand of mucus on the web of skin between Santo's thumb and forefinger.

"That's right," Santo said slowly, brushing his other hand against Rasmin's forehead. "Just relax. Now listen to me. I'm going to take my hand off your mouth and then you're going to answer some questions. Don't yell out. Do you understand?"

Rasmin nodded his head.

"Good. Now like I said, I'm not going to hurt you. But it is very, very important right now that you keep quiet, because whoever's after you will hear you, and then we're all fucked. Okay?"

Rasmin nodded again, relaxing more.

Santo slowly lifted his hand. Rasmin gasped spasmodically, staring at Santo's grizzled face.

"What's your name, stud?"

"Ras-Rasmin. Newton Rasmin."

"Why were you running away from your campsite like that?"

Rasmin began breathing hard, gasping, and a low moan gurgled from the bottom of his throat. Santo put his hand back on Rasmin's mouth.

"Just take it easy, Newton Rasmin. Like I said, we're not going to hurt you." Rasmin relaxed. Santo pulled his hand away, and the other man gulped audibly. "Now, tell me everything."

"I—I—I was sleeping in the tent—my girlfriend—my—oh, God, my girlfriend and I were . . . this—this man, a big man, came in and—and—" Rasmin broke off, crying softly and sputtering.

"Shhh . . . shhh . . ."

Rasmin regained his composure. "This guy . . . came in the tent and killed her with his hands. Just snapped her neck, man, like—"

"How did you get away?"

"David—a guy climbing with us—he came back to camp and fought the other guy with the gun outside and the guy in my tent went back out and killed him with a stick and . . ."

Minutes later, Rasmin finished the story, and he lay back against the pine needles, crying softly, curled up into the fetal position. Santo and Greeley exchanged glances.

"Looks like we've got company for sure, Boss."

Santo picked up the PRC-68. "Keep an eye on him, Ted." He pressed the talk button.

Saxon tossed a pebble in the direction of Barkowitz, who had slept entirely through the storm next to the little cliff. The rock, a tiny specimen of red-tinted granite laced with spots of mica, bounced lightly on Barkowitz's head, which was wrapped up in the hood of his rain parka.

Barkowitz opened one solemn eye and stared at Saxon.

Saxon swallowed. "Uh . . . time to get up, big guy." He broke eye contact and studied the contents of his half-drained canteen cup.

Barkowitz muttered something unintelligible and sat straight up. Then he yawned, arms outstretched, and came to his feet.

Saxon picked up the canteen cup, showing it to Barkowitz—a peace offering. "Hey, there . . . fresh brew. Want some?"

Barkowitz walked over to Saxon, who was amazed that a man so big and solid had such an easy, flowing grace. "Yeah. Thanks." Saxon handed him the cup. Barkowitz slugged all of it down in a couple of gulps. He belched lightly, and worked out the kinks in his neck by twisting his head to one side with both hands until it popped. Then he repeated the process on the other side.

They were in position now, scant meters away, in the shadows, on their bellies, behind the rocks joining the small cliff face by the Americans' position. Each clenched a knife in one hand and a pistol in the other. Chelstovsky had his spade beside him. Navarro's thumb caressed the trigger button on his spring-knife.

"Hey!" Saxon got up to his feet, his eyes scanning their perimeter.

"What is it?"

"Did you hear something?"

"No."

"Yeah—like something is moving."

Barkowitz, fully alert now, glanced all around. *Goddam!* He'd left his rifle by his poncho! He walked calmly toward it. "Must be a squirrel or something," he said.

Saxon pulled a .45 out of his shoulder holster.

The radio broke squelch.

"Charlie-Sierra, this is Romeo-Sierra Two, over."

Saxon glanced back at the radio, then looked over at Barkowitz, who had retrieved his M16 and was walking back to the radio.

"Charlie-Sierra, this is Romeo-Sierra Two, over," the message repeated.

"That's Santo," Barkowitz muttered, grabbing the mike. "Keep an eye on things."

Saxon nodded his head and stared out at the perimeter. *Where had the noise come from? Caffeine rush playing tricks on me? Yeah, that's it. Fucking caffeine rush.*

"This is Charlie-Sierra, go ahead, Two," Barkowitz spoke lowly into the mike, staring out at the perimeter.

"Flash sit-rep, Charlie Sierra: We've got one of those climbers from this afternoon. Says his friends were murdered back at the campsite. Enemy's somewhere in the AO. How copy, over?"

"Roger that, Two," Barkowitz replied. "I'll notify FOB ASAP, over."

Saxon's heart skipped a beat. *That scraping noise—he'd just heard it again. What the fuck was going on?* He moved a little closer to the perimeter where Barkowitz had been sleeping.

"We're keeping this guy with us for the time being. Send Maslow down to retrieve him, and then detain him at your location. In the meantime, flash-priority this info back to the FOB. Tell them to stand by with the reaction force, over."

"Wilco, Two, I copy that—"

A metal clinking sound and a whish, immediately followed by the sound of a meat cleaver striking a side of beef. Saxon belted out a hoarse, choking sound. Barkowitz sprang to his feet, his M16 at the ready, his thumb flicking off the safety switch. Saxon dropped his .45 and stumbled backward toward Barkowitz, clutching at his throat. When Saxon turned around, mouth opening and closing, saying nothing, Barkowitz stared at the knife blade sticking in the left side of the DEA agent's throat, blood pumping out in sheets from his severed carotid artery. Saxon collapsed at his feet, blood pooling around the stove.

In the next seconds, Barkowitz saw two things: two blackened figures jumping over the nest of boulders leading away from the small cliff face and running toward him, and one of them at the same time throwing a long bladed object at him, whirling, hissing, cutting a trail through the mist of blood Saxon had choked out of his lifeless body—

And it clanged off the receiver of Barkowitz's M16, which he held out in front of his face. The spade deflected away and sliced into his hand between the forefinger and middle finger, where it cut halfway down into his palm. His trigger finger was useless.

In those split seconds, Barkowitz let his instinct and training take over, ignoring the pain, his adrenal gland surging huge spurts of energy into his stomach and circulatory system. He roared, charging the two figures running at him, and he slammed his M16 into one man's cheek. The man went down, stunned and bleeding from where his face had been ripped open.

But before Barkowitz could switch hands and pull the trigger on the other man, the muzzle of a pistol had already been shoved into the fold of flesh between his rib cage and left kidney. The pistol fired. Barkowitz felt the muffled report and muzzle blast and powder burn sear into his side and the lead of the bullet flame through his intestines, knocking him off balance and making him stumble over the body of the man he'd slammed down with his M16.

He lurched about on his feet, dizzy and confused, staggering around like a lanced bull before a matador. The other man lunged at him with a knife, and Barkowitz managed to ward off the first slashing movement with his M16, and then countered the knife thrust with a jab of his M16's muzzle into the man's solar plexus, bayonet-style.

The other man screamed and doubled over, backing away. Barkowitz, his face as pale as the moon above him, charged on lead feet for another thrust with the M16 to finish him off.

Then, a scraping sound, a movement behind him. He whirled around, losing balance, and slammed the butt of his M16 back into the first man's side, and at the same time, received a blow to the side of his head with a rock the size of his hamlike fists.

Chelstovsky fell, twice beaten by the American, fighting to maintain consciousness.

Barkowitz sank to his knees beside the Russian. The horizon and the lights of White Sands Missile Range far below on the desert plain swam before his eyes. A distant ringing hummed deep inside his head, and he knew he was dying.

Before he could fall over, the Mexican had withdrawn his sheath knife and plunged it deep into Barkowitz's throat. The big man toppled over, crashing onto the prostrate body of Saxon.

Their blood mingled into a pool that surrounded Saxon's stove, which amazingly had not been knocked over while it boiled water, its steam floating up into the cool, thin mountain air.

Noise! A shot, muffled and hollow-sounding, but nevertheless, it *was* a report filtering down from the commo site . . .

Huddled over the slit trench he'd dug, Maslow froze inside the tree line fifty meters downslope from the communications site, taking in the noises, his mind analyzing their meaning in the rapid sequence of a computer. He thought of the body of the dead Russian soldier they had discovered early in the morning, high up in a rocky, talus-covered canyon, the steel filings in his teeth and recent battle scars on his body, the discovery of the hypodermic needle hole in the crook of his arm . . . *Spetsnaz* . . .

Maslow leaped up, yanking on his trousers. He grabbed his M16 lying beside him, hoping beyond hope things weren't too entirely out of control back at the communications relay site.

But if things were . . . his eyes scanned the route he'd traced down the mountainside. A finger of trees led back up to the summit, which was steep going. Nevertheless, his movement would be quieter on the pine-needle-carpeted mountainside. He had to go that way.

His mind racing, Maslow flew up the mountainside, picking through the rocks and cactus, nerves on high, his jawbone muscles gritting his teeth together, his heart churning adrenaline and blood through his head and ears.

Chelstovsky groaned and tried to get on his feet, while the Mexican hustled about the commo site, smashing the main and backup radios into pieces and gathering weapons. The communications sergeant collapsed and lay still for a few moments.

He hurt all over. By all rights, he alone should have killed the two Americans. It had been purely bad luck. First, his spade had only sliced the American's hand. Then, the counter with the M16, leaving him stunned and useless for precious seconds while Navarro engaged the American with the knife. But he had managed to hit the big man with a rock, setting him up for Navarro's coup de grace.

Lying near him, Chelstovsky nodded at the lifeless face of the American, a broad, peasant face similar to his own Ukrainian countenance. Different cultures, different countries—but the other man had been a soldier, and he therefore deserved respect. He had died fighting, with dignity. By contrast, the way he had been killed was like two Neanderthals beating a water buffalo to death.

Chelstovsky moaned in pain. Yes, the American deserved his respect. But if it hadn't been for Navarro . . .

The Mexican stood over him. Chelstovsky held up his hand, grimacing from the pain of his lacerated face and cracked, splintered ribs. "Eh, comrade, we make quite a team, yes?"

Navarro stared back at him. It was time. Hopefully Pushtkin was doing the same with that bastard Antonov. If not, then he'd have to do it for him.

"I save your life, and you save mine . . . think of the vodka we will drink in—" Chelstovsky broke off suddenly when he saw Navarro's hand tighten around the knife he was holding. Cold, hard realization set in.

Before he could roll over, Navarro had opened his throat from ear to ear. Chelstovsky's lungs gasped out his remaining air through his severed trachea, while his feet drummed the ground. For a second, he stared up at the Mexican, bewildered. Then the light went out from behind his eyes and he lay very still.

"Yes, my stupid Russian friend," Navarro muttered. "Quite a team."

Navarro took in the campsite. The radios! He had destroyed the main one and another one just like it. Where were the others? He had much work to do. He spied a hand-held radio the size of a brick. He picked it up and smashed it against a rock. Then he dragged the two Americans apart from one another and rifled through their pockets, looking for maps, frequencies, orders . . . there were none.

He surveyed the carnage. All the blood . . . yes, it was good. It was good and finished.

A noise! Whirling around, knife hand outstretched, Navarro spotted a flying figure sailing toward him, his jungle boot aimed at his face. Immediately he ducked, and he heard and felt the tip end of a knife slice through the air and nick him just underneath the right eye. Any closer and . . .

Like a cat, Maslow landed on his feet, surprised at having missed the man he'd just witnessed killing someone who appeared to be his partner. Before attacking, he'd drawn his knife from his web gear and laid the rest of his equipment on the ground to ensure silence. Any shots from his M16 would have warned the rest of the Spetsnaz team elsewhere in the canyon below—ruining any chance for Santo, MacIntyre, and the others to pinpoint them and call in the reaction force. But how old was the man he was fighting? Certainly younger than himself. He'd would be forty-two in October. He'd have to be very careful.

He threw a glance at Barkowitz and Saxon, their twisted bodies crumpled on the rocks over to his left by the other dead man. Then, as he looked back at the Mexican, hate and revenge curdled in his eyes. The other man turned toward him with his knife, circling it to his front, upright, preparing for a quick jab up into Maslow's intestines. Maslow hefted his own knife in the palm of his hand. He knew how to fight with a knife too.

When he had reached the periphery of the communications site, he'd had to numb his mind to the sight of them . . . his teammates, his friends, his family . . . entwined together in eerie, surrealistic detail, their lurid, twisted positions covering the commo site in pools and rivulets of dark blood.

Barkowitz and Saxon. Not that Saxon had qualified as a friend—he'd barely known him—but still, he had been on the team for this mission, and . . . and Barko. Before Maslow had been able to quell the hurt and pain from seeing his dead friend, thoughts had flashed through his mind of the volleyball games on organization day back at Bragg, how Barkowitz had always been able to spike a volleyball into some poor slob's face from whichever opposing team had the misfortune of playing theirs, his little girls cheering for him on the sidelines . . . and Barkowitz, always reliable, always making commo, steady, mature, strong, the mainstay of their team . . . Now he was dead, dead and laid out alongside Saxon. It was plain, however, that he'd put up a good fight—a fight he'd had no chance of winning.

Maslow would make it up to him, though, and now, as the Mexican agent dressed in civilian outdoor clothes circled around him with a knife, he'd personally ensure that.

Navarro lunged first, and Maslow stepped off to the side, countering the thrust with one of his own. The Mexican danced away. Maslow wished he had time to wrap something around his left arm. To fight with a knife properly, one had to use his arm to ward off a blow, to take the risk of his arm being laid open like a filet, giving him a chance to counter with a blow deep into the guts or throat of the other man. It was really the only way.

Eyes narrowing, Maslow moved in—and received a slice on his arm that burned and cut all the way to the bone. When he shot his knife hand forward, it drove into Navarro's guard arm to the hilt, sticking through the forearm bones and lodging there.

The Mexican screamed and reflexively slashed his knife across Maslow's rib cage, opening Maslow up but not cutting any organs.

Maslow drove his knee hard into Navarro's testicles. The Mexican grunted hoarsely, spittle flying from his lips. Then Maslow drove his guard arm's elbow into Navarro's nose, shattering it. He stepped back, yanking his knife out from Navarro's forearm.

Navarro wobbled on his feet, doubled over, bleeding from his nose and arm and clutching at his testicles with his good hand. His knife hand was useless.

Maslow knew he had to keep the Mexican alive for information, take him apart piece by piece, disarm him . . . he moved forward and delivered a sharp kick to the other man's kneecap.

The Mexican fell down, screaming. A foot-stomp cracked his wrist and sent the knife flying out of reach. He was powerless. Blood, streaming out of his nostrils, pooled around his eyes, blinding him in salty, crimson stickiness, as he lay supine beneath Maslow's boot. Navarro knew he had only one other weapon—*the spring-knife, thank the Holy Mother he had reloaded it before his attack . . . his pocket . . . if only he could get to his pocket . . .*

Maslow planted his knee on the Mexican's chest with enough pressure to make his rib cage give. His own blood dribbled from his lacerated side and forearm onto the other man's body. So much blood, so much . . .

"Tell me," he rasped, "where the others are." Maslow applied more pressure with his bony knee. The other man was helpless, his left arm pinned under his hip, struggling like a bug on a biologist's pin, his other arm motionless on the ground, the broken wrist bent at an off angle.

"No . . . *señor*," the other man groaned, whining, begging, "my English is . . . my English is not so good. . . ."

Maslow switched to Spanish. He'd pulled more than a few tours down south. "Where are the others!"

The Mexican's eyes widened, and he croaked something inaudible under the pressure of Maslow's knee.

Maslow released the pressure on the other man's sternum.

"The canyon . . . the mining sluice . . ."

"How many?"

"One."

More pressure.

"Two, two!" Navarro gasped. *The spring-knife, he had it now, oh, sweet Virgin Mother, he had it*. His hand pulled away from his pocket.

"What is your mission?"

Navarro, summoning what he had left of his strength, yanked his hand out from underneath his hip with the spring-knife. *"Die!"*

Maslow twisted away with the movement, but not before something snapped and flashed up into the flesh of his pectoral muscle. A hot, searing pain burned underneath his collarbone and lodged there.

Screaming, the Mexican tried to struggle to his feet.

But not before Maslow backhanded the butt-end of his sheath knife just underneath the Mexican's nose, cramming the splintered bone into his brain and killing him.

Maslow, weary and bleeding, staggered to his feet, dizzy, disoriented, discovering a knife blade underneath his collarbone. When he pulled it out, a wave of nausea hit his gut, and he plopped back down on the rock where Saxon had sat just fifteen minutes earlier, brewing coffee. He'd been gone for just that amount of time, yet so much had happened, so much blood, so much death . . . his eyes misted over, and his chest throbbed deeply from the pain and the emotional drain.

He had to grab hold of himself. The others! He had to get to them, to warn them, there were more of the enemy in the mountains, at least two others. . . .

He scanned the perimeter. The radios were useless. His friend was dead. Saxon was dead. The two Spetsnaz men were dead. The mountaintop was dead. Lifeless in the cold breeze of the spent storm . . . the stars were back out above, and the full moon shone brilliantly down upon the bloody, black mess. His mind drifted.

For one wild instant, Maslow thought he would lose touch with reality. His sole mind focus centered on a van Gogh painting, a print he'd framed and centered on his living room wall back at Bragg—it was the "Starry Night" painting, with huge fireballs swarming through the night above in swirling oil strokes of the artist's brush, the winking lights of the town below minute and helpless underneath the universe; so utterly alone, yet so many stars, so helpless, so . . .

Maslow shook his head. He had to get a grip on things. Retrieving his web gear from where he'd left it, he pulled out a first-aid packet from its case where it was bound to the left shoulder strap, and bound the cravat around his forearm to stem the blood flow. Then, doing the same with Saxon's and Barkowitz's first-aid packets, he strapped up his side. He plugged the bleeding hole underneath his collarbone.

He had to get off the mountaintop, find Santo and Greeley, the others. A klick's worth of movement through rocks, cactus, pine trees, mesquite. Being on the lookout for any others. He had to get to Greeley's first-aid kit and get help before he bled to death. He needed an IV. He had to warn the others. He had to . . .

Lurching forward, Maslow staggered down the mountainside.

CHAPTER TEN

The sky lost some of its stars and turned into the darkest shade of gray. Venus was still out, Mars too—but now it was BMNT, Beginning Morning Nautical Twilight. Master Sergeant Manny Santo confirmed that with his watch, which read 0532.

"Damn radio," he muttered, digging through his rucksack for fresh batteries. "That's all we need is for commo to go out. Barkowitz never breaks off contact like that unless he's got a damned good reason."

Sergeant Ted Greeley, scanning the perimeter of their R & S site they occupied with a prostrate and very scared Newton Rasmin, glanced over at Santo, and a shiver stole up his spine. It was the third time Santo had tried to reestablish radio contact with Barkowitz's communications relay site on top of the mountain. What had happened?

"Maybe it's not . . . maybe it's not the radio, Manny."

Santo jerked his head up, eyes flashing. "What do you—"

Squelch broke in through the brick-sized radio in Santo's hand. *"Romeo-Sierra Two, this is One, over."*

Both men stared at the radio still clenched in Santo's hand. Neither moved.

"Two, this is One, over," MacIntyre repeated, from his and Hanlon's position across the canyon.

Santo pressed the talk button. "This is Two."

"Two, have you lost contact with the Charlie-Sierra, over?"

"Roger that. Try to raise them from your position, over."

All sat in silence as MacIntyre, from a better vantage point across the canyon, one that was not masked by overhead trees and rocks like Santo's position, tried unsuccessfully to raise Barkow-itz.

Moments later. *"You copy last transmissions, Two?"*

"Roger."

More silence. Santo began to think the unthinkable. Then, he knew what had to be done. "One, this is Two. I'm going up on top to locate them."

"Roger that, Two. We'll stay put at present location and try to pinpoint the enemy. Call in a sit-rep every fifteen minutes, over."

"Wilco. Two, out."

Santo leaned over Rasmin, who had watched the interchange with fascinated silence. "You stay put, Mister Rasmin, you got that?"

"Yes . . . yes."

"Keep an eye on him, Teddy. Your PRC-68 working okay?"

Greeley pulled his hand-held radio out of the extra ammo pouch on his web gear and turned it on, breaking squelch with the talk button. "Check," he said. The medic scooted around where he could observe both Rasmin and the perimeter.

Santo grabbed his M16 and stood up. "I'll be gone half an hour at the most," he said "If I'm not back by then, wait another fifteen minutes, and if I still don't show up, notify the captain. He'll establish a rendezvous for you. Got that?"

"Just be careful, Big Sarge."

Santo clapped a paw around Greeley's shoulder and held it there for a moment. Then he glanced quickly away and started to hike up the mountainside.

Maslow crashed heavily against a pine tree to rest and regain his bearings, as early morning light began to help him pick his way down the mountainside. He was losing blood fast; it was soaking through the gauze first-aid packets he'd strapped over his wounds.

Weak from the loss of blood, he hugged the tree trunk to keep from rolling down the mountainside, his head resting against the tree bark. Thick, white resin glued to his forehead, and Maslow's sense of smell reacted to the pungent pine odor, making him more alert. How far had he come? When would he find Santo? When would he . . . his knees buckled, and he fought for balance, struggling back to his feet.

When would he . . . ?

Winston Maslow fell to the ground, rolled fifteen feet down the mountainside, and lay very still against a tree trunk.

Santo spotted him just before he fell, knowing something was wrong, very wrong. When he reached him, he immediately saw the knife wounds and bound Maslow up, stopping the heavy bleeding.

"Manny . . ."

"Chrisakes, Chief, what the hell happened?"

"Spetsnaz . . . Barkowitz, Saxon, they're dead . . . had to kill . . . those . . ."

"Save your strength, Chief. I'm going up for a look."

"They're dead. . . ."

Santo swallowed, feeling goose flesh streak across his shoulder blades, down his spine, and spread out along the small of his back. His breathing picked up. Maslow stirred. Hastily, he angled Maslow's head downhill to prevent him from going into shock, and then resecured his bandages. "You stay put, Chief. I'll be back in a few minutes."

Time passed. Santo returned, his face pale and his eyes deep pools of black premeditation for the revenge he would seek. Maslow was awake and coherent.

"It's bad, Manny."

Santo said nothing. He picked the warrant officer up and hauled him down the mountain in a fireman's carry. Fifteen minutes later he returned to the R&S site where Greeley scanned the perimeter. The medic had just removed the night scope from his M16 and was now watching his front with binoculars. The early morning gray was just light enough to cancel out the image he'd see with the light-enhancing night scope, so it was useless. Still, at this hour, the naked eyes could see only in grays and blacks, so it was best to use the binos. Upon hearing Santo's return, Greeley spun around, aiming his M16. Then he saw Santo.

"Jesus H. Christ, Manny, what the—" Greeley broke off when he saw Maslow. Santo laid the warrant officer down on a bed of pine needles next to the civilian.

"He's been hurt bad, Teddy, cut up."

Greeley stared at Santo, beginning to say Barkowitz's name. Before he could say it, Santo's black eyes answered him.

Greeley ripped open his field medical kit, hunting for sutures, gauze, iodine, morphine. His eyes grew hot and salty, and he had to force himself to concentrate.

Captain Matt MacIntyre lay prone with his binoculars, studying the shadow of the campsite below, as dawn began to break. Hanlon was catching a few winks five feet to his left. During the night, they had found a crevice in the rock apron which linked their position up with the tree line for an unimpeded view of the campsite below them. They had masked their R&S site with deadfall and pine needles and an assortment of rocks. It was still quite dark—there was only light enough to make out the shapes of the tents seventy-five meters below their position, masked by trees. Now that day was breaking, he felt a growing nakedness he did not experience with the concealment of the night.

He cursed softly under his breath.

Finally, things had gone wrong. Somehow, they always did. No plan, regardless of even perfect planning, was ever flawlessly executed as anticipated. Murphy's Fucking Law.

Then, five minutes ago, Santo had informed him about Maslow. About Barkowitz, Saxon—both dead. There was no doubt now about who they were up against. Like themselves, the Spetsnaz were a special unit, consisting of special people, people who would put the mission first and use their initiative and equipment and intellect to carry it out, unconventionally and within the principles of guerrilla warfare.

Two men dead. One seriously hurt. For what? A drug bust? No. Capturing enemy espionage agents, just a couple, as Saxon had told them about back at the FOB? Hell, no.

And what about himself, the team leader of his detachment? There's a good one. What did he have for experience as the leader of his team? Four years of college back in Oklahoma? Basic and Advanced Officers training; Airborne, Ranger, Special Forces qualification; Survival, Military Free Fall, and Jumpmaster schools? He had the schooling. And six months so far as a team leader. But when you compared all that to Santo's and Maslow's combat experience in Vietnam and over eighteen years' team

experience apiece, and the rest of the team members'
experience—none of them had less than four years on a team
together—then what the fuck was *he* doing as their team
leader?

Yeah, there's a good one.

Two men dead . . . two men . . . Maslow . . .

"What do you think, Dai-uy?"

MacIntyre grunted and looked over at Hanlon, who had been
watching him. "Huh?"

"Bad situation."

"Yeah."

"We'll make it."

MacIntyre swallowed, feeling impotent and full of rage. He
glanced away and brought the binos back up to his face. Then, he
saw two men climb out of the gorge below, from lower down, and
wind their way up toward the campsite.

"Dai-uy, look—"

"*Shhh . . .*"

The skin on Antonov's neck crawled every time Pushtkin fell
further behind, as they climbed out of the gorge en route to the
campsite. As tired as he was, he could not afford any more
mistakes. Trusting the Moscow party-line-quoting son of a whore
behind him who had gotten his team into this mess had cost him
his senior sergeant the day before. Now that the linkup with
Chelstovsky and the Mexican had not taken place as planned—
they should have been back down from the mountaintop at least
half an hour ago—he was beginning to assume the worst.
Chelstovsky was too good to have been spotted by any American
surveillance elements reconnoitering the area. Also, they had not
located the one civilian who had escaped the campsite earlier in
the night. They should have. But that man had vanished, and they
could not spend any more time trying to find him. Besides, the
rendezvous with the sleeper agent was to take place in only
another hour.

They had to get back to the campsite! Dawn, light, compromise!

A wheezing gasp to his rear as Pushtkin fell.

Antonov wheeled around and caught the KGB man by his arm.

He had stepped on a loose rock and twisted his ankle. "Bloody hell . . ."

"Quiet!" Antonov hissed. "Keep quiet, you fool!"

"Help me. . . ."

Antonov glared at Pushtkin with contempt. *This idiot has been what was wrong with this mission. He, Sergei Antonov, could have accomplished this mission alone if* . . .

He then had an idea.

He helped Pushtkin to his feet. "Come, comrade . . . the light . . . dawn is breaking."

"Yes, yes, I am all right." Pushtkin hobbled around on his foot, testing it at first, and then stepped out more boldly as they trudged up the canyon, up the flooded gorge, toward the campsite. With each step, dawn progressed. Soon, the campsite and mining sluice came into view.

Antonov appraised Pushtkin's sprained ankle, and thought of his senior sergeant. Now, quite literally, the shoe was on the other foot. He wondered if Pushtkin was thinking about the shot of bliss. "It hurts much, comrade?"

A frightened look. "No!"

They reached the tents. Outside the one, the body of the young man whose throat had been crushed by Antonov the night before lay on the rocks by the flooded gorge, his body half submerged in the water where swirling currents threatened to carry the tent away.

"We'll push the bodies in the stream," Pushtkin said, with the semblance of an order.

Antonov started. He'd already planned out how to dispose of the bodies. Evidently, so had Pushtkin. What was running through his mind now?

Grimacing, Pushtkin gripped the leg of the young man and pushed him out into the rain-swelled stream. The rushing current caught the body and flipped it across the rocks, down the mountainside, down into the larger mouth of the gorge farther below them. Antonov dragged the two women out of the tents and did the same. It was done. Then they brushed over their tracks and the signature of the struggle that had taken place, and made the scene look like the campers were the victims of the flash flood. Then they were finished.

They climbed back into the tree line on the western side of the canyon where they had established their hide site the day before upon spotting the campers. Four civilian backpacks—theirs—lay hidden underneath the leaves and flora they had camouflaged them with. But still, no Chelstovsky or Navarro.

By the time they climbed into the tree line, Antonov made sure Pushtkin led the way, under the guise of helping him along with his injured ankle. It was only a light sprain, and he could tell the pain would not last. Too bad. He wanted to deliver the shot of bliss personally into the Muscovite. But he had climbed up to their hide site behind Pushtkin for a reason, and that was to catch Pushtkin's reaction. When they reached it, he noted sudden confusion and disappointment etched into the KGB man's face.

"He should have been back by now," Pushtkin muttered, scraping the leaves off Navarro's pack.

"Yes, *they* should."

Pushtkin opened his mouth in surprise, realizing his mistake, and fought for a normal voice, choosing his next words carefully. "Something must have . . . happened to them."

"Both of them are good men, comrade. They have probably located something of interest."

"Yes . . . yes, they have found something."

"But if they're dead . . . then so much the better."

Pushtkin blinked. "What?"

"All traces of the mission can thus be eliminated. They are burned. So much the better for operational security."

"Yes . . ." Swallowing, Pushtkin fumbled around with the top flap of his backpack, unzipped it, and retrieved a wad of toilet paper. "Excuse me."

Two minutes later, Antonov followed Pushtkin deep into the tree line, silent, with grace, noiseless like a cat of prey. Not to violate Pushtkin's privacy, but to sneak up on him and watch him break open the emergency escape-and-evasion corridor plan hidden within the lining of his windbreaker, as Antonov had assumed.

Antonov's suspicions were confirmed when he found the KGB man scanning his notes in furtive glances. The plan obviously did not include him or anyone else within the team.

Pushtkin met Antonov back at the hide site. He was brewing tea on the civilian stove he'd packed in.

"Tea, comrade?" Antonov offered.

Nervous eyes, a quick nod. Pushtkin, hand shaking, took the offered cup. "It will not be long now," he murmured between sips.

Antonov glanced at his watch. Early morning light was finally showing on the peaks surrounding the canyon in a dull, reddish hue, and now it was almost 0600 hours. The contact was scheduled to take place in less than an hour. "Not long at all, comrade," he said evenly.

"The time—they must be here very shortly or else—"

"Yes."

"If they do not show up, we must leave! Moscow will forgive a missed contact."

Antonov threw Pushtkin a laconic glance, knowing better. "Moscow will *not* forgive a missed contact." Pushtkin couldn't even lie very well. He pictured the KGB man putting a pistol to his head once under way on the exfiltration. No, he would not put it past him—to erase all vestiges of why his mission had failed. "We will wait an additional hour, and *then* leave."

Pushtkin glanced away, unable to hold Antonov's steel-gray eyes. The next hour was critical. The exfiltration! There were many possibilities—the dirt bikes they'd cached in the southern canyon on the first night out, the safe house in Las Cruces— Pushtkin had personally coordinated that one—always a way, a technique, a contact. He knew El Paso well. If only Navarro— *Damn him, where is he?*—were here, it would make killing Antonov easy.

Grzniecki, the deputy chief of the Juarez *residentura*, was his only hope, along with the safe house in Las Cruces. It was bad joining two operations, but Grzniecki would help him.

Either way, if the sleeper agent and the scientist failed to show up, he would have to do away with the Spetsnaz major and then head out for the safe house near Las Cruces. He would not allow himself the luxury of nodding off, as all they had to do now was wait.

But neither would Antonov.

"I say again, Two. Two rabbits located on our side of the canyon. They dragged the bodies out from the campsite and dropped them in the stream. Then they climbed about a hundred meters up in the

tree line on *our* side of the canyon, over." MacIntyre released the
talk button on his PRC-68 and watched Hanlon scan the perimeter
of their surveillance site in the direction of the Soviets' position.
Only two hundred meters separated the two elements.

"Roger that, One," Santo's voice crackled over the radio. *"We
can rendezvous at your location in about forty-five minutes for the
snatch. XO is stabilized, wounds are superficial, and can leave
him here to cover the civilian. Over."*

MacIntyre paused before answering, not sure if he should have
the team capture the remainder of the Spetsnaz team or not. Why
were the Soviets here? Who were they to meet? What if Santo and
Greeley were seen approaching his side of the canyon?

But what else could he do? Communications with the rear was
out. There was no way he could call in the reaction force.

MacIntyre realized that the decision had to be made, and made
now. His team was stronger with firepower times four, rather than
two separate two-man buddy teams if it came down to it.

Santo's plan and recommendation were the better course of
action, given the developments. He, MacIntyre, could counter
it—as team leader, he had the final decision, he was responsible,
that was what he was paid for. But no . . . they had to link up.
It was the only way to accomplish the mission, even if it
demanded *their* action and not that of the reaction force back at the
FOB as planned. And it meant taking the risk of exposure, now
that it was light.

"Roger that, Two," MacIntyre spoke softly into the radio.
"Link up in thirty minutes. And watch out for other infiltrators."
"Out."

Santo shoved his radio back into his carrying pouch on his web
gear and then checked his M16's action. After oiling his bolt with
some lubricating gun oil, he slid the receiver back and forth gently
with the charging handle, so as not to make the loud metal-on-
metal snapping sound. Greeley did the same.

Finished with his M16, Santo examined Maslow, who by now
had some of the color restored in his face. Earlier, Greeley had
stuck an IV in the warrant officer's arm, and had stopped his
bleeding. Maslow was weak, but at least he was alert. He was
propped upright against Santo's rucksack, and he watched
them.

"Better?"

"Yeah."

"Okay, Chief, you know the deal. Me and Greeley are going to link up with MacIntyre and Hanlon. We're gonna have to catch the bad guys ourselves. That means you've got to watch Mister Rasmin here, and make sure he doesn't sky out on us." Santo looked hard at Rasmin, who acknowledged the statement with wide eyes. "That means you stay put. Got that, Mister Rasmin?"

"Yes!"

"Good." Santo handed Maslow a pen flare gun he detached from the left shoulder strap of his web gear, where it had been cinched next to his strobe light. "Chief, you run into any trouble and you shoot this thing a couple of times."

Maslow took the device with his good arm, his right, and nodded.

"Sure you're okay?"

"I'm sure."

"Then we're outta here."

Maslow suddenly grabbed Santo's upper arm, squeezing it tightly.

"Hey, Chief, what the—"

"You *remember* what they did to Barko, Manny."

Santo winced from the pressure of Maslow's fingertips. While dressing Maslow up, they had all tried very hard not to talk about Barkowitz. But now, he thought of Barkowitz, and the other man his team had been responsible for, Saxon. He thought of having to see Sue Barkowitz back at Bragg, and how he would have to explain to her about how Ed had died on a classified operation—which meant no details—leaving her and the twins behind forever.

A lead weight sank in Santo's mind as he thought about how a man, a good man, and friend he had known for over eight years had died. That man had been a friend and confidant who had helped him keep his sanity during that bleak and desolate period of his life when his wife and daughter had been cremated in the family car after a drunken driver had slammed his pickup into them with a full gas tank. Ed had been a friend. How could you explain the depth of friendship like that? The people who stood by you regardless of the depth of your tragedy? You could only count them on one hand.

It had not been the first time Manny Santo had seen death. There had been, of course, his assignment in Thailand and the covert operations in Laos, followed by a tour in Africa, and his missions in El Salvador and Honduras. There had been death in those places—instigated by the drug chiefs, the prostitutes, the mercenaries, the death squads. Always, when Manny Santo had seen death, it had arrived in the form of evil and clothed in shame and degradation. There was no honor, no glory. You could save those cliches for the armchair warriors and the comic-book readers and the moviegoers. Always, he had seen death perpetrated in the debased, hollowed vacuum of man's ultimate and inventive statement of hate, ignorance, and depravity.

And the smell. Always there was the smell of feces in death, and the complete disintegration of the soul, which was no longer mirrored in the eyes when you contemplated the face of death you had created. It was bad. It was obscene.

Staff Sergeant Edward Barkowitz's throat had been cut open like a slaughtered bull's in a charnel house. When Santo had found him in a pool of blood on top of a desolate mountain in southern New Mexico, the memories of death revived by this new outrage had balled into a slick, greasy knot deep inside his solar plexus. Then, the physical feeling in his gut had rebounded into the mental feeling of incredible sadness tinged with disgust—and the involuntary relief that *he* hadn't died that way, closely followed by accompanying guilt. And then there had been the smell of drying blood and the smell of feces—always, always the stink.

Santo had thrown up and scrambled back down the mountain for Maslow as fast as he could. Scared. Wanting more than anything to be back home, relieved of any further responsibility and warm in his bed. Alone. Finally, he'd choked back the panic boiling underneath his skin only after realizing that he'd been foolish enough to think he was used to death. Only then had he grown numb and unemotional.

And Maslow had the goddamned presumption to tell *him* to remember. That's right. Maslow had actually said, *You* remember *what they did to Barko, Manny*.

Santo grunted and shook his head. It was time to leave. He

peered deeply inside Maslow's black eyes, locked in on pupils shrouded in twin glints of moonlight. "You think I won't, Chief?"

A brief silence. Mutual understanding. A nod of the head.

Then Santo and Greeley stole down the mountainside, quiet, stealthy, and with the mission on their minds.

CHAPTER ELEVEN

A thick fog coagulated in Lieutenant Colonel Andrei Volensky's mind when his alarm went off. It was his own self-protection system designed to shut off and block out unwanted noise when his sleep was at its deepest.

But the damn thing was just too obnoxious. With a swipe of his hand, the little Toshiba hershey-bar clock-radio crashed to the cement floor of his quarters and splattered its electrical contents.

Just a minute more, he thought. *Just a minute . . .*

He bolted upright.

No. As he squinted hard through the dark, early morning light, his old Rolex read 0553 hours. Goddam. *Goddam!* He'd overslept by three minutes!

He leaped out of bed at the same time the knock came on his door.

"Colonel Volensky!"

Volensky cursed under his breath. That would be Hutton, last night's watch NCO.

"Colonel Volensky, sir, it's time to—"

"I'm up!"

"Uh, yes, sir. Sir, there's a couple of three-piece-suiters waiting for you in the FOB. They're making an awful lot of noise, sir."

"All right, all right!"

Footsteps faded away, and Volensky knew that Staff Sergeant Hutton was on his way back to the FOB.

The FOB!

"*Hutton!*"

Running footsteps, returning.

"Yes, sir!"

"Come inside!"

The door swung open, gently. A white-faced young man, about twenty-six, whose normally worldly smile and countenance now vanished into one of respect and fear for the big guy, the Old Man, the Mad Russian. "Sir?"

"Where's Wiggins?"

"Uh, sir?" Hutton, whenever he was around the Old Man at this hour in the morning, was at a loss for words. Ian Lange Hutton of all people! He was the battalion S-4 NCO, but more importantly, he was the main man who ran the Oro Grande Range Camp's club. He was the one was responsible for importing the babes in from El Paso for the battalion party that got put on hold because of this mission. Shit, he, Ian Lange Hutton, was the guy who could get anything for anyone (he, of course, named the price) who provided the necessary funding—

"I said where is that worthless motherfucker?"

Hutton's eyes expanded. He wasn't used to hearing someone he usually referred to as "sir" with a capital S as motherfucker. Hutton swallowed and licked his lips. "Uh, sir, I think he's still in the sack. As a matter of fact, sir, he can probably hear you. He's rooming in the hootch on the other side of your wall."

Volensky blinked. Hutton was right. The DEA special projects point of contact that organization had sent over to supervise their part of the mission had been put up for the past couple of nights in the room across from his on the other side of the battalion staff's billets. Volensky shook his head, trying to rid it of the cobwebs spun around in his brain.

What had started as a drug operation for the battalion had sure as shit turned into a bureaucratic cluster with DEA involvement. He had suspected as much, but he had been briefed and personally ordered by the 1st SOCOM commander to support it. And his earlier suspicions about a possible penetration of White Sands Missile Range were confirmed when it was discovered that there was much, much more to all of this than drugs—Spetsnaz of all things!

Volensky scratched his gray-grizzled cheek and yawned. Then he glared at the staff sergeant standing before him. Hutton stood erect and looked directly back at the Old Man, not flinching under Volensky's stare.

Volensky, liking that, beamed at the young sergeant. He didn't like timid, shy people. He reached out and pinched Hutton on the cheek, and then slapped him there gently a couple of times. "Pardon my foul mouth, Sergeant. You did not hear me call Mister Wiggins a worthless motherfucker." Volensky winked. "Sometimes I speak too loudly."

Hutton grinned back at the Old Man. The Mad Russian's habits: Just like his bear hugs and violent slaps on the back, accompanied by loud, uninhibited gales of laughter, Volensky's mannerisms when he was pleased never failed to surprise and somewhat embarrass the people who worked with him—who would suddenly realize that Volensky's ethnicity was still Russian down to the core. The Old Man was nothing if not colorful.

"Tell me, Hutton, about the 'three-piece-suiters.' "

"Well, you know, sir, they're like beeper-boys."

"Old? Young? In or out of shape?"

"They look like civilians, sir. Agency types."

Volensky scowled. More complications in his life, especially now with this DEA mission, he did not need. He thought of the ineptitude Wiggins, the DEA man, had demonstrated with his lack of understanding for special operations. Perhaps there had been a security leak.

"Wake *Mister* Wiggins up. Tell him I want to see him in the FOB ASAP."

"Yes, *sir*." Hutton shot out the door.

Five minutes later, Volensky had swiped his electric razor across his face, combed his hair, climbed into a freshly starched uniform, and was walking across the compound gravel toward the FOB, a hundred meters away. He immediately noticed two late-model dull and neutered beige-colored sedans parked outside the door. Each car had its own government insignia, and he recognized those insignias.

Government, he thought, eyeing the van as he pushed open the door to the Forward Operations Base. Inwardly, Volensky shuddered. DEA. And now, the FBI and CIA. When he'd worked with the CIA in Vietnam, he'd had his fill of civilians controlling military special operations. With them, the words duty, honor, country (and yes, it was a cliche, but as usually was the case with all cliches, duty, honor, and country were imperative prerequesites for the job) all too often took a backseat to careerism and making the figures right on paper at all costs. Zero-fucking-defects.

Then Volensky caught himself up short—he had to admit that it was true in the military as well.

How many times he had seen his own peers—now colonels, and even a few having recently been promoted to general—sell out their own integrity for merely looking good on paper, to get that silver eagle pinned on their collars or the first star. And more stars. It all boiled down to whether an individual's character and integrity overrode personal ambition, whether you were a soldier or a civilian. There was a syndrome in the country of having to look good at all costs in this day and age of mass telecommunications and media super-exposure. All manner of leaders in high-visibility environments were prone to tell half-truths, distort reality, place higher priorities on appearances. As a result, far too many people in positions of authority and power were eager to conform to the status quo: to lie if necessary, and above all, cover their respective asses—whether they wore a uniform or a three-piece suit.

When Volensky entered the FOB and strode down the short hallway to the war room, he saw them, haggling with the guard standing by the entrance. Hutton, the graveyard-shift NCO in charge of the FOB, stared back and forth between them and the colonel, waiting for the explosion to come.

"Young man, I said I am Special Agent—"

"Now open the door, see this badge, kid?"

"Where's the boss around this place? Who the hell is in charge of—"

"*I'm in charge!*" Volensky's voice boomed above the chaos.

Silence as the two men turned around and stared at the battalion commander. Hutton smiled and handed a freshly brewed cup of coffee to Volensky, murmuring that Wiggins was on the way. "What can I do for you gentlemen?" Volensky asked them.

Two badges flashed before him.

"CIA. Agent John Peterson, Colonel."

Rail-thin, Volensky noted. *Balding, wife, three kids, one in college, et cetera, et cetera . . .*

"FBI. Special Agent Fred Dixon."

This must be the water-walker, a little pudgy, probably di-

vorced, workaholic . . . seems to be the de-facto leader between the two . . .

Hutton quickly arranged three chairs, two facing one, for the meeting to follow.

"Please have a seat, gentlemen, and tell me what I can do for you."

Cups of coffee magically appeared in their hands. Hutton was busy this morning. Volensky acknowledged his quiet efficiency with an appreciative nod. Hutton placed another chair by the others for Wiggins, the DEA man, to sit in when he arrived. Then Hutton vanished.

"Colonel," the man called Dixon began, "my headquarters has word that the DEA has initiated a highly unauthorized project with you."

The door banged open. "Excuse me," broke in a grating voice, interrupting Dixon. Wiggins strode in to the room excitedly, holding up his frail, nicotine-stained hands. He was a thin, nervous man in his forties. He swiped a lock of wispy gray hair out of his eyes and then looked pleadingly at Volensky. "You people are not cleared to be here, you had better—"

"Well, excuse the hell out of me!" Dixon retorted. "Listen, you DEA people are in deep shit back in Washington. You had best learn not to—"

"Hey, everybody," Peterson, the peacemaker, broke in, "we're not gonna get anywhere with all this haggling."

Volensky let them argue. He checked his watch. When the time read 0605, he rose to quiet them down. "Gentlemen . . . gentlemen, may I have your attention, please? Thank you. Please understand that I am nothing more than a simple, dumb Russian who has been blessed with the command of this battalion. Kindly inform me what the problem is. As far as my chain of command has told me, the only agency authorized to be here is the DEA, represented by Mister Wiggins. Elements of my battalion are supporting a classified operation under DEA jurisdiction and authority."

"That is exactly the problem, Colonel," Dixon, the FBI agent, responded. "We have just learned that this operation was secretly authorized and executed by the Drug Enforcement Administration without coordinating with its sister services."

Volensky arched an eyebrow toward Wiggins. No, he wouldn't

put it past him and his agency. The CIA, DEA, and FBI competed against each other for their shares of the budget pie just like the Army, Navy, Air Force, and Marines. The fact that this competition could endanger the lives of his men in the field enraged him.

"As a matter of fact," Dixon continued, "my department has sent me here to investigate why and to put a stop to it until further coordination is effected between my boss and Mister Wiggins's boss."

Peterson nodded in agreement.

The color drained from Volensky's face. He leaned forward in his chair. "I have men in the field *now*, gentlemen." He flashed an angry look toward Wiggins. "Why did you not tell me this earlier?"

Wiggins shrank underneath Volensky's glare. Dixon, thinking that was that, stood up from his chair and downed the final slug of his coffee. "Colonel, I'm afraid we'll just have to shut down this operation immediately. There will be no further military operations conducted at this headquarters until my investigation team arrives from FBI headquarters in Albuquerque."

Volensky fought to retain his composure, his suspicions of the DEA running a renegade operation now confirmed. "Gentlemen," he said calmly, "I have men deployed in accordance with a mission authorized by the DEA and approved by my chain of command. A last-minute change might endanger those men who are now deployed in the area of operations."

"Colonel," Dixon said, pulling a letter out of his breast pocket and handing it over to Volensky, "we already *have* notified your chain of command."

Volensky immediately recognized the 1st SOCOM commander's signature and his own Group Commander's initials on the routing address. The paper shook with Volensky's barely checked rage.

The front door flew open. Hutton ran up to Volensky. *"Sir!"*

Volensky wheeled around, still clutching the letter of authorization.

Hutton thrust a message from the communications center in the Colonel's hand. "Sir . . ." He looked away from the group, so he could speak to Volensky in private. What he had to tell him was classified. Taking the cue, Volensky took Hutton's elbow and led him into the hallway out of earshot.

"What is it?"

"Sir, the team did not radio in their 0600 situation report. We've got a missed contact on our hands."

Volensky glanced at his watch. A missed contact? Already, it was fifteen minutes after the team's last scheduled communications check with the FOB. Radio trouble? No, the team had plenty of lithium batteries and spare parts, and Barkowitz was the finest communicator in the battalion. And it certainly could not be forgetfulness. The team was too good for that. No, something was wrong.

The civilians! His own command! What about them and the message he clutched in his hand, telling him to abort the mission—to leave his men out in the field until some mother *fucking* FBI investigation team showed up? Why hadn't the team contacted him? What the hell was going on?

Volensky forced himself to calm down, and he released his iron grip on Hutton's elbow. He pulled a pack of More cigarettes from his fatigue trousers pocket and lit up. Hutton massaged his elbow and looked at the Old Man for instructions.

Inhaling deeply, Volensky put his arm around the young staff sergeant's shoulders. "Hutton, find Major Richards and the battalion executive officer. Get them both in here ASAP."

Hutton nodded. Richards was the Charlie Company commander, Santo and MacIntyre's parent CO in the chain of command. The company made up the bulk of the reaction force Volensky had chosen to support the team on the mission. Major Blane, the battalion's executive officer, would be out on his morning run.

"And get those Blackhawk pilots in here too." Volensky turned around and stared thoughtfully at the haggling civilians from three different federal agencies. "My men will not become casualties because of sloppy government administration," he muttered. Then he thought of his own chain of command. "Or military," he added, regarding the sludge of grounds at the bottom of his styrofoam coffee cup.

Sorens wondered why his backpack was so heavy. Then he remembered that Vicki had packed it for him.

He wondered what that meant, if all they were going to do was hand off the RAIL device. *Why is it so heavy? And why did Vicki have to . . .*

Blake Sorens had received his first shock earlier in the night when he watched his lover kill the security guard. Then, just ten minutes ago, he'd received his second shock when Victoria Sanchez had ordered him to assist her in pushing his beloved Jeep Cherokee off the trail into the still-flooded gorge at the foot of the canyon they would soon enter.

Whether he wanted to admit it or not, the reason his pack was so heavy was because he was leaving. Leaving the country.

Gray, pre-dawn sky, rain-soaked ground with green cactus and wet rocks slipping underfoot. And the uphill climb. Blake Sorens, feeling all of his thirty-nine years with a fifty-pound backpack cutting into his shoulders, followed meekly behind Sanchez, too stunned and acquiescent as a result of her dominance to say anything. He tried to blot the murder out, tried to forget the twin blobs of mucus in the corners of the security guard's eyes, eyes that had flown open in surprise when Sanchez stuck her poison-laden syringe between his shoulder blades. Eyes that stared at nothing moments later in his death.

What had she said? A heart attack was what Bloodworth died from? That no trace would be found? He remembered how the security guard had clutched frantically at his chest and then fallen heavily on the cold tile floor, staring at the ceiling with those goddam sleep-filled eyes. . . .

"Please keep up with me, Blake."

Startled out of his thoughts, Sorens glanced up and stopped his plodding. The sun had finally peeked behind them in the east, and the first few rays lit up the tanned smoothness of Victoria Sanchez's skin. The physical effort of their hike glowed agreeably in her face, her black, shoulder-length hair, her muscled, tawny legs bared by the khaki hiker shorts and mountain boots she wore. She too carried a backpack, but somehow she was a little more erect, more sure of herself. And what he saw now in her dark eyes was a hard glint that he'd seldom seen before.

Sorens knew that score. She was in charge and she was telling him to keep up. He stared at his own mountain boots, knowing that somehow the new definition of his masculinity just didn't matter anymore.

"Why'd you have to kill him, Vicki?"

"You know the answer to that. You've known all along."

Sorens shrugged off his backpack. The RAIL device was inside, and it added to the weight. But why was his goddam backpack so heavy? "Is this really so important? Important enough for you to have killed that man?"

Sanchez kept staring at Sorens. Sorens suddenly saw the muscle on the right side of her jawline pump up as she gritted her teeth. It scared him.

"Yes, Blake," she finally said. She took off her backpack and set it down on the rocks by her feet. Then she walked slowly toward Sorens and put her hands gently on his shoulders. She reached up and massaged the back of his neck. Despite everything, Blake Sorens thought she never looked more beautiful. He swallowed. "Yes, Blake, it was necessary. I had to kill him. He would have alerted security. Then we would have been caught. We would have been—"

Sorens grimaced and tried to pull Sanchez's hands away from the back of his neck, but her fingers curled into his muscles there and would not move away.

"We would have been compromised, Blake! You *know* what would have happened then!"

"No!" Sorens twisted away suddenly and gave his backpack a kick. It flopped over and rolled a few feet downslope, then came to a rest against a boulder.

Trying to keep her patience, Sanchez glanced at her watch and realized they had only another half hour to rendezvous with their exfiltration team up in the canyon. They had to get moving.

"Blake." He was sulking over by the backpack. She walked to him and pulled him around to face her. "Blake! Listen to me! We will meet some people thirty minutes from now. What's happened so far has happened! If we do not move soon, then we will be captured when the base authorities initiate a manhunt. Stay with me and you will be all right. You will be all right, Blake! Do you understand?"

Sorens acknowledged with a barely perceptible nod of his head. Thoughts flashed through his mind of protest marches when he was a college student in the sixties. Then, there had been all-night bull sessions with pot and cold beer during backyard cookouts. He remembered those old memories of burning his draft card, Johnson-bashing, and Nixon-bashing. After graduating, he'd bashed Ford and Carter, still the idealist, still the moral suprem-acist. Finally, as he reached that state of nirvana that the eighties defined as yuppiedom, he'd bashed Reagan and Bush—always knowing that the system was fucked no matter what you did or said, and that America was always fucking up. So what the hell did you do about it? In these years, the prime years of his thirties, he'd outgrown LSD for occasional, and then more frequent, blows of snow. He'd reaped debt, divorce, alimony; then there had been loneliness, ah, God, the loneliness, and how for just sweet Jesus once he had finally come up with something good, RAIL, *his* project, and he'd been sold a bill of goods by being forced to come to White Sands. . . .

And, well, he'd just wanted a goddam piece of the pie with Vicki and what she'd had to offer too. . . .

Was it bad? Was it really so awfully bad?

Blake Sorens knew the answer. What he'd tried to suppress all along no longer lay hidden and dormant inside his bowels, occasional tendrils of guilt licking his guts. Now, he could focus on his relationship with someone whom he knew to be working for the other side with clarity and utter, absolute reality.

He was a traitor.

"Let's go, Blake." She squeezed his hands.

When he glanced up from his boots, Blake Sorens thought for one second he saw compassion in the eyes of Victoria Sanchez.

But he knew it was contempt.

CHAPTER TWELVE

Maslow dozed.

Newton Rasmin did not, and now, as he watched the wiry man before him rest his chin on his bloody, gauze-covered fatigue blouse, Rasmin realized that the radio clenched in the soldier's hand was available.

But Rasmin was scared. The tall pines overhead swayed in the crisp air of morning, and he did not know if he was shivering more from the cold or the fear of the night before. Very soon now, the sun would crest the horizon and spill light across the valley floor into White Sands Missile Range complex below them. He gazed down the long slopes of the mountain, welcoming the day. Daylight was safety. No more Army people holding him at knife-point. No more Army people . . . killing his friends.

Rasmin's eyes widened suddenly. Far below, at least a mile away, he could make out two figures approaching the entranceway to the canyon. Backpackers!

Trembling, he glanced back at Maslow, who hadn't stirred in the past five minutes. The soldier was still leaning against the thick resin-spotted base of the pine, quiet and relaxed, made oblivious by the dose of pain killer the Army medic had given him an hour earlier.

If he was going to do it, if he, Newton Rasmin, was going to escape and save himself, well, he'd better get on with it. He had to get out of here! And then, by God, he'd contact some kind of authority down in the missile base and have these men arrested! He'd been chased down by murderers. His friends were dead.

He'd been bruised and hurt and brutalized by these men . . . well, fuck them!

He could—he could take this guy's radio, his weapon—yes, that too—and then he could run down, meet the two backpackers below, and get the hell off this mountain, down to the missile range, down to safety.

Rasmin reached out with trembling fingers and touched the radio in Maslow's hand. He pulled it away, slowly, gently. Little crumbles of gravel slipped from underneath the gray plastic casing of the brick-sized radio. He had it now. Rasmin grinned nervously, as he picked up the radio—

Just in time for Maslow to lock his bony hand on Rasmin's wrist.

Rasmin yelped in surprise.

"Sit down." Weakly, Maslow started to raise his M16, fumbling with the tubing connecting the IV bag suspended on a tree branch above him and the IV needle inserted in the vein of his forearm.

Rasmin grabbed the M16's barrel. "No!" He pulled hard on the barrel and both the rifle and Maslow's grip on him gave. Rasmin yanked harder, and then fell down hard on his hip with the M16 in one hand and the radio in the other.

Maslow grunted in pain, where his lacerated side pulled and bled from the effort, and then he fell back against the tree trunk. Rasmin leaped to his feet, still holding the barrel of the M16, not sure what to do.

"Give it back, son," Maslow panted, beads of sweat forming suddenly on his forehead and upper lip.

Rasmin stuck the radio between his legs and fumbled with the M16 until he had it aimed at Maslow. "F-fuck you."

"You're going to hurt yourself." Maslow concentrated on staying calm. This kid would screw everything up. If he made any noise, it would alert whoever was in the canyon other than his team.

"I'm not sticking around any more, man . . . you Army pukes! *Baby-killer-fascist-pigs!* Fuck you! Fuck you and your buddies! I hope you all die! Like my friends! You killed them!"

"No. You're wrong."

"You killed them!"

Maslow shrank back against the tree trunk, staring at the

business end of his own M16, silently cursing himself for falling asleep. What a goddam mess! He inhaled deeply, smarting with the cuts on his side and forearm and shoulder. Then he exhaled. He still felt dizzy. But he had to talk to this fuzz-head, had to make some sense with him. "Where do you want to go?"

"Away from here, man!"

"Down to White Sands?"

"Yeah!"

"Think about it . . . the Army runs White Sands. Don't make things hard on yourself. We're here to find whoever killed your friends—"

"I don't want to fucking well hear it!"

Maslow got to his feet.

"Stay down, man!"

Maslow stood up, holding his side. He stretched his hand out. "Just give me . . . the weapon."

Rasmin gasped in fear and panic. "No," he whispered. He backed slowly away, reaching down with the other hand to retrieve the radio he'd stuck between his legs earlier. Rasmin shook his head and aimed the M16 at Maslow's face. "Don't make me do it. . . ."

"Hand it over, son," Maslow said soothingly, taking a step forward. You'll be down off this mountain soon enough. Today, this morning even. Just give it time."

"Christ almighty, no!" Awkwardly, Rasmin brought the M16's stock up to his shoulder, but he couldn't shoot the man standing before him. Suddenly, he spun away from Maslow, lost his balance, and tumbled ten meters down the mountainside, the M16 flying from his grasp as he stretched his hands out to break the fall. The radio smacked against a rock lying by his head. Numb, Rasmin got to his hands and knees, disoriented. He found the radio and picked it up.

Maslow thanked God he'd left his M16 on safety, or else it might have blown off a round. He glanced at the IV Greeley had planted in his arm earlier, the M16 lying in the dirt between him and Rasmin, and the scared young man writhing in the pine needles and cactus below. Then he ripped the catheter out of the crook of his arm and scrambled down to the weapon before Rasmin could react.

Rasmin got back to his feet before Maslow could close his

hands around the stock. Scrambling on all fours, he slipped farther downhill and then raced away from the soldier.

Victoria Sanchez felt a stitch in her abdomen as she climbed over a boulder with Blake Sorens, their backpacks swaying awkwardly and pulling them off balance as they climbed. She clamped her hand there and breathed hard, trying not gasp.

She cursed silently at the pain, yet she was relieved that finally, her period had come. She'd been a week late, and the last, absolutely the last thing she needed now was to be late and possibly pregnant.

Sorens climbed to the top of the car-sized granite boulder ahead of her and extended his hand to help her up. "You okay?"

She climbed to the top without his assistance. Sorens averted his eyes and let her do it. "I said . . . are you okay?"

"Yes," she replied curtly. "Please keep going, Blake."

Sorens walked on ahead of her. Sanchez regained her pace. The cramp passed, but she knew it would be followed by others. Her mood worsened. She despised the man in front of her and tried to focus on something else. Then she shook her head, trying to clear her mind. The mission! Time was critical. A missed rendezvous spelled disaster. She glanced at her watch as they reached the mountain switchback trail winding upwards into Ash Canyon. Another fifteen more minutes until 0700, the designated rendezvous time. She quickened her pace, and soon, she was ahead of Sorens.

Finally, they paralleled the gorge. They stopped for a moment in silence, each pulling a canteen out from their backpacks. Sanchez, drinking deeply, traced the gorge's trail up the canyon with calculating eyes. Another five hundred steep meters would bring them in sight of the sluice, the old mining apparatus.

Then she froze.

A body lay twisted and quite dead in a tangle of branches fifty meters to their front in a stand of rapids. She knew it was dead by the way the force of the current bobbed a bloody face up and down, up and down, crashing it on an algae-stained rock. The face was a bloody, pulvertized mess with long brown hair.

Sorens walked up to her and then she saw it.

"My God."

"Let's go, Blake."

"But that body—"

She followed the trail paralleling the gorge, growing more uneasy with each step. Sorens hiked on ahead of her, trying to reach the body first. Sanchez concentrated hard. It had to be a civilian. The contact and exfiltration team she was to meet—it all had to be related. Her mind raced for contingency plans. Were they compromised? Under surveillance? Perhaps. But what to do? She imagined being caught, being in possession of the RAIL model and blueprints and the irradiated microchip circuitry in Sorens's backpack.

She thought of the bomb she had rigged in her own backpack. It was homemade, yet powerful enough to knock anyone within five meters down and kill them as if it were a grenade. *That* was her contingency, one of them anyway. Her sixth sense had told her to make it before she met with Sorens in the missile range the night before. If she had to, she could break contact with the explosive and the three tear-gas cannisters she had rigged to a thirty-second timing device.

So she had the bomb and she had her pistol—a Walther PPK.380-caliber—and she had her own wits. What if everything *had* turned to shambles? A surveillance team, White Sands security, her contact team, the body . . . *had they been compromised?*

She'd use her own net if she had to. On the side, Sanchez had recruited her own four-person cell in El Paso. It was easy enough with the cash she had received over the past two years in her dead-letter-drops—that was a contingency plan too.

"Vicki . . . there's someone down there by that body."

Sanchez shot her head up, her thought-train broken. She had fallen behind again. "Where?" She climbed the slope faster until she reached the spot where Sorens had paused by the side of the gorge, just off the trail.

"There," he said weakly, pointing a trembling finger, then dropping his arm to his side. He wanted to throw up.

The body was in plain view now. Kneeling beside it, crying softly, was a young man with longish light-brown hair pulled back in a ponytail.

Leaning heavily on his M16, Winston Maslow climbed down into a tributary of the gorge, and then started up the next five meters that would bring him to the top of a small ridgeline that kept him out of view from below and from which he could observe Rasmin's progress. He'd had Rasmin in sight most of the time, but Maslow didn't know how much longer he'd be able to keep up the pace. The knife fight had just taken too much out of him. But somehow he had to keep close to Rasmin—wait for the younger man's panicky state to make him fall down, break his leg, sprain his ankle—anything to give Maslow a chance to catch up and keep Rasmin quiet.

Maslow crested the ridge, and then he immediately took a knee behind a barrel cactus. There were *three* people down there now, no more than a hundred and fifty meters downhill.

Maslow opened the top of the extra ammo-pouch he had strapped to his web belt and retrieved a miniature set of Zeiss binoculars.

"Lady, for God's sakes, I said there are two others up there by my campsite who are dead!"

Blake Sorens walked away from them in disgust and sat on a nearby boulder on the trail, watching the charade. Vicki was putting on an incredible act with the young man in tattered jeans they'd found. She toyed with the man's radio he'd brought along, staring at it.

"And you said that soldiers did this?"

"Hell, yes!" Rasmin pointed at his bloody feet. "I've been running from them all night. They caught me once, held me for a few hours. But I got away." He tried to stand up. "Gotta go get the authorities, man. Fucking Army fascists, why the hell did they have to do this!" He blanched suddenly and sat back down.

"So." Sanchez put the radio down by her feet. She opened the top of her backpack and pulled out a first-aid kit. "You were attacked last night and you've been held prisoner during some war game the Army's playing?"

"Christ, I don't know, must be something like that. All I know is that my girlfriend and two other people are dead, and that's . . . " He looked back at the gorge. "That's all that's left of . . . Sarah." Holding his hands over his ears, Rasmin put his head between his legs and began crying again.

"We will go with you."

Sorens shot his head up at that and locked eyes with Vicki. She had the same cold gleam in them from the night before. He looked at the first-aid kit she had opened.

This time Rasmin was able to make it to his feet. "C'mon, lady, we don't have much time." He saw a syringe in her right hand. "What's this?"

"Your feet. Look at them."

They were a bloody mess. Rasmin stared at them and then back at the syringe. Sanchez pulled out an alcohol pad and walked over to him.

"I'm a trained nurse. You need antibiotics."

"Yeah . . . I guess so."

"No!"

Both of them stared up at Blake Sorens, who stomped over to them.

"Blake, he needs help."

"No Vicki! Not this time!"

"Hey, what gives?" Rasmin got back to his feet and started to edge away. Something was going on and he didn't like it.

"Give me that thing, Vicki."

"Blake, move away."

"Give it to me!"

Sanchez turned away from Sorens's outstretched hand and grabbed Rasmin by the arm. Sorens darted forward and tackled her by the waist before she could stick Rasmin with the syringe. Cartwheeling around, they fell together in the dirt, Sorens on top of her.

She lay there for several moments fighting for consciousness, the breath knocked out of her. Finally, she pushed Sorens off. He was limp, his eyes glassy. He stared up at the blue sky above, his mouth opening and closing.

The syringe was planted in his side.

She said nothing and stared at him for the few seconds it took for him to die. When she looked up, she saw Rasmin's fleeing figure now over two hundred meters away, downhill, running down the trail for the missile range.

She breathed long and hard for the next several minutes, letting a thick fog gel her emotions into numb detachment. All the death. The mission. Stress. Pain. The pain.

No pain. No more. Get on with it. Stand up! She stood up. Two backpacks were at her feet, side by side. One had a bomb in it.

The other, the RAIL device and the irradiated microchip circuitry and papers. That one belonged to a dead man.

Five minutes later she moved out, with her contingency plan riding along in the bottom of her backpack.

Maslow watched it all long enough to see the woman fumble around with the two backpacks—transferring part of the contents of one and placing them in the other—and then get underway in his direction after dumping the body in the gorge. Wincing, he got to his feet in a crouch and made back for the place where Rasmin had escaped earlier in the morning.

The woman was an agent. The contents in her pack and the man she killed had to originate from the missile range. He put it all together with the Spetsnaz team in the area. Whatever was in the backpack represented the White Sands Missile Range, national security, SDI, and for the love of Mike, the genesis of World War Three.

Clamping his hand against his bloody side, Maslow climbed higher into the tree line. There was plenty more pain killer in Greeley's aid bag back at the R&S site. He had to get it.

And then he had to stop her.

Hanlon refocused his binoculars from where he and MacIntyre kept watch on the two men in the tree line to their right not far from the mining sluice. "Boss . . . they're moving around again."

"Let me see."

Hanlon handed him the binoculars. MacIntyre shifted around, trying to peer out from the screen of pines and prickly-pear cactus and rocks to his front. They were in a well-concealed position, but so were the two agents below them deep inside the canyon. Starting from the reference point of the mining sluice, he shifted the binoculars up the canyon where the swollen stream started. Higher up, fifty, maybe seventy-five meters, he let his focus rest on a clump of trees and rocks where he finally spotted movement. It was still hard to see, as the entire canyon was shrouded in the half-light of early morning shadow.

"Yeah, I see them."

Hanlon glanced at his watch, "Santo and Greeley should have been here by now."

"They've got to move slow," MacIntyre muttered, concentrating on the movement in the trees below. "They're probably coming in to our left rear, where that draw will keep them from being—" He stopped in mid-sentence.

"What?"

"A radio. Those guys below have a radio."

Noise to their left, scuffling rocks and the sound of bushes parting branches. Both men turned around, hands tightening on their weapons.

Then the faces of Master Sergeant Manny Santo and Sergeant Ted Greeley came into view. They were high-crawling through the rocks, trees, and cactus. A jackrabbit scampered away from its hiding place and sprinted across Hanlon's boot, from which it then bounced down the slope below them.

Santo and Greeley quietly joined them. MacIntyre handed the binoculars back to Hanlon, who maintained surveillance on the two men below.

"How's Maslow?" MacIntyre asked his team sergeant.

"He'll be all right. He's watching the kid. Greeley left him some painkiller and bound him up pretty tight." Santo breathed deeply, wiping the sweat away from his forehead with the sleeve of his fatigue shirt. He left a trail of sand glistening on a smudge of camouflaged face-paint.

"Barkowitz . . . Saxon . . . "

"They're dead, sir."

Just as he'd been told two hours earlier over the radio, MacIntyre told himself. Somehow, he had just hoped that it wasn't true, wasn't the way it actually happened, and . . . He glanced back up at Santo's face. The older man's eyes clouded in fury.

"You've spotted them yet?"

"Down there. Hanlon's got them under surveillance."

Santo spotted them with his own binoculars. Several minutes later, he put them back inside his shirt, where they wouldn't dangle from the strap around his neck.

"What do you think, Manny?"

"I think we're going to get those bastards. They're waiting here for something, or else they'd have skyed outta here a long time ago after what all happened last night." Santo looked up at the sky, and then contemplated the shadows in the canyon. "We've only got so much concealment left before the sun lights up the canyon enough for easy observation. I'd say maybe half an hour at the most. I think two of us should flank those guys down from the rear. Greeley and I can do that. You and Randy should move in a little closer from above."

MacIntyre crawled forward and looked downslope. "Okay," he replied. "You guys move out first. It's fairly open from this position for my and Hanlon's route, but there's a draw below us that'll conceal our movement. If you and Greeley stay in the tree line to the right, you can haul ass and get in position sooner."

"Then we'll call you up on the PRC-68 when we have them in sight."

"Roger that. I'll give you an up when we're in position."

"Then what?"

Both men stared at each other for several long seconds. "Like you said, Manny, they're waiting for someone. We'll snatch them when they link up."

"Look!" Hanlon was aiming his binoculars toward the opening of the canyon. All eyes followed Hanlon's line of sight. A lone figure was climbing through the trees and boulders, winding up the trail toward the mining sluice.

Maslow stared at the IV bag still suspended on the tree branch, breathing hard. Each inhalation spread the lips of the long knife wound along his rib cage. It was the least serious of his wounds—including the one along his upper pectoral muscle where the spring-knife had lodged earlier, almost severing an artery, and the long slash on his forearm—but the one along his rib cage hurt the most. So far he had been able to follow Rasmin, see the others, witness the murder, and return.

But how much more strength did he have?

He thought just then of his wife back in their condo in Fayetteville, the town just outside Fort Bragg. Jane. *Janie, you are right, sweetheart. You've been right all along. I am getting way too old to keep on being a green-beanie*. Maslow loved his wife, and she deserved his being with her more than four or five months out of the year. She had stuck with him through every deployment and had never complained. She did not succumb to the alcohol, gossip, and neuroses the other wives in the battalion fell prey to when their men were gone, and she never did run around on him. Over the past couple of years, though, Maslow had broken his ankle, sprained his back, and was developing arthritis in both knees. He was in outstanding cardiovascular shape, yes, but one just had to face it when it was time to leave. He had twenty-four years in now. He would put his paperwork in for retirement when they returned from this deployment. Then, together, he and Jane could open that computer store back home in Albuquerque. Or buy the ranch up near Taos. Be happy.

First things first, though.

Maslow spied Greeley's aid bag, where he'd left it by the IV before moving out with Santo hours earlier. Carefully, he knelt down and unzipped the medical kit. He searched around until he found an amber bottle of Motrin. Then he slugged two giant orange-colored capsules down with half a quart of canteen water.

The woman. Where was she? Had he kept ahead of her?

He had no time to waste. Quickly, he took stock of his situation. Santo and Greeley had to have reached MacIntyre's and Hanlon's position across the canyon, ready with a plan of action of their own—whatever that was. But the woman he'd spotted earlier was the wild card. What would she do? The others couldn't know about her yet.

Inventory time: Like the others in his team, he still had his M16 and fresh, unspent magazines in his ammo pouches. He had a .45 in his pistol holster on his web belt and his old Ka-bar sheath knife over his left hip. He patted his web gear's left shoulder strap, and squeezed his strobe light. He could signal oncoming helicopters with that, and he had a VS-17 signaling panel for that purpose as well. He still had the pen flare Santo had given him stuck inside his ammo pouch. Team SOP, everyone had the same.

And all that would come in handy later, if Volensky back in the rear came looking for them. They'd missed their 0600 commo check with the FOB, so that was a likelihood.

That was it. He would have to make do, but it could be worse.

No more time. He had to move out now. For the next ten minutes, Maslow crept silently along the contour of the mountainside, angling down toward the mining sluice, staying in the shadows, stopping frequently to ensure he began each twenty-meter movement with a good solid screen of trees and boulders to his front while keeping a wary eye out for the woman paralleling his route below.

He saw her again when he neared the mining sluice and the two brightly colored dome tents nestled at its foot, half-submerged in the water from the night before. Cautiously she picked her way through the debris-strewn trail now exposed from the receding rapids of the flash flood. He looked at her for several moments, admiring her long, tawny legs as she stepped along. Whoever she was, she was in good shape. But, cuts and all, he was ahead of her and that was good. It was going to be at least another five minutes before she reached the tents and sluice.

Maslow picked out an overwatch position adjacent to the sluice thirty meters away and ten meters above the apparatus, where he had a clear field of vision. There, he could watch both incoming and outgoing avenues of approach for the mining sluice. After setting up a field of fire covering both routes with his M16, he waited.

Maslow's stomach growled, and he grinned. At least he didn't have a fever. Plus there was an assault ration packed away in his left fatigue trousers cargo pocket. He opened it, and munched on a few sticks of beef jerky and ate the chocolate bar.

The wounds were bad, but he'd made it okay up to this point.

Maybe he wasn't half the pansy he thought he was.

CHAPTER THIRTEEN

Major Jake Blane strode purposefully inside the battalion headquarters, where he immediately noticed two new civilians (both dressed in three-piece suits, and he knew what *that* meant) and the DEA representative, all squabbling among themselves. His boss, Lieutenant Colonel Andrei Volensky, was fuming.

That was no good. Immediately, two purplish veins stood out on each side of Blane's forehead. He knew something was up as soon as Volensky'd had Staff Sergeant Hutton run him down from his early morning ten-miler out on dirt roads criss-crossing the long slopes of Elephant Mountain overlooking Oro Grande Range Camp. After alerting the two standby teams to prepare for deployment, he'd broken starch on a fresh uniform and headed for the FOB.

He was in Special Forces this tour, but by God, let no one ever forget that Jake Blane, the battalion executive officer and second-in-command, was a Ranger at heart. A stiff shadow of prematurely gray hair on top was all that adorned his head. Just under five ten, weight only five pounds under his original muscled bulk of 190 when he'd wrestled for Texas A&M fifteen years earlier, Blane still retained the edge. There were only two types of people as far as he was concerned. Those who led, and those who followed. The ones who led were the people—no, the *leaders*—who made things happen, got the mission accomplished, people who used initiative and drive and perseverance for unit success. And that was his motto: *Make it happen*.

But now, something haywire was happening, and he did not

like the look on his boss's face. Inside his hand, Volensky clenched a paper.

Blane walked up to him and leaned close to his ear. "They're ready sir—two detachments from Charlie Company. Got the pilots squared away too."

Despite his mood, Volensky grinned. That meant his battalion XO had kicked the door down to the pilot's hootch at sunup hours and had them shaking in their boots to get ready. Then the grin vanished. Volensky waved the paper in front of Blane's face. "This goddam paper has just fucked everything up. We have troubles, XO. Come inside the war room." He glanced at the three civilians sitting on folding chairs and drinking the coffee Hutton kept plying them with. "Gentlemen, we are working on the situation. Now, if you'll excuse us, please."

Volensky clapped his arm around Blane's broad shoulders and walked him inside the FOB's war room. Immediately, Blane studied the map covering the entire wall behind the podium delineating the Fort Bliss and the White Sands missile range boundaries.

Volensky stuck his finger in the area of Ash Canyon behind the missile-range complex. "That's their location. As you know, it is MacIntyre and Santo's team. Our last contact with them was at 0300 this morning. They failed to make the 0600 situation report."

"They missed a contact?" Blane stared thoughtfully at the floor, hands on his hips. "Not good." Looking back up, he said, "Sir, the two teams I got ready this morning have a hell of a lot of questions, and so do I. I thought we were working as a reaction force for some type of drug operation."

"It's more than that, Jake." Volensky told him the entire story—the mission and the mission's cover while the rest of the battalion stood down for the Labor Day weekend. He told Blane about how the team had discovered a body the day prior—no identification, the steel bridgework in his mouth—how MacIntyre's team had deduced that the corpse had belonged to a Soviet Spetsnaz commando team. Then, after MacIntyre had deployed his team into the two recon-and-surveillance sites and the commo-relay site, communications had gone nil during the night.

Blane studied the map closely. "Drug op my ass, sir. Something's going down at White Sands."

"Up until now, I could not even tell you this much."

Blane glanced up in surprise. Volensky nodded this head. "Confusion reigns, Jake. These representatives from the CIA and FBI have arrived with a signed document from Bragg to cease and desist with the mission. Everything—even the deployed team. We are supposed to freeze in place until an FBI investigation team arrives in the afternoon to help smooth out the mess."

"So that's what's going on." Blane shook his head. "And they're telling us we can't even get our men out of there?"

"Yes."

"Christ, sir, the team missed their radio contact! Anything could be going on . . ." Blane set his jaw and threw an angry glance toward the civilians in the other room. "Fuck 'em," he growled. "If we're going to 'cease and desist,' then we simply have to get our team back home. We can't leave them out there. And a missed contact means trouble!"

Volensky stared hard at his battalion XO. "It's not as easy as that Jake. I have proof that the FBI has complete jurisdiction and authority here and now. Legally, we're powerless to do anything."

"Goddam civilians!"

"That attitude will not help at all, Major," Volensky said, his voice rising. "Whether they are right or wrong, civilian control over the military is the law—despite how incredibly fouled up things are now."

Blane's face turned red as he fought for control. "Sir, how can you say that when the lives of our men are at stake? Jesus, Colonel, you're not going to—"

"Roll over and play dead? No." Volensky raised the tilt of his chin as he regarded his XO. "But you will not accomplish anything with belligerence, regardless of how right you may be. We are going to talk to them, and, Major, *all* of us are going to lay off this crap about who is in charge. *They* are in charge—that man out there, Agent Fred Dixion. We are going to work with him."

Blane took a deep breath. "Yes, sir. Of course. I'll keep my temper in check."

Moments later, Volensky had led the three agency representatives inside the war room and was showing them the situation map. Blane stood off to the side, watching the Old Man's Byzantine machinations. He glanced at his watch. He'd better hurry. Already it was 0635—thirty-five minutes after the missed contact.

"Gentlemen," Volensky told them, "if I seemed rather upset a few moments ago when you arrived, please understand that my overriding responsibility as the commander if this battalion concerns the safety of my men." Volensky looked at Dixon. "I also fully understand how events between the DEA and the FBI have transpired, regarding the legality of this mission."

"I'm glad you do, Colonel," Dixon replied.

"However, please understand our immediate situation." Volensky nodded at the situation map. "Yesterday, I sent a six-man Special Forces team and their DEA attachment into the Organ Mountains to conduct a reconnaissance. They discovered a corpse with no identification on it in one of the canyons. We have reason to believe that that corpse belongs to a Soviet commando team which has infiltrated across our borders for an operation against the White Sands Missile Range." Volensky paused, letting the effect of his last statement sink in.

"Go on, Colonel," Dixon said, satisfied that his authority remained intact.

"Now, my team is deployed on one of the main avenues of approach into the southern boundary of the missile complex—Ash Canyon. They have been in position since 2100 hours last night. As per our unit standing operating procedures, my team reports to the FOB—this headquarters—every three hours. They do this under strict orders to report any and all activity—even if they have observed nothing—so that I may know that they are still on site without having been compromised by the enemy. They made their first contact at 2100. They radioed back at 2400, and then at 0300, but they failed to make their next scheduled contact at 0600." Volensky glanced at his watch. "Mister Dixon, that was over forty minutes ago."

Dixon shrugged. "They fell asleep."

Volensky inhaled sharply. "No. They did not fall asleep. They missed their last radio contact, and we have every reason to believe that they are in trouble."

Dixon chewed the inside of his cheek.

"Mister Dixon, my team is in some sort of danger," Volensky repeated, keeping his voice on an even keel. "There could have been a confrontation between my men and the object of their surveillance—possible Soviet commandos. Anything. I want to take my helicopters into the canyon and retrieve them. Then we can stand this entire operation down for your investigation. I have nothing to hide, nothing to cover up. I only want my men safely returned."

Before Dixon could reply, the door to the war room burst open. It was Hutton. "Sir—flash commo on the secure line from White Sands. The commanding general there wants to talk to you. And a vehicle from White Sands security just pulled up outside."

"Mister Dixon, you may wish to listen to this."

Together, Volensky, Dixon, and Blane left the FOB for the quonset hut behind the building housing the communications center. Outside, they met a captain and the MPs.

"Take care of them, Jake."

"Roger that, boss." Blane led the MP captain back inside the FOB. Volensky and Dixon followed Hutton into the communications center, where they passed two banks of secure radios fronting the main work area. The battalion communications and electronics officer met them inside the secure room at the rear of the communications center, where a sergeant handed Volensky a phone. Volensky waved everyone outside, expect for Dixon. The door closed behind them.

"Lieutenant Colonel Volensky, sir." Volensky held Dixon's gaze as the FBI man picked up the other phone to listen in.

"Hawkins, here, Colonel. Got a situation I'd like you to handle."

"Yes, sir." Major General Glenn Hawkins, commanding general of the White Sands Missile Range, was not in Volensky's chain of command, but whatever this was, it was urgent. Volensky admired the man—he'd been a big help in supplying his battalion with available logistics and training-area support during the deployment to Oro Grande every six months, in exchange for the battalion's offering of foreign-weapons, patrolling, and rear-echelon-security training by some of Volensky's "A" teams. Having spent a tour with Special Forces himself in the sixties, Hawkins on occasion would visit the range camp for some brews with Volensky and his officers, relaxed, without all the protocol and unnecessary broohaha that usually heralded a general's visit. Not many generals had served in Special Forces, but Hawkins was an execption. It was the brotherhood.

"Andrei, we've got a problem here on the post. Last night, a security guard in one of our research labs was found dead of an apparent heart attack. That means that for several hours no one was on watch. We've got a security leak, Colonel."

"Yes, sir."

"And now, one of our scientists is nowhere to be found. He'd been in the same lab the night the guard died. I've got to assume the worst. We're increasing our security, and I've ordered my MPs to seal off all avenues of approach to the complex. I'd like to use some of your people to sweep the mountains to the south. You should have one of my officers out at your location by now for coordination."

Volensky exchanged glances with Dixon, whose eyes had widened with mounting concern. "He just got here, sir, and my XO's talking to him." Volensky paused. Then; "Sir, have you contacted the 1st SOCOM commander at Ft. Bragg about this? Has anyone informed you about what we're doing here?"

"No."

Volensky paused. If he disclosed his mission—the team in Hawkin's back yard—he knew he didn't have authorization. But maybe if he . . .

"Call my commanding general at Bragg, sir, for the necessary information. In the meantime, I have two teams on standby now to sweep the area." Volensky glanced at Dixon, who listened intently on the other line. After a moment, Dixon looked up and nodded his head. Volensky then said, "I can have another company out there by midday."

"Give me the rest of the story, Colonel."

"Sir, I'm not at liberty to disclose that information."

"Cut the bullshit."

Volensky frowned. Call my CG at Fort Bragg, sir," he replied firmly. He wasn't about to be intimidated, whether the general was a friend of Special Forces or not.

"You're right, Colonel. Sorry I snapped at you. When can you have the teams out?"

"In the next fifteen minutes, sir."

"Good. Do it."

"Sir, do I have clearance for live ammunition? It has to be that way."

Hawkins paused before answering. He knew Volensky. If Volensky wanted it, then it was necessary.

"Yes."

Volensky nodded his head. "Sir, I'll have my communications officer coordinate with yours for radio frequencies. We'll be in touch via FM communications before we move."

"Good. Meanwhile, I'll talk to Johnny."

Volensky grinned. Generals could more often than not get things done by dealing directly with each other, bypassing respective staffs and bureaucracy.

"Out here, sir."

"Out."

Dixon replaced his phone on the hook and unbuttoned his coat and loosened his tie. "Soviet infiltration, huh?"

"Yes. It appears that way."

"Then we've got one hell of a situation here, Colonel, if your theory is true. In any case, White Sands seems to have problems today. I'll allow you to retrieve your men from the field and support that general's request."

"Hutton!"

Staff Sergeant Ian Lange Hutton popped his head inside the door. "Sir."

"Get the communications officer up to the FOB, and tell him I want us wired into the White Sands security people ASAP!"

"Yes, sir!"

Volensky and Dixon strode back inside the FOB. There, Dixon informed the other agency representatives that he and the battalion commander were en route to retrieve Volensky's men from the operation.

Fifteen minutes later two teams were standing by at the chopper pad behind the range camp, aligned in their respective on-load sticks with weapons at the ready. Two Blackhawk helicopters warmed up, rotor blades swirling dust all around, as the teams prepared to mount.

With Blane in charge back at the FOB, Volensky sped to the helicopter pad in his CUC-V rough-terrain vehicle with FBI Agent Fred Dixon in tow. Before coming to a complete stop, Volensky leaped out of the four-wheeler, buckling his web gear together around his middle. Running toward the first bird, he pulled his beret off and stuck it inside his trousers cargo pocket. Dixon followed him, and they climbed inside the Blackhawk. The two waiting teams scrambled on board behind them.

Seconds later, they were airborne.

Santo and Greeley picked their way up the reverse slope of the ridgeline concealing both sight and sound of their approach from the two Russians. They had stayed in the trees after leaving MacIntyre and Hanlon, and they had moved rapidly, unencumbered by their rucksacks, the well-worn soles of their jungle boots padding quietly on the pine needles underfoot. They finally reached the U of the canyon, where the contour of two adjoining ridgelines met in a crescent, peaked in the saddle with a false hilltop that led in a southerly direction toward Soledad Canyon. They paused for water.

"Check yourself, Teddy."

"You too, old man. People your age suffer from senility and incontinence, you now."

"Stow it, dirtbag."

Greeley patted his gear, ensuring nothing was loose, that his tie-down cords held his gear in place and that his sheath knife was strapped securely to his thigh. The buckles on his M16 carrying strap had been taped down with OD-green hundred-mile-an-hour tape. Satisfied with his external gear, Greeley then pulled his signal mirror out of the extra ammo pouch on his web belt. With a tube of face-paint, he streaked his smooth complexion down with heavy strokes of forest-green and loam camouflage. Santo did the same. Greeley pulled a camouflaged first-aid cravat out of his pouch. It was his drive-on rag and, after pulling off his bush hat, he tied it around the top of his head, securing the tails with a square knot in back.

"Terry and the Pirates, huh?" Santo grunted. "Volensky'd throw a fit if he saw you."

"Helps you hear better on these deep dark woods, Team Daddy."

"Gimme one."

Seconds later, they were high-crawling over the ridgeline, feeling minute cactus barbs gouge their way into their knees, thorns sticking their elbows, and oblivious to all except the pounding of blood through their ears.

The trees thickened and thinned. Sometimes, they had no

choice but to skirt open areas through what remained of the shadows receding from the canyon walls. Their descent grew steep. When it got steep, they got closer. When they got closer, they moved slower, and finally they crawled, quiet, unobtrusive, with the stealth and grace and with adrenaline pounding sweat through their pores.

When they stopped near the stream that would eventually lead them below to the site where they had seen the two men earlier, Santo reached out and grabbed Greeley by the shoulder. "I'll go first," he whispered. "Follow me."

"But—"

Santo's eyes left no doubt in Greeley's mind that he'd go first. Santo looked away for a second. His team. Greeley was his team. MacIntyre and Hanlon and Maslow were his team.

Barkowitz.

"You've got . . . water in your eyes, Big Sarge."

Santo said nothing for a moment, breathing deeply and evenly. Then he said, "Follow me. And keep your eyes peeled."

They slithered down the mountain.

Antonov and Pushtkin crept quietly downhill from the darkest of shadows where they had cached their backpacks. To Antonov, it seemed like an eternity of time since they had all been one, four of them, stronger, deadlier, stealthier.

Now, there were only two of them left eighteen hours later. Antonov thought of Chelstovsky. Why had he not returned? His earlier suspicions of Navarro, the Mexican, had remained unspoken with Pushtkin. Yes, there was always a plot within a plot. The underworld's chief characteristic. His own organization, Spetsnaz, was largely unknown throughout the breadth of the Red Army, as was its parent organization, the GRU.

And let us not forget the KGB, he mused, with its own Byzantine twisting of secret organizations and a paramilitary branch of its own similar to Spetsnaz. Contemptible bastards! Pushtkin had allowed himself to be watched hours earlier as he examined maps and codes he should have had the sense to memorize and burn before the mission.

Sooner or later, Antonov would have to confront the swine about it. He kept Pushtkin to his front as they slipped down toward the mining sluice. *Yes*, he thought, *when they had been stronger*.

What would this day bring? He hefted the H&K 9-millimeter submachine gun in his right hand, and parted a pine bough away from his face with his left, as he and Pushtkin stole downhill, concentrating on staying in the shadows.

Finally, they reached a cluster of boulders mixed with a stand of pine saplings and prickly-pear cactus. The mining sluice was now in sight. The vegetation grew thicker next to the receding water of the canyon stream feeding into the gorge farther below. The bodies from the night before they'd dumped in earlier had been washed away, now out of sight. He glanced at his watch. So much had happened during the night.

Now, the sun climbed higher and the shadows of the canyon receded. The fresh smell of drenched and dried granite mingled with the pine-resin sap of the trees. It was going to be a beautiful day, but what the hell did that matter anyway?

Antonov let his mind reflect on his own upbringing near the Gorky forests where his father had been the local conservationist and gameskeeper. The forest. It was his friend, and as a boy he lived for days at a time off the land from which his father and the wildlife and flora divulged the secrets of survival. Then, later, there were the long survival periods with his Spetsnaz company in the Karlovy training grounds outside Moscow. Higher headquarters would turn his team loose on an escape-and-evasion exercise, after having alerted the local villages and collectives that hardened criminals had escaped from prison . . . *rapists, murderers, beware! Catch them, and rubles from the state will flourish in your village! Catch them!*

Armed with no more than their authorized allowance of fifty rubles apiece and their sheath knives and compasses, their prison uniforms and boots—and their wits—they evaded hundreds of their own citizenry during those exercises. They even had to kill a man, a gameskeeper like his own father, who was determined to track him and his four-man cell down in the woods. Chelstovsky buried him with his spade. The same spade he had killed the gameskeeper with.

It had been the same in Afghanistan when the Mujahideen rebels raided the communications outpost from which his team had been basing their reconnaissance operations high in the Hindu Kush Mountains. With no logistical support, they made it back to Kabul, near brushes with death constantly on their heels, knowing

that the Muslim fanatics with their bloody .303 Lee Enfields—
World War I British rifles!—would eventually find them and
mutilate their bodies during a slow death that always ended up in
castration and decapitation.

Major Sergei Antonov stared at the back of Pushtkin's head.
The radio on his back pulled at his shoulders, and he knew he was
weakening from the strain of the past thirty-six hours of almost
constant movement and killing and . . .

The swine! What did *he* know of hardship? Pushtkin was a
complainer out of his element, here in these mountains. Urban
guerrilla warfare was his forte. Terrorism, sabotage, assassination, But now, the so-called leader of this mission was out of his
natural environment. And surely now, he was planning how to
eradicate all traces of this mission after the handoff and exfiltration of the scientist and agent.

Pushtkin's neck flushed and he turned and faced the cold gray
eyes of Antonov behind him. He blinked. "It is time," he finally
said, unslinging his backpack.

Antonov grunted noncommittally and set his own backpack
down next to the cluster of boulders that would conceal them from
the mining sluice.

"Your radio, comrade."

Antonov arched an eyebrow and stared hard at the KGB man.

"We must call the support element."

Yes, the support element, you bastard. Call them, call them!
"You have not informed me of this," he said evenly.

"You know how these things are."

"The Mexican knew."

"Yes . . . things are different now . . . we must plan for
our own exfiltration."

Antonov toed his backpack with his boot. "You are very good
at covering your ass, Comrade Pushtkin. You know how to set up
the radio. Set it up."

Antonov and Pushtkin stared at each other for several long
moments. Pushtkin knew he could never get out of this American
canyon without Antonov's assistance. Later, when they rendez-
voused with his support team—men from Juarez, drug operatives
advised by his own cell of agents from the *residentura*—he could
take care of Antonov. Grzniecki would help him.

Pushtkin opened the flap of the civilian backpack where the

radio was strapped inside the pouch next to the back side, and he dialed the tuning knobs onto the emergency frequency. His codes—he could easily forewarn the others at the safe house of the additional company he'd be bringing in—they'd know and understand. Antonov would be taken care of. Soon, he had the radio tuned in, and he braced the backpack containing it against the rocks concealing their position. He knelt beside it and scanned the descending slopes of the canyon to their front, which was no longer obscured by the dim light of early morning.

"Show me, comrade."

"Eh?" Pushtkin turned and faced the open bore of Antonov's submachine gun lying carelessly across the Spetsnaz major's lap, his hand clasped loosely around the pistol grip, his index finger brushing the trigger. Pushtkin swallowed. "What?"

"The papers," Antonov responded wearily. "You are still very much the unprofessional, my friend. I know of your papers and codes and maps. Show them to me."

"I . . . have nothing to hide from you." Pushtkin hastily unzipped the hidden lining to his windbreaker and hesitantly pulled out several documents wrapped in plastic. He handed them over to Antonov, hands shaking. *Was he actually aiming the submachine gun at him or was it just the way he was sitting?*

Antonov glanced alternately between the papers and the KGB man kneeling beside him. Then: "So this is what you've been hiding from me. It's too bad the Mexican and Sergeant Chelstovsky cannot share this information with us."

"You never know . . . they might return anytime now. . . ."

Antonov gave Pushtkin a look of utter contempt. Then, glancing at the inside of his wrist, he watched the second hand of his watch sweep past 0700 hours. He shifted his weight around, careful to keep the submachine gun in Pushtkin's direction. Cautiously, he peered over the rocks at the mining sluice and the canyon and stream descending beyond. Then he locked cold eyes back on Pushtkin. "We will wait an additional fifteen minuites. By that time, it will have been thirty minutes with no contact, and we can be sure that the mission has been compromised. We will move out of here at that time."

"Yes! 0730. I must contact the others."

"You do that, comrade. You do that. Your codes are very crude, you know. They train us to a higher standard in your sister service, the GRU. We pride ourselves on our professionalism, you know. You and your kind have the millstone of politics hanging around your necks. Your leader sits at the right hand of the Party Chairman in the Politburo. I am only a soldier, but I know these codes—I've seen the format before. Let me assure you: When you call this in, I will be listening closely. If I begin to think you are setting me up, I will kill you on the spot and let the skunks and coyotes of this forest feed upon your carcass."

"There is no need to—"

"Call it in!"

Two minutes later, the transmission process was complete. Although the message was not sent in the clear, Antonov knew that the rendezvous time for Pushtkin's KGB support team was set for 0200 hours. They were to meet them in a canyon they had crossed a day earlier, somewhere in Soledad Canyon. Now, all he had to do was sit and wait.

And while they were waiting, they saw a distant figure with a backpack approach them from the gorge far below.

Twenty meters behind them, Master Sergeant Manny Santo and Sergeant Ted Greeley also watched as the two Soviets waited for the backpacker, a woman, to wind her way up the canyon trail towards the mining sluice. They had seen the Soviets speak into a radio. There seemed to be a tension between the two.

Fifty meters away, on the western slope of the canyon, Captain Matt MacIntyre and Sergeant First Class Randy Hanlon were in position behind a screen of trees facing the Soviet agents' left. They too followed the lone backpacker's movement with binoculars and the front sight post of their M16's.

And from his location on the opposite canyon wall above the sluice, CW2 Winston Maslow stopped thinking about his wife.

The next few minutes would decide everything.

Chapter Fourteen

Maslow held his breath as the woman walked not ten meters downslope from him, heading toward the tents and abandoned mining site. He studied her face: brown, Hispanic, dark pools for eyes—and yes, sensuous. Her face was also a study in control and concentration; her jawline worked and popped, the determined set of her mouth indicating total awareness of her surroundings. Any confusion, stress, or guilt she might have felt from killing a man only a half hour earlier was not present in her countenance now.

Maslow wondered if she had a weapon, and assumed that she did. If so, it wasn't visible. Of course, it would be concealed. And what was in the backpack?

Silently, he watched her approach the tents.

Victoria Sanchez paused before the mining sluice. It was rusted brown, and huge nuts that had fallen off their bolts lay scattered on the gravelly surface near the sand of the streambed where debris of leaves and sticks and pine cones covered the area, leftovers from the flash flood.

And the tents. One blue, one red on blue. Both deserted. She spotted the metal glint of a cooking stove that had been knocked over. A sleeping bag lay half in and half out of the tent closest to the stream, partially submerged in the water. It would eventually be pulled loose from its moorings and get caught in the current—and probably lash up in the tangles farther below, where she'd seen the first body and then the others higher up upon climbing into the canyon.

183

Like Blake Sorens, she thought, *torn up and twisted in the gorge far below, death etched in the pallor on his face, his lifeless pale . . .*

She shook her head and concentrated on her surroundings. She was late, but this was the right place. If she was to be given a grace period by her contact team, then the next few minutes would tell.

The signal—she must hurry!

Quickly, she set her backpack down on the stream bank and carefully unzipped the top flap. She hesitated. She had placed the explosive and the tear-gas cannisters—her contingency plan—in the bottom of the backpack, underneath her clothes and wrapped up in a canvas tote bag. There was enough padding surrounding it for the bulk inside to seem innocuous. Would she need it? Yes, of course, leave no door shut. Always have a contingency plan, a backup plan, a go-to-hell plan. It was the only way. The smokeless fuse ran up the inside of the backpack to the outside front left pocket. If she popped open the closure snap to that pocket, it would galvanize the fuse into action and thirty seconds later burst the device. The concussion alone would kill anyone within five meters, and enough smoke and tear gas would immediately cloud a radius of twenty-five meters with confusion, but also concealment. It was SOP. It was common sense.

Her far-side signal was a cup of tea on the sluice.

"Yes, it is her. But where is the scientist?" Pushtkin glanced at Antonov, as if he would know the answer, but got a grunt for a reply. "Something has gone wrong."

Antonov peered at Pushtkin with one eye. Had he met with this woman before? Did he actually know her? How could he be sure it was her without the near-side signal? Yet another interesting flaw in KGB professionalism. One simply did not conduct operations such as this with known contacts.

Antonov watched the slender brown woman of delicate, yet strong features and ebony hair boil water with her metal hiker's cup on top of a hissing stove. The rest of her signal came then when she pulled a blue bandanna from her backpack and tied it around her head, while waiting for the water to boil.

"Is the signal good, Pushtkin?"

"Yes . . . yes, it is. It is her. We will leave our packs here. I'll go down first to meet her, while you cover me."

"We'll go down *together*, comrade. I'll be right behind you."

Pushtkin eyed Antonov's H&K as they got to their feet. "As you wish."

Antonov opened his windbreaker, which concealed the tiny machine pistol resting in his shoulder holster.

Then they walked out into the open to meet her.

Static hissed quietly in Santo's ear, where he'd been holding his PRC-68 radio. "We have them in sight," MacIntyre's voice crackled to him. "How's your view?"

"Too many trees in the way over here," he replied. "You've got better fields of fire."

MacIntyre paused before answering. "Then initiate the snatch when ready. This thing's going down."

"Roger that. Out." Santo stuck the radio back in the carrying pouch attached to his web gear and glanced at Greeley, who trained his M16 on the agents below them. He reached out, tapped him on the shoulder. "Let's go get the bad guys."

"Yo, blood. Let's do that."

Santo got to his feet in a crouch and moved out first, Greeley on his right, both at the ready.

Victoria Sanchez's eyes widened as she watched two men approach from higher up in the thicker woods covering the top of the canyon. Two men—one with a lean, slender build, short, thick black hair, hard steel-gray eyes; the other . . . she knew him.
She knew him!

She immediately recalled the pockmarked face, the thin lips, the fleshy gut of a man who'd once called for a personal meeting in Juarez when Sorens was ready to reveal everything to White Sands security. The meeting had been necessary, covers would have been blown if immediate action was not taken. This man had been the one to set Sorens up in the whorehouses where the prostitutes and then the transvestites had plied him with tequila and perversion and had taken the pictures, the pictures sent to him with the money that had ensured Blake Sorens' silence.

And now he was here for the handoff and exfiltration. This was not good. It violated procedure and the principles of underground operations. If he was ever caught, their entire *residentura* staff in Juarez and in El Paso would be blown. Surely he had done this other times with other agents.

She studied the two men as they walked toward her. The other one—he had the gait, the look, the *feel* of a professional. She spotted the bulge in his windbreaker below the man's left armpit. And that would be his weapon. Of course. She thought of the Walther PPK in her shoulder holster, but did not reach her hand toward it, which would be a giveaway.

Pockmark Face spoke first. She immediately braced for anything to go wrong. "Is there a bus for El Paso leaving from the range today?" he asked her in perfect English.

"Yes. It leaves in thirty minutes."

"Too bad, we'll miss it. Might we have some tea with you?"

"It's Lord Grey, if you care for it."

There, she thought, now that they had passed the bonafides code phrases between them. It was done. She nodded at her contact.

They came closer. "Where is the scientist?"

"He's dead."

Pushtkin exhaled softly and glanced quickly all around. He licked his lips and then said, "When?"

"I have no time to go into it," Sanchez replied, walking over to her backpack. Antonov had already reached it, and was poking around with the contents. When she saw him begin to open the outside pocket she grabbed his hand. They locked eyes. "No," she whispered. "Let me do it."

Antonov cursed himself silently. That had been a stupid thing to do. It was *her* carrying device, and she might have had it booby-trapped. He looked back at her appraisingly.

Within seconds, she had pulled out a shoe box and handed it to the KGB agent.

"This will take time to verify," he said.

She shouldered on the backpack, anxious to move out.

"We have no time," Antonov told him. He looked at the woman.

Sanchez nodded her head quickly. "We must leave now. I will brief you as we go, but now we must leave."

"Nobody's going anywhere."

Startled, the Soviets gaped uphill at a man in uniform ten meters away with camouflaged face-paint streaked in green blotches over his face. He had an M16 leveled at them. He had crept up on them while they were talking, and was now half covered by a boulder adjacent to the mining sluice.

"Get your hands up."

As the three of them complied, Antonov's eyes scanned their perimeter. *I deserve this*, he told himself, *for being such an ignorant fool*. He suddenly grew very tired. *My mind is weakening*. He fought to clear his head. *Wake up! This is no time for sniveling like a recruit. . . .* His eyes picked up the soldier's partner off to their left who also covered them. Were they completely surrounded? If they did manage to break contact, they'd be forced to go uphill, and that would be hard.

"We're coming in, Manny," another voice called down from Antonov's left. From the western side of the canyon, Antonov spotted two more figures leapfrogging each other as they neared the first two for closer fields of fire.

"Sir, you'd better keep some distance," the first man called out.

Antonov clenched his teeth. All was lost.

A tap on his hand. The woman standing next to him was looking at him intently. She nodded her head. Antonov knew then that she had a contingency plan.

Santo caught the movement. "You two . . . separate. *Now!* You, lady—put that backpack down and step away from it."

Sanchez did as she was told.

She also deployed the thirty-second timing device.

"I didn't say to open it!"

Sanchez rejoined the others.

Antonov and Sanchez moved apart, Sanchez in the middle, Antonov farther uphill, Pushtkin downhill with the shoe box in his hands, licking his lips. The backpack was several meters to their front.

"Now back away. You—put that shoe box down by that backpack. Now everyone move over there with that sluice to your backs."

They did as they were told.

"Teddy!"

"Yo, Boss!"

"Come on down here and check this stuff out while I cover them. Keep out of the Dai-uy's and Hanlon's line of sight."

"Why are you men doing this to us?" Pushtkin whined. "We are on a backpacking excursion."

Santo ignored the question. "Shut up. All of you . . . down on your knees. Put your hands behind your heads. *No habla Ingles*, huh? Right. *Callate! Bajen a sus rodillas! Ponganse sus manos detras sus cabezas!*" He repeated the order in Russian. The three agents stared at him, stupefied.

Greeley scrambled down the slope, keeping his M16 on the agents.

"It's okay, Teddy. I've got a grip on things. See what they've got."

Sanchez's eyes followed the younger soldier's movements, as Greeley opened the shoe box.

"Holy shit, Manny . . . this box has some kind of wiring in it with silicon chips all over. Christ, there's radiation signs inside, skull and crossbones."

"Check out that backpack." Santo studied the Russians. Suddenly, the color just seemed to drain out of the woman's face. "Something in there you don't want him to see, lady?"

She backed away, closer to the sluice.

Greeley stared at the backpack. "Something's not right, here, boss. I smell sulfur."

God, no! "Teddy—"

The woman and one of the other Russians bolted. In slow motion, Santo raised his M16 to fire and smelled the sulfer from the fuse in his nostrils. He jerked back around for Greeley, who was stepping away from the pack. Santo tackled Greeley to the ground, where they then tumbled together downhill into the streambed.

Ka-wham!

Gas, smoke, concussion. Gagging, they crawled out of the stream, soggy from the water and with their eyes burning from the gas and smoke. *"Get them!"* Santo roared. He tugged on Greeley's shirtsleeve, but the younger soldier didn't budge. Mortified, he saw a huge chunk of splintered wood imbedded deeply in his side. Greeley's face was pale and his pupils were dilated, as he slipped quickly into shock.

The bastards! He shot his head up at the ridgeline, where he could barely make out the figures of the man and the woman

running back for the backpacks he and Greeley had passed on the
way down to carry out the snatch.

Greeley pulled on Santo's sleeve. *"Manny . . . it hurts, oh,
God . . ."*

"Take it easy, you're gonna be all right!" Santo hauled his team
medic out of the stream and scanned the perimeter, trying to locate
the fleeing agents. Already, Hanlon and MacIntyre were shooting
at them as they escaped into the tree line higher up the canyon.

Pushtkin, disoriented and confused, ran for the ridgeline behind
the sluice.

Choppers, inbound! They glanced up at the sky—there was no
mistaking the steady whir of Blackhawk rotor blades. MacIntyre
and Hanlon met Santo by the streambed to guide them in. They
would enter the canyon at any second. "It's the backup teams!"
MacIntyre yelled at Santo. "We'll get them."

Santo grabbed MacIntyre's arm, and pointed at the ridgelines
higher up at the canyon's end. "Someone's gotta stay hot on their
asses!"

MacIntyre glanced back and forth between Greeley and Santo
and back up the canyon, where by now the Soviets were out of
sight. Santo grabbed MacIntyre's arm.

"Greeley will make it. Sir, you gotta round up the rest of the
team, brief Volensky, then come for me. We've got to maintain
visual with those agents. I'm outta here."

Before MacIntyre could reply, Santo sped off uphill, his M16
leveled out in front of him.

Pushtkin crashed wildly through the trees, pine boughs slapping
him in the face. Powder burns from the blast had seared his
exposed hands and arms, but had miraculously spared his eyes—
although his face was sheared clean of eyebrows. His eyelashes
had curled into tight balls of seared hair. His nose felt as if
someone had scrubbed it with hydrochloric acid.

But he was alive! He would escape! The safe house—he had to
get to the safe house on the other side of the mountain range!
Running downhill was easier; he could scramble away from the
confusion, the chaos, button-hook around, get up on the ridges
and reach the motorcycle cache, speed into Las Cruces, link up
with Grzniecki—

No time for thinking, just run!

Panicking, Pushtkin clawed his way up the steep mountainside over the mining sluice. He had to get away before the others could fire upon him. He clawed forward at the ridgelines above the mining sluice, careful not to lose his balance and tumble over a rock wall flanking a cut within the mountainside.

Did he hear helicopters? My God, yes, he did! What to do, oh . . . he fought the mountainside, climbing higher and higher, grasping frantically at tree branches, spikes from the cactus stabbing at his knees and thighs, his mind discounting the pain. Only one thing counted and that was to—

A jungle boot protruded in his path and Pushtkin's feet went flying. He sprawled in the scree and pine needles of the slope, his hands clawing at the shoulder holster strapped across his chest . . . *A cliff! He was slipping toward a cliff! Another meter and he'd—*

He slowed to a stop, suspended upside down, his head scant inches away from the cliff ledge . . . and then he saw the bore of a Colt .45 staring him in the face. Past that, he looked into the glinting eyes of a wiry black American soldier dressed in bloody fatigues.

Pushtkin froze into position upside down on the slope of the mountain, little rivers of granulated pebbles and dirt pooling around his neck and running across his face. His arm cramped, but he didn't dare work out the cramp. One miscalculated move and he'd tumble over the ledge.

"Pull it out slowly with your forefinger and thumb," the soldier told him, pulling back the hammer on his .45. Pushtkin heard it snap into place with a loud click.

Pushtkin's eyes clouded. He had failed. The soldier could easily kill him. If he tried to get up, he might just tumble over the cliff and smash his head on the rocks below. There was no escape, no safe house, no one to rescue him. . . . Slowly, Pushtkin reached inside his shirt and retrieved his pistol from its shoulder holster.

"Hold it by the barrel."

Laying the pistol on his chest, Pushtkin grasped the pistol by the barrel and handed it to the American. The slight movement started him skidding again. "*No—*"

Maslow grabbed the Soviet by the foot with his other hand, wincing in pain where the lips of his side wound pulled and bled.

He ground his teeth and kept a slight pressure on the Russian's ankle.

"You move and you're a dead man."

"I won't move, I swear it! I . . . I *defect*!"

Maslow spotted a tree root underneath the Russian's hips. "Oh? That's rather decent of you. Hold on to that root, and you won't fall."

Pushtkin grabbed the root.

"Now, no other movement."

The Russian nodded his head, and felt more dirt and pebbles run from across his neck, over his chin, across his lips, and up his nostrils. He could not ever remember feeling more vulnerable. His very life depended on what this American would do.

Maslow listened. The sound of the helicopters grew louder. Shouts, orders, the team . . . his team below was guiding them in. What the hell had happened? The explosion. The woman, the other Russian—what of them? This man had the answers.

Maslow pressed the muzzle of his pistol in the hollow of Pushtkin's throat. Then he looked up and scanned the canyon below them. Through the branches, he spotted Hanlon and MacIntyre carrying Greeley onto level ground. Two Blackhawk helicopters hovered above the mining sluice, where soldiers spewed out of them with ropes hanging from their sides like a dragonfly moored in mid-flight by the strands of a spiderweb. He spotted the battlion commander. Where was Santo?

Then he remembered the red pen flare that his team sergeant had given him earlier. He could signal them with that.

"I am going to let go of your foot," he told Pushtkin slowly. "You hang on to this root and you won't fall. But if you try anything . . ."

"I won't, I won't, just get me out of this!"

Maslow let go of him and opened the flap to his ammo pouch on his web belt, where he pulled out the pen flare.

Sergeant First Class Randy Hanlon jumped when he heard the hiss and a splat against the mining sluice beside him. *What the . . . ?* Immediately, he took cover and aimed his M16 at the smoky trail the pen flare had left behind. He followed the trail up the mountainside into the trees, where the smoke slowly dissipated.

"Get down, sir!"

MacIntyre flopped down beside him. One of the teams that had just flown in and fast-roped out of the helicopters hovering above formed a quick security perimeter around the mining sluice and campsite. MacIntyre spotted the starched uniform and easy, loping gait of his battalion commander and a necktied civilian running toward their position. The other chopper maintained its hover, awaiting orders from Volensky.

"What is it?" he said, looking back at Hanlon. Splat! Another flare smacked against the mining sluice beside them. "What the hell is going on?"

Hanlon squinted upslope. "It's a goddam pen flare, Dai-uy!" He unstrapped his binoculars from around his neck and peered through them uphill. He spotted movement. "I'll be a son of a bitch! It's Maslow!"

Ten minutes later, one team from the reaction force had consolidated around the mining sluice. Volensky had ordered the other to sweep the gorge, where they were discovering the bodies. Dixon walked up to Volensky, as the battalion commander debriefed MacIntyre and Hanlon in the center. He said nothing, letting Volensky run the show. Glancing upwards, he spotted a four-man party escorting Maslow and another man down from the mountainside.

"Captain MacIntyre, where is your team sergeant?"

"He took off after the others, sir." Moments later, MacIntyre had told Volensky the entire story—the killings from the night before, Barkowitz and Saxon, their movement through the canyon and capture of the agents. How, just as the choppers were approaching, an explosive had blown, affording the agents an escape.

How Santo had taken off in chase after them.

"He's right, sir. He did the right thing. We caught that Soviet team red-handed, but then that explosive blew. Someone had to stay in line-of-sight contact, so we can pick them up later."

Volensky nodded his head. That was just like Santo. The four-man retrieval party walked into the perimeter. Two men supported Maslow, who was struggling to hold his head up. The other two men held a civilian between them, whose hands had been bound behind him with a strip of quick-close plastic cufflets—faster and simpler than ordinary handcuffs. The man was haggard and beaten. He hung his head in surrender.

Volensky guided Maslow down into a sitting position in the shade, where one of the reaction team's medics attended to his wounds.

MacIntyre and Hanlon joined them, and Pushtkin was placed in a squatting position in front of them for questioning.

"So, Team XO . . . what is your story?"

Maslow lifted his weary head. "Sir, you'll find some bodies down in the gorge, heading back toward White Sands. Apparently, this guy here"—Maslow jerked his head at Pushtkin—"infiltrated with a Spetsnaz team to link up with two people coming from White Sands to rendezvous with them, a man and a woman. Some campers got in the way last night here at their rendezvous site. The Sovs killed them. Now this guy says he wants to defect."

Volensky's left cheek twitched and he swung his attention to the Soviet before him. Pushtkin glanced away.

Dixon could retain his silence no longer. "Colonel, I'd like to know what in Christ's name is going on around here."

"A lot of chefs stirring the stew pot, Mister Dixon," Volensky replied. "Looks like even the FBI lacks the agents to comb these mountains." Volensky led Dixon away from the group congregating around the Soviet agent, preparing him for extraction back to the FOB.

"Mr. Dixon," Volensky began, "we can either work together on this, or we can continue to butt heads through needless bureaucracy. The simple fact remains that there are enemy agents on the loose, and I have the assets and manpower standing by to track them down. You could shut this entire operation down and do it by the book, by calling in your reinforcements. On the other hand, you could allow me to retain control of my men and I'll report to you."

Dixon pursed his lips. "What do you propose?" he said finally.

Volensky pulled an acetate-covered map of the area out of his cargo pocket and, squatting, spread it over his knee. Dixon knelt next to Volensky and squinted at the map. "We can reasonably assume that this whole thing has been a Soviet attempt to steal SDI secrets," Volensky began.

"But what about *glasnost, perestroika,* all that jazz?"

"What about the fact that maybe we have a workable SDI

system?" Volensky countered. "Don't you think that maybe the other side had a mole on the base, gathering information? Hell, look at it this way, Mr. Dixon . . . if the Soviets actually did plan this operation, you can bet it's without the blessing of their President. My bet is that this is a KGB adventure. If their mission succeeds, then so much the better when considering the Star Wars race. If the mission is a failure, then the hard-liners can blame the president, and let the fiasco discredit him in front of the rest of the world."

"Well . . ."

"At any rate," Volensky said, pointing to their location on the map, "according to what my detachment commander told me, there are two other agents on the loose. One of my team sergeants is following them. His name is Santo, a fine soldier. I also have a helicopter scanning the area intermittently which spotted the two agents as we flew in. The question is when to pick them up."

"You could do it easily enough now. You can mobilize your entire battalion, chopper them out into these mountains, form screen and blocking positions, then hunt them down that way."

"Or," Volensky said slowly, standing up, "we can finesse this situation."

"What?"

"What you suggest is too heavy-handed. Let's find their reception party—people supporting their operation, such as an exfiltration team. We can maintain surveillance on the escaping agents, as my man Sergeant Santo is doing. That will give us time to interrogate our new prisoner," Volensky added, tossing his head toward the captured Soviet over by MacIntyre and Maslow. "We could blow the entire spy network in this part of the country."

Dixon glanced at the Soviet prisoner. "I'd like to know what he's got to say."

Volensky grinned. "Let's find out." The two men approached the wide-eyed Soviet.

"Your name?" Volensky asked him.

"Boris—" Pushtkin started, then stopped, his mouth an O. The American officer had spoken to him in Russian.

Volensky reached out and squeezed the KGB agent's cheek, then clapped him lightly there three times, as if they were good friends. "Tell me your name, my friend."

"Boris *Petrovich!*" Pushtkin lied. "I—I defect!"

"Yes, of course. We will take very good care of you, Boris Petrovich." Volensky stood up and clasped his hands behind his back, looking down on the agent with contempt. A Blackhawk returned to their position, maintaining a low hover. The group then walked toward the helicopter, Pushtkin in tow.

"Tell me everything, Boris Petrovich," Volensky told him after they had climbed inside and buckled up, Pushtkin handcuffed to the seat beside him. "Your mission, how many of you there are, your contacts . . . everything."

Pushtkin babbled other lies.

CHAPTER FIFTEEN

The morning sun popped out over the canyon walls at the same time Major Sergei Antonov and Victoria Sanchez emerged from what was left of the shadows onto the top of the main series of ridgelines that would lead them into Soledad Canyon.

They knew they were exposed. For the past two hours of running, they'd only had time to rest briefly amidst the rocks and overhangs of intermittent cliffs paralleling their route south— south to safety and escape.

And south, Antonov knew, to the dirt-bike cache his team had established two days earlier. An eternity of time earlier. Where was his team now? he thought bitterly. What of Grodniko, his senior sergeant, of Chelstovsky, his communicator?

Antonov took his rage out on the mountainside, the slopes of this damnable American mountain desert not unlike the terrain he'd encountered in Afghanistan. His team now consisted of the woman with him—but he could have done worse. At least she was keeping up, unlike the KGB swine he'd carried so far during his mission.

"We must find a hide site."

Antonov became suddenly alert. It was one of the few times his new partner had spoken. They stopped alongside a cliff wall at the top of the ridgeline, and each pulled a canteen of water from their backpacks, now lightened by the necessity for speed. When the bomb had blown, they'd barely had time to grab his and Pushtkin's gear left behind at their surveillance site prior to linking up. They carried only the essentials—weapons, two rations apiece, and water. And soon, they would be out of water.

"It is no use running like this during the day," Sanchez added, appraising her new partner. Would this man be a burden like Sorens? No. This man was a soldier. She could easily tell by his sense of urgency and his cool actions when she'd blown the bomb earlier at the handoff sight. And now, Ash Canyon was three kilometers behind them.

"You're right. A cave would be perfect. We must rest."

"I know of a place. Let me see your map, comrade."

Antonov pulled an acetate-laminated map out of his hiking trousers and handed it to the strong, dark woman by his side. *So, she knows how to read a map*, he thought. *That is good. Her training must have been far more complete than that fool Pushtkin's.*

Moments later, Sanchez pointed at a series of contour lines jumbled tightly together in the general vicinity they had reached. "I know of a mining site at this location." She stood up and walked the few meters left to the top of the north-south ridgeline they had been following. Antonov walked alongside her, his ears alert for the noise of the helicopters that had been sweeping the area. Then they were on top, the rest of the Organ Mountain chain sprawled at their feet.

Sanchez pointed to an adjacent ridgeline south by southwest of their present location. "One more kilometer—we travel downhill, careful to stay near the canyon walls, then we climb up that scree slope in the distance. See that hole in the ridgeline over there? That is a mine. We can stop there."

Suddenly, the whir of approaching helicopter blades cut through the desert morning air. Sanchez and Antonov scrambled down the slope in the direction of the cave, where they holed up in a gully twisting the rest of the way down the mountain. Cactus, stunted pines, lizards—and rocks. They hid in the rocks with the lizards and the snakes.

A Blackhawk helicopter swept a hundred feet overhead, and the two Soviets felt the blast of heated desert air blow sand around them, stinging their skin. They hugged the dry rocks and scree of the gully. The helicopter passed, and continued its search pattern throughout the area. When they saw it pass by the next ridgeline to the south, they sprang to their feet and fled down the mountainside.

Five hundred meters away, Master Sergeant Manny Santo crouched on top of the same ridgeline, watching them make for the opposite mountain. Where were they going? His eyes traced their direction of travel, and then he spotted the abandoned mine. Of course. To travel anymore during the day spelled suicide for them. They were going to hole up in the cave. Before they could reach it, Santo raced down the mountainside in a gully that twisted and turned to the base of the mountain.

Another helicopter zoomed in from the north, the first helicopter's partner. Santo hugged the ground to blend in with his surroundings, not wanting the people he was following to know of his whereabouts. At the last second, he yanked out the sand-camouflaged netting for his rucksack he'd stored in his web belt's butt pack and spread it over him.

The helicopter passed overhead and kept going.

Santo stuffed the camouflaged netting back into his butt pack and raced down the mountainside, his senses fully alert and every footstep calculated and sure. One slip, one fall, and he'd have a sprained ankle. He didn't need that.

What he needed were the two Russians left—the man and the woman—who had hurt his family. His team. Barkowitz, dead. Greeley, hurt and hurt bad. Maslow, cut. He would get the bastards.

Was it that? Revenge? And wasn't it guilt too, that he had let Greeley down by not suspecting the booby-trapped backpack? He had to assume the blame, he should have known better.

Santo had to admit that he had initially given chase to the fleeing agents for those two reasons—guilt and revenge. But also, and more importantly, if his team's operation was going to mean anything, if whatever Barkowitz had died for was going to amount to anything . . . no, it wasn't just guilt and revenge. There was a mission to complete. The intent of that mission was to capture Soviet agents violating the security of the United States, and specifically, the security of the White Sands Missile Range. They had to be caught, and they had to be caught with the remainder of their contacts, however many of them there were.

He would follow them and somehow contact the FOB. There

were ways. The helicopters in pursuit, scanning the desert mountains, ridgelines, and valleys—MacIntyre had told them to be on the lookout for him. Hopefully, they had the sense not to compromise his pursuit. He could signal the choppers at the right moment.

For now, if he could just keep going, he could reach the ridgeline above that cave and then watch them from there, and then he too could rest. He hadn't had time to think clearly, to make a plan.

But when he stopped, he'd think of something.

There *was* a way for the mission to succeed.

Inside the abandoned mine, Victoria Sanchez laid two civilian Mountain House freeze-dried rations on a smooth shelf of granite. The shaft was clean, blown dry and sterilized by the relentless heat of the desert and the lack of moisture. Inside, it was cool. She so badly needed rest. Too much had happened. She stared at the foil packets of dehydrated rations, calculating if they had the water to spare to rehydrate and eat them.

She looked up at her new partner. Could she trust this man? She knew it was better to trust no one. But in this situation, survival demanded cooperation.

Antonov stood by the entrance of the cave, staring out at the twisted valleys and slopes of sun-blasted rock and cactus below. Sanchez walked up behind him.

"We must rest, comrade."

"Do not call me comrade. I am a soldier."

"Then what do I call you?"

"Major Sergei Antonov."

"I am Sanchez."

"Pushtkin told me your name."

"That ass!"

Antonov grinned. "My sentiments exactly."

"He is responsible for this colossal mess."

"It does not matter, Victoria Sanchez. What matters now is our escape."

She nodded her head. Then she climbed to her feet and walked out the ledge, where Antonov resumed surveilling the valley below.

"I'll take first watch," Antonov muttered.

"Wake me in two hours."

Antonov walked back inside the mine shaft and retrieved his binoculars from his backpack.

"What is it?"

"I thought I saw something below." Antonov brought the binoculars to his eyes.

Sanchez tensed, automatically reaching for the Walther PPK in her shoulder holster. Antonov caught the movement and uttered a short, dry laugh.

Sanchez lowered her eyes. "It is futile."

Antonov shrugged his shoulders. "No, there is nothing out there. My mind is playing tricks."

"Perhaps."

"And then again, perhaps not, eh?"

"We must level with each other, Antonov."

A slight pause. Then: "Yes, it is the only way. I take it you kept some of the documents on your person. The technology we came to get—it was destroyed in the explosion, yes?"

Sanchez opened her mouth in surprise. "Yes . . ."

"Good. Keep them. We could always use those documents for bargaining."

"Our plan, Sergei Antonov—we must make a plan and decide on how we will escape from this desert and from this country."

"Yes. I presume you have other contacts?"

"And *I* presume you had an exfiltration team?"

They stared at each other for several moments. Antonov spoke first. "Pushtkin had arranged for an exfiltration team—his agents in Juarez. They have a safe house near Las Cruces."

Sanchez spat onto the floor of the cave. "Consisting of men from the Mexican drug cartel his *residentura* monitored and advised. It is madness to work with the drug people. They will sell you out."

"I saw what drugs did to the Red Army in Afghanistan . . . opium and heroin . . . I agree. They are cutthroats."

"And do you think we should contact this exfiltration team?"

Antonov's brow furrowed in thought. "Pushtkin gave me the coordinates for the linkup site before we met you and radioed in the actuation signal."

"And do you really think, Major Antonov, that Pushtkin's people will protect us and exfiltrate us without our beloved

Comrade Pushtkin? Do you suppose that even *with* Pushtkin we would be allowed to live?"

Antonov thought for a moment. This woman was shrewd and had been reading his mind. "Our mission here was to exfiltrate you and the scientist. . . ."

"The scientist, maybe. With him alive they would have kept me alive as well. But as for you and your team, conducting this deniable operation for the *Rodina*? How many men did you come here with? How many are now dead and in the hands of the Americans? Do you really think Pushtkin's people in Las Cruces will save you? I think you know the answer to that."

Antonov slowly nodded his head. She was right. The mission had been compromised. Before charges could be leveled against the Soviet Union, his own country would eliminate all traces of the mission. And that demanded his head. If he was lucky, he'd be shot. A chill snaked across his shoulder blades as he thought of the oven back in GRU headquarters.

"Of course you do," Sanchez continued. "I believe our fate was determined by Pushtkin and his people long before this operation began. They were to eliminate all traces of the operation if anything went wrong."

"You are right. There could have been no other way."

"I have contacts of my own."

Antonov arched an eyebrow.

"When we ran from the Americans in the canyon, I saw Pushtkin trying to escape in a different direction. He had to have been caught by the helicopters and the other Americans."

"Yes, I think so. His kind is never at home in the field. He was more suited for the urban environment."

"Then let us assume he was caught . . . alive. The Americans would not be fool enough to kill him. At this moment, he is talking to save his own skin."

"I agree."

"Then the exfiltration team is entirely out of the question."

"You are perceptive. I agree. So tell me of *your* plan."

Sanchez studied Antonov's gray eyes. "The less you know, the better. But have faith in me, Major. Your map—show it to me."

Antonov gave her the map. "The Las Cruces–El Paso highway is only twenty-three kilometers away from here traveling due west," she said after a moment. "I have contacts in El Paso. From there, we can get across the border."

"And how will I know you won't burn me as well?"

Sanchez handed the map back to her new partner. "You will have to take my word for it."

"A rare commodity, trust."

"But a vital one."

Neither spoke for several moments. Antonov resumed scanning the valley below with his binoculars. Sanchez turned to go back into the dark confines of the mine shaft and rest.

"I have a motorcycle cache about two kilometers from here in a ravine adjacent to Soledad Canyon. At night, that will cut our traveling time by two thirds."

Sanchez turned about, incredulous. "What of the helicopters—we'll be easier to spot!"

"How much water do *you* have, Comrade Sanchez?"

Sanchez said nothing.

"Have you a better idea? Or would you rather travel over these mountains without water?"

Victoria Sanchez nodded her head at the man standing before her. Then she lay down on the cool sandstone of the mine shaft, cautious and alert. Any sudden move from Antonov would automatically awaken her. Her mind focused on the bulge inside her shirt, her pistol. Then she thought of the plastic bag strapped around her waist containing the RAIL blueprints. Insurance on both counts.

She trusted no one. But she had to work with this man. For now, it was the only way.

Antonov continued to scan the ridgelines with his binoculars. *Had* he seen movement earlier? Had they been spotted? If so, then by how many? How many more of the Americans trailed him and his new partner?

Time would tell.

Two hundred meters away from them, Santo sipped continuously from the two-quart canteen he'd lifted from his rucksack before giving chase to the two agents. For the past hour since he'd spotted the two enemy agents entering the mine shaft, he'd crawled up a narrow gully littered with loose rocks to the top of the adjacent ridgeline of their position. He'd just kept out of sight from them. Finally, when he emerged, he had spotted a good observation post near the top of the mountain. It was sheltered on three sides from the wind. It offered shadow and that was good. For today, he would rehydrate himself with the two-quart canteen. When it was gone, he would have two one-quart canteens left, which were suspended on his web belt. He'd have to save those for the cross-country movement tonight.

And when those were used up, then . . .

Well, he'd just have to make do.

Now, he needed to conserve energy. Get some sleep. They wouldn't move before nightfall. He glanced at his watch and then looked at the sun. It was midday on both counts. That meant at least eight hours before the two would leave the cave.

He had to sleep.

Tumbleweeds bounced across the desolation of Oro Grande Range Camp, driven with abandon by the mid-morning heat and wind. A few of them hit against the quonset hut that had once housed MacIntyre's team. Now, one team member was dead, two in the hospital at Bliss, and one still out in the field.

And now, the team hootch was the location for Pushtkin's interrogation.

"Contrary to popular belief, mate, we soldiers and spooks, if you will, in the American Army . . . will not torture you to make you a little more, ahem, cooperative. You see—we know you've been lying to us."

Pushtkin swallowed and opened his eyes a little wider at the sandy-haired man standing before him at his full height of six feet three inches. Every now and then, that man—who had openly introduced himself as intelligence and interrogation specialist Staff Sergeant Bernie Haywood—would pop his hands behind his back, legs slightly apart, and rock on his heels. Pushtkin despised the British and their fastidious ways. But what was a Britisher doing in the American Army?

"Does that come as such a great big bloody fucking surprise, mate?"

"I have already told you everything!"

"But you've been fibbing, Boris. Come now—you're with the KGB! You're a smart cookie!" Haywood smiled thinly at the Soviet seated before him. The battalion commander's decision to debrief the KGB agent after an hour-long wait upon return to the FOB had been a good one—it had given Pushtkin time to worry. And his decision to have him debriefed in the snatch team's sterilized isolation area had been equally as good. There had been no fuss, no attention. The remainder of the teams throughout the battalion were conducting business as usual, with the exception of the STRIKE force company, which was gearing up for an operation later on that night. The nature of that operation was predicated on the outcome of Pushtkin's interrogation.

Pushtkin swallowed again and stared at the bodies of Navarro and Chelstovsky, the dead Spetsnaz communicator, that the Americans had laid out on ambulance stretchers before him. "You play with me," he said nervously. Pushtkin could not take his eyes off the ant that crawled in and out of Navarro's right nostril. *Why were the Americans doing this?* "Mind games . . . all of it is a game with the mind to make me say anything."

"I admit, Comrade Pushtkin—"

"My name is not Pushtkin! It is Petrovich!"

Haywood leaned close to Pushtkin's face. "Your name is bloody well Boris Pushtkin."

Special Agent John Peterson, CIA liaison, walked up to Haywood and handed him a manila folder, which contained the data Dixon had requested through Interpol's fax line and data bank. Peterson had to admit that the intel specialist working for Volensky was good. Haywood was a transplanted Brit who, once having emigrated to the States, could not keep his finger out of the cloak-and-dagger business. He'd once been an intelligence analyst for the elite British Special Air Service.

Haywood glanced briefly through the file. Volensky and Dixon were seated next to MacIntyre and Hanlon near the opposite wall of the isolation area, listening closely to the interchange. Haywood nodded his head at Volensky.

Volensky acknowledged with the smallest of smiles. After muttering something to Dixon, he got up and wandered over to Haywood and Pushtkin, lighting up a fresh cigarette.

Pushtkin fidgeted in his chair. *What kind of Army is this? Russians, British? Who else belongs in this American Army?*

"As I was saying, Comrade *Pushtkin*," Haywood continued, "we have enough information on you from this morning's events and what we have gathered through our data banks to extract the rest of what we need to know through other means." Haywood grinned boyishly and finger-combed his sandy hair back over the crown of his head. "For example, we know that you are a KGB agent under diplomatic cover at your *residentura*, as you call your intelligence headquarters, stationed in Juarez. Also, we have discovered your photo located in our Drug Enforcement Administration's files, depicting your meetings with one Luis Munoz, a drug-trafficker in Mexico they keep tabs on. We've matched that photo with the personnel file the CIA maintains on all Soviet diplomats serving in Mexico and Cuba. Further investigations on your activities in the past reveal that you are suspected of having constructed the Cuban Intelligence drug-contacts liaison department for operations throughout the Caribbean basin. So please, Boris *Pushtkin*—feel free to open up."

Pushtkin's mouth hung open, and then he clamped it shut, swallowing, saying nothing.

Volensky barked a short, brittle laugh. He brought his cigarette up to his mouth and kept his hand suspended there while he cupped his right elbow in his left hand. Then he blew smoke in Pushtkin's face and scowled at him.

Pushtkin paled. His eyes darted back and forth between the bodies and the two men standing before him. He licked his lips. "Torture then. I thought so. That won't work and you know it." Somehow, he didn't think he sounded convincing enough, as the sweat stains growing underneath his armpits attested. The American Russian standing before him blew more smoke in his face. Pushtkin found himself staring at the ash drooping on the end of the cigarette. How would it be? Burns? Electric shock? The file? There were infinite techniques. He, of course . . . knew them all.

"Yes," Haywood continued, "there are quite a few ways indeed, Comrade Pushtkin, with which we could find out what we need to know. And, my friend, we *do* have a need to know. A man's life depends on it—not to mention national security."

"That's for damned sure," MacIntyre uttered from the rear of the room, thinking of Santo. A quick glance from Volensky cut him short.

"You say you defect," Volensky said to him for the first time. "Then why don't you tell us of your exfiltration team? Tell us how and when you planned to escape from the country after your rendezvous in Ash Canyon with your White Sands mole. Her name, I believe"—Volensky paused for dramatic effect, glancing back at Dixon and then back to Pushtkin—"is Victoria Sanchez."

"We were to exfiltrate on our own," Pushtkin said quickly. "We had a motorcycle cache planted to do that."

"Why do I refuse to believe that, Boris Pushtkin? Eh?" Volensky smiled at him, arching his eyebrows. "They say here in America—never bullshit a bullshitter. I know how your mind works. Now tell me of your exfiltration support team. Who were you to meet and where?"

Pushtkin had already chewed his lower lip into bleeding chaps. Maybe he could tell them a little more, mislead them with half-truths. Yes, that was the only way. "We were to meet a contact team in El Paso tonight, on the boundary of the Fort Bliss Military Reservation."

"Time?"

"22—no, 2300."

"And then?"

"We were to link up with our auxiliary network in town to get across the border."

"Bullshit!"

"What?"

Volensky shot a dark look at Peterson, the CIA agent, who had taken a seat in the background. "Take over! You know what to do!"

"No . . ." Pushtkin whimpered, "no . . ."

Peterson walked slowly over to the KGB man, letting him squirm. In his hand, he clasped a little black bag, not unlike a country doctor's tool kit. This was going to be easy. The FOB had enough information now to ask him the yes-and-no-type questions. So let him think it was going to be torture. Comrade Pushtkin really thought his nuts were going to be squeezed. Good.

"Relax, buddy," Peterson told him. "You're in the good old U. S. of A., not KGB headquarters in Dzerzhinsky Square. We have a different style." He unzipped his black bag slowly.

Perspiration beaded on Pushtkin's upper lip.

Peterson pulled out a syringe and a vial from the black bag. He loaded the syringe with a clear fluid from a vial marked Sodium Thiopental.

"Truth serum?" Pushtkin asked incredulously.

Haywood clapped him on his shoulder and then rolled up Pushtkin's sleeve, as Peterson prepared the syringe. "Of course, laddie. We aren't barbarians, you know. Now do be a cooperative chap and try to relax for us."

Pushtkin flinched and then sighed as the needle stuck him in the hollow of his arm. Well, he had tried.

When it was done, Volensky and Dixon sketched out a tentative course of action against the safe house near Las Cruces Pushtkin had told them about. Volensky had left the interrogation team with Pushtkin to mop up remaining traces of information, and had given specific orders to be left alone while he conceptualized the overall game plan.

Five minutes before, Volensky's communications and electronics officer had delivered a message from the White Sands Missile Range that said the level of priority on the RAIL project had been downgraded three months ago, given alternative radiation-enhanced micro-chip-circuitry research that would eventually supersede it. RAIL was still a viable plan for SDI missile-guidance systems, but would probably be scrapped in the near future, given the now-apparent alternative and potentially better systems currently under development.

"The helicopter we have out scanning the area spotted the agents again about an hour ago. I was told right before the interrogation. Pushtkin confirmed their names—Major Sergei Antonov and Victoria Sanchez." Volensky bent back over the map and stuck his finger over a grid square. "There," he told Dixon. "The helicopter spotted them there. Santo was following them from about five hundred meters behind."

Dixon scanned the map until he found the town of Las Cruces indicated on the western side of the Organ Mountains. Starting from the safe house's location Pushtkin had informed them about, he counted the grid squares between the safe house and the two agents on the run. "No more than twelve to fifteen kilometers. They can cover that distance in one night."

"Well, then—we either snatch them now, or wait until they link up with their rendezvous team. Plus, I have reaction force on standby, waiting for an operations order to take the safe house down."

Dixon weighed the pros and cons in his mind. If they took the two agents now, then they had two agents. If they took the safe house, they could capture Pushtkin's entire KGB cell and their drug contacts, but that might allow a chance for the two agents to escape. It had to be one or the other. If they took the two agents now, it might alert any enemy surveillance in place at their rendezvous point. They might have snipers poised, ready to terminate the agents before a snatch team could capture them. On the other hand . . .

"Colonel," Dixon said finally, "I can downlink satellite data from FBI headquarters onto your monitors inside your headquarters building—uh, your FOB as you call it. The DEA rep—Wiggins—he can do the same from his data banks. That'll provide us a constant eyeballing of the safe house area for all movement in and out of the access roads. That safe house—if we were to hit it with one of your STRIKE teams—would be of more importance than those two agents from the canyon this morning."

Volensky gnawed the inside of his cheek. Manny Santo was loose in the mountains chasing Antonov and Sanchez down. Logic said he was doing it to maintain human visual contact for future military operations, like the snatch he and Dixon were considering. Another thought, a less professional thought, said that Santo was following them for revenge. . . .

As Volensky considered this, two men entered the isolation area and approached him.

"I wish to be left alone for now, Team Leader."

MacIntyre exchanged looks with Hanlon as they stood before Volensky and Dixon. "Sir. Sergeant Santo is out there by himself. Greeley's in serious condition and Maslow's cut up pretty bad. Barkowitz is dead. That leaves me and Sergeant Hanlon."

"Get on with it."

"Sir, include us on this mission."

"I have fresh teams standing by. You two rest up."

"Sir, we know who and what to look for. We've seen the agents. We know the Organ Mountains better than anyone else in the battalion. And we'll have all the rest we need by the time you deploy any kind of reaction force."

"What are you doing, Team Leader, testing me?" Volensky

squinted hard at the young officer standing before him. "Go on. Get the hell out of here."

MacIntyre worked his mouth in anger, starting to speak. Hanlon grabbed his arm. MacIntyre shrugged it off. Then he wheeled about and headed for the door.

Hanlon saluted his battalion commander. "Sir . . ."

"Beat it."

Dixon stared after the departing soldiers. "Their team got chewed up pretty bad, Colonel," he said after the door closed behind them.

"Yes, well the score is fucking well fifty-fifty," Volensky replied bitterly, thinking of the corpses they'd made Pushtkin look at during the interrogation earlier. He shook his head and then glanced back at the map. "The safe house it is."

"We'll wait until tonight to hit it, say around 0400, 0500 hours, and snatch all personnel there. That will give time for me to lay on FBI support to seal off the area, time for continual intelligence updates from the NSA and the CIA. It'll also provide you more time to get your teams ready."

"I'll send in some people early to put point surveillance on it."

Thirty minutes later, Volensky summoned the officers and team sergeants from MacIntyre's company into the isolation area.

"We have all the information now. We scared the KGB agent a little to open him up. The Sodium Thiopental did the rest. Company commander!"

"Sir!" Major Halley Richards, MacIntyre's boss, popped up before his battalion commander like a marionette. They came in all shapes, attitudes, and personalities in Special Forces, and Richards was no exception—he was the archetypical bachelor who had blazed a trail of tears and broken hearts over the past fifteen years of his adult life. He was blond, a weight lifter, and an egomaniac when it came to downhill skiing and driving. He loved talking about himself. He wore tailored fatigues. He was hyperactive. He could be as obnoxious as hell.

But he was also a good soldier and leader, and that was why Volensky had him commanding one of his companies.

Volensky pointed at the map on the briefing board. The officers from the two joint STRIKE teams and their operations sergeants and team technicians clustered around the map board. "Your mission, Company Commander, is to infiltrate this area of operations on my order and capture approximately twenty personnel who are drug-smugglers working in tandem with a KGB drug-subversion cell from Juarez. These people are also supporting the exfiltration of the Spetsnaz team who penetrated White Sands security this morning."

"No guts, no glory, sir!"

Volensky scowled at the company commander. "Spare me your platitudes, Company Commander, before I reach a higher plane of existence."

The cluster of men around Richards chuckled, then fell silent. All liked the Old Man, the Mad Russian. They were more than willing to go to hell with him in gasoline-soaked drawers. The Mad Russian was the kind of commander who would do the same for his men and not think twice of it. They liked his gruff way.

"How you accomplish this, Company Commander, is initially up to you. Brief me on your concept in one hour, and then we will finalize your plan together. You will conduct the STRIKE on the enemy's safe house before daybreak, say around 0330 hours. Time on target is on my order. I will brief you on exact details upon receiving your concept."

"Clear, sir."

Captain Matt MacIntyre and Sergeant First Class Randy Hanlon shouldered their way up front. Volensky caught their movement. "You three stay behind with me," he told them, clapping Richards's shoulder. "Okay, that's all for now." He took the men before him in with one sweeping gaze. "You men from Charlie Company do your duty and make me proud of you," he told them sternly.

A respectful murmur assented, and then the assembly of officers, warrant officers, and master sergeants dissipated toward their respective team-isolation areas to prepare for the mission.

"And if you fuck it up, I'll kill you!"

They laughed before exiting the door. Volensky turned toward Richards. "One more thing for your plan, Company Commander."

"Sir."

"These two will be your point-surveillance trolls."

MacIntyre and Hanlon breathed sighs of relief. Richards nodded his head.

"It's their team sergeant out there," Volensky added with his sardonic grin. "Let *them* call in the STRIKE force."

Chapter Sixteen

Santo shot upright, his head butting the desert camouflage netting he'd stretched over the cactus beside him for shade. He glanced at his watch, and confirmed mechanical time with his own biological clock as 2030 hours. He'd overslept by thirty minutes.

The agents! Santo peered out from underneath the camouflaged netting down the slope toward the cave. The shadows were back. Off to the right across from the north-south ridgelines, the setting sun threw its last rays of light in his direction.

Santo pulled out the Zeiss binoculars that were buttoned inside his fatigue shirt and scanned the mine shaft along the ridgeline three hundred meters away. He saw movement. Thank God, they were still there. The woman squatted at the mine's entrance, her head just visible over a jumble of boulders guarding the opening.

He glanced up. Already, the moon was out, its pale, shimmering face suspended in the darkening blue sky. The planets were out too—Venus and Mars—and the evening's first stars from Orion. EENT (End of Evening Nautical Twilight) was being ushered in quickly, as usually was the case in the desert, along with a rapid drop in temperature.

Santo ate the remainder of his assault ration for his evening meal, consisting of jerky sticks and dry cocoa powder. He drained the remainder of his two-quart canteen, rolled up the bladder, and stuffed it inside his trousers cargo pocket. He shivered—the temperature had already plummeted from the daytime high of 105 degrees to seventy, and the drastic change alone was enough to put a steady drain on his body heat that would last all night when the mercury bottomed out at sixty. He pulled out a field-jacket liner from his butt pack and shrugged it on. Once he moved out, he would put it away and let the calories from the assault ration burn and give him the energy he needed.

Thirty minutes later, when the sun had disappeared, EENT came. Enough moonlight existed for easy observation when he started tracking the agents. Santo's binoculars amplified the moonlight, and he could still see the cave. He took off his field-jacket liner and shoved it back inside his butt pack, waiting for the two agents to come out.

The agents exited to resume their hike south. Santo followed them slowly, masked from their sight by always staying in a gully or behind a sand mogul or a knoll in the ridgeline.

An hour passed. Two. The two agents stopped for a breather once they had crested the top of a long and steep ridgeline leading to the top of a shallow canyon. Santo eyed their position for a moment, and then angled up the mountainside, scanning them from above, keeping them in sight with his binoculars. The terrain looked familiar. He pulled out his map and studied it for a moment. After making a compass bearing and studying the major terrain features of hilltops and ridgelines, he knew he was at the top of Dorsey Canyon. Two and a half klicks almost due south would lead them to the major east-west approach throughout the breadth of the Organ Mountains known as Soledad Canyon.

Soledad Canyon. He wondered why the two agents were heading in that direction—it was a broad canyon, a valley, actually, flanked on both sides by an endless series of ridgelines from adjacent mountain chains and other canyons. It was a main avenue of approach from the Las Cruces area into the White Sands Missile Range/Fort Bliss military reservations. Both White Sands and Fort Bliss security would have observation posts littered all along the roadway there, looking for the agents.

Santo deduced then that they were heading for a contact team for a rendezvous somewhere in the canyon. A cache, contact team, anything. But at least the chase would not go on much longer.

Five minutes later, after the agents resumed their hike south, the helicopter returned.

Santo started, upon hearing the Blackhawk's approach. Strangely, it had been silent for the past three hours, and he hadn't remembered his sleep being interrupted during the daylight from aerial surveillance. This had been the first time the chopper had flown by in at least eight hours. Quickly, he got a fix on where the Soviet and the Mexican woman lay hidden in the rocks. Santo was in a more exposed position, and the sector of ridgeline he was on was only dotted by enough brush to conceal him laterally, but not from above.

Santo swore softly under his breath, hoping the bird would not get a fix on him. If it did, and if it started hovering above him with its spotlight, the two agents would get away without anyone on the ground to watch them and tail them.

Blast it! As little cover as he had now, he might as well bring the bird in with his strobe light. . . .

The strobe light! Santo recalled the clandestine aerial communications classes he and Barkowitz had been working out with the chopper pilots back in the rear. . . .

Santo yanked out his strobe light from its cord-laced pouch on his left shoulder strap. The strobe light emitted a pulsating flash of light normally used to beacon incoming aircraft toward a pickup zone on the ground. It had an infrared cover for usage with pilots wearing night-vision goggles for clandestine signaling behind enemy lines. The chopper pilots above had to be using AN/PVS-5 night-vision goggles now that it was nighttime.

Barkowitz'd had an idea the previous week on how to jury-rig all team members' strobe lights with a bypass switch controlling the flash sequence. With that switch, a man on the ground could communicate by infrared Morse with incoming helicopters, provided they knew of the technique.

People had laughed at the idea, but Ed Barkowitz had made his idea happen with Santo's eager blessing. A couple of the pilots out of the crew of six assigned this year with the battalion out at Oro Grande had displayed more than a passing interest.

Now was the time to see if it worked. It was either that or be lit up like a Christmas tree with the incoming bird's spotlight.

Santo swallowed and flipped on the switch.

"Movement at four o'clock, Chuckie," CW3 Tom Delano told his copilot, CW2 Chuck Pence. Delano adjusted the focus knobs of his night-vision goggles. "One man—he's in uniform. That's gotta be Santo!"

"Anything else?"

"No, can't make anything out."

"Still must be following the two rabbits."

"He was driving on pretty hard earlier in the day." Delano remembered seeing Santo on the ridgeline, and then, moments later, he had disappeared. He had standing orders from Volensky to maintain visual contact with Santo, but to make it appear as if he was on a dry run, not to blow the team sergeant's cover during the chase. "Make a pass, and don't let it seem like we spotted him, Chuckie."

"Rog-o, Boss."

A splash of light! "Christ, Chuck, slow down!"

Chuck Pence cut the throttle and lost a little altitude. Delano only called him Chuck when he was serious.

Delano whipped off his PVS-5's. Nothing. He put the night-vision goggles back on, and saw more flashes of light. "We've got one of those Morse messages on infrared, bubba. I'll keep Santo in visual, and you fly around in a lazy-eight like he isn't there. Also, keep an eye out for the two rabbits."

"Rog-o, Boss."

More flashes, some of them sustained, some short. Delano spelled out the message: AM IN CONTACT EN ROUTE SOLEDAD HAVE STRIKE ON STANDBY FOR SNATCH MY SIGNAL ACTIVITIES.

Delano waited for more. There was none. Unfortunately, he hadn't received one of the special strobe lights so he could reply. Then he remembered that would be useless, unless the man on the ground had night-vision goggles as well.

But at least he had listened to that one team's idea concerning infrared Morse ground-aerial communications, and was glad that he had. It seemed that the best training in Special Forces came from the ground up.

"Back to the FOB, Chuckie. Got a hot one for the Old Man."

"Most ricky-tick, Boss." Chuckie Pence grinned hugely underneath a regulation-defying pilot's mustache and opened the throttle.

The whir of the blades rescinded back into the quiet of the cool desert night. Sanchez pulled on Antonov's shirtsleeve. "Come."

She started to climb out from behind the rocks and barrel cactus they'd been hiding in.

"Wait." Antonov scanned all around their position with his binoculars.

"See something?"

"No," Antonov eventually answered.

"Are you . . . sure?"

"No. I'm not. But what difference does it make now?"

Santo waited until they took off down the long, winding canyon, contouring the eastern ridgelines. He followed them, hoping his message had gotten through. The choppers would fly back in intermittent scans, so as not to set up a pattern. He'd just have to make do. At least they hadn't identified him with the spotlight, so maybe that meant they did get the message. The next go-round with the birds would tell.

He followed the agents until 2200 hours, when they took another fifteen-minute break. They entered a draw just before exiting Dorsey Canyon into the east-west expanse of Soledad Canyon.

The fifteen-minute break turned into twenty. Then twenty-five. Santo crawled out from one of the endless series of gullies slashing all mountainsides throughout the Organ Mountains, and made quietly for their position. What the hell were they doing? Could this possibly be their contact site? There was only one way to find out.

He crawled on his belly the last few meters until he spotted them below. When he saw them, he let his hand caress the black-ribbed plastic of his M16A2 rifle, wondering when and how he should use it.

For the first time during the chase, he could hear their voices.

After Antonov had cleared away the brush guarding the entrance of a hole in the rocks by the cliff face, she stared openmouthed as the Soviet Spetsnaz major wheeled out a dirt bike.

"I don't believe it."

"Believe it. We cached three of them here."

"But the noise of the engine . . . the helicopters. . . ."

"How much water do you have?"

Sanchez ran her tongue over her lips, which had been chapped rough by the constant blow of wind throughout the night. She had drained her remaining canteen six hours ago.

"A stream parallels the Soledad Canyon road," Antonov said, pointing south.

Sanchez followed his gesture and, three hundred meters away, could barely make out a strip of dirt that passed for a road, running the breadth of Soledad Canyon. "It will be dry," she replied. "The rainwater from last night has already been sucked dry by this desert."

"That storm from last night left enough water behind to form pools in the stream junctions. According to the map, there are a series of stream junctions by some ruins about two and one half kilometers from here. Maybe there is a well. Have you a better idea?"

Sanchez thought for a moment. "I have backpacked around those ruins before. Yes. You might be right." She glanced at the bike where Antonov was wiping down the black anodized finish of the paint. It was dark-colored with no chrome, painted flat black. It was a Japanese model, a Suzuki, with a 250-cc engine.

Antonov read her mind. "A special adapter on the muffler keeps it quiet. They are not as loud as conventional motorcycles."

"I see. . . ."

"Well." Antonov climbed on top of the motorcycle and then stared at her, waiting. His eyes played over her body; her hair was tied in a loose braid behind her head, the swell of her breasts—not large, not small, rose and fell with her breathing. He saw the sweat stains beneath her armpits, and how the moonlight glinted off the moisture collected in the hollow of her neck. Most women were not desirable in the field and under these conditions, but Sanchez . . . had not lost her sensual charm. How very much he would like to . . .

Sanchez straddled the motorcycle behind him. "Let's go."

Antonov kicked the engine over, letting the moment pass.

And then they took off.

When they had gone, Santo stole inside the cache site. He spotted the other two motorcycles. After a quick search, he found that one of them had had the wiring cut and the carburetor removed. The other bike merely had the spark plug removed.

Santo snorted. He removed the spark plug from the one bike and reinstalled it in the other. *That was simple enough,* he thought. *Too simple. Why?*

But did he have a choice, if he was to keep up with them? He'd just have to be careful and not fall into a trap.

He rolled the bike out of the cache site and listened for the agents' engine. He could still hear its fading sound in the distance. By now, they should be close to the road, if they followed the canyon's streambed.

He had to take the risk. Speed was security. Santo kicked the engine over and then wound his way down the streambed toward the Soledad Canyon road.

Hanlon slugged his team leader on the arm and pointed outside the helicopter. "*The CO!*" he yelled above the din of the Blackhawk's rotor.

Straining against his free-fall rig, MacIntyre peered out of the cabin at the figure running toward them, just as their bird started to lift from the helicopter pad. They were to parachute into the AO (area of operations) and set up point survelliance. The chutes and equipment with which they were jumping in made movement inside the bird difficult. The others inside the Blackhawk consisted of the security teams, whose mission it was to surveil the avenues of approach to and from the objective and then seal them off when the STRIKE went down. MacIntyre spoke into the intercom attached to his flight helmet, and the pilot set the Blackhawk back down.

Richards, his face camouflaged by face-paint like MacIntyre's, leaned inside and yelled above the roar of the engine, "We just got a visual on Santo!"

"Is it still a go?"

"Yeah. They're in Soledad Canyon now. He's following the two that got away."

MacIntyre grabbed his company commander by the sleeve. "Snatch them now!"

"No way! First priority remains the safe house as planned. That's where the Soviet exfil support team is located. You keep an eye out for Santo if he follows them there."

MacIntyre thought about it. It made sense. Too much sense. "Roger that!" he yelled back, bitter and mad.

Seconds later, the bird lifted off. MacIntyre and Hanlon glanced at each other, and then studied the terrain below them, as the Blackhawk flew the twenty-minute approach to Las Cruces.

CHAPTER SEVENTEEN

Sergei Antonov decelerated the bike as they approached the ruins.

"We have farther to go," Victoria Sanchez told him. She tightened her grip around his wrist, and Antonov did not mind that.

Antonov spotted a subsidiary dirt road on the left, which appeared to circumvent a large hill. Automatically, his mind made a mental picture of the map, and he knew that tributary streambeds joined in two junctions with the main streambed of Soledad Canyon.

Before he made the turn the chopper came back, speeding low over the horizon.

Sanchez glanced to her rear, horrified. "Hurry!"

Antonov raced the bike into the first streambed junction for cover.

Santo spotted them just as they bolted off the road. He pulled his bike behind a small rise and dismounted, so the two agents could not spot him. He yanked out his strobe light to signal the chopper whirling above.

But the Blackhawk continued its southwest line of flight.

Santo wheeled his bike forward across the desert valley floor, as the helicopter swooped on past Soledad Canyon in the direction of Las Cruces. They hadn't seen him. Or maybe they had. What was going on?

Onward he trudged, waiting for the sound of the two agents restarting their engine first.

• • •

Exiting their cover of trees, Antonov and Sanchez scrambled up to the top of the rise between their position in the streambed and the man Antonov now knew was following them. "Quickly!"

"What is it?"

"There is no time. On the motorbike, now!"

Antonov gunned their motorcycle into the dark hue of the desert night. They circled the mountain standing at the foot of the ruins they had approached from the Soledad Canyon road. Antonov wheeled right again once past the mountain massif. Soon they'd be back on the Soledad Canyon road.

"What are you doing?" Sanchez demanded.

Antonov did not reply. Quickly, he gunned the motorcycle up the slopes of the mountain. He angled into a draw and shut off the engine.

"Do you hear that?"

Sanchez shook her head to rid it of the vibration and shock of the rough cross-country movement. Then she did hear it.

"Yes. Another . . . another engine. Like our own!"

"I left one of the motorcycles operable so I could determine whether or not we've been followed. One man is following us, surely no more than that. I've suspected it all day. We *have* been followed."

"But why just one man?"

"They say that in the American Army, oftentimes an individual deviates from his orders—they change things as the situation warrants. Perhaps this man is from the group that . . . no time for this now! We must set a trap!"

Sanchez got off the bike. Antonov followed suit, and they backtracked several meters to look down the curve in the trail behind them, waiting for the other engine.

Suddenly there were silence.

"He has stopped."

Antonov stared back at Sanchez, his mind whirling.

Suddenly, a flare of light sparkled off two hundred meters away from them near the Soledad Canyon Road, by the ruins.

"Look!"

Antonov whipped out his binoculars. The illumination from the full moon above helped him pick out two people by a Coleman lantern and a small campfire. They had missed seeing them during their partial ascent up the mountain on the dirt bike. He handed the binoculars to Sanchez and went back to the motorcycle to conceal it in the rocks.

Sanchez walked over to him. "We are being followed then, yes?"

"There is no other explanation. But surely no more than one. Two at the most."

"Then I have an idea."

Santo debated on whether or not to leave the bike. It was a hindrance to push it up the mountainside, and he hadn't heard the agents' engine start back up yet.

He decided to leave it in a gully by the trail he'd followed partially up the mountain. Then he crept up the mountainside, quiet, catlike, his M16 at the ready. He glanced all around. The shadows! Where were the goddamned shadows? He felt naked on the mountain. What trees there were only grew in sporadic stands by the road at the base of the mountain.

Suddenly, Santo's gut felt hollow. Was he being watched now? When was the last time he'd heard the agents' engine? Fifteen, twenty minutes ago when the chopper had passed by? Maybe he'd better sit tight for a while.

Santo took a knee by the biggest boulder he could find, and listened.

And listened.

Five minutes later, he noticed a flash of light downslope, and immediately recognized it as someone below starting up a Coleman lantern. The two he was following had to have seen it. What to do? Locate the camp or whatever it was down below? He did have to get to a better vantage point than the naked hillside he was on now for better observation. He waited, growing impatient and pissed at himself for climbing up on the hillside like this. Movement now was no good. But to stay here all night without finding out what the two agents were up to was no good either. He had to do something.

And then he saw a walking figure fifty meters in front of his position, heading toward the light that had flashed below. Santo brought his Zeiss binoculars back up to his eyes. *The woman!*

But where was her partner? Were the people in the campsite below part of their network?

There was only one way to find out.

He waited until the woman neared the campsite at the foot of the mountains. Cautiously, he picked up and shadowed her, scanning his periphery every fifteen seconds with the binoculars to make sure he wasn't being followed.

When he neared the camp, the mesquite grew thicker and, using the concealment to crawl even closer, he saw a Toyota four-wheeler and an older couple sitting back on a pair of lawn chairs before the lantern and a small campfire.

And then he saw the woman walk into their campsite to greet them.

"C'mon, old girl, let's turn in." Sean Harley patted his wife on her knee upon hearing her begin The Snore. It was definitely unbecoming for his wife, Liz Harley to snore. Besides, even at the not-so-tender age of sixty-three, Lizzy still had the body of a woman twenty years younger in good shape.

"What—what, dear?"

"Come on, sweetheart. Time for bed."

Liz Harley pulled her graying, once-raven-black hair back into the loose ponytail she'd tied it into the morning before, and arched her back, looking at her husband with soft, loving eyes. Sean Harley grinned, displaying a set of huge, pearly teeth that age had spared. It was that same big grin that had won his Liz forty years ago when he was flying the Berlin Airlift and Liz was a nurse in the Rhein-Main base hospital.

"Ain't you glad you married me, Liz?"

"Of course, dear."

"We're gonna get rich as hell, you know."

Liz Harley smiled wistfully. Her husband's recent obsession with metal detectors and panning for gold had yet to turn up any nuggets. But still, they'd needed to get away from Albuquerque for a few days before going to see their daughter and son-in-law in Oklahoma, and a little camping with the Toyota four-wheeler and each other out in the desert was sort of nice. Sean's government pension from the Air Force wasn't much, but they were comfortable.

"Very rich, darling." She smiled and took his hand, ready to climb out of the lawn chairs and back to their trailer. She lowered her husky voice. "Time for bed."

Sean Harley grinned and started to get out of his chair.

"Hello? Hello there?"

The couple started. The evening had been so quiet. The voice. Where was it? Sean and Liz Harley squinted at the horizon beyond the campfire, where they saw a person, a woman, a young woman materialize out of the dark and limp toward them.

"Please . . . please help me." The girl pitched forward and fainted.

Antonov watched his pursuer followed Sanchez's route toward the camp. She was there by now, and he could see her talking to the couple in the camp by the fire where they had heated up soup for her and had laid her on one of their lawn chairs. Antonov watched the man climb inside his four-wheeler to retrieve a blanket, exit, and then put it over Sanchez's shoulders.

What an act! And her idea had been brilliant. Why hadn't he thought of it first?

From his vantage point on the mountain Antonov switched his gaze back to the man who had been following them. The man was crawling along in a draw tracing an unseen route down the mountain. A thick brush chain of mesquite paralleled the draw. Antonov would be able to follow the man into the camp through the trees, sneak up on him, and disarm him. Interrogate him and then dispose of him.

After Sanchez killed the couple below. At least that would attract their pursuer's attention. Things were finally looking up. They would dispose of the civilian couple below and their pursuer in one fell swoop. New identification cards, the legally registered four-wheeler below. They would be able to drive into El Paso and escape across the border before any kind of alarm for this elderly couple could be sounded.

But, of course, he had to catch the man sneaking *his* way toward the camp first.

"Try some of this, sweetheart." Sean Harley handed Victoria Sanchez a glass of ice cubes with Jack Daniel's Black Label splashed over them.

"Sean!"

"Relax, Lizzy. This poor girl's tuckered out, and a drink will do her good. She needs a rest."

Sanchez took the drink and sipped it as she lay curled up on a third lawn chair before the fire. "Could I . . . also have some more water, please?"

Liz Harley scooted her chair closer to Sanchez with a canteen, frowning at her husband in the process. "Of course you can, dear."

The couple stared at the young Hispanic woman for several moments while Sanchez gulped from the canteen.

"Easy there, young lady," Sean Harley told her. "Don't be making yourself sick, now. By the way—I didn't catch your name."

"Victoria. Please call me Vicki."

"Vicki. . . ." Harley waited for the young woman to tell him her last name. She didn't. He looked at her closely, immediately drawn to her eyes and the lines of her mouth and face . . . the confines of her hiking shirt and shorts. He was attracted. Abruptly, he turned away and examined the bottle of Jack Daniel's he clenched in his hand. "By God, I'll think I'll have a slug of this myself." Automatically, he glanced up at his wife, as if to ask permission.

Liz Harley frowned. Sean hadn't drunk very much *this* trip, and she had hoped he would continue that way. "Sure," she told him curtly. "Why not?"

Sean Harley poured himself a glass and set the bottle down by the fire, where the glow from the coals made the amber whiskey inside light up in a reddish hue. Harley studied his drink, occasionally stealing a glance at the quiet girl sitting with them. "Now tell me," he said, after draining half the contents of his glass, "what in God's name are you doing out in this part of the desert alone and at night."

Sanchez leaned back in the lawn chair to stretch and felt the bulge of her Walther PPK in the small of her back. So far, so good. "I'm a geology student at the University of Texas in El Paso—UTEP. My friends had invited me on a campout this weekend up here in the canyons, and I couldn't go because of a previous commitment . . ." She looked up shyly, then lowered her head. "My boyfriend, you know. Well, he's kind of a rat, and we had a fight. I decided at the last minute to drive out here earlier today and find my friends. I got lost on these trails, and late this afternoon my pickup's radiator blew. I've been walking west ever since. I had drunk everything in my canteen hours before I saw your campsite."

"Well, dear, you just spend the night with us and we'll get you back to El Paso tomorrow," Liz Harley told her. "We're on our way to Fort Sill, Oklahoma, so we'll just drop you off when we pass through."

"By God, that's *exactly* what we'll do," Sean Harley added, a little loudly. "Our daughter for cryin' out loud married an Army officer there. *Army*. Hell, the least she could'a done was married an Air Force fella like me."

Liz Harley shot an evil look at her husband. *So you're going to get drunk after all tonight. Sean, you had best stop looking at this girl.*

"And you don't have any business 'tall wanderin' around these hills at night. They're dangerous. I almost fell in an old well I found here today."

Sanchez noticed the friction developing between the couple and decided to capitalize on it. "A well?" she asked, the picture of innocence.

"Yep. These old ruins around here"—Harley made a sweeping gesture with his arm—"ain't much, but some of these here Indians must'a dug 'em a well at one time or another." He leaned close to Sanchez where he could get a better look at her cleavage. "We ain't really supposed to be campin' here, you know," he stage-whispered.

Harley caught another reproachful look from his wife and leaned back in his chair, swirling the dregs of his whiskey for a moment. Then he drained the rest of the glass and his face grew serious. "Yep. Damned near fell in that well. Dropped a rock in it, you know, to see how deep it was. Didn't hear a splash for five long seconds."

"Sean, you're rambling."

"So I am . . . so I am." Harley grabbed the bottle of Jack Daniel's. "Like some more, Vicki?"

"No, thank you. Maybe some water, please."

Liz Harley handed her the canteen. "It's time for bed, dear," she told her husband.

"Think I'll stay out here a little longer, Liz."

"Well I'm going to bed! Good night!" Liz Harley strode angrily toward the camp trailer hooked behind the couple's Toyota.

"Aw, Liz, stay on out here for a while."

Harley received the well-slammed door of their trailer for an answer.

"Could I see that well?" Sanchez asked Sean Harley after several moments.

Harley blinked. "What for?"

"Well, like I said . . . I'm a geology student. I just enrolled in an anthropology course in school, and—"

Harley glanced back at the trailer. "Tomorrow would be better."

"Look," Sanchez said, smiling sweetly. She placed her hand on the older man's knee, which trembled at her touch. She supressed her sudden desire to break out laughing. "This may sound weird, but I have this thing about old ruins and stars. It is so lovely tonight, and well, I'd really like to see it. I can put the description down in my diary and use it for my class."

Harley threw a quick glance back at the trailer. The light inside had just been snapped off. He knew his wife was pissed. For what? Staying outside while he talked to a young woman? Hell, he wasn't gonna do nothing. Those days were long gone. So if she wanted to get in a tizzy, then let her. He let the girl before him keep her hand on his knee a while longer. *Hell, she's harmless enough . . . damned good-lookin' too.*

"I suppose it wouldn't hurt none—"

"Then let's go," Sanchez said excitedly.

Santo's gut churned when he saw the old man lead the woman he'd been following out of the campsite. This wasn't a contact team. This was bad. Where the hell was her partner? What could he do, just sit behind a sand mogul by this campsite and let the woman murder these people?

That would happen.

He had to stop her.

Santo stole through what scrub brush existed near the campsite, weaving his way through the sand moguls and mesquite, paralleling the woman and the old man's route to the well he'd heard them talking about.

Then they stopped. Santo heard the old man mumble something inaudible and toss a rock inside the well. Seconds later, the woman laughed and clasped the old man's hands in her own.

Santo sweated. He had to do something. But where was her partner? He had to be stalking him. He had to—

Something brushed across his leg. Starting, he scrambled away from the sensation, a crawling, wriggling sensation, trying to catch the cry in his throat when he saw a diamondback rattler as thick as his wrist making S twists over and past his leg toward the campsite.

Santo's heart pounded. A goddam snake! He'd almost yelled out. He swung his attention back to the old man and the woman. She was still holding his hand. Their voices grew softer, and he strained to hear them.

A light! Glancing to his left, he saw a flashlight bobbing back and forth as the old woman walked from the campsite toward the well.

Santo checked the safety on his M16 and flipped it on the fire mode, gently easing the selector switch with his thumb to keep it from making a snapping sound. He'd have to be quick.

He got up into a couch, and edged a little closer to the clearing and the well.

At first, Antonov had seen nothing of their pursuer when Sanchez had gone into the camp. While Sanchez talked to the old couple, Antonov had remained up on the ridgeline, scanning the terrain below with his binoculars.

When he spotted another figure weave his way into a sparse stand of trees by the campsite, he knew he had the advantage.

For the next ten minutes, Antonov had crawled down the ridgeline, trying to get his bearings back on whoever it was that was following them. Then, when the old woman broke away from her husband and Sanchez, entering their trailer, he had noticed movement on the edge of the campsite.

Twenty meters below him was the same man who had held them at gunpoint earlier that morning. He recognized him now. He had almost walked on top of the American! If the American hadn't moved so suddenly then . . .

Antonov silently drew in a deep breath of relief. So far, so good. He had him in his own sights now, not the other way around. He followed the American, who now trailed Sanchez and the old man toward some ruins where they stopped before a well.

Sanchez was ready to kill the old man; it was the logical thing.

And that meant that he, Major Sergei Antonov, would have to get the American before the American got Sanchez. Antonov looked at the H&K submachine gun clenched in his hands. To shoot him? No, it would be too loud, and besides, he wanted the American alive. Not only that, but it would bring every hunting party in the area down on him. He still had his knife . . . but the American had an assault rifle. He would have to be very, very careful.

Antonov tiptoed down the ridgeline.

Sean Harley tried to pull his hands away from the girl who had introduced herself as Vicki. "I see my better half coming," he muttered, watching a flashlight trace its way through the dark of the night toward them.

Sanchez tightened her grip and moved in close to Harley. "It's all right, " she murmured. "Later, perhaps. . . ."

She's actually coming on to me. "Now listen here, Vicki, I gotta go to—"

"*Aargh!*" Sean Harley doubled over, trying to clutch his testicles where Sanchez had delivered her first blow. She held tightly to his hands and yanked them up. Then she spun around and planted her heel in his chest.

Harley wheezed out like a lung-shot mule deer, feeling the pain of three broken ribs splintering into his lungs.

"Sean? *Sean!*"

Victoria Sanchez finished the old man off by slamming her hand into his throat slightly below the Adam's apple, where the web between her outstretched thumb and forefinger crushed his larynx like rotten wood. The old man dropped.

"*Sean, what's wrong?*" Liz Harley screamed out again, running toward the well.

"Something's happened, Mrs. Harley!" Sanchez told her excitedly, supporting the old man by his armpits. "I think it's his heart—"

"*No! Oh, God, no!*" Liz Harley ran toward her from ten meters away, the flashlight bobbing up and down as she clenched her fists and pumped into a fast jog toward her.

And that suited Victoria Sanchez fine. How would she do it? Yes, her hands could do it, just as she had killed the old man. The woman came closer. Sanchez tensed for the right moment when she would drop the old man and let loose on—

Suddenly, everything happened at once. A blur on the left, a ninety-degree angle away from the woman's approach. A uniform! A rifle!

"Lady, get the hell outta here!" a voice cried out.

Liz Harley stopped in her tracks, trying to locate the voice and what it meant. She glanced back at Sanchez and her husband the young woman clenched in her arms. *"Sean!"* She lurched forward.

"NO!" Manny Santo bellowed.

Sanchez dropped the old man as the rushing newcomer sprinted closer, now only meters away. She leaped out and grabbed the woman by the hair, flinging her down on the ground. Sanchez immediately whipped her PPK out from behind her back and scrubbed the muzzle vigorously against Liz Harley's scalp. The old woman screamed and tried to claw toward her dead husband, who stared at the stars above the well in death, his mouth wide open.

Santo reached the agent, leveling his M16 at her. "Let . . . her . . . go." He had to be very careful now. He was exposed and he did not know where her partner was. It would have been better to wait for both of them to arrive in the campsite, but there was no way he could have let the old people die. He would have always remembered the looks on their faces, as he stood impotently on the sidelines. Like now.

Sanchez yanked harder on the old woman's hair, using her as a shield, forcing her head up close to her own as she maintained a low squat on the ground. The old woman shrieked. Sanchez then noticed a black silhouette creeping up on the American from behind.

"I said put her down!" Santo aimed his M16 and centered the front sight-post in between Sanchez's eyes. He thought he heard something then, but it was too far away. He had to wait for the right moment.

"You are so noble, my American friend," Sanchez chuckled. She broke out into a laugh, and tried to control it, but she couldn't. She kept laughing and tightening her grip on Liz Harley's long graying hair, twisting it into knots and listening to the old woman scream.

Antonov stepped up closer.

Santo's forefinger pressured the trigger of his M16, wanting to go through with it, to end the chase now, to blow the bitch away and deal with the . . .

Footsteps!

Santo spun around just in time with his M16 to ward off the newcomer's butt stroke. The butt end of Antonov's submachine gun clanged noisily against the receiver of Santo's M16. Both men locked weapons together, each straining to bash the other's face. They began a slow circling movement like rams in a fight with their horns locked up. Santo pulled back on his M16, catching his opponent off guard, then butted his forehead into his face. He followed that by kicking the other man between the legs. Antonov weakened and dropped his submachine gun.

But before he could slam another kick into Antonov's groin, the Soviet countered by raising his right leg to ward off the blow, and then completed the movement by sticking his right foot into Santo's midsection. He then grabbed hold of Santo's shirt, rolled to the ground on his back, and threw Santo in the air behind him.

Simultaneously, Sanchez slugged the old woman on the head with the butt of her pistol and jumped out of the immediate area.

Santo landed six feet away on his arched back, heels first, arms outstretched to break the shock of the fall, his weapon clattering off to the side. Unhurt, he scrambled to his feet and snatched up his M16, knowing he had to rush his opponent before he recovered from the groin kick earlier.

Then he knew he had him. The agent was too beaten from his earlier blows. He raised his M16 at the agent, who now looked back at him with a hollow stare. At the agent's feet were two bodies. The energy and adrenaline of the fight made spots appear in Santo's eyes, and he blinked several times. It began to register that the old woman was now alone, supine before her dead husband and the well.

And that was when the back of Santo's head exploded.

He dropped to his knees, detached, all at once numb and confused. He felt like he was out of his body, and he was seeing everything in a movie theater. Himself, down. The bad guys, up. The dead old man, down and out for the count. Some old lady lying down in the sand face-first, blood pooling around a cavity in her graying hair.

In slow motion he watched his rifle strike the ground butt-first, then fall over sideways. He weaved. Then the pain came. A crushing, concussed pain that sent his brain slipping all around, rattling every crevice and seam of his skull. . . .

Standing behind him, Victoria Sanchez, rock in hand, planted her foot on his back and gave him a push.

Santo slumped to the ground, face-first, unconscious. A small trickle of saliva drooled on the sand underneath his mouth.

CHAPTER EIGHTEEN

Lieutenant Colonel Andrei Volensky walked away from the situation map where Dixon and the other two representatives from the CIA and DEA all huddled around, pointing and talking.

Volensky exited the hum of the war room's activity, pulling a vial of aspirin from his pocket and unscrewing the safety top. He dry-swallowed a tablet, followed by a gulp of water from the fountain in the FOB's entrance hallway in front of his office. *At least things have smoothed out*, he thought. His gut was settling down too.

Through Dixon's constant flow of communiques to Washington, they'd finally gotten "official" clearance through Group headquarters and 1st SOCOM back at Bragg all the way up to the National Security Council to run a joint operation with the civilian agencies. That was the cover for the media's sake when news of the operation broke out after they raided the safe house. News and publicity were inevitable. Now, with Dixon's authority, Volensky was in complete control of the military aspect of the mission—the STRIKE—once it was enacted.

Too many chiefs and not enough Indians led to confusion, paperwork, bureaucracy, and chaos. Thankfully, Dixon had taken legal, civilian command of the situation without micro-managing the tactical aspect of this special operation. He had also organized and streamlined the local police and sheriffs and Border Patrol departments for emplacement of patrols to cover the avenues of approach leading in and out of the safe house. The FBI would also conduct the mop-up on the objective after the STRIKE went down. The CIA's representative, Jon Peterson, cleared the tele-communications computer link to Langley and gathered intelligence concerning known and suspected KGB agents under diplomatic cover in Juarez. Volensky and his men would conduct the raid, neutralize the objective, and exit the area when the FBI people arrived on the scene.

The commanding general of White Sands Missile Range had notified Volensky earlier of a ranting college student half-crazed with fear who was discovered trying to scale a fence that morning on the missile-range complex's southern boundary. After telling the MPs about a woman who had tried to kill him, and of the murders in Ash Canyon the night before, Newton Rasmin had been treated at the base hospital. Later on in the day, Staff Sergeant Haywood and the CIA liaison had debriefed him for any bits of knowledge untapped. When everything was over, the college student would be turned loose.

The information Pushtkin had told them, coupled with MacIntyre's debriefing and the information gleaned from the college student, confirmed all earlier theories—that an active penetration campaign of SDI by the Soviets, camouflaged by the cover of illegal drug-smuggling, had occurred. The myriad of drug-trafficking routes, trails and roads networking back and forth along the Rio between Mexico and the United States, overtaxed the Border Patrol and the DEA. By working in tandem with the drug cartel, the Soviets and Cubans had been able to infiltrate spies, commandos, and terrorists whenever the need arose—for more than the past twenty years.

And Volensky's battalion was the only unit in the area that could do anything about it. The STRIKE had to happen soon if they were to prevent the exfiltration of the two agents still on the loose and take down the wasps' nest of agents and drug smugglers in position to rendezvous with them. It all led to the safe house near Las Cruces.

The safe house itself consisted of a ranch tucked up in the mountains east of Las Cruces and west of the White Sands Missile Range. Staff Sergeant Haywood had built a terrain model showing the ranch's layout and the surrounding fences, mountains, vegetation, and other structures in the area of operations by requesting and receiving NSA spy-satellite overflight photos of the ranch earlier in the day.

The continual flow of intelligence and aerial reconnaissance

had allowed the leader of the STRIKE element—MacIntyre's
company commander, Major Halley Richards—to compose a
detailed operations order he had briefed hours earlier to Volensky
and Dixon. A change here and there—not much—and Volensky
had "blessed" it. Richards, two teams of twenty-four men for the
fire support and assault elements, a two-man point-surveillance
team, and a six-man team for security comprised the entirety of
the STRIKE force. Within minutes MacIntyre and Hanlon would
be positioned on-site near the safe house, ready to make commo
and verify the presence of the agent exfiltration team at the ranch
as the point-surveillance team.

The mission's concept was simple: Get point-surveillance and
security teams in first; maintain close-up visual communications
for in-flight objective activity communications updates while the
STRIKE force flew in; and then go in heavy with tear gas and
ordnance around the perimeter. Secure the tops of the buildings by
fast-roping from the Blackhawks. Subdue the enemy. Corral the
drug-traffickers and Soviet agents in a holding area, secure them,
and then turn them over to the FBI mop-up team that would follow
the STRIKE.

It was a simple plan. Volensky believed in keeping things
simple, because any real-world mission's execution was bound to
change once things started happening. When bullets flew, confusion reigned. What was important, and what he continually
stressed to his men, was the *intent* of the mission and operation.
The commander's intent was the *why* of the mission. When the
men on the ground executing the mission understood the *why*,
then they could use their initiative to make the right on-spot
decisions at the right time and place when Murphy's Law took
over.

As it always did, whether in conventional or unconventional
warfare.

Volensky walked up the hallway to where his office was
located—empty and forgotten. Everything now happened in the
war room, and secure communications had been set up to converse
with the point-surveillance team now en route to the safe house.

Now it was time to wait. Volensky entered his office and stared
at a book he'd been reading over the Labor Day weekend which
was opened facedown on his desk. It was a biography of Peter the
Great. Russian culture and history. A study of a leader determined

to pull eighteenth-century Russia out of the jaws of ignorance and barbarism, the legacy of centuries of Mongol control.

But now, Volensky simply stared at the book, transfixed, thinking not of his heritage but of his men on the ground. He had three men out there now—nine including the six-man security team—each *taking the risk.* Santo had taken the risk. Master Sergeant Timothy Manuel "Manny" Santo. Hopefully, MacIntyre and Hanlon would spot him out in the area of operations and bring him back.

Volensky shook his head. What was it he had come in here for? He patted his pockets for a smoke and then remembered. He opened the drawer to his desk and retrieved a packet of cigarettes. He lit one up and pulled on it deeply.

Goddam you, Team Sergeant, you crazy sonofabitch . . .

Volensky had been working for the CIA when he had first met Santo in Thailand. Santo had been a junior communications sergeant on his first overseas deployment with his Special Forces team—and at that time, a specialist fourth class. But the low rank did not matter. It was the man that mattered, and that man's contribution to the team and the mission.

Volensky's mission at that time when he had been working with the CIA was to infiltrate Laos and destroy an opium field lab sequestered deep in the jungle that processed morphine and heroin for the drug mafia controlling Southeast Asia's Golden Triangle. Volensky's own communications man had stepped into an old punji-stake pit along the Thai-Laotian border and had to be evacuated. Under orders to support Volensky's mission along the border where they were training an infantry company from the Royal Thai Airborne Rangers, Santo's detachment commander had attached the junior communicator to Volensky for the mission.

There had been many casualties. Eleven men dead, shot on the objective, or killed when their exfiltration bird was downed by a Soviet-made Strela surface-to-air missile. One of the few walking wounded, Santo had carried Volensky out of the kill zone and back to safety of the jungle; back ultimately to their staging area in Thailand. A close friendship had formed.

Often, when their careers criss-crossed back in the States and on other assignments overseas, they would crack the seal on a good cognac and wax philosophical about the purpose of that mission, and its futile attempts to stop the flow of drugs into the U.S. They would try to understand the nature of covert operations enacted by an open society. What had been their government's intent in Southeast Asia then? Military intent? Political intent?

They had long ago decided that Vietnam and its legacy was a war that military and civilians leaders alike neither understood nor knew how to fight—a war of *Low Intensity Conflict*. Clausewitz's first stated principle of war was *objective*—to identify one's goal and one way or another achieve it. There had been no clearly defined strategic objective in Southeast Asia—there had been no policy to take Hanoi and destroy the Communist government in the north. Wars of containment—the insipid alternative the Johnson Administration had decided upon for political expediency—led toward eight years of non-commitment and ethnocentric decision-making in Washington. You either fight a war or don't. But the resultant lack of objective had developed a "career-first" mentality within the senior military leadership, who were unwilling to challenge nebulous and immoral dictates from Washington. Drug use rose. Morale plummeted. Casualties mounted. Why?

After 58,000 deaths, the United States had pulled out. There had not been a major encounter lost to the North Vietnamese. Tactically, the North Vietnamese had been beaten. Hanoi had finally been bombed into submission when Nixon carpeted the skies with B-52's during the Christmas bombing campaign of '72. But 58,000 American lives and countless Vietnamese civilian deaths had meant nothing in the long run when no clear political and strategic objective had ever developed within the conduct of the war itself. There was plenty of blame all around to share— with the senior political *and* military leadership.

The war in Southeast Asia inexorably culminated in the domino effect, dismissed by vocal and naive liberal crusaders as reactionary rhetoric. But in the spring of 1975, the victorious North Vietnamese Army seized Saigon, radically extending the Bamboo Curtain in Southeast Asia. Laos fell. Millions died in the spectacle of Cambodian genocide perpetrated by Pol Pot's Khmer Rouge that for so long the rest of the Western world ignored. Burma and Thailand continued to fight Communist aggression and infiltration. But what was the domino effect to the average American when the alternative on the television set was "Monday Night Football" and any number of sitcoms?

The same war was happening now in the Western Hemisphere. A war of Low Intensity Conflict with no clearly defined front, a war of terrorism, espionage, and subversion through drug-trafficking that divided the entirety of Latin America into two camps of political and economic turmoil, rape, and chaos. There was either the political right wing replete with death squads and minority wealth, or the political left wing that spread insurgency, drugs, and Moscow-puppeted revolutionaries throughout Latin America. Whom to support?

How indeed was an open society, a democracy, to wage covert warfare against the nebulous tools and proxies of totalitarian-inspired insurgency within the Western Hemisphere without violating the principles outlined by the Constitution that he, Andrei Volensky, and every other military officer and the civilian leaders of his country had sworn to uphold and defend against all enemies foreign and domestic?

He had no immediate answer. What was immediate now concerned the attempted Soviet penetration of the White Sands Missile Range, the capture of all agents involved, and the drug-traffickers in the area they were working with.

Volensky's mind returned to Santo. There was one man who was concentrating very hard on staying alive, who was following the two escaped agents on his own initiative by adhering to the *intent* of the original mission they had deployed on two days earlier to conduct.

Volensky continued to stare at the book open-faced on his desk, and the ash on his long, brown cigarette grew.

"When you gonna quit smoking those coffin nails, sir?"

Volensky wheeled around and saw his battalion executive officer standing in the doorway. "I'll quit smoking these goddam things when I quit drinking cheap wine, XO. Never!"

Major Jake Blane grinned at his battalion commander, trying to loosen the Old Man up. Blane admired Volensky. Two different men, different in personality, in age—Volensky was fifteen years older—different in styles of leadership. But the two different types of strength combined into a more powerful, collective strength, and that was one of the many things that had made their Special Forces battalion the best-trained, with the highest morale, throughout the 1st Special Operations Command.

Blane grinned, and then his face turned serious again. "We just got commo from the war room that the point-surveillance and security teams on board the HALO Blackhawk just crossed Phase Line AMBER on our aircraft-movement chart. They're on time and should now be climbing to altitude for the jump."

"Phase Line AMBER. That crosses Soledad Canyon, does it not?"

"Yes, sir."

"Any more visual on Santo?"

"No . . ."

"Goddam."

"Yes, sir. I agree."

"Goddam!" Volensky fell silent, brooding.

"He'll make it, sir. He's one tough son of a bitch."

"Tough between the ears, that simple bastard."

"That too. But he'll make it happen, sir. Santo will simply make it happen like he always does."

Volensky looked up and saw the unwavering sincerity in Blane's eyes. Different personalities, different modus operandi. Blane was a good man and an effective XO. They all were in his battalion.

"Let's get back to the war room, Jake." He paused, thinking that by now the point-surveillance and security teams should have just reached the objective and were now free-falling toward their assigned positions. "And like you say—make this STRIKE operation happen."

Ricky Vargas's stomach growled, and he grew steadily more pissed at his buddy Chico, who was supposed to have brought the burgers and coffee over half an hour ago.

Boring, he thought. *That's what it is around here, boring.* He gripped the steering wheel of his Silverado pickup and glanced over at his gringo partner, Tracey. Tracey always got sleepy when he was stoned. Now he was asleep and that meant that he, Ricky Vargas, was pulling their first shift. He had started it when they relieved the midnight watch at 0100. Now it was 0200 in the fucking early morning hours, with four more to go. He'd just give Tracey another thirty minutes and then it would be his turn.

His head drooped. He jolted suddenly, remembering to scan the trail before him with the binoculars his boss had given him. Maybe it would be better to get outside the truck and walk down the trail a little. And—and, yeah, man, another reefer. Christ, but he'd be glad to get this two-day job over with—it was boring, man, boring. He could use the bucks, though.

"Tracey. Hey, Tracey, m'man! Wake up!"

"Uh?"

"I'll be outta the truck for a few minutes. Okay?"

"Yeah." Tracey sat up, rubbing his eyes.

Vargas climbed out of the Silverado, slinging his Mini-14 over his shoulder. Tracey then slumped his chin back on his chest and went back to sleep.

As Ricky Vargas walked away from the truck, he shivered in his work shirt and hitched up his Levi's. He'd left his jacket back in the cab of the pickup. But that was all right, the night desert chill would keep him awake. He glanced back at the truck every now and then during his walk, to make sure he could still pick it out of the shadows. He and his partner had parked it in a cluster of pines just off the trail where they could overlook the approach from the south.

When he had walked twenty meters, he stopped and pulled a skinny joint from the front pocket of his blue work shirt. As soon as he struck the match, the burning sulfur flames stung his nostrils, and like always at night, made him see spots in his eyes.

At 12,500 feet, Captain Matt MacIntyre exited the Blackhawk with Hanlon, the wind lashing his face into a numb, frozen mask. Free-falling, he got stable and immediately linked up with Hanlon. When their altimeters read 8500 feet, both men started tracking for the lights below them.

There would be no drop zone for them, manned by a reception party. They were going in blind. And the lights below were from the safe house—a ranch with a dilapidated old bunkhouse once used in the days when the ranch had been a prosperous one.

The ranch itself was situated on top of a broad knoll about a hundred feet above the valley floor. According to the terrain model back at the FOB and the aerial photographs they had studied prior to infil, enough vegetation and ridges and rolling terrain were in the bowl to mask their movement upon landing. The bowl area itself was created by a complex of east-west and north-south ridgelines that crisscrossed one another, leaving the ranch area in a broad, boxed-in valley.

An improved dirt road ran the breadth of the valley, with trails leading out through the passes from the ranch house like spokes from the hub of a wheel. Their goal was to land between 500 and 1000 meters south of the ranch, behind a small ridgeline that would mask observation. Then, once on the ground, they'd parallel one of the trails over the ridge to emplace point surveillance 200 meters away from the ranch with their night-observation devices—both thermal and starlight—packed in the small rucks lashed behind their legs under their chutes.

MacIntyre continued to study his altimeter. Five more seconds, and he'd pull at 1200 feet. He glanced at Hanlon in mid-flight. Everything was good; they were within fifty feet of one another.

When MacIntyre pulled, the pilot chute deployed first and he barely slowed. Then, when the main chute swished out of the sleeve, he brought his knees up and the opening shock came with a pop. MacIntyre felt his balls crammed up into his groin, but he was too adrenaline-rushed to feel them cramped under the pressure of his rig. After the initial jolt, he grabbed the toggles of his chute, and in tandem with Hanlon, steered toward an open spot below them where a trail switchbacked up the ridgeline they'd soon be climbing en route to the objective.

Seconds passed. So far, so good. MacIntyre stared at the horizon and saw the lights of the ranch to his north. It was hard to see anything else—at 0200 the moon was sinking toward the horizon, and darkness below varied in shades of pitch-black. They were due south of the objective, maybe three or four hundred meters off azimuth for their foot approach. He looked down and grasped the straps for his lowering line that would deploy his rucksack away from him before landing. One hundred and fifty feet. One hundred feet. It was time.

And then, just as he yanked on the straps, he saw a match flare into the palms of a man lighting a cigarette.

Ricky Vargas watched the match flare as he lit the end of his joint, and when he took the first drag, it immediately revived the receding buzz of the first joint of the night he'd smoked an hour ago. He knew how to handle it. Hell, he'd been getting stoned for the past fifteen years, ever since sixth grade.

He flung the match to the ground when it burned the ends of his thumb and forefinger, and inhaled deeply, still seeing the flame in his eyes like the negative of photograph.

Thump.

What the . . .

Thump!

Vargas shot his head up and saw a black shadowy thing cascade to the ground in a billow, not thirty feet in front of Him. He spat out the joint.

Thump!

He jumped when a black bundle landed five feet beside him. He opened his mouth to yell out in warning—

THUMP!

Vargas crashed to the ground and rolled into a cactus plant, the breath knocked out of him. He heard the sound of metal and brushing cloth and padding feet. He fought to get to his feet, and then something clouded over him, soft, silky, confining.

"Tuh-Tracey!" Vargas fought with the parachute silk draped over him and caught his feet in the parachute's suspension cord. He fell again.

"Tracey!"

Something crashed against his skull. Ricky Vargas became oblivious and all went dark. And silent.

Hanlon raced for the pickup he'd spotted just as he'd climbed out of his free-fall rig. MacIntrye had already taken care of the guard or whoever it was smoking the cigarette. No, it was pot. He recognized the smell.

Hanlon tripped over a cactus plant and sprawled by the front bumper of the pickup. Before he could get to his feet, the door opened. A tall man stepped out.

"Ricky, man, what's going on? Hey, Ricky!"

Hanlon's eyes widened, he drew up into a crouch. *Now, do it.* Do it!

He leaped out from behind the door and grabbed the figure by his shirt. He stuck his hip inside the taller man's gut and heard him wheeze out in surprise. Hanlon threw him as hard as he could over his hip into the dirt and gravel of the trail. The rifle the man had been carrying flew out of his hands. Hanlon slipped on the gravel and fell down by the other man. Both men scrambled to their feet, and Hanlon got smacked in the face by an elbow.

Hanlon's head spun from the blow, and he knew automatically

he'd lost a tooth when the blood from his lip sprayed and he felt the new cavity with the tip of his tongue. He fought to regain balance.

The other man scrabbled away from him for the rifle lying just out of reach on the dirt road.

Hanlon kicked the guard with a roundhouse, the heel of his jungle boot sinking deeply into the taller man's gut. The guard flipped over on his back, gasping. Hanlon dropped his knee onto the man's chest and slapped his palms over the guard's ears, breaking his eardrums, the pressure from Hanlon's knee keeping the guard from yelling out. Then, Hanlon clouted him hard on the side of the head and he went limp.

Hanlon retrieved the guard's weapon and scrambled away on all fours, fighting to get back to the pickup. He was dizzy from the blow he'd received in the mouth, and could feel his lips ballooning. Were there others? Where? He glanced at the weapon in his hands. It was a Mini-14, a good civilian carbine, modeled on the M14 the military had once used twenty-five years earlier. A choice weapon for paramilitary outfits, legal and illegal.

Like dope-smugglers. It made sense.

He raced back for his free-fall rig where his M16 was still strapped. MacIntyre met him there.

"Jesus," MacIntyre wheezed, "that was close." He had climbed completely out of his rig now, and knelt on one knee by Hanlon, covering him while the sergeant retrieved his M16 and wadded up his canopy. "I got the guy with the cigarette. He's out."

"He had a partner in the truck. He's in the trail over there."

"Use your chute to tie him up."

Hanlon pulled out a handful of quick-close plastic ties from his trousers cargo pocket. "We've got these cufflets too, Boss."

"Good idea. Give me a couple and I'll secure the asshole with the cigarette. Whattya think, we ought to put them back in the truck?"

"I don't know. We've got to do something with them."

"Better hurry." MacIntyre darted off for the guard he'd taken out. After binding him by the ankles and wrists, he dragged him back to the pickup and laid him in the bed, making sure he was covered by the parachute canopy.

Hanlon followed suit with his guard. MacIntyre studied the unconscious man for a moment.

"You sure knocked the hell out of him."

"Look at my lips, Dai-uy."

"Aren't you pretty."

"Yeah. Got a tooth knocked out too."

Seconds later, both guards were secured, and hidden in the bed of the pickup. A panel cut out of one of the canopies was hundred-mile-an-hour-taped inside each man's mouth.

"C'mon, we can't stick around."

Hanlon glanced at the two prostrate figures. "What about them?"

MacIntyre showed Hanlon two billfolds. "I checked out their IDs. Driver's licenses, pictures, that sort of thing. Found marijuana on them too. They've got to be guards for the safe house. No telling how many of them are out here."

"We'll have to hide the truck."

Headlights suddenly beamed on them.

"Got company, Boss." They watched another pickup crest over a rise in the trail, 500 meters to their front.

"Holy Christ! Get in the truck!"

Hanlon took the wheel, and MacIntyre got in on the passenger's side. He spotted hats and a couple of jackets. *Maybe, just maybe* . . . MacIntyre fought to get control and think. "Randy," he whispered, opening one of the billfolds. "You're . . . you're Tracey Rhoads. The guy's a blond, like you."

Hanlon yanked out his .45 and kept it palmed in his lap with his right hand. "Ooo-kay." He swallowed. "Brilliant idea, Boss. Fucking brilliant."

MacIntyre slapped one of the hats over his head. It was a beer-stained Stetson, ancient and torn at the brim. "My name's Richard Vargas. I'll act like I'm asleep. I've got my M-16 aimed toward your window."

MacIntyre handed him a baseball hat with a nylon mesh crown and a foam front proclaiming the excellence of Beech-nut chewing tobacco. Hanlon pulled the brim low over his eyes, and drew one of the civilian jackets around his shoulders to conceal his .45. MacIntyre did the same.

"Oh, shit! There's something else!"

"What?"

"Face-paint! They'll see it!"

Hands, arms, and elbows flurried. The truck got closer.

"Try not to shoot my dick off, Dai-uy, if it comes to it."

"Just play it by ear, Randy. Play it by fucking ear."

The approaching vehicle was now only a few feet away. Both men tensed. It was another pickup, a late-model Chevy Silverado like the one they were sitting in, with mirrored windows and a high, stiff suspension.

The pickup slowed to a stop beside them. Hanlon slouched with his Beech-nut hat pulled low over his eyes. The newcomer's window rolled down, revealing a blare of hard-rock music. Hanlon almost grinned. *At least the shitheads listen to AC/DC,* he thought, his hand tightening on the .45 in his lap.

The newcomer thrust a bag at him from the open window.

"Sorry I'm late," a young voice, overly loud, overly stoned, told him. "Had to make a couple of other stops for the rest of the guys."

Hanlon took the bag of hamburgers, and cleared his throat. "Thanks," he garbled. He swallowed, hoping the truck would drive on by. He peered out at the new arrival. It was a young, skinny kid with a partner nodding off in the passenger's seat.

"Hey—you're that guy, uh, Tracey, right?"

"Yeah."

"You sound kind of funny."

"Got laryngitis." Hanlon opened the door of the pickup and banged it lightly against the door of the other. MacIntyre turned as if he were asleep, ready to follow Hanlon's lead to spring out of the pickup and cover him.

"Hey, do you mind? I just got this truck."

"Oh, sorry, man," Hanlon rasped. "Wanta get out and stretch my legs."

"We're outta here."

" 'Kay."

"Change is in the bag. Oh, yeah. There's a couple of trucks coming your way in about an hour from the mountains east of Las Cruces, so watch for them."

" 'Kay."

The pickup sped off, leaving them in a cloud of dust, with pings of gravel in appreciation for the door bang.

MacIntyre exhaled. "Jesus."

"Shit almost hit the fan."

"Yeah."

Hanlon jerked his head at the unconscious guards in the back. "What about these two?" He got out of the truck and inspected the two guards. "They're still out and sleeping hard."

MacIntyre climbed out with him and retrieved his rucksack from where he had concealed it in the bed underneath the parachute canopies, more than a little glad that there'd been no questions asked about the "cargo" back there. Immediately he turned on the radio strapped inside the carrying pouch in the ruck. "One thing is, we've gotta call back to the rear and give them a situation report."

"Yeah. Hurry, though—we don't have much time." Hanlon pressed the illumination button on his watch. "And time is now 0223. That means we've got exactly thirty-seven minutes to be on surveillance."

MacIntyre thought for a second. "I got an idea."

Ten minutes later, they had the truck cached not three hundred meters away from the ranch at the foot of the hill. Fortunately, there had been enough trees in the area to conceal it far enough off the road. They'd eased the truck into the dried-out riverbed that paralleled the main access road to the ranch.

And ten minutes after that—and one hundred meters away from the boundary of the ranch—they had the objective under surveillance from the opposite ridgeline nestled in the boulders and the trees, with the PRC-70 tuned in for their first contact of the night with the FOB.

It would be time for the STRIKE soon.

CHAPTER NINETEEN

Santo came to when he heard the bodies being thrown into the well. A dull, hollow splash, long seconds after the bodies were dumped in, brought him slowly back to reality.

He opened his eyes, trying not to get sand in them. The pain in his head blazed in concert with a knot on his crown that had spurted up like a baby volcano.

"He's coming to," Santo heard a feminine voice say. He tried to locate the voice. Where had he heard it? Why was he looking at two piles of clothing in front of his face?

A centipede crawled across his hand. He stared at it for a moment, trying to remember what *that* was, and developed a gnawing fear that it was not a good thing. The centipede crawled rapidly across his arm and up to his neck. Then he remembered. *Christ!*

A kick sent Santo sprawling back down on the sand as he shook the centipede off. He stared at the 9-millimeter bore of a tiny submachine gun.

"You're well equipped," he heard himself say to the Russian soldier. Hours earlier he'd had the drop on the Russian. Now, all he had was a high-pitched whine in between his ears. He'd been slugged a good one.

"Kill him."

"No."

"Kill him now, Antonov. You should have killed him with your knife when you had the chance."

"We need information."

Squabbles, squabbles, Santo thought, almost laughing. *Yes, why not kill me now and be done with it?* His eyes narrowed. He had to find a way. Any way. Adapt, improvise, overcome, all that hu-yah bullshit. *Yeah, c'mon, Manny, think . . .*

"Put the old woman's clothes on now, Sanchez. I will cover you."

"Kill this American!"

"We have more important things to do! First, we need information, and to get information requires what we don't have—time!"

Sanchez stared long and hard at Antonov, wanting to put her hand on the comfort of the pistol in the back of her trousers. Why did she want to counter Antonov's decisions? Were they decisions? Was *he* in charge? Was she? Did it matter? He was right. At any rate, they had to be gone from this place and back in the city, where they could melt into the crowds, the indigenous population of southern New Mexico.

She nodded her head. She stripped and put on the old woman's clothes.

"I went through her things and found her identification card," Antonov informed her, keeping a wary eye on Santo. "Memorize her name and numbers. I'll do the same with the old man's clothing. If we are stopped by any American paramilitary like sheriffs or the Border Patrol, we will have identities. We can use this man here—this Master Sergeant Timothy Santo—to—"

Santo winced and immediately patted his front shirt pocket. His identification card was missing. They'd been ordered to carry their identification cards on the mission. They should have gone in sterile. It was the best way, but DEA dictated that their mission be aboveboard and legal.

"Stay still!"

Santo scowled at the Russian. "Relax, pal. You guys really think you can get out of this?"

Antonov reached in his pocket and flipped Santo's ID card back to him. "Yes, Comrade Santo. You will drive."

"Hey, spare me that 'comrade' bullshit. I'm *Sergeant* to you, bud."

Santo received a kick in the ribs for a reply. He clutched them; the kick hadn't been as hard as it could have been. He glared up into the eyes of the Russian. There was a humorous glint in them.

"*Sergeant*, then. I am Major Sergei Antonov."

Sanchez walked up to them and nodded at Antonov, having exchanged her hiking shorts and flannel shirt for the old woman's long canvas trousers and denim blouse. She covered Santo while Antonov changed his clothes.

It gave Santo time to think. Why *hadn't* they shot him? They would not, of course, want to draw attention to the area; plus the gunfire would more than likely draw any MP security patrol monitoring the Soledad Canyon road. Still, he could not do anything rash. Just because they hadn't shot him as of yet did not mean they wouldn't. The clothes they were all changing into would give them new identities. That was why they had murdered the old couple. Santo clenched his teeth in disgust. *Murdered for their clothes.*

Seconds later, Antonov threw his old clothes to Santo. "Put them on."

"Let me guess—you're gonna make me look like a civilian and you expect me to drive you people out of here. You're giving me back my ID card to make it all appear legal in case we run up against an MP patrol."

Victoria Sanchez thumbed back the hammer of her Walther PPK and centered it on Santo's face. "Yes." Then she added, mockingly, *"Sergeant."*

Santo knew she was not bluffing. Besides, he could think of something to do while he was driving. At least he would have a little more time. He glanced at the well. At least more time than the old couple had had.

He'd have to be very careful with these two. Cold-blooded professionals were hard to kill. Santo put on Antonov's discarded clothes. His uniform, rifle, and web gear were tossed into the well. Minutes later, they had broken down the couple's camp and were driving west out of Soledad Canyon. The trip grew in irritating silence as Santo weaved back and forth between the sand moguls, cactus, and rocks while driving out of the campsite. When they reached it, the main canyon road was not much better comfort-wise. Years of neglect and bumps and potholes kept their top speed limit down to no more than twenty miles an hour.

Antonov kept his submachine gun's muzzle pressed against Santo's back as Santo drove. Sanchez had her pistol palmed in her lap with the business end also aimed at Santo.

"If we encounter any law enforcement," Antonov informed him from the back seat, "I am a sick camper, a friend of yours, who has been food-poisoned. You are taking me back to a doctor. If you say anything different, *Sergeant* Santo, rest assured that you will not live."

"By golly, looks like you've got all the bases covered."

"When we reach the Las Cruces highway, you will drive toward El Paso," Sanchez added. "You will maintain the legal speed limit and under no circumstances try to escape. You will be shot."

"No shit, Sherlock."

"What?"

Santo quickly slowed the vehicle, as he approached a series of potholes in the road. They'd be out of the canyon in another ten minutes. If he could slow them down, maybe they *would* be pulled over. He spied a barrel cactus ten meters in front of him, its thorny spikes jutting out in the roadside by the potholes. *Now that,* he told himself, *is an idea.*

"What are you doing?"

"Hold on, this part of the road is pretty rough."

Santo collided the left wheel with the barrel cactus and drove partly over it as he "wrestled" the four-wheeler back onto the road.

Sanchez brought her PPK up to Santo's temple. "I think you can drive better than that."

As they crested a rise in the bumpy road, they came to a three-way intersection overwatched by the mountains and ridgelines that opened the jaws to Soledad Canyon. From their vantage point now on the main north-south ridgeline marking the boundary of the Fort Bliss military reservation, the lights of Las Cruces sprawled before them. Santo slowed to make the turn, wishing the tire had blown earlier.

"Which way?"

"Left!"

As Santo turned the wheel, a muffled pop, accompanied by a rotating left lurch, made him grin. *Delayed reaction,* he congratulated himself.

"Fool!" Sanchez snapped at him, thumbing back the hammer of her PPK. "Change the tire!"

Santo snorted in disgust. He was getting tired of this woman's hammer-cocking.

They pulled over to the side of the road to stop. As soon as they did, headlights from another vehicle, hidden and parked behind them in a road-overwatch position, illuminated their Toyota.

Antonov pressed his submachine gun harder against Santo's back. "Victoria Sanchez! You cover him while he changes the tire." He glanced to his rear. The Bronco approaching them had Border Patrol markings on it. "Remember your identity and cover story. If things go bad, I'll think of something. Hurry!"

"You get out after I do," she said to Santo.

Sanchez exited the Toyota, keeping a careful eye on Santo.

The Bronco pulled up behind them and stopped. Clouds of dust were illuminated in surrealistic beams of blue and red from the patrol vehicle's strobe light. Sanchez saw two men in Border Patrol uniforms exit their vehicle and walk toward them. One man was tall, lanky, out of shape with fish-belly white skin contrasting with a thin black fringe of hair hanging outside the rim of his hat. The man's partner was swarthy, Hispanic-looking, and in bad need of a haircut and shave. *Border patrol?*

"You seem to be in trouble here," the tall man said, speaking first in a scratchy voice, somewhere between a baritone and a tenor.

His partner immediately walked up to the passenger side of the four-wheeler with his gun drawn. He stepped around Santo, who was changing the tire, and peered inside.

"My boyfriend is sick. We were out camping, you see—" Sanchez broke off suddenly. *Something about that voice* . . .

"And where are the other friends you went camping with?"

Santo noted the Border Patrolman carried a Smith and Wesson stainless-steel .45 double-action. *Odd . . . maybe blowing the tire wasn't such a hot idea.* The Hispanic-looking Border Patrolman withdrew his head from the four-wheeler and returned to the first man. He nodded his head curtly at the tall man, saying nothing, and then put his hand on the butt of his .45.

"Excuse me?" Sanchez asked sweetly. "We were only by our—"

The tall Border Patrolman walked up closer to Sanchez and took off his hat. When he smiled, Sanchez recognized the row of yellowed, crooked teeth and his black eyes. The foul breath.

"Where is Comrade Pushtkin, Victoria Sanchez?"

"Grzniecki," she whispered.

Santo ground his teeth as he pumped the four-wheeler's lift jack. *Grez-nyeckie,* he repeated to himself. *Fucking intrigue around this place kills me. How the hell does she know a Border Patrolman with* that *typical Irish name?*

"Ah. You remember the time in Juarez."

"Yes." Sanchez wanted to throw up. On orders from Pushtkin, the *residentura* chief, she once had to deliver a package to this man in a filthy barrio near the center of Juarez. That package contained this man's—Grzniecki's—payment to his runners. Grzniecki, a transplanted Pole, ran Pushtkin's locally recruited illegals. Illegals—indigenous, locally recruited agents—were used by all worldwide KGB *residenturas* for any purpose, but in Juarez they were used primarily for dope. Juarez illegals were dope-smugglers who also ran messages to the agents across the border in El Paso, Alamagordo, Colorado Springs—all major cities located next to American military bases—where designated recipients of those packages containing cocaine, heroin, and crack turned over microdot messages to their network case officers.

Grzniecki was a reptile, as far as she was concerned. A clammy-handed, hairless reptile.

"You are off course, Major," Grzniecki called toward the back seat of their four-wheeler. Antonov exited the vehicle with his submachine gun. "You should have turned *right* at the intersection, as I so informed Comrade Pushtkin." Santo listened closely as he changed his tire. Grzniecki glanced at Santo. "I do not know this man."

"Auxiliary," Sanchez quickly explained, moving closer to him. Santo let her do the talking, as he tightened the wheel nuts with the tire jack. "He was ordered to report to me in Soledad Canyon for our emergency exfiltration from this area. Much has happened."

"Where is Comrade Pushtkin?" he asked Sanchez for the second time.

"Pushtkin is dead. And so is the scientist. It is a long story."

"I see. Then you will have much to tell me back at our little hideaway."

"Yes . . ."

Grzniecki broke away from her stare. There was enough time for the debriefing later. He regarded the tall, lanky Spetsnaz major standing before him with the submachine gun. He did not care for the submachine gun.

"Stephan!"

Grzniecki's partner stepped forward.

"Escort the good major and Sanchez's driver back to their vehicle, and—please, Major—hand your weapon to my assistant. He will return it to you later after it has been cleaned."

"I clean my own weapon."

"Yes, of course. Give it to him anyway. My sniper may get the wrong idea."

Antonov's eyes scanned the ridgelines above them. There was no choice. He handed Stephan the submachine gun. He supposed it was the best way. They weren't being frisked, and he still had his pistol in his shoulder holster. He could think of something later. The main thing now was to stay calm, keep up the appropriate appearance, and then think about breaking away from these KGB bastards when the opportunity presented itself.

If, in fact, it ever did.

Antonov eyed Victoria Sanchez. *And what role does she truly play? Is she a friend, or is she everyone's mercenary?*

Grzniecki slicked his black, oily hair over his balding pate with long fingers and put his patrolman's hat back over his head. "We leave now. There is a plane due to arrive at the ranch. We must meet it in less than an hour."

Santo climbed back into the four-wheeler, his stomach churning. Things were really screwed up now and one hell of a lot more complicated. Now he had two roles to play—Special Forces team sergeant, and auxiliary driver recruited by a woman who was either KGB like this slime-ball newcomer, or GRU like this Spetsnaz major sitting on the passenger side.

Stephan sat in the back seat, covering both men with his newly acquired H&K MP5 submachine gun. "Stay close behind them," he muttered, nodding his head at Grzniecki and Sanchez as they entered the Bronco to their front. A slight, wiry man descended from the ridgeline with a night-observation telescoped rifle, and he took the driver's wheel. They waited for Grzniecki to move out first, and everyone fell silent.

Grzniecki slammed the door behind him as he entered the Bronco after Sanchez. Together, they sat in the back seat, where he could better cover her. They stared at each other for several wordless seconds.

When his sniper entered the vehicle on the driver's side and started the engine, Grzniecki broke off his gaze. He would have to ask her questions later. He didn't like the way things were going at all. What was important now was to get out of this country and back into Juarez.

Grzniecki regarded Victoria Sanchez's looks again, tracing the curve of her neck where it met her shoulder. She returned his look with a Mona Lisa smile. She was playing up to him, but he knew she was simply playing it cool until she had a chance to escape. He would not let that happen. From here on out it was a game. Something had gone wrong with the White Sands operation, and she was trying to escape when he found her.

When his sniper started to drive the Bronco out of the area, Grzniecki was brought back to a more immediate train of thought. He had to get the exfiltration actuated as soon as possible. He had to consummate the arms deal with Luis Munoz. He had to burn all traces of the mission, this direct penetration of U.S. borders, by making it simply appear as another drug operation under the cover of Luis's men. It was part of the plan.

Now, confusion reigned. Antonov was still alive. Pushtkin was dead. There was this unknown American Sanchez said was a member of her private auxiliary. He had to, of course, be disposed of. Then it occurred to him that maybe the American could explain why Sanchez and Antonov were attempting *not* to link up with the exfiltration team in accordance with Pushtkin's radio message earlier in the previous morning.

"Give me the microphone." Grzniecki took the dashboard radio's black squeeze mike from his sniper and depressed the talk button. Once his transmission was completed thirty seconds later, his contingency exfiltration plan was in effect. The man he'd talked to back at the safe house would radio in the aircraft from Juarez immediately, and the special tilt-rotor plane would be on the landing zone at the safe house within the next forty-five minutes. It would all be over very soon.

Once again, he faced the woman sitting beside him, his mind racing. "You may now tell me exactly what happened in Ash Canyon, Victoria Sanchez."

Santo drove fifteen meters behind Grzniecki's vehicle, paralleling the ridgelines on dirt roads separating the Fort Bliss and White

Sands military reservations from the outlying desert and mountain reaches of Las Cruces less than sixteen kilometers to their west.

Santo's eyes popped open suddenly. He still had his identification card on him! For sure, he'd be strip-searched upon arrival to wherever the hell they were going. He'd have to get rid of it somehow. But if he tried it now, the fake Border Patrolman sitting behind him would surely see it.

He felt the crawling sensation of someone looking at him. It was Antonov. The Russian's eyes conveyed a feeling, a mood, a message. Santo knew what he was feeling and what he was thinking. The Spetsnaz major had lost his edge again, and was in as bad a spot as Santo was.

Which meant that everything now was a free-for-all.

CHAPTER TWENTY

Staff Sergeant Ian Lange Hutton burst into the war room. *"Sir!"*

Volensky jolted from a semi-doze, typical of the almost catatonic waiting period before any mission went down. Dixon followed the NCO inside the war room, having just refilled a styrofoam cup with freshly brewed coffee. "What is it?" Volensky asked Hutton, already on his feet.

"Flash traffic, sir, back in the commo center!"

"C'mon, Mr. Dixon." The two men followed the NCO outside.

Seconds later they were in the quonset hut commo center behind the FOB building, watching a cipher clerk decode the message that had just come in over the radio. When the cipher clerk was finished, he handed the paper to Volensky, who quickly scanned it.

"God-*dam*," he whispered. The paper tightened in his hand as he handed it to Dixon to read. Dixon had to tug on it. "Hutton, get the STRIKE force commander and S3 in here ASAP!"

"Sir!" Hutton bolted for the door.

"And the XO!" Volensky called after him. "Get the XO!"

Major Jake Blane strode inside the quonset hut from the opposite entrance. "Right behind you, sir . . . what's up with—"

Dixon handed the message to Blane. "That was MacIntyre and Hanlon," Volensky told his XO. "They've already made enemy contact on their drop zone and had to take a couple of them out. We're moving the STRIKE up"—he glanced at his watch—"by one hour."

"Christ, sir, that means it's going down at . . . at 0345. That's only thirty minutes from now."

"We have no choice, if this thing is going to succeed," Dixon said.

Blane scrubbed his knuckles around the back of his high-and-tight sheared scalp. "I'll run down to the airstrip and get the pilots squared away."

"I'll be down there too, as soon as I talk to Richards," Volensky said, yanking his beret out of his trousers cargo pocket. He stared hard at Dixon. "And you tell CW3 Delano he's got another passenger."

After Blane had left the room, Dixon said, "Are you up to it? I didn't know that fifty-year-old colonels did this sort of thing."

"Those are *my* men, Dixon. Talk is cheap, and any commander can talk. I intend to be on the objective with my men. Blane will remain behind here with you to hold the fort down."

"I don't think it's a very good idea, Colonel."

But Volensky's look in reply left no doubt in Dixon's mind that the Mad Russian thought it was.

As their Bronco approached the last few kilometers to the safe house, Grzniecki feigned interest in Sanchez's story:

1) Under specific instructions from Moscow, Antonov had eliminated his own team, for secrecy; Pushtkin was forced to be eliminated when he fell and broke his leg after the handoff;

2) She herself was forced to kill the scientist when he tried to escape from them shortly after their linkup in Ash Canyon; and

3) As with any plan, one must have a backup plan for exfiltration. Anticipating that heightened White Sands Missile Range base security would compromise existing exfiltration plans, she had secretly arranged for a member of her El Paso auxiliary to meet them in Soledad Canyon for emergency exfiltration.

Of course, Grzniecki believed none of it. He, as Pushtkin had cryptically dictated in his earlier radio broadcast that morning, would kill them all upon debriefing back at the residentura in Juarez, and burn all traces of the mission.

"Why do you not have the RAIL model as promised?"

"It proved bogus upon Pushtkin's inspection. The scientist misled us. It was why he tried to escape, because he thought he had us fooled." Sanchez thought of the bomb in her backpack she'd blown, and how the RAIL model, months in preparation, was now scattered bits of circuitry. She had no contingency plan now, unless . . . yes, she knew Grzniecki wanted her. She would have to force herself to . . .

"You do have—"

"Yes. The blueprints. I have them on my person." She took Grzniecki's hand and placed it on her waist. "Here, covered in plastic and wrapped around me like a money belt." She kept his hand on her waist.

Grzniecki squirmed in his seat. Before killing her, he would let her try to whore her way out of the trouble she knew perfectly well she was in. *So let her lie. Let her lie and pretend you believe it.*

Lights appeared on the horizon as they crested a rise in the road, then dipped out of sight as they entered a new valley. Sanchez glanced out the window. For the past fifteen minutes they had been driving, they had entered a complex of ridgelines and mountains about sixteen kilometers away from Las Cruces which sprawled below the main mountain massif they paralleled now. They continued for another five minutes into a broad, boxed-in valley. The lights she'd seen earlier had to be the ranch, and now they approached a low hill where the ranch sat on top. The Bronco they rode in slowed and then stopped.

A figure walked out from the side of the access road and popped his head in the passenger window, looking at the back seat where Sanchez and Grzniecki sat. Grzniecki snatched his hand away from Sanchez's lap.

"Ah, Pietrov. What is it?" Pietrov inhaled deeply. He was the drug chief's main arms advisor, a blocky, thick-trunked man with a deep bass voice. His dark appearance helped him to blend well with the indigenous populations with which he worked.

But Pietrov, Grzniecki knew, had nothing but contempt for Luis Munoz—drug chief, thief, and opportunist. The inbound plane from Juarez contained the other half of the American Redeye missiles due the drug lord. It was the only way to deal with the bastard, Grzniecki realized.

"We seem to have 'lost' two of our men who were stationed

here earlier this evening. Munoz's recruits. When they failed to report in for their hourly checks with the radio, we came out. Their truck is gone as well."

"Contemptible bastards!"

"They will be found tomorrow somewhere in town and punished."

"And what is our friend Luis Munoz doing about his lack of control over his own men?"

"He will find them and kill them."

"Yes. Pietrov, Luis will meet us there at the ranch house. Come up in a few minutes and get him off my hands. Luis's men will need to off-load the plane."

"I will keep him out of your way."

They drove past the guard, and over the next hill, and then Sanchez knew they were almost there as they turned onto the access road leading uphill toward the ranch.

Unaware that seventy-five meters away they were under observation.

"Just got a message in, Dai-uy. Things are gonna start poppin' soon."

"Vehicles coming—two of them!"

Sergeant First Class Randy Hanlon popped out from underneath the poncho they had rigged over the radio where they could use a red-lens-filtered flashlight to code and decode messages. He brushed away the pine boughs draped over their position on the boulder-littered ridgeline above the streambed where they'd hidden the truck. He crawled up to MacIntyre.

"Check 'em out with the thermal," MacIntyre said, adjusting the focus on the AN/PVS-4 mounted on his M16. The starlight scope gave them good observation on the ranch below, but the thermal-imagery device Hanlon used would give them a definite count on the warm bodies the STRIKE force would have to deal with.

Hanlon spotted the boxlike chassis and monocular snout of the thermal-imagery device lying next to his team leader. He flipped on the motor switch, and brought the device up to his face, pressing the rubber eyepiece against his brow. Immediately, he spotted the glows of two vehicles, where the engines up front radiated heat. The heat outlined the brakes and chassis as well.

Sparks flew underneath the chassis as the vehicles ground their way up the hill across from the men's position where they had the ranch in clear view. He also saw the people inside the vehicles.

"I count six of them, boss."

"Uh-huh." MacIntyre continued fiddling with his starlight scope's focus lens. "What was the message, Randy?"

"Volensky moved the time-on-target up by one hour. STRIKE's going down in another thirty minutes."

"Holy shit. I hope security's in place by now." MacIntyre thought of the two three-man security teams that had jumped seconds after he and Hanlon had infiltrated the ranch house area. Their mission was to secure the north and south avenues of approach into the ranch site. Upon STRIKE initiation, they were to seal off the road from incoming and outgoing personnel.

"They should be." Hanlon leaned forward as he watched the vehicles to their front stop by the ranch house's entrance. "They're getting out."

"Randy!" MacIntyre whispered excitedly, "Check out the first vehicle. I see the woman. It's the same woman from this morning in Ash Canyon. Get ready to radio this in."

"Roger that." Hanlon crawled back for his poncho hootch. MacIntyre continued scanning his front as he watched the occupants from the second vehicle get out.

"Okay, sir, prepared to copy."

"Wait . . ."

"What is it?"

"Oh, God."

Hanlon sidled back up to MacIntyre. "What is it, Dai-uy?"

"They've got Santo."

As he and the others drove toward the top of the hill, Santo automatically scanned the area for its military applications. Just what in hell was he up against? How would he get away? What about the goddam helicopter he'd been in touch with before 2400 hours?

Throughout the approach, Santo had closely examined the terrain changes as they went from the lower altitude of Soledad Canyon to the higher reaches of the Organ Mountain chain that separated Las Cruces from the White Sands Missile Range. He glanced at Antonov sitting at his right on the passenger side, and knew the Russian was doing the same.

The ranch house itself was more of a dilapidated old one-story frame structure with probably only four or five rooms in it. It was located toward the western crest of the broad hilltop, a dozen thirty- and forty-foot pines surrounding it. More pines were staggered down the hill toward a grassy area, a stream, and a shallow ridgeline facing the ranch from due south. Located a short walk east of the ranch house—twenty meters, give or take—was a bunkhouse, now used more than likely as a barn.

Santo thought of the stream they'd crossed just before driving up the hill. The higher elevation, cooler temperatures, and the natural screen of terrain-trapped clouds absorbed most of what moisture this part of southern New Mexico offered before the clouds could escape over the dry confines of the White Sands Missile Range and the expanse beyond.

That was it. Two buildings on top of a broad hilltop. The grass—hardy, wiry desert weed—and scrub oak covered the hill in knee-high thatches. Enough water from this particular summer's rains and the altitude within this complex of the Organ Mountains had kept enough foliage around to allow a dismounted approach into the area.

He gritted his teeth and thought bitterly, *At least,* my *team could do it. What there is left of it.*

Santo made a mental picture of the one-over-fifty-thousand-scale military map he'd used for the past three years since deploying to Oro Grande. He knew the terrain like the back of his hand. He'd never been to this area, but he knew it was isolated well enough—a couple of rundown buildings at least twenty kilometers away from Las Cruces on the west and ten to fifteen from White Sands on the east.

He wished the helicopters had come back when he had been knocked unconscious by Antonov. Now, he no longer had his strobe light. It was sitting at the bottom of an old, forgotten well in Soledad Canyon with his weapon, the rest of his web gear, his uniform, and a couple of bodies.

The Bronco pulled up to a stop before the ranch house entrance. Two men walked out to greet them. Santo parked the Toyota behind the Bronco. When Santo saw the man called Grzniecki exit the Bronco with Sanchez, the guard behind him nudged him in the back.

"Both of you—get out."

Santo kept his mouth shut. The less he said, the better. He and Antonov exited the vehicle, their guard walking behind them as they approached the others by the doorway of the ranch house. One of the men Santo had seen walk out of the ranch house first joined Grzniecki on the porch.

"Vasily, you have contacted the team in Juarez. . . ."

"Yes, Chelmno Grzniecki. It shall be here"—the man called Vasily, a black-haired, pale man with a cigarette in a nervous, trembling hand glanced at his watch—"within the next half hour."

"It is the special aircraft, as planned. The one with greater speed and the radar."

"Yes, comrade. It will be flying a low-level route under radar scrutiny through the corridor we reconnoitered two weeks ago."

"Good . . . good."

"What is wrong?"

"Yes," another voice interrupted, striding toward the two KGB operatives, "what is wrong? I trust nothing has happened to the cargo you promised." He was a mustachioed, swarthy man of medium height.

"No, of course not, Luis," Grzniecki said soothingly.

"I have fifteen other men to pay for their efforts tonight! You'd best have both the cash and the missiles!"

"My friend," Grzniecki replied, "let us discuss this in Juarez. Rest assured you will receive your shipment."

"I trust no one. You bring the missiles in on that aircraft. I have already satisfied my portion of the bargain by taking this place over."

Overhearing, Santo began to put two and two together. The missiles—what could they be, if they were being transported on an aircraft, a small aircraft that would land here? He glanced around the area, trying to let his night vision encompass the terrain. What aircraft *could* land here? Only a helicopter could land here, unless . . . unless one of those new rotary tilt-wing aircraft— half helicopter, half airplane—was going to arrive. What kind of missiles? They had to be shoulder-fired missiles. But for what purpose?

A chill stole up his spine. Shoulder-fired SAMs could bring down anything from a Piper Cub to a Boeing 747. In the hands of anyone.

The new man had spoken in Spanish. Santo looked at Sanchez and Antonov to gauge their reactions. Who *was* this guy? He was obviously independent of the Russians. Santo found himself remembering what Saxon had told them back at the FOB before the mission, of a possible narco-terrorist link between the KGB residentura in Juarez and the Latino drug cartels throughout Mexico and Central and South America. What about the KGB and GRU residenturas in *every* major city down south?

Grzniecki noticed his movement. Santo looked away from the KGB chief. Grzniecki walked up to him.

"Stephan!"

"Yes, Chelmno Grzniecki!" Santo's guard said.

"Take this man to the bunkhouse. I don't know him, but I will find out later. I have some questions for our newcomers before our transportation out of this place arrives."

"*Da!*"

Grzniecki led the others into the ranch house.

Santo felt the nudge of Stephan's submachine gun in his back, and he turned toward the bunkhouse, trying to think of a diversion.

"Christ almighty, sir, they've *got* to kill him! What else would they do?"

MacIntyre felt sweat pop out on his forehead. Hanlon was right. Their team sergeant was not going to last long. "The STRIKE will happen in the next twenty or thirty minutes."

"In twenty or thirty minutes, Manny could be dead."

MacIntyre said nothing. Hanlon scrambled back to his rucksack, which lay next to the radio underneath the poncho hootch he'd rigged. Seconds later, he reemerged holding a pistol in one hand and a tubular device in the other. MacIntyre stared at it.

"Where'd you get that?"

"You know the rules, Dai-uy. This silencer doesn't exist. And I made sure I had an adapter for this Browning's muzzle when I first got it."

"Volensky'd have your nuts for that. If you were ever caught

264 Mark D. Harrell

with that silencer back in the rear, you'd be spending time busting rocks at Leavenworth."

"Yeah, but that doesn't really matter right now, does it?"

"So what are you thinking?"

"The radio, sir . . . we can remote it. Leave the transmitter up here. We've got another transmitter for a backup. Ed Barkowitz showed me this once. You remote one part of the radio, and then use the extra transmitter like a walkie-talkie. We can get in real close to the objective and still maintain commo with the FOB and incoming birds."

MacIntyre picked up on Hanlon's reasoning. What was the *intent* of their mission? Volensky wanted point surveillance on the objective, radioing back last-minute intelligence updates before the strike. They were also to spot targets of opportunity with M203 flares to guide in the STRIKE mission. They could do a better job close up.

And save the life of their team sergeant at the same time.

He picked up Hanlon's thermal-imagery device and scanned the perimeter of the ranch house. During their surveillance thus far, they'd spotted three pairs of men surrounding the perimeter. Including the two guards they'd taken out near the access trail they'd infiltrated an hour earlier, there had to be another pair of guards on the opposite trail that led into the ranch from the north.

"Randy," MacIntyre whispered, "there are two guards located in the grassy area by the trees leading away from the ranch house." He handed Hanlon the thermal. "See 'em?"

"Yeah." Hanlon handed the thermal back to MacIntyre and began to screw the silencer on his Browning Hi-Power. "They're smoking cigarettes."

"What kind of rounds you got?"

"You sure you want to know? They're as illegal as this silencer."

"What kind?"

"I hollowed them out myself and inserted a full clip's worth with mercury drops. Then I cross-hatched the ends and sealed them up with Teflon."

MacIntyre inhaled sharply, and then let it back out. "Jesus. That'll do the job." Indeed it would. When the nine-millimeter slug entered the target, the round would begin tumbling because of the mercury inside and disintegrate where the round had been cross-hatched. The Teflon coating would ensure penetration, even if the bullet encountered body armor.

"So when did the IRA recruit you?"

"What?"

"Never mind."

Hanlon scanned the ranch house's perimeter once again. "There's another pair of guards on the north end of the ranch, by the access trail. The others are out of sight—no telling how many men are manning listening and observation posts in the tree lines. That bunkhouse they put Santo in is lit up, so there's probably more of 'em inside."

"We'll have to time this with the STRIKE."

"Roger that, but does that give Manny enough time?"

MacIntyre gritted his teeth. "It doesn't matter. We can't blow this whole operation for one man. You know that."

Hanlon looked away. "Yeah," he said bitterly. Then he felt MacIntyre grip his shoulder, hard.

"We can damned sure play it by ear, though. Manny would do the same for us."

Hanlon quickly nodded his head. "I'll get the radio set up."

Santo was led to the bunkhouse, from which occasionally a burst of laughter brayed out through the thin walls. Stephan pushed him through the door.

"Watch it," Santo snarled at him, stumbling inside. He saw two men playing a hand of blackjack on a card table inside a Coleman-lantern-lit cabin room, reeking of urine and of wood smoke from a potbellied stove. Both men had long hair, and beard stubble covered their faces. One was fat and Hispanic. One was skinny with light brown hair. Both had automatic weapons, Ingram MAC-10's, slung over the back rests of their chairs.

A gnarled fist smacked him in back of his head. Santo sprawled down by the card table, and immediately saw something else leaning against the corner of the tiny room. It was cylindrical, about four feet tall. The olive-drab color and yellow lettering confirmed what he thought it was—a Redeye surface-to-air anti-aircraft missile. Santo began to understand what was going on.

The fat man grabbed him by the hair and yanked his head

around. "You're not very polite." Santo looked up into the face of a man that reeked of tequila and had the red eyes of an all-night pot smoker. "You apologize, now."

Santo fumed. He grabbed the fat man's wrist and thumb-pressured the delicate bones on the underside. "Let go."

The man's eyes bulged, and a low keening began in his throat. Then Santo felt the cold barrel of Stephan's submachine gun nuzzle up against the hollow underneath his ear. "*You* let go."

Santo released his grip. The fat man stood up, his potbelly bulging out of his armless T-shirt and bouncing up and down over his belt. "It will be a pleasure, shithead, to rip your balls off." He kicked Santo hard in the ribs. Santo grunted and rolled over to the side.

Stephan intervened. "Okay, okay, Marín. Save him for later. Grzniecki wants to question him with the others in a few minutes. For now, stick him in the back room with the old man, and I'll come back for him in a few minutes."

"Hokay." The fat man grabbed Santo by the hair and dragged him toward the back room, Stephan's submachine gun still parked against the team sergeant's head. They threw him inside, and Santo crashed against the opposite wall, stumbling over the prostrate form of an old man, thin, wizened, and dressed in overalls. He was dead. Santo guessed him to be the owner of the ranch.

Marin and Stephan hovered over Santo as the team sergeant got back to his feet.

"Something about this guy bothers me," Marín told Stephan in Spanish.

Santo glanced away from them, pretending he didn't know what they were saying.

"This guy . . . he looks like one of these Army guys in El Paso from Fort Bliss. I see them all the fucking time in the mall, in the restaurant, in the movies, in the clubs. . . . Look at his haircut. He looks like one of these Army guys, you know, like he's got this . . . this *appearance*, man."

Stephan studied Santo. No one had told him to search Sanchez's auxiliary driver yet. No one had paid him that much attention. Maybe he should. "How about it, asshole. You in the Army?"

Santo listened to them both laugh, imagining the surprise on their faces when he'd eventually figure out a way to cave both their heads in.

MacIntyre exited the tree line masking their surveillance site on his belly, and he slithered through the weeds and grass toward the stream below. Hanlon covered the approach with his silenced nine- millimeter. Every ten meters, MacIntyre stopped behind a rock or a bush, and then Hanlon would follow suit.

They had to be silent, slow. They'd taped down their web gear and taped their trousers and re-camouflaged their faces before leaving as insurance to keep from being seen and heard. They had to blend in with the terrain like a chameleon, glide over it like a snake. For the next five minutes, both men crawled in the direction of a bush-covered knoll on the opposite side of the stream. Across the stream and higher up the hill toward the bunkhouse, at least one man sat on a rock with his rifle propped up between his legs, smoking a cigarette. Only a few trees separated his position from the stream. The other man they'd seen earlier was out of sight.

They reached water, and gingerly hopped across the stream over rocks that glinted in the moonlight. Hanlon spoke barely above a whisper when they reached the bushes. "Dai-uy—I can go first." He pointed at the cigarette trail tracing an arc every so often between the guard's lap and his mouth. Hanlon flared his nostrils, and inhaled in short, sharp sniffs. "He may be smoking dope. There's a couple of bushes over on his right. That's where I'll go. I'll get a close look, and then zap him."

"Keep low. I'll stay a few meters behind and cover you."

Hanlon led out, high-crawling from bush to bush. He got closer. When he was fifteen feet away from his target, he stopped for a few seconds behind a tree where weeds and mesquite clustered around the tree trunk. He put his hand down to lower himself prone to the ground. The earth was damp. What the—

Hanlon raised his hand to his face and winced from the smell. It was the watering bush. He glanced at MacIntyre behind him, made a face, and pinched his nose. Suddenly, there was a rustling sound, and Hanlon saw MacIntyre's eyes widen like plates. MacIntyre raised his weapon. Carefully, heart pounding, Hanlon turned back toward the guard.

The guard was walking straight toward him!

Hanlon raised his Browning, cursing silently. If he took the guard out now, he'd get an awkward shot off at best. With his other hand, he fumbled for the sheath knife on his web belt.

The guard stopped five feet away from him, slung his rifle over his shoulder, and unzipped his pants.

Hanlon sprang to his feet, grabbed the surprised guard by the lapels of his surplus-store Army-issue jungle fatigue shirt, and sunk his sheath knife into the guard's throat up to the hilt. Then he yanked the dying man down into the bush and clamped his hand over the guard's mouth. Arterial blood from the guard's severed carotid artery sprayed a dark red smear all over Hanlon's face, sliming with the green of his camouflaged face-paint. In seconds, it was over.

Hanlon, shaking, wiped the blood off his knife and tried to stick it back in the sheath. After three tries, it finally went in.

MacIntyre had watched everything in horror, covering Hanlon with his M16 the entire time.

There was another noise, a scuffling sound, as another figure from the same guard site sat up from the prone. Apparently, he'd been sleeping.

"Jose! Where'd you go, man?"

Jose, of course, could not answer. Hanlon decided to use his suppressed Hi-Power this time. He got ready.

The other guard, a taller man, made cautiously for the trees, holding his rifle at the ready. Hanlon licked his lips and held his breath, not daring to breathe. The element of surprise was virtually gone.

"Jose," the man muttered. "What you doing in that bush, man?" He brought his rifle up to his shoulder.

MacIntyre flipped a pebble back at the man's guard position.

The guard wheeled around.

Hanlon stood straight up and aimed. His suppressed Browning spit mechanically into the night.

MacIntyre watched the guard arch his back, as if he'd been hooked around the spine with a winch and pulley, and his forehead splintered off the rest of his crown in a bloody mist. The guard fell over, making a hollow clump against the rocks. Hanlon let go of his breath and joined MacIntyre at the corpse, trying not to vomit.

Seconds later, after they had dragged the body into the bush where his partner lay, MacIntyre and Hanlon wove through the remaining bushes and rocks and trees leading toward the bunkhouse, where their team sergeant was held prisoner.

Silent. Stealthy. And with the mission on their minds.

CHAPTER TWENTY-ONE

Santo doubled over in agony where Marín's boot sank into his gut. He slumped down on his haunches against the wall, trying not to cry out. He had to endure the pain. With the submachine gun staring him in the face, any wrong move now would get his head blown off. Of course, they'd find his ID card. He simply had not had the time to get rid of it.

"Frisk him," Stephan ordered the fat man.

Marín fingered through Santo's pockets. Seconds later, he pulled a green and white laminated card out of Santo's front breast pocket that had his name and picture on it. "What did I tell you, Stephan." Marin grabbed Santo's cheeks and pinched his mouth together. "This guy *is* Army."

"Let's take him in to see Grzniecki."

Marín paid him no mind. He slapped Santo in the face twice, front- and backhanded.

Santo tuned it out. He had to absorb the pain. He had to. . . .

"I said, let's take him to—"

Marín spun around with a gleam in his eyes. "Just softening him up, you see." Then he kicked Santo between the legs.

Hanlon froze. MacIntyre crawled up next to him. "Did you hear that?"

"Yeah," MacIntyre muttered. "At least he's still alive." Hanlon checked the safety on his Hi-Power. MacIntyre pointed at the bunkhouse, which was now only another twenty meters away.

They were at the last clump of trees. Any further than that was clear going, and they could be spotted.

Hanlon grabbed MacIntyre's sleeve, pointing up at the top of the bunkhouse. "Check it out, Dai-uy. They just put a guard up there."

MacIntyre brought his M16 up and peered through the starlight scope. He saw one man with a rifle. Leaning against the bunkhouse's chimney was a tubular device about four feet long. "That's not all that's up there, Randy. Shit. Looks like a LAW, only bigger." He handed Hanlon his rifle for a look.

"That's no anti-tank weapon, sir. I think it's a shoulder-fired SAM. Can't tell what make it is."

Another yell penetrated the walls of the bunkhouse. Both men looked at each other.

"We've got to warn the STRIKE force."

The two crawled back into the tree line and made commo with the FOB, informing them about Santo's presence on the objective and the possibility of an unknown amount of shoulder-fired SAMS in the area. Minutes later, they returned to their vantage point.

"How much more time, Randy?" MacIntyre asked his partner, surveilling the guard again with his starlight scope.

"Anytime. STRIKE will be inbound within the next ten minutes."

"Let's get Santo. Can you hit that rooftop guard from here?"

Hanlon licked his lips. It was at least a thirty-meter shot. "I want to get a little closer."

Voices!

MacIntyre and Hanlon shrunk back behind the trees as a group of three men walked up the trail, each with an automatic weapon. MacIntyre scanned the group with his starlight scope. "They're headed toward the bunkhouse."

Hanlon gently slid open the breech to his M203 grenade launcher attached beneath the barrel of his M16, and replaced his flare round with one of the six buckshot rounds he'd jumped in with. MacIntyre scanned the immediate area for any more guards.

"Give it just a few more minutes till we hear the birds incoming. Then we'll take 'em out."

Hanlon nodded his head.

Suddenly, the bunkhouse door opened, and the sagging figure

of Master Sergeant Manny Santo was dragged out, supported by two men. The three others escorted the procession toward the ranch house.

Hanlon tensed and brought the M203 up to his shoulder. MacIntyre gripped his arm. He put his forefinger up to his lips, and then pointed at the guard on top of the roof.

Chelmno Grzniecki walked back into the main room of the ranch house from the bedroom, having just exchanged his Border Patrol uniform for bland, nondescript outdoor clothes and hiking boots. He met Sanchez and Antonov sitting across from one another in silence. Pietrov, who had met him at the door when they arrived, kept a wary eye on Sanchez and Antonov. His assistant, Vasily, was engaged in heated conversation with Luis Munoz, both men standing in the center of the room.

"I demand to know what is going on!" Munoz yelled.

"Señor Munoz—your merchandise is inbound even as we speak."

"I have this strange feeling that your side of the house is not in order. You told me only one person would meet us here. Instead, you bring three. Where is Pushtkin? I demand to speak with Pushtkin!"

I'd like to know that myself, Grzniecki thought, walking up to the two men. Grzniecki leaned against one of the four interior support beams that crossed the room, where once there had been a wall. "Luis," Grzniecki said soothingly, holding the drug chief by the arm, "we have done business for a while, you and I."

Munoz shrugged away from the KGB man's grasp. "Where is Pushtkin?"

"Pushtkin is dead," Grzniecki muttered, looking straight at Victoria Sanchez. "But—all goes as planned. Our people here"— Grzniecki swept an open hand toward Sanchez and then Antonov—"were more than capable of satisfying our mission requirements. Our payment to you will be here any moment. I suggest that you and your men prepare to off-load the aircraft."

Antonov stared at the KGB man, saying nothing. It simply went on and on and on, the lies, the deceit, the treachery. The only thing Grzniecki had in hand was the RAIL blueprints Sanchez had turned over as soon as they had reached the safe house. No RAIL model. No RAIL scientist. And as for Pushtkin—Grzniecki suspected the worst. Antonov knew he was a dead man.

Sanchez read Antonov's thoughts as she stared at him from across the room. This time there was no bomb in a backpack, no uncertainty in a canyon in the mountains. They were trapped. She glanced from man to man, surmising their weaponry. *Unless* . . . The man called Pietrov, standing next to Munoz and Grzniecki, was a virtual armory of personal weapons. Strapped to his body in a crisscross of web gear were grenades, a pistol, magazines of ammunition; slung over his arm was a submachine gun. Perhaps she could create a diversion. Perhaps she could enlist Antonov's help, as before. . . . She concentrated very hard on catching Antonov's eye.

And then Antonov saw her.

Munoz softened a little. "If this is a double cross, so help me—"

"*Señor!* We have done business together many times," Grzniecki said, putting his arm across the shorter man's shoulders. "You already have half of what I promised you. I would be a fool to cross your organization—an utter fool! We share the same goals, you and I. And when have we ever withheld payment?"

Now Munoz grinned. "Yes, you *would* be a fool, and no, you have never withheld payment." Munoz laughed loudly and shook Grzniecki's hand. "But in my business—I trust no one."

The door banged open. All stared as two men flung Santo inside, his bruised and battered face striking against the floor. Stephan entered with the fat man. "That's enough, Marín. Bring the others up to the bunkhouse to off-load the aircraft when it comes." The fat man left.

"What is this!" Grzniecki demanded. "I told you to keep this man in the bunkhouse."

Before answering, Stephan glanced at the drug chief. Grzniecki took the cue. "Vasily! Help Señor Munoz get his men together to off-load the aircraft."

"What is this, Grzniecki!"

Vasily took the mercurial Munoz's elbow. "This is between the Russians, my friend. Family business. You understand."

Munoz made a face. "I warn you. . . ." He stomped toward the door. "I'm ready to call everything off! By God, I will!" Vasily followed the drug chief out the door, calming him down.

Grzniecki turned flaming eyes on Stephan. "Now what!"

Stephan handed him the identification card. Grzniecki read it. "Master Sergeant Timothy M. Santo, this says. United States Army." He squinted at Santo, who by now had gotten back to his feet. Santo's two escorts grasped the team sergeant tightly by his upper arms. Grzniecki flipped the card over. "Serial number H092138." Grzniecki looked around the room and then slapped his palm against the upright beam he'd been leaning against earlier. It was sound. "Bind him between these beams," he ordered Santo's two guards.

Grzniecki walked up to Sanchez as his guards complied. "You did not tell me you had recruited someone in the American Army, Victoria."

Sanchez lifted her chin. "I have my reasons. This man works in Fort Bliss and has access to White Sands. As I told you earlier, he was a part of my auxiliary network."

Antonov's ears perked up. He hadn't had a chance to match stories with Sanchez yet. He'd have to follow her lead.

"Enough," Grzniecki barked. "We will talk in Juarez." He turned his attention to Antonov. "I think, Major Antonov, that Victoria Sanchez is not as smart as she thinks she is."

Antonov made no comment. *Diversion, diversion! Think of something!* He too, as with Sanchez, had cased the room for weaponry. If he could only get that guard Pietrov's submachine gun. He glanced at Stephan, who oversaw the two other guards binding Santo in spread-eagle fashion between the roof support beams. *Maybe . . .*

"I think, Major Antonov, that our Spetsnaz friends are more than capable of extracting information from American counterespionage agents." Grzniecki swung his attention to Santo, walking toward him.

Santo didn't know *what* to say. Either way, he was fucked. The corners of his mouth slowly upturned, mocking the KGB officer. "Chill out, Grez-nyeckie. You'll give yourself an ulcer."

Grzniecki wheeled away from him. "Major Antonov! Interrogate this American pig!"

When MacIntyre and Hanlon saw a Soviet and one of the Mexicans leave the ranch house and head toward the southern trail, the Mexican gesticulating wildly and cursing, they knew the odds were improving—the more internal confusion happening within the enemy element, the better. But there was still the rooftop guard above the bunkhouse to consider. They had to take out the SAM position before the STRIKE force arrived. There was no telling how many others were in the area.

"Ready, Dai-uy?"

"Yeah."

Hanlon skirted back up the hill the last few meters up to the clearing around the bunkhouse, MacIntyre following closely behind. Hanlon slung his M203 around his shoulder and thumbed back the hammer of his pistol. They watched the guard walk from one side of the roof to the other. When he was on the side opposite to them, the two sprinted one at a time across the twenty-meter clearing.

They hugged the splintery wooden side of the bunkhouse, breathing in deep, controlled breaths. Hanlon glanced at MacIntyre with both hands on the grip of his Hi-Power and nodded.

MacIntyre reached up with a stick and tapped the lip of the bunkhouse's roof.

Footsteps, approaching. MacIntyre shrank back against the wall of the bunkhouse and split the full moon in half with the muzzle of his M16 he held upright in front of his face. Hanlon held his pistol above his head with both hands, ready.

The guard leaned over the rooftop. Hanlon leaped out and double-tapped him twice in the face with the Hi-Power—two spits and a clump when the guard collapsed backward on the roof. He lay very still.

Hanlon and MacIntyre crept around the side of the building and they cautiously peered around the corner. Another guard was stationed at the ranch house entrance, having just shot upright from the chair he'd been sitting in. The coal on the end of the cigarette he was smoking lit his face in an orange glow.

Hanlon and MacIntyre exchanged looks. They had to move. To waste time and stay out in the open like this for more than a minute would spell disaster.

Then MacIntyre grabbed Hanlon's arm, tapping his own ear and pointing skyward. It was the faint whir of helicopter blades. MacIntyre mouthed the words—*STRIKE force*. Another minute and it would be onsite.

Hanlon nodded and peeped back around the cabin at the guard.

The guard had heard it too. He left his post and walked directly toward them to investigate the strange sounds he'd heard moments earlier.

"Hey, Lacey," MacIntyre heard the guard say softly, craning his neck up at the bunkhouse's rooftop. "The bird's inbound. Keep a sharp eye out for anything that doesn't look right."

The guard received no answer.

"Lacey! You asleep?" He came closer to the bunkhouse.

When he walked around the corner, MacIntyre yanked his head back by the hair and slashed his throat in one fluid movement. He threw him down to the ground. Hanlon put a round in his head to ensure his silence. Both men looked at each other, wondering what to do with the body. "Out of sight, out of mind, boss," Hanlon whispered, his face pale as the moon.

They stuffed him underneath the bunkhouse.

Silently, they stole across the clearing between the two buildings up to the front door of the ranch house, careful not to make the porch boards squeak.

The whir of the approaching aircraft grew louder. MacIntyre glanced at his watch. It was time for the STRIKE.

Then the both of them heard something else.

Voices. Several of them.

MacIntyre brought the starlight scope mounted on his M16 up to his face and saw a half-dozen men on the southern approach walking toward the ranch house.

"Comrade Major," Grzniecki told Antonov, smirking, "I believe that our friend Victoria Sanchez has not been telling me the truth."

Antonov glanced at Sanchez, who was now standing just ahead and off to the side of her guard Pietrov to watch the "interrogation." Pietrov watched her closely, ready at any moment to seize her on Grzniecki's signal. Santo was spread-eagled and bound between the support beams of the ranch house's living room, straining against the thin nylon cord that cut off the circulation to his wrists and ankles. His shirt had been ripped off, and Antonov stared at a long scar that ran in a diagonal slash from Santo's right armpit to his navel. Clearly, the man had seen combat before. Antonov identified with the scar. He had a few of his own.

Grzniecki now turned his attention to Santo. "Tell me, Master

Sergeant Santo, exactly why our friend Victoria Sanchez has *recruited* you. What was your duty position at Fort Bliss? What was your mission concerning White Sands, your directions from Sanchez, your payment?"

Santo squinted at the KGB chief, saying nothing. His mind raced, wondering how long he could hold out. Was there any sense in holding out? They'd kill him either way. If he stuck with Sanchez's story about his being a member of her auxiliary—which Grzniecki apparently did not believe—things were going to get rough. If he spilled the beans about what *really* happened . . .

"Stoic, eh?"

Santo cleared his throat to speak.

Grzniecki leaned forward. "Yes?"

"Listen very carefully."

"Yes?"

"Suck . . . my . . . shorts."

Grzniecki shrieked in outrage and slapped Santo twice across the face. "Oh, I see now! Yes, indeed. You will talk, American spy, yes, you will talk!"

The KGB agent pulled something out of his pocket and thumped it repeatedly in the palm of his left hand. Antonov stared at it. It was an eight-inch mill bastard file, used for sharpening saws, knives, axes . . . it did one hell of a job on human teeth. Antonov had used the file technique many times. One or two strokes would flay the front incisors down to raw, screaming nerve. It was one of the quickest ways to coerce information out of anyone.

Why does he want this charade to go on like this? Antonov thought. "Perhaps this is best done in Juarez, Comrade Grzniecki."

Grzniecki drug the handle of the file, more of a tapering metal point, slowly across Santo's scar, smiling a big smile. "We still have a few minutes before our plane arrives, Major." Santo stared back at him in contempt.

Antonov's mind raced. When he did get the information out of Santo—and he would—both he and the American would be shot on the spot. He was being used merely as a tool to inflict torture, a charade, a game for Sanchez's benefit before Grzniecki burned her mind out with drugs.

Grzniecki's smile vanished. "I want information from this man now, Antonov. I don't understand why, if he is merely an auxiliary, he refuses to talk. And that . . . bothers me a great deal." He nodded at Pietrov. "Hold her." Pietrov grabbed Sanchez's arms to hold her fast. Grzniecki nodded at his partner Stephan, who was watching the process in grinning interest. "Assist Major Antonov, would you?"

Stephan nudged Antonov toward the bound American, covering him from the rear. Grzniecki grabbed Antonov's hand and slapped the file in it. "I don't believe her story, you see, Comrade Antonov. I have yet to question you. But—you *will* get the story out of this American. The real story. Now . . . make the American talk."

MacIntyre and Hanlon looked around from the corner of the ranch house. The voices they'd heard turned out to be over a half-dozen men. They'd entered the bunkhouse and then exited, walking toward an open area on the other side. Another ten joined them from the opposite wood line. They were now out of their lines of sight and had not seen the dead guard on top of the bunkhouse. The hum of the approaching aircraft grew louder.

"Dai-uy—they act like they're expecting the STRIKE force."
"Makes no sense."
"Maybe they're expecting something else."
MacIntyre nodded his head. "We've just gotta play it by ear, Randy. We'll have to wait till the STRIKE force gets on site." He pointed at the ranch house's side window. Hanlon followed him to it and flicked off the safety to his M203. MacIntyre slowly raised his head and peered inside. Seconds later he ducked back down. "They're gonna give him the third degree. Some guy's got a file. Take a look." Hanlon raised his head and scanned the room. Then he ducked back down.

The hum of the aircraft grew louder as it made its approach, but it was not the steady whir of a Blackhawk. Both men squinted at the horizon. When they spotted the incoming aircraft, their eyes widened upon spotting a tilt-rotor inbound to the ranch. As it landed, engines still idling, a crew of six men raced toward it for off-loading.

"No—that's not them!" Suddenly, static crackled on MacIntyre's transmitter. *"Papa-Sierra, this is Sierra-Foxtrot One—Tango*

Oscar Tango in one minute; I say again, time on target in one minute, over."

"This is Papa-Sierra—be advised, another aircraft is on the objective; unknown armaments; approximately sixteen to twenty enemy personnel in the clearing by the ranch house, over."

No answer. MacIntyre repeated the message. Then, the crackling reply: "*. . . three-zero seconds, time-on-target . . . we're coming in, over."*

"Let's go," MacIntyre whispered.

They returned to the porch. MacIntyre stuck his transmitter back into the spare ammo pouch on his web belt. Their lives would depend on their commo in just a matter of seconds after they sprang Santo.

Hanlon stood on the right side of the door where he'd follow MacIntyre in with his buckshot-loaded M203. MacIntyre looked at his watch, as they crouched down low, ready to spring inside in twenty seconds.

"Open the American's mouth, Stephan, so the major can do what he does best."

Grinning, Stephan slung his submachine gun over his left shoulder and walked over to Santo with a stick of wood he'd ripped out of the window paneling earlier.

Antonov's eyes widened. *That, my friend, was a mistake.* He moved his grip up on the file, so now he held it as he would a dagger. The point of the handle would easily penetrate skull bone.

Stephan yanked back on Santo's hair, exposing his neck. "Open your mouth."

"Fuck you."

"Open your mouth, American pig!" Stephan kneed the team sergeant deep in the gut. Santo sagged between the beams. Then he tensed and glared at the Soviet, murder in his eyes. "Open your mouth!" Stephan ranted.

Santo opened his mouth.

Stephan shoved the wood paneling in it to bare Santo's teeth. When he did, Santo jerked his head around and sunk his teeth into the Soviet's fingers.

Stephan lost all composure and shrieked. Frantically, he slammed his knee into Santo's groin and the team sergeant's bite on him relaxed. Stephan yanked his torn and bleeding fingers away from Santo's mouth.

Grzniecki shifted around to Sanchez and put his hands on her shoulders, momentarily masking Pietrov's line of fire. "Fool! Hurry up! Watch closely, Victoria Sanchez! Remember when you debrief me in Juarez how you will talk!"

A cascade of obscenities, in Russian, poured from Stephan's mouth. *"Pig! Bastard! You will pay!"* He yanked back on Santo's hair and struck the small of his back with his right fist. Santo grunted.

Stephan glared wildly at Antonov, who moved in with the file. *"File his lips off! Rind the gums from his skull! Shove his teeth up his ass!"* Stephan yanked back harder on Santo's hair, clenching Santo's bicep with his left hand. His submachine gun slipped off his shoulder and hung half way down his arm.

MacIntyre palmed the door handle in his left hand, his right clasped tightly around the pistol grip of his M16. The other birds were clearly inbound now, and they could see the enemy look up in the air in surprise as they off-loaded the tilt-rotor that had just landed in the clearing. Swallowing, MacIntyre brought the stock of his M16 up to his shoulder and whispered, "On three. *One . . . two . . .*"

A Blackhawk doing over a hundred knots flying nap-of-the-earth makes little noise at treetop level until it's actually over its destination. The sound the rotor makes is a steady hum, and it does not make the wop-wop sound of a Huey.

Lieutenant Colonel Andrei Volensky sat in the front passenger seat of the lead Blackhawk, as the bird skimmed just meters off the ground, tensed, adrenaline flowing, his heart thumping hard in his chest cavity. They'd been flying through canyons, in between ridgelines. Within seconds they'd be on the objective.

With Redeyes on-site. Volensky's stomach churned when he thought of them.

Now, surprise was largely cancelled. They were already inbound when his point-surveillance team radioed the information about the SAMs. They could no longer fast-rope on top of the buildings as originally planned. Success on this mission depended on how fast the two teams could dismount from a spot where the Redeyes were unable to get at the birds and sweep the entire objective area. Hopefully, being dope-smugglers, the men on the ground would run like scared rabbits and become ensnared in the FBI nets all along the objective's avenues of approach.

Then again, they might fight. They just might.

Antonov moved in closer with the file and raised it up to Santo's mouth.

"Now! Do it now!" Stephan ranted.

Antonov raised the file back up to Santo's mouth. Both men stared at each other for a second. Beads of perspiration formed on Santo's forehead. Antonov's grip tightened around the blade of the file, the point sticking out of the bottom of his fist and the knuckles of his hand gleaming in the dark, poorly lit room.

Then, wheeling around, he slammed it into Stephan's forehead. Stephan shrieked, and Antonov ripped the submachine gun away from him as the dead man slunk to the floor.

Split seconds! Everything happened at once!

Grzniecki moved first, shoving Sanchez away from Pietrov's line of sight so the other could fire. They darted for the back door.

Antonov spun back around to shoot.

The door burst open!

Santo, wide-eyed, watched his team leader and heavy weapons sergeant leap into the room.

The roar of Hanlon's M203 blew Pietrov backwards head over heels.

Antonov hesitated and made for the back of the room. Where was Grzniecki? Sanchez? He scrambled for the rear entrance.

MacIntyre shot him.

Antonov felt a crushing blow pound his head, a burst of light, a numbness. And then he was dead.

MacIntyre whisked out his sheath knife and started to cut his team sergeant down.

"Hurry, Dai-uy!" Hanlon yelled, rushing toward the back rooms of the ranch. No one. The others had gotten away. He reentered the living room, where MacIntyre was cutting at the cords around Santo's ankles.

"Cover the door, Randy!" Santo yelled.

Hanlon kneeled by the door, flipped open his M203's breech, and slammed in another buckshot round. He spotted movement to his front and fired. The corner of the bunkhouse splintered into fragments, where two men were blown into oblivion. More came. Many more. "Goddam, there's a bunch of 'em by the bunkhouse!" he yelled. Pinging rounds smacked into the doorway and windows. Hanlon belted out another round at the bunkhouse, and the firing subsided.

"There's a STRIKE going down, Manny!" MacIntyre informed his team sergeant.

A second passed as Santo stared at the dead Russian on the floor. The Spetsnaz leader. There was no way MacIntyre could have known. "Come on, we've gotta stop their exfil bird!" Santo whipped up the submachine gun and checked the bolt. Then he grabbed two more clips of ammunition from the corpse with an eight-inch mill bastard file planted in his forehead.

"The STRIKE force—Manny, these guys have SAMs!"

Santo stared at MacIntyre and Hanlon, remembering the Redeye he'd seen in the bunkhouse. Hanlon continued blasting M203 rounds at the bunkhouse from the front door.

"There's one in the bunkhouse. We gotta take those guys out before they blow up the Blackhawks. Let's go out the back way."

The three men bolted out the back door, and then circled around and flanked the bunkhouse.

A rain of fire met them there.

CHAPTER TWENTY-TWO

"Sierra-Foxtrot One, this is Papa-Sierra," MacIntyre yelled into the transmitter. "You're coming in hot, over."

"This is Sierra-Foxtrot One, read you loud and clear," came the reply, hissing over MacIntyre's hand-held receiver-transmitter. He recognized the voice belonging to Major Richards, his company commander and STRIKE force leader. *"We will dismount the birds in one-five seconds and assault over your northeast ridgeline on foot, over."*

MacIntyre ducked, as rounds pinged the tree trunk by his head, blasting pine bark into his face that stung and cut. Hanlon and Santo were still firing at the bunkhouse.

"Keep the Blackhawks away from here," MacIntyre replied to Richards. "I repeat, there's an undetermined amount of SAMs in the AO of the Redeye type, I say again, *Redeye*, over."

"Roger that, our force will be at your location in another five minutes. Out."

MacIntyre stuffed his transmitter back in its pouch, realizing that things were not looking good at all. The dope-smugglers on the LZ were no more than seventy-five meters away from them, hurrying to off-load the tilt-rotor. More were scrambling in the perimeter over by the bunkhouse, caught between the STRIKE force and themselves. It was rapidly turning into an every-man-for-himself situation if they were to escape, and that meant they had to get back to the bunkhouse where the bulk of their ammunition was stored.

Santo crawled over to MacIntyre, while Hanlon pumped out

M203 heat rounds on the bunkhouse, keeping the enemy's heads down. "Sir! We gotta take out that aircraft before it takes off! There's a Redeye in that bunkhouse we can grab."

Somehow, the three had to hold their own and keep the bad guys from controlling the bunkhouse while the STRIKE force pressed them in that direction. Even cornered rats would fight, and the druggies would have to fight for the bunkhouse if they were to survive.

But MacIntyre knew they had to prevent the aircraft's escape. If it took off with the RAIL information the woman had stolen from White Sands, then the entire mission would have been a failure. "Let's go!" MacIntyre yelled.

Hanlon spotted two rushing figures in the distance, making their way toward the tilt-rotor. "Hey, those are the agents—the woman and the guy who was interrogating you, Manny!"

"Hold 'em down, Randy. We'll be back as soon as we get that Redeye!"

With that, Santo and MacIntyre broke contact and rushed in three-second bounds toward the bunkhouse.

"Go, go, go!" Lieutenant Colonel Andrei Volensky shouted at Richards. The company commander needed no encouragement. He and his two-team STRIKE force fast-roped off the two helicopters maintaining a ten-foot hover just on the military crest of the northern ridgeline facing the objective. Two men remained behind with Volensky, armed with M203's.

Volensky watched his STRIKE force race into the trees scattered over the top of the ridgeline. It had been a good thing that his point-surveillance team had located the SAMs and radioed the information in, or else the Blackhawks would have been destroyed upon the assault. MacIntyre and Hanlon were alert and thinking.

Things were happening fast. Already, he could hear the sound of gunfire on the objective. Then it occurred to him that his point-surveillance team had to have been pretty goddam close to the objective to have seen everything they had reported in as much detail.

Volensky turned toward his pilot in the Blackhawk's cockpit. "Stay on the periphery of the camp. Be ready to duck back behind the ridgelines in case we get any of those SAMs coming our way. I want to see how this little battle develops. When Richards assaults the objective, be prepared to move in with our door gunners to support them."

"Roger that, sir!"

The helicopters started a slow circle just over the ridgelines, and Volensky saw the tilt-rotor aircraft below. It had to be the escape bird.

That aircraft had to be destroyed.

Major Halley Richards and crew silently rushed over the top of the ridgeline. Speed was security as it stood now. They simply had to assault the objective and secure it as soon as possible.

Gunfire on the left! The STRIKE assault element hit the ground.

Richards counted the muzzle flashes as his STRIKE force returned fire at them. There were only four of them, probably an enemy security position. There was no choice. They had to go through them.

"Assault!"

The STRIKE force laid down a murderous base of fire. The muzzle flashes disappeared.

After rushing forward, they located two bodies. The others had broken contact and were rushing down the opposite side of the ridgeline toward the ranch house.

"What's the status, Seven-Three?" he yelled out in the dark of the night.

"No casualties here," the team leader answered from his left.

"Three-Five's got the team leader down—broken ankle during the rush!" the other team added from Richards's right.

The sweep was going to be simple. All they had to do was assault the drug-smugglers, and they'd run into the traps and ambushes the FBI contingent had emplaced farther down along the opposite avenues of approach.

"Move out!" Richards yelled.

The STRIKE force picked up and gave chase to their would-be ambushers.

MacIntyre and Santo hugged the side of the bunkhouse. Just around the corner, two men were returning fire at Hanlon. Both MacIntyre and Santo glanced at each other. It was very simple. They had to rush them.

MacIntyre stepped around the corner, and saw them behind the porch blocks of the bunkhouse. He leveled the muzzle of his M16 and emptied half his magazine in their position. Santo covered his rear. Another man jumped out of the front door with a drawn .45. Santo blew him over the rail with a three-round burst from his submachine gun.

Santo bounded up the steps to the side of the door and sprayed the room before bursting in. MacIntyre ran up the porch steps and followed suit. Both men jumped inside one after the other, their weapons at the ready for anyone who might have survived the initial burst of fire. Santo spotted a fleeing figure exiting the back. It was too late to get him. Immediately, he saw what they'd come for—the Redeyes. Already, crates of the missiles had been carried from the tilt-rotor on the landing zone into the bunkhouse for storage, and three of them were laid out on the poker table Santo had seen earlier.

"Sir, cover me while I get this thing ready."

"Roger that!" MacIntyre posted himself by the front door.

Santo opened up one of the missile crates and ripped away the foil vacuum seal. He stared at the olive-drab-colored missile for a second, and then gently pulled it out of the styrofoam encircling the heat-seeker. A cursory glance and a few movements of his fingers later after checking the safety and arming device, he slung his submachine gun over his shoulder and ran for the back door with the Redeye. "Cover me!"

MacIntyre moved out ahead of his team sergeant. When he reached the back door, he popped his head outside before darting out to identify any enemy. There were none. He could still hear Hanlon's M203 firing, so things were still maintaining. "Manny, c'mon! He can't hold out much longer!" He flew down the back steps.

Then a man ran past his front from the right side of the house. He wheeled around in surprise as MacIntyre quick-fired his M16 at him. When MacIntyre squeezed the trigger, the man's face disappeared in a red cloud.

Santo dashed down the steps upon hearing the front door behind him open. He spun around just in time to snap his submachine gun up and fire at the men entering.

"They're hitting us from the other side," MacIntyre yelled. "The STRIKE force must be closing them in. Get on back to Randy and take out that exfil bird! C'mon, move it, Manny!"

Santo needed no additional prodding as he sprinted for the ranch house twenty meters away, while MacIntyre laid down suppressive fire. MacIntyre worked his way back for the scant safety of the porch, where Santo got the Redeye ready.

Santo now had a choice. Save his team leader's ass, or blow up the tilt-rotor. He hesitated, and then rushed back up to MacIntyre, spraying the remainder of his magazine into the men firing at them, offering MacIntyre a chance to change magazines.

"Goddammit, take out that aircraft!"

"Cover me while I arm this thing—I can get it from here!"

Swearing, MacIntyre popped another magazine into his M16 and returned fire, his mind a flurry of thoughts and emotions and questions and decisions. How much longer could Hanlon hold out? How much longer could any of them hold out?

The pitch of the tilt-rotor changed into a shrieking whine as it prepared to take off.

Hanlon pumped out the remaining buckshot round he had left, and then clawed back at the ground and pine needles and cactus beneath him as he received an answering barrage from the enemy perimeter around the exfiltration aircraft eighty meters to his front. He roundly cursed himself for not having brought more heat rounds. Now, the five personnel who had been off-loading it had formed a tight security perimeter around the aircraft while Grzniecki and Sanchez crawled toward them under the safety of their suppresive fire.

He realized they stood a good chance to escape, unless Santo got that Redeye in action, and that had damn well better be soon. There was no way he could get at them with the rock chips and tree bark flying at his face from barely missed rounds. Hanlon hugged the ground and crammed a fresh magazine in his M16. The only thing he had left for his M203 were flares, and a fat lot of good that would do him now.

He crawled to the side of his covering boulder and blasted away at the perimeter, and saw one man grab his forehead and fall back. *One more. That's good. Now if I can just—*

A spray of dirt erupted in his face. Blinded from dust, Hanlon crabbed around to his side, bringing his M16 up. Before the rushing figure on his right could assault his position, he pulled the trigger and rattled a six-round burst into the man. The man twisted around and the momentum of his assault carried him over Hanlon, where he fell and tumbled face-first into a bed of prickly-pear cactus.

Hanlon shuddered and fought to clear his irritated eyes of dirt. Already, tear streaks ran muddy trails down his cheeks.

The aircraft! Gotta get that bird!

The whine of the aircraft, as it climbed into a two-foot hover, grew louder.

When Hanlon could see again, he watched one man climb inside. He brought his M16 back to his shoulder to fire at him, but it jammed. He yanked back at the charging handle, and then burned his fingers trying to pull two 5.56-millimeter cartridges loose where they had crammed against one another in the chamber.

Victoria Sanchez made her own choices and chose her own destiny. To escape from the incoming American force via this exfiltration aircraft made sense, even if it meant crawling through rocks and cactus and deadwood and thorns to get to it. Even if it meant following Grzniecki back to Juarez.

But as she lurched toward the aircraft, she also knew that Grzniecki would get all the information from her she had left in her cerebrum upon arrival, and then dispose of her. She knew this too.

But was she trapped? Not if she could help it. America was a land of opportunity, and she damned well intended to stay here. She would, by God, take the aircraft over as soon as she got on board.

Rounds shot dirt sprays all around her. *Blast it!* The Americans left behind in the woods would kill her before she could get on the aircraft.

"Hurry!" Grzniecki screamed at her from up front. She glanced up and coiled, ready to spring at him and propel them both toward the open cabin doors of the tilt-wing, which was now maintaining a hover two feet above the ground. Each of the men returning fire at the Americans back at the ranch house were now glancing around in fright, knowing that it was time to board the tilt-rotor, but wasn't the aircraft trying to take off without them?

A double cross!

One man, a smelling, long-haired fat man, sprang to his feet to run away, to run into the tree line and evade his way back into the safety of Las Cruces and El Paso, dependent on his own wits. For this man, Marin, it was the wrong decision. As soon as he got to his feet, Sanchez saw him get drilled in the forehead by the Americans' persistent fire from the ranch house. Sanchez started to crawl past him, keeping her head down, knowing the aircraft was her only hope.

"Hurry!" Grzniecki shrieked at her. He had by now reached the cabin door and was climbing inside the aircraft. He turned away to save his own skin. The tilt-rotor climbed to a hover of three feet, and started to fly across the LZ.

It was her chance. She grabbed the dead man's machine pistol he'd been firing. It was an Ingram MAC-10, and that suited her just fine. She could deal with Grzniecki on board the tilt-rotor. She slung it around her neck and bolted for the aircraft.

Before it could gather lateral speed, she latched her hands on the skids and clawed her way up toward the cabin door. She was off balance. The lurching of the aircraft made her feet slip. The aircraft skimmed the ground faster now, and her hiking boots brushed the cactus and the scrub oak flashing below. What remained of her strength ebbed slowly, inexorably away from her forearms as she fought to maintain her grip. She had to hold on, had to. . . .

When she looked back up, she saw the bore of Grzniecki's 9-millimeter staring her in the face, and behind that, the smirk of a man who had just won the Monopoly game creasing his thin lips.

Mortified, Santo watched the aircraft take off and drew his lips back in a scream of outrage. *"Goddammit, no!"*

MacIntyre released a barrage of fire with his M16 at the newcomers approaching the bunkhouse, and Santo did the same with his submachine gun while Macintyre slammed his last magazine into his weapon to reload. The rounds pinging around them were lessening now.

There was only one thing to do, and it had to be done now.

MacIntyre started firing again.

Santo leapt out from behind the protective cover of the cement blocks comprising the ranch house's porch. Rounds pinged all around him as he planted the Redeye's sight against his right eye and thumbed the arming device onto the fire mode. He did his best to ignore the heat of the battle erupting and flaming all around him.

And when a round burned its way into his calf, he tried to regain his balance and ignore that too.

"You die, Victoria Sanchez!" Grzniecki thumbed back the hammer of his pistol. His finger started to squeeze the trigger.

Sanchez released her grip on the aircraft and tumbled into the void below.

Where she disappeared in the mass of cactus and scrub brush and pine trees that grew along the stream junction at the foot of the hill.

"Faster!" Grzniecki screamed at the pilot. "Faster!" His mind raced in a multitude of disjointed, panicking thoughts. *Sanchez is dead, at least. The Americans will not find out about anything—all traces of the operation are finally burned.*

RAIL!

He sighed suddenly in relief. He, as Sanchez had done, had wrapped the RAIL blueprints in plastic, and it was now taped around his waist like a money belt. The mission would be successful after all, and now he would be in charge of the *residentura* in Juarez. Pushtkin was no longer around. He might even get one of the more choice *residenturas* . . . there was always Vienna or Paris to consider. . . .

The tilt-rotor gathered more speed and Grzniecki leaned out toward the cabin door to pull it shut. Already, he could see the tops of the two buildings below. All was done. The drug people—well they had known the risks. And the Redeye SAMs his own people had taken from the Mujahideen rebel bases in Afghanistan could only be traced back to the American pig CIA agents who had given them to the rebels in the first place. There would be a public outrage when the news was leaked to the American public about Redeye missiles in the hands of the drug cartel. Political heads would roll. Yes, there had been casualties this mission, but now, all traces were burned.

As thoughts of promotion passed through Grzniecki's mind, and as the KGB chieftain reached his hand out to close the cabin door, he saw one last thing below that . . . for a moment confused him. It was a bright red dot. It was a bright red dot that grew bigger.

And when it got really big, and when Grzniecki's face started to melt in the heat milliseconds before the explosion, the last thing he thought about was the goddamned Redeyes the American pigs had supplied Mujahideen rebels with in Afghanistan.

The explosion's concussion threw Santo to the ground like a discarded doll. His leg was on fire, where he'd been shot. The heat and flame lit up the entire area, and debris from the blast smacked all around the ranch house. A weapon that had been firing at him was now silenced, and when Santo looked up, he saw a man clutching at his chest with a huge metal fragment lodged in there.

MacIntyre!

Yelling in pain and outrage, Santo lurched back to MacIntyre's position.

No—no, it wasn't MacIntyre . . . his team leader lay in a dazed stupor where he'd caught a round that had grazed the side of his head, tearing his right ear almost in half. Blood from the wound covered the side of his face and neck.

"C'mon, Boss . . . got to get out of here . . ." He yanked at MacIntyre's web gear. The dazed captain's eyes blinked rapidly, and then he started to move.

"Out of ammo," he gasped.

Rounds! Firing from everywhere! Chips of concrete from the porch sparked and stung Santo's face, as what was left of the off-loading detail now tried to rush theirs and Hanlon's positions from the landing zone.

Santo ducked, pushing MacIntyre back to the ground with him, his leg screaming in pain. His submachine gun! He glanced around and spotted it in the dirt, where he'd left it when he'd fired the Redeye. *Please, God, let there be ammo left.* . . .

His fingers clawed around the pistol grip just in time to take out one enemy guard trying to get to them from the entranceway of the bunkhouse.

MacIntyre, regaining his senses, crawled to his feet. "Manny, let's get the fuck out of here!"

More fire!

In horror, Santo spotted uniformed men laying down a base of fire as he clung to MacIntyre's uniform shirt, leaning on him for support. They were firing at him! He realized then, that he was dressed in Antonov's discarded civilian clothes. The STRIKE force!

MacIntyre threw Santo behind the protective cover of the ranch house, and then scrambled after him, his hand groping for the transmitter in his web gear. Santo crabwalked toward Hanlon's position.

MacIntyre brought the radio up to his mouth. "STRIKE force, this is Papa-Sierra, STRIKE force, this is Macintyre, *Goddammit!* You're firing on us, you're . . . *cease fire! Cease Fire!*"

MacIntyre glanced up. Santo was crawling toward Hanlon's position. He was still receiving fire from two of the enemy from where the tilt-rotor had taken off. Hanlon was curled up into a ball, clutching at his chest, his weapon empty.

He watched the remaining enemy on the landing zone aim their weapons toward Santo.

"Manny, get down!" MacIntyre ran after him.

Major Halley Richards led the STRIKE force into the objective's perimeter, where they had chased what was left of the armed drug-smuggler force up the hill, driving them back like cornered rats to where they would capture or kill them. There were now precious few left, and they were raising their hands in surrender.

The Blackhawks reappeared on the horizon, suddenly opening up on the landing zone. They had been following the skirmish the entire time, as the STRIKE element drove the undisciplined crew of drug operatives back toward the ranch.

Suddenly, Richards's radio crackled to life, and his RTO handed him the mike.

". . . this is MacIntyre, goddammit! You're firing on us, you're . . . cease fire! Cease fire!"

Richards raised his night-vision goggles to his face. There! He spotted MacIntyre and a civilian crawling toward some rocks behind the ranch house. What was he doing with a civilian?

Santo!

"My God, cease fire!" he yelled above the din. *But wait . . . there were other civilians on the opposite side of the ranch house, also heading toward the rocks, firing at something. What the hell about that?*

"Shift fire! Shift fire! Targets on the right of the ranch!"

The STRIKE force bounded in elements of two on both sides of the ranch house.

"Okay, go in!" Volensky yelled at the pilots. "Door gunner—take them out!"

As Volensky's Blackhawk screamed into the ranch house's perimeter, the door gunner manning a 7.62-millimeter mini-gun sprayed hundreds of rounds onto the landing zone, where what was left of the drug-smugglers' force died in the midst of red tracers that consumed them like a horde of locusts.

Hanlon finally freed his Hi-Power away from its shoulder holster inside his fatigue shirt, whipping it out in time to sight it in on a civilian druggie hobbling his way toward him—

No! It was Santo!

A fresh volley of fire blasted his position from the side of the ranch house! Santo flipped to the ground.

"NO, GODDAMMIT!" Hanlon raised up and emptied his Browning Hi-Power into two of the enemy racing for his position.

Simultaneously, MacIntyre jumped out from around the corner of the ranch house and blew his remaining magazine into Hanlon's targets. With cold satisfaction, he watched one man's face turn into a red, raw cavity where Hanlon's double-tap had hit him. Before, that face had belonged to the petulant, gesticulating drug chief he and Hanlon had spotted leaving the ranch house before they sprang Santo earlier. MacIntyre's target had fared no better.

The two Blackhawks swooped in low suddenly over the northern ridgeline, the front support wheels of one banging a cactus plant down the slope. The choppers came in low, very low, emptying a stream of red tracers from the door gunner's position into the bunkhouse.

One swerved and pointed its nose at Santo. It seemed as if the helicopter was trying to make up its mind whether or not to blast him into infinity.

"Help me, Randy!"

Lurching for Hanlon's position, MacIntyre grabbed his team sergeant by his shirt.

Hanlon jumped to his feet, and together, they dragged Santo behind the rocks.

"Reload!"

"With what?"

"Fucking *anything!*"

"I'm out!"

MacIntyre gave Hanlon a wide-eyed stare. "Me too."

Santo mumbled incoherently. He'd been shot through the thigh on the same leg wounded earlier, and was bleeding badly. "Get my . . . get the clip in my . . ." He fumbled for the pocket of the hiking trousers he wore.

"There!" MacIntyre yelled, sticking his hand in Santo's pocket. He pulled out the last clip Santo possessed.

"Get ready with that!" Hanlon said, this time loading his M203 with a flare. It was all he had left. "More of 'em coming from around the ranch house!"

MacIntyre fought with Santo's H&K and stuck the remaining clip into the submachine gun. When he had it loaded, he pulled the bolt to the rear and made sure the selector switch was on fire.

He aimed the submachine gun at the running figures approaching them. He started to squeeze the trigger.

And then he relaxed.

Hanlon dropped the barrel of his M203-mounted M16.

This time, they would have been firing at friendlies, and the STRIKE force clustering around them now would not have liked that at all.

Volensky ordered the pilots to set down, ready to retrieve the STRIKE force and security and point-surveillance elements immediately after the civilian authorities arrived. As the two Blackhawks landed on the LZ, a dozen assorted four-wheelers from the New Mexico state police and FBI drove into the area to mop up.

Lieutenant Colonel Andrei Volensky jumped out of the helicopter. Inhaling deeply, he smoothed down his uniform and put his beret on his head. Slowly, he walked up to the spot where the STRIKE force had set up a perimeter.

Where he recognized the survivors of an "A" team he'd sent out two days before to conduct a recon mission.

CHAPTER TWENTY-THREE

Captain William "Wild Man" Fulmer leaned back against his bunk with a sigh of contentment, an A&W root beer in hand. Finally, he'd been able to rest. With all the excitement of the past several days, he, as the battalion adjutant and personnel officer, had had to hold civilian law-enforcement officers at bay and coordinate back and forth between the intelligence, operations, logistics, and communications officers from the battalion staff in trying to run the FOB's message center. All the paperwork! No sleep! It had been so exhausting!

And that for-crying-out-loud party the Old Man wanted. He'd really been scrambling lately.

Now, having just returned from the makeshift club over by Oro Grande's tiny quonset hut that was supposed to be a PX, he was ready to relax. Tonight was the battalion commander's party, and everyone was "invited." All morning, while the FOB conducted its classified mission debriefing to a Special Operations representative for the Chairman of the Joint Chiefs of Staff and the 1st SOCOM and Group Commanders, he'd been scurrying around like one of those lumpy, disease-ridden desert Jackrabbits trying to throw this party together. The XO had been hounding him non-stop too, trying to get him to "make it happen" a lot faster.

The XO.

Fulmer hated the battalion executive officer. He honestly thought that Major Jake Blane was the most unfeeling, intimidating, and loud-mouthed officer he'd ever met. But Blane also scared the hell out of him, so he did as he was told.

Fulmer sighed and ran his long, slender fingers through his thinning red hair. Had he done the right thing by volunteering for Special Forces training from the relative comfort of the AG Corps?

The answer was a definitive no. Fulmer pulled off his glasses and looked at them. His XO called them "faggot glasses," and had been harping on him to procure and wear only Army-issue "birth-control glasses." The reason for calling them birth-control glasses was that whoever had the misfortune to wear the ugly glasses with the heavy-duty black frames would never get laid. Fulmer sighed and took a long sip on his root beer.

Outside Fulmer's hootch, the wind picked up. When the wind picked up it banged his door open. Wearily, Fulmer got up from his bunk to close the door. Before he reached it, doom struck.

Major Jake Blane filled up the door space.

"Sir?"

"What are you doing, S-1?"

Fulmer cringed. He was either being called Adjutant or S-1, his duty position as the battalion's personnel officer. He'd only been assigned to the battalion for two months, and this was his first deployment. He seriously wondered if his superiors would ever learn his name. "I'm, uh . . . taking a break, sir." He noticed that Blane was holding something in his hand that looked like the stock of a disassembled rifle.

Blane nodded his head sagely, squinting at the battalion's newest officer. He had so much to learn. "How's preparation for the party going, S-1?" he said gruffly.

Fulmer swallowed and ran his mind through the entire twenty-six-point checklist he'd written up just the night before when they'd brought the team back that had conducted the mission. Colonel Volensky had gone over the list personally with him, telling him not to mess (fuck) it up or else he'd *walk*.

"Well?"

"Sir, all is taken care of. We've got steaks, booze, beer, and soda pop for those who don't drink. We set up the grills over by the club and—"

"You got cooks assigned?"

"Roger that, sir. Colonel Volensky said all battalion officers were to take a turn doing that—himself included."

"And did you get that goddam movie the Old Man wanted?"

Fulmer recalled the state of near-panic he'd gone through the day before in El Paso as he hunted up a copy of the movie video *The Road Warrior*. For some strange reason, Colonel Volensky wanted everyone to see it at this party, which, of course, everyone was invited to and darn well better attend if he knew what was good for him. "Yes sir, I got it. Checked it out on the clubhouse's VCR, and it works fine."

"All right, S-1. Sounds like you got your little rubber duckies in order."

Fulmer beamed. It was the first, the very first compliment he'd ever gotten from his XO.

Though he didn't show it, inwardly, Blane was pleased too. Maybe his new adjutant would work out after all. Yes, even he himself had been a nerd at one time like they all were. The kid just had to be provided opportunities from those who cared to develop a tough hide so he'd quit acting like a wimp. It would serve him well later on in his career as an adjutant.

"I only got one more thing for you to do, S-1."

Fulmer paled and pushed his "faggot glasses" back up on his nose. "Sir?" he asked meekly.

Blane thrust the rifle stock in the battalion S-1's hand. "The old man wants desert food on the grill tonight. You know how he is about tradition and ceremony. He's starting up a *new* tradition with desert food. You, S-1, are going to make it happen. That's your job, you know, ceremonies and bullshit."

"Sir?" Fulmer stared at the black plastic rifle stock. It was hollow, and a large, rounded metal plug was screwed just above the pistol grip and things rattled around inside. It was a disassembled rifle.

"That, S-1, is an AR-7 survival rifle. You *will* procure rabbits, snakes, and lizards with it for the party tonight."

Fulmer swallowed. "What, sir? You mean to *eat*?"

Blane gave him an evil scowl. "Did I stutter, S-1?"

"But sir, isn't this . . . illegal?"

"It won't make much noise, S-1. Just don't get caught. Of course, if I were you, I'd take Sergeant Major Avery along for guidance and advice." Blane knew that Avery was lurking outside the door.

"But—but we don't get along too well, sir, and . . . and I don't think he cares much about military courtesy and—"

Blane cut him off with a cold stare. "Are you snivelling, S-1?"

"No, sir!"

"Then make it happen." Blane strode purposefully out into the sun and the wind of Oro Grande and headed back for the FOB, where he could be of further use.

Another man entered the hut. He was a big, grizzled man who liked to drink beer, free-fall when he had the chance, run an out-fucking-*standing* S-3 operations center, and have a little fun every now and then with the new officers in the battalion.

Big, helpless eyes. "Yes, Sergeant Major Avery?"

"C'mon, sir, I'll give you a hand. Wouldn't want you to get in trouble, you know."

"Sergeant Major, I'm more than capable of—"

"Oh hell, I know that, sir." The big man clasped his hand around the adjutant's shoulders. "C'mon, we'll even drink a few brews and bullshit around."

Fulmer stared at the survival rifle for a few moments. Then he slugged down the remainder of his root beer and crumpled the can in his fist. Ten minutes later, he and the S-3 Sergeant Major were prowling the gullies and sand moguls surrounding the perimeter of the Oro Grande range camp, hunting for lumpy, disease-ridden jackrabbits.

A CUC-V rough-terrain vehicle pulled up to the FOB at 1400 hours and joined the government sedans in the parking lot. Master Sergeant Manny Santo and Warrant Officer Two Winston Maslow hobbled out of the vehicle, patched, slung in casts, and rehydrated from their wounds in the desert. They'd just returned from an overnight stay in the Fort Bliss hospital, and the battalion medic was more than trained to oversee their outpatient recovery back in Oro Grande. Now there was a final debriefing to settle in the FOB for the benefit of the general who had flown down from the Pentagon's Special Operations Division. He was also the personal representative for the Army Chief of Staff.

Captain Matt MacIntyre and Sergeant First Class Randy Hanlon met them in the parking lot, unsmiling. The news they'd received an hour before their team sergeant's arrival was bad.

Santo bounced out first. The color had been restored in his face, and he handled his crutches well. "Hey, guys—what's the scoop? Are we gonna debrief a big hitter or what?"

MacIntyre put a hand on his team sergeant's shoulder.

Instantly, Santo spotted the dark look on his team leader's face. His forearms started to shake where they were tensed up already from gripping his crutches.

"Teddy's dead."

A moment's silence. A tumbleweed blew across the parking lot and glanced off Santo's right crutch.

"He had a relapse. He had a relapse and . . . oh, hell, he died last night, Manny."

Santo was numb. He clenched his jaws tightly together and looked away.

MacIntyre's hand fell from his shoulder.

"We found out about it—"

Santo spun around and almost lost his balance in the compound gravel leading up to the FOB headquarters. Tears streaked his face. "We'd . . . better attend this briefing."

"Manny—"

Santo hobbled for the door. The others followed.

Three hours later, as dusk approached, the Special Operations representative for the Army Chief of Staff and his entourage of colonels and majors left, after having conducted the debriefing with the FBI. The general conducting the interview with the team said he'd be back to visit the Special Operations community at Fort Bragg, "to talk to the community from the ground up."

The remaining members of the team exited the FOB headquarters and slowly made their way back to their hootch—a five-minute walk across the dusty compound, turning into a ten-minute excursion because of Santo's crutches. Santo had refused another ride in the CUC-V, opting instead to be around his teammates, despite his black mood. Charcoal smoke and roasting meat wafted through the air, and other teams in the battalion were gathering around the grills by the camp's club, laughing, yelling, having fun.

"Looks like a party," Hanlon said. He didn't feel like going to a party. Two members of their team would not be there.

"My mouth got a little loose in there," Santo muttered to MacIntyre.

"You've got to tell it like it is, Manny."

"Do you think that general got the message?"

"What?" Maslow joined in. "Your point about recognizing the threat down south and how it is necessary to fund Special Operations forces and let them conduct realistic training instead of pulling detail support back at Fort Bragg? In other words, getting them ready for war before Mexico and the rest of Central America falls?"

"Yeah," Santo said.

"Well, you say what's on your mind, and then you can look yourself in the mirror. That general did say he was coming back to Fort Bragg."

"Yeah."

"And that remark about having to face the Banana Curtain when Mexico goes was a nice touch too."

"Yeah. It's all bullshit, though. That general won't listen. They never do. They just cover their asses and never learn. That's all what that debriefing was, just a cover-your-ass charade. Of course people are gonna get hurt when you do something for real. So far as the generals and politicians are concerned about 'down south,' they're just gonna make the same mistakes now like we did in Vietnam." Santo crutched along faster. "Just another no-win situation," he muttered.

The team entered the barracks portion of the compound and walked slowly to their quonset hut. When they entered, they spotted a field table erected in the middle of the hut. On top of the table was a bottle of Courvoisier, five glasses, and two large coins.

Santo hobbled toward the table. "What's this?" He picked up one of the coins. They were Special Forces coins. "This is Greeley's. The other one is Barkowitz's." He looked at MacIntyre, who was equally as confused.

"They weren't here when we left to link up with you guys for the debriefing," MacIntyre told him.

"*I* set it up for you."

The team turned around and saw Lieutenant Colonel Andrei

Volensky silhouetted in the doorway against the approaching dusk. He entered the team hootch.

"Detachment . . . 'ten—*chun*!"

"Relax," Volensky told them, walking toward the table. "I figured we could talk a little and drink some of this cognac."

"What gives with the coins, sir?" Santo asked. "They should have been sent back to the families."

"They *have* been sent back to their families," Volensky told him. "*This* family."

Santo turned away, feeling a lump grow in his throat. "Ah, it's all just a bunch of bullshit, sir." He recalled how Greeley had "coin-checked" him in the latrine, just four days ago. An eternity. "Coin checks . . . who needs 'em?"

"Tradition, Team Sergeant."

"Traditions are bullshit, sir. They just don't make any goddam difference."

"That's not what you said and thought sixteen years ago, Team Sergeant."

"Times change."

"And that's not what you said in the FOB to the general just an hour ago either. You told it like it was—honestly and with conviction." Volensky looked at MacIntyre. "You as well, Team Leader."

Volensky redirected his attention to Santo, who was now concentrating very hard on the two bunks and wall lockers where once two members of his team had lived. "So don't tell me that our traditions, philosophies as soldiers, and what we stand for are bullshit. You owe Greeley and Barkowitz more than that. And don't give me that crap about how you could have prevented their deaths. They were *Special Forces* soldiers.

"And they did their *duty*, Team Sergeant, as good Special Forces soldiers are supposed to do. Always remember—a Special Forces soldier or any other officer or enlisted man in the military does not owe his allegiance to his commanding officer, or to a general. That soldier owes his allegiance to the Constitution of the United States of America, and has sworn to uphold and defend the Constitution against all enemies, foreign and domestic."

Volensky gritted his teeth suddenly, turned around, and walked for the door, where he inhaled deeply of the late afternoon's desert air. The others, knowing he was in pain, watched him in silence. Facing them again, Volensky went on.

"You men . . . as Special Forces soldiers . . . must never lose sight of the way, the *intent* of what your profession entails—to support and defend the Constitution in your own unique way as a special operator. Otherwise, you're no different than Hitler's Waffen SS. So—the words duty, honor, country— still mean something to me. And it goddam better not be thought lightly of in *this* battalion."

The group of men parted as Volensky walked back to the field table. He poured a drink for each of them and passed out the shot glasses. He charged his own glass and raised it up for a toast.

"Philosophies, coins, traditions . . . our profession. It all may seem like . . . bullshit . . . to those who don't know of them, to the uninitiated. But *you* men know better."

Volensky locked eyes with each man on the team and continued. "We are drinking to the memories of Staff Sergeant Edward Barkowitz and Sergeant Theodore Greeley—good Special Forces soldiers. We are drinking to everything that made them special on this team and in this battalion. Their mutual talents. Their communications and medical expertise. Their high physical and intellectual standards. Their strength in life and sacrifice for their team and their mission in death. Their courage. And above all, their honor and integrity in defending our Constitution. Gentlemen, here's to our fallen comrades."

They downed their glasses and Volensky charged them again. "These coins now belong to you. Keep them well." Volensky cast a searching look at Santo. There were so many more things he wanted to say. He wanted to tell Santo that it was now time to take the baton from an old Russian and drive on with it, that it was time to teach someone of his own. That it was time for Santo to remember the philosophy of Special Forces and to keep it well for the new generation, because the battalion demanded good men to populate and lead it into the next century.

But some things have no meaning when they are merely spoken.

"And now, let's drink to the battalion!"

Before they started the next toast, Santo picked up Greeley's coin. On the back, it had an inscription. It read, "We, the

Professionals." That was an unusual inscription. Some people had
other things, like "Take the Risk," or the SAS's motto, "Who
Dares Wins," or something like "No Guts, No Glory." Greeley,
the perpetual jokester, had "We, the Professionals." And that was
serious for little Teddy.

Santo thought of Greeley's wisecracks and Barkowitz's dour
countenance. Opposite personalities, different moods. But the
thing that had bound them both as with the rest of the team
members was Greeley's inscription . . . "We, the Professionals."

He faced Volensky and nodded his head, taking in a deep
breath. "We'll mount them up on a plaque for the team room back
at Bragg, sir. You know—in memory of them and all."

Volensky grinned. "Charge your glasses, gentlemen."

Five minutes later, the bottle of Courvoisier was demolished.

Volensky glanced out the door and checked his old and worn
Rolex watch. Kegs of beer had been tapped and the rest of the
battalion was fully gathered around the club across the compound
for the party. Later, he'd pull Santo aside and talk to him again
about the direct commission. Pass along some thoughts. Volensky's eyes grew suddenly warm. Facing the team before he got
emotional on them, he smiled broadly.

"Tonight," Volensky told them with his sardonic grin, "we are
having a party. I want all of you to attend. As a matter of fact,
there is a fantastic movie the entire battalion will watch inside the
club. It's about this desert warrior called Mad Max who avenges
the death of his family in the wake of nuclear destruction. You
know, lots of blood, guts, gratuitous violence, that sort of thing.
The sort of stuff you heathens are used to . . .

"This *is* family night, you know."

Santo and the other members of his team exchanged grins.

Then they walked out the door with the Old Man.

GLOSSARY

1st SOCOM: U.S. Army's 1st Special Operations Command, headquartered at Fort Bragg, North Carolina. Subordinate units include all Special Forces Groups, the 75th Ranger Regiment, and a mix of other units consisting of Psychological Operations, Military Intelligence, and Civil Affairs.

ADA: Air Defense Artillery.

AG: The AG Corps is the personnel management/administration branch of the Army.

AK-47: Kalashnikov semi-automatic/automatic assault rifle produced in the Soviet block. Fires 7.62-millimeter rounds.

AN/PVS-4: Army telescopic night-observation device that can be mounted on a rifle or a machine gun. Operates on starlight technology that enhances moon and star illumination at night.

AN/PVS-5: Army night-observation goggles. Operates on same starlight technology as with the AN/PVS-4.

AO: Area of Operations.

Article 15: Military non-judicial punishment; authorizes unit commander to legally pass judgment on offenses within his unit that do not warrant a court-martial or felony record. The commander is authorized to punish the individual by withholding part of his pay, confining him to quarters, and putting him on extra duty for a specified period of time.

ASAP (pronounced ay-sap): As soon as possible.

Assault Ration: Lighter, more compact, yet packed with more calories than the conventional field ration, the MRE (Meal, Ready to Eat). One assault ration can sustain a soldier for an entire day.

Auxiliary: The element of an underground network established to provide logistical support to an intelligence agent's, resistance movement's, or terrorist's operation. Members of the auxiliary maintain outward appearances in following their normal, already established life-styles, while supporting their recruiter's operation in a clandestine manner.

Azimuth: Direction of travel, using map and compass.

Blackhawk: Current, state-of-the-art Army multi-purpose helicopter; will eventually replace existing stocks of the UH-1H "Huey," prevalently used throughout the 1960's and 70's.

Cache: A secure storage site where weapons, water, food, and ammunition can be hidden for future recovery in operational or emergency usage.

C&E Officer: Communications and electronics officer of a battalion.

CG: Commanding General.

CO: Commanding Officer.

Commo: Slang for communications.

CUC-V: Chevrolet four-wheel-drive diesel Blazer, modified for military specifications under government contract.

Dai-uy (pronounced Die-wee): Vietnamese for boss, or captain; often-used slang term in Special Forces in reference to the team leader.

Demo: Demolitions.

DMDG: Special Forces secure communications device that resembles a small digital typewriter. Sends "burst" transmissions in seconds from the deployed ODA in the area of operations to the FOB, and vice versa (see ODA and FOB).

DZ: Drop Zone; a specified site for parachute-infiltrated men and supplies.

FOB: Forward Operation Base; operated by a Special Forces battalion headquarters element. This element is the command, operational, communication, intelligence, air, and logistics lifeline to a deployed Special Forces Operational Detachment "A" team, during the conduct of that ODA's mission.

FALN: Puerto-Rican separatist terrorist group.

FTX: Field Training Exercise.

GRU (Glavnoye Razvedyvatelnoye Upravleniye): Soviet Army's military intelligence organization, rivaled by the KGB. Known officially as *Chief Directorate of Intelligence of the*

General Staff. Independent of the KGB, the GRU operates a worldwide network of agents for military intelligence acquisition during peacetime and wartime. Sometimes, KGB and GRU activities overlap. The GRU's overriding mission is to gather military intelligence on other countries, hostile to the Soviet Union or otherwise, and to continually recruit agents in those countries for ongoing intelligence acquisition. *Spetsnaz* (Soviet Special Purpose commandos, SF's counterparts) are directly subordinate to the GRU; they are trained in subversion, infiltration, sabotage, and assassination. The GRU also trains foreign terrorists and operates a training division within its hierarchy for international terrorists in support of "Liberation Movements."

HALO: High Altitude Low Opening; military free-fall parachuting technique.

Heat Rounds, 40-mm: Ammunition for the M203 grenade launcher; means high-explosive.

Higher: Slang for the next higher headquarters, or the element in overall command.

Hundred-mile-an-hour tape: Olive-drab green duct or insulation tape, used for general purposes.

Infil: Slang for infiltration.

IR: Infrared

KGB (Komitet Gosudarstvennoi Bezopastnosti): Officially known as the Soviet Union's Committee for State Security, the KGB is a security and intelligence-gathering organization that operates both within and outside the Soviet Union and throughout the world. The KGB conducts many different types of operations through its five major departments, including: disinformation in the Western media; foreign espionage operations; counterespionage; internal security and surveillance; and control of internal dissent—political, religious, and ethnic. The KGB also maintains a well-trained and equipped military force to patrol the Soviet Union's borders, similar in concept and usage as the Nazis' Waffen SS during World War Two.

Kilometer: Metric unit of measurement, which is .62 mile. The military expresses all distances metrically, and all military maps are delineated metrically.

Klick: Slang for kilometer.

LAW: Light, Anti-tank Weapon; official nomenclature—

M72A2 LAW. A 66-millimeter rocket encased in a disposable firing tube for usage against armor and bunkers.

Low Intensity Conflict: Low-key form of warfare, usually conducted in Third-World nations, in which revolution, guerrilla warfare, subversion, terrorism, and sabotage are some of the key techniques used for the internal seizure of power. The techniques and tactics of Low Intensity Conflict can also be conducted between two or more powerful nations who do not want to or cannot accept the political or psychological brunt of public opinion that would evolve if their conventional forces (troops, tanks, warplanes, ships) were brought to bear against each other for the accomplishment of a strategic goal.

M14: A 7.62-millimeter semi-automatic rifle used by U.S. forces in the early sixties. Was replaced by the M16, but is still retained for use as a sniper rifle.

M16A2: U.S. military automatic/semi-automatic assault rifle that fires 5.56-millimeter rounds, which is currently replacing the "A1" version. This version has a molded pistol grip; rounded, ribbed forearm assembly; more accurate sights; three-burst selector switch; and a heavier barrel for a longer maximum effective range.

M203 Grenade Launcher: A tube-shaped, breech-loading grenade launcher, fastened underneath the forearm grips of an M16 rifle. Fires forty-millimeter grenade shells with a four-hundred-meter maximum effective firing range.

M-19 (terrorist group): Left-wing Colombian guerilla/terrorist group that fund their operations through support of the Latino drug cartel.

Meter/Kilometer: One meter is 39.37 inches, little more than a yard; one hundred meters is approximately the size of a football field. One kilometer is 1 meter X 1000, or .62 mile. The military, when expressing distance, does so metrically.

Mike: Military phonetic term used for the letter "M." Also used as slang for minutes.

MI: Military Intelligence.

Mole: A deep-cover intelligence agent infiltrating a target area/country legally, and under a false identity. After having established a time-proven routine as a model citizen, the mole can thus actuate intelligence-acquisition and indigenous-agent-recruitment operations under the cover of his or her everyday life-style.

MP: Military Police.

MRE: Meal, Ready-to-Eat; Army field ration, semi-dehydrated and contained in a brown plastic bag. Replaced the C-ration in the early 1980's.

Mujahideen: Islamic Afghani guerrillas that fought Soviet oppression in their country as a holy war, given the dictates of their religion. The most effective Soviet counter to the Mujahideen was the Soviet Union's Spetsnaz forces, who are highly trained in counter-insurgency operations.

Nap-of-the-Earth: Pilot lingo for flying an aircraft along treetop level to avoid detection by enemy radar; it's also useful when conducting a helicopter assault on an objective.

NCO: Non-commissioned officer; ranks include corporal through command sergeant-major.

Night-observation device: Telescopic, hand-held and/or weapon-mounted, infrared, thermal, or starlight technology that enables the viewer to observe and engage targets at night. Such technology includes the AN/PVS-5 and the AN/PVS-4.

OD: Olive drab.

OBJ: Objective.

ODA: Operational Detachment "A"; more commonly known as the twelve-man Special Forces "A" team; a unit consisting of twelve highly trained men with basic and specialized military skills consisting of light and heavy weapons, demolitions, communications, operations and intelligence, and medicine. Capable of organizing, supplying, training, directing, and controlling indigenous forces up to battalion strength in all aspects of guerrilla/unconventional warfare, Special Forces also conducts STRIKE (raid) and deep reconnaissance operations. Capable of infiltrating the area of operations through Military Free-Fall (High Altitude, Low/High Opening) parachuting techniques; static-line parachuting; SCUBA; and general military mountaineering.

Op-order: Operations order; the plan for movement, execution, and exfiltration of a mission. Also known as briefback.

PRC-68: A small, two-way radio, used primarily for intra-team communications if the team splits up.

PRC-70: Backpack-mounted FM radio; used for transmitting and receiving messages over long distances.

Prone: Lying down on the ground behind cover, facing with weapon toward possible enemy contact in assigned sector.

PT: Physical training, usually in the form of a five-mile run, accompanied by an hour of vigorous calisthenics.

PZ: Pickup Zone; the site for helicopter exfiltration from an area of operations.

Q-course: Slang for the Special Forces Qualification Course. The Q-course is one of the Army's most physically and mentally demanding schools. Any soldier can volunteer, provided they meet the physical and mental screening requirements and graduate jump school prior to attendance. It is headquartered at Fort Bragg, North Carolina, and successful completion of the Q-course is mandatory before a soldier's assignment to an ODA. Initial and mid-course training includes land navigation, survival, patrolling, and individual specialty training (either commo, demo, weapons, medic, or operations and intelligence). The Q-course culminates in a three-week collective field training exercise; called ROBIN SAGE, whereby the students, organized into twelve-man "A" teams, infiltrate their assigned areas of operation in North Carolina's Uhwarrie National Forest. Upon linking up with their mission's "guerrillas" (who are in fact various members of their training cadre), the students put the skills they have learned into practice, utilizing the techniques, tactics, and principles of Unconventional Warfare. Length of the course is between six and eighteen months, depending on military occupational specialty.

Rabbits: Military jargon for targets or persons being surveilled or snatched during an operation.

R&S Team: Recon and Security team.

Redeye: U.S.-manufactured, shoulder-fired, anti-aircraft surface-to-air missile (SAM).

Release Point: A pre-planned spot near the objective where a unit splits up to conduct simultaneous missions or contributing elements of the mission.

Rodina: Russian word for motherland.

ROTC: Reserve Officer Training Corps.

RPG-7: Soviet-block, exposed-warhead, direct-fire, anti-tank weapon.

Ruck/rucksack: Army-issue heavy nylon rucksack with an external frame; olive-drab in color.

S-1: Personnel officer of a battalion headquarters. Also known as the Adjutant.

S-2: Intelligence officer of a battalion headquarters.

S-3: Operations officer of a battalion headquarters.

S-4: Logistics officer of a battalion headquarters.

SAM: Surface-to-air missile.

SAS: The British Special Air Service; an elite commando unit whose specialty is combating international terrorism.

SDI: Strategic Defense Initiative.

Sit-rep: Slang for situation report.

SOP: Standard operating procedure.

Spec-4: Slang for specialist fourth class, rank of an enlisted man in the Army that falls between sergeant and private first class.

SF: Special Forces.

Special Forces (aka Green Berets): The basic Special Forces unit, the ODA, consists of twelve highly trained men with basic and specialized military skills consisting of command and control, light and heavy weapons, demolitions, communications, operations and intelligence, and medicine. Special Forces units are capable of infiltrating any target area by land, sea (SCUBA), and air (static-line or military free-fall parachute). Capable of organizing, supplying, training, directing, and controlling indigenous forces in all aspects of guerrilla/unconventional warfare, Special Forces units also conduct STRIKE (raid) and deep reconnaissance operations. During the conduct of an operation, the Special Forces ODA is controlled, isolated, infiltrated, supplied, and exfiltrated by the ODA's parent battalion headquarters through the FOB (see FOB), where secure communications are maintained throughout the mission.

Spetsnaz (Spetsialnoye Nazhacheniye): Soviet Special Purpose commandos, similar to U.S. Special Forces, specially trained in sabotage, subversion, assassination, terrorism, counterinsurgency, and guerrilla warfare. Their overriding mission is to penetrate strategic nuclear-missile sites and make them inoperable during the period of heightened tension immediately before war breaks out. They operate in small units consisting of two to twelve men, and their role is to sabotage key targets within the military-industrial complex, such as oil refineries, airfields, missile bases, and electrical plants/power supply stations. The Soviet Union's

Spetsnaz forces are controlled by the GRU (the Red Army's Military Intelligence branch; see GRU).

T-10: Nomenclature for a parachute used in the Army throughout the 1960's and 70's.

Team Leader: Commander of a twelve-man Special Forces ODA. Rank is captain. Responsible for everything the ODA does or fails to do.

Team Sergeant: Senior non-commissioned officer in a twelve-man Special Forces ODA. Rank is master sergeant. Usually has the most experience of anyone on the ODA.

Team Technician (aka Team XO): Second in command of a twelve-man Special Forces ODA. Rank is warrant officer two. Commonly referred to as "Chief."

TOT: Time-on-Target.

VS-17 Panel: A signaling panel made out of cloth, international orange on one side and red on the other. Used for guiding helicopters onto an LZ.

Web gear: Shoulder straps connected to a web belt and butt-pack; used for securing canteens, ammo pouches, strobe light, first-aid kit, and sundries.

XO: Executive Officer.